KISSING EMILY

"Surely you are not serious?" Emily said. "You cannot really think me as attractive as Lady Meredith?"

Sir Terrence shook his head. "Not *as* attractive," he said. "*More* attractive. In fact, to state the matter bluntly, I think you are beautiful."

Emily took away his sherry glass. "Obviously you have had more than enough to drink this evening."

"I am not intoxicated, Emily. What I said was in simple earnest. Why will you not believe me?"

Something within Emily snapped at that moment. "Very well: I give you the chance to prove what you have said. Prove that you think me beautiful."

"By God, I will," he said, and the words were a solemn vow rather than an irreverent oath. The next thing Emily knew, she was enfolded in Sir Terrence's arms and being kissed with a passion that left no doubt of his sincerity. . . .

Dear Romance Reader,

In July, we launched the **Ballad** line with four new series, and each month now we offer you both new and continuing stories set everywhere from medieval England to the American West—the kind of passionate, romantic stories you love best, written by the most gifted authors. At the back of each book, we'll tell you when you can find subsequent books in the series that have captured your heart.

Rising star Joy Reed continues her charming Wishing Well trilogy with *Emily's Wish* as a spirited young woman fleeing her past stumbles into a celebrated author . . . and a chance at a love story of her own. Next Candice Kohl sweeps us back to the medieval splendor of The Kinsmen as *A Knight's Passion* becomes a breathtaking romance . . . with a Welsh heiress the king intends for his brother.

New this month is veteran author Linda Lea Castle's Bogus Brides series. The Green sisters must invent "husbands" to remain in the charter town of McTavish Plain, Nebraska—and love is an unexpected complication in *Addie and the Laird*. Finally, we return to the bayous of the Louisiana Territory as Cherie Claire offers the second book of The Acadians. *Rose* dreams of romance . . . but loses her heart to the one man her family has forbidden. Enjoy!

Kate Duffy
Editorial Director

Wishing Well

EMILY'S WISH

Joy Reed

ZEBRA BOOKS
KENSINGTON PUBLISHING CORP.

http://www.zebrabooks.com

ZEBRA BOOKS are published by

Kensington Publishing Corp.
850 Third Avenue
New York, NY 10022

All Kensington titles, imprints and distributed lines are available at special quantity discounts for bulk purchases for sales
promotion, premiums, fund raising, educational or institutional
use.

Special book excerpts or customized printings can also be cre-
ated to fit specific needs. For details, write or phone the office of
the Kensington Special Sales Manager: Kensington Publishing
Corp., 850 Third Avenue, New York, NY, Attn. Special Sales
Department. Phone: 1-800-221-2647.

First Printing: November, 2000
10 9 8 7 6 5 4 3 2 1

Printed in the United States of America

For Wilma, with love

Chapter 1

"No, please, sir, you mustn't! Your aunt would dislike it very much."

Emily spoke sharply, keeping the table between her and the young man opposite. He shook his head, an amused smile on his handsome face.

"Just one kiss, Emily," he said in a wheedling voice. "Auntie needn't know anything about it. Just one little kiss." He gave Emily a beseeching smile. "One little kiss, and then I won't plague you anymore. You wouldn't be so cruel as to deny me just one kiss, Emily? When you know how crazy I am about you?"

"I only know how much your aunt would dislike it," said Emily. She spoke doggedly, but her eyes were angry as she contemplated the young man opposite. "Please let me be, Mr. Bartholomew. Your aunt will be wondering why I am such a time fetching her medicine."

"Let her wonder," said the young man, and made an abrupt lunge across the table. Emily was prepared for the move, however, and took several quick steps backward. But though Mr. Bartholomew's maneuver was ineffective in itself, it had forced her away from the table that had been her chief protection. This new vulnerability was quickly noted and taken advantage of by her enemy. Emily saw the intention in his eyes and made a dash for the door, only to be caught just before she reached it. Mr. Bartholomew pinioned her arms to her sides with a cry of triumph.

"Now I've got you!" he said. "Emily, you little coquette, you've been snubbing me for weeks, but you shan't snub me now. Give me a kiss, do, and show me you like me a bit!"

"Let me go," said Emily through clenched teeth. "Let me go, Mr. Bartholomew. I must insist that you let me go!"

She might as well have saved her breath. The young man merely laughed and pulled her closer. "All in good time," he said, regarding Emily with a bold smile. "You must know I don't intend to let you go until you kiss me. And while I'm at it, I'm going to make you give up this ridiculous business of calling me Mr. Bartholomew. I've told you at least a hundred times you might call me Ronald. It's only right that friends like us should call each other by their Christian names."

"We're not friends," said Emily, trying vainly to twist out of his grasp. "I am your aunt's hired companion, Mr. Bartholomew. And it is very improper of you to keep me from my duties like this—very improper and very unkind."

Ronald's face assumed a hurt look. "Unkind?" he repeated. "Emily, how can you say so? When you know how I feel about you! Why, I'd do anything for you—anything at all."

"Then let me go," said Emily in a voice verging upon despair. "All I want is to attend to my job, Mr. Bartholomew. Can you not see what a position you are putting me in?''

It was evident that he could not or would not see. A scowl disfigured his handsome face. "I only see that you're a damned coy girl with a damned standoffish manner," he retorted. "What the devil do you want to make such a fuss about a simple kiss for?" With a return to his former coaxing manner, he added, "I tell you I'm wild about you, Emily. I should think if you liked me at all, you wouldn't grudge me one little kiss. You do like me a little, don't you, Emily? Don't you?"

No, I despise you. Emily did not speak the words aloud, but she wished she did dare speak them. Looking into Ronald's spoiled, handsome face, however, she recognized that such an action would have been very imprudent. He unquestionably had the upper hand with her at that moment, and he had also (what was still more important) a great deal of influence with his aunt. Emily knew how easy it would be for him to get Miss Morris to discharge her on some trumped-up excuse if he ever chose to do so. Since she wished to keep her position, a measure of diplomacy was clearly in order, but Emily registered a silent vow that someday she would give the Honorable Ronald Bartholomew her real opinion of him.

In the meantime, she contented herself with saying as lightly as she could, "Oh, Mr. Bartholomew, you will embarrass me if you insist on asking me questions like that. Please let me go, and don't tease me anymore."

"I won't if you'll kiss me," he answered promptly.

Position of power or not, Emily was not about to go this far. He must have seen the resolution in her face, for his own face darkened. "By God, if you won't kiss me, I'll—" he began menacingly.

Fortunately for Emily, the threat was never completed. The door to the parlor opened, and Nell, Miss Morris's maid, came into the room. She took in the situation at a glance, but when she spoke, her voice was expressionless. "Excuse me, Miss Emily, but Miss Morris was wanting to know why you hadn't brought her her drops. She's been waiting to take them this half hour."

Emily felt her face must be scarlet with embarrassment. Ronald appeared to be embarrassed, too, for he let go of Emily, strolled over to the fireplace, and began studying his face in the chimney glass with close attention. "I have Miss Morris's drops right here," said Emily with as much composure as she could muster. "I meant to bring them down directly, Nell, but I was delayed a moment in—er—talking to Mr. Bartholomew."

She threw Ronald a savage look. Nell threw him a look, too, and a smile appeared briefly on her round red face. "Be that as it may, you'd best be taking those drops to Miss Morris this minute," she told Emily. "She's not half in a state about your being so slow about it."

As Emily followed Nell out of the parlor, she reflected gloomily that she was passing out of the frying pan only to fall into the fire. Miss Morris was not an easy person to deal with at the best of times, and in one of her "states" she was nearly impossible. Another fierce surge of resentment against Ronald rose in Emily's breast. *How I despise him!* she told herself, grinding her teeth with impotent fury. Nell glanced at her curiously.

"You look as though you're in a state yourself, miss," she told Emily. "Mr. Ronald's been pestering you again, has he?"

"Yes," said Emily simply but forcefully.

Again Nell looked at her curiously. "It beats me why you let that put you in a temper. Me, now, I'd be happy to have a handsome young man like Mr. Ronald trying to steal a kiss from me. I expect most girls'd feel the same."

Emily did not allow herself to comment on this speech.

Her face was expressive, however. Nell saw the expression, and when she spoke again, her voice was sharper than it had been before.

"If I was you, I wouldn't be so quick to turn up my nose at such a chance. Seems to me you're foolish not to make the most of it. It's plain to see Mr. Ronald's nutty about you—yes, and no wonder, neither. You're a handsome girl if you do have red hair." She glanced disparagingly at the cluster of red-gold curls pinned atop Emily's head. "Why, if you was clever about it, there's no saying what might not come of it. I heard tell the other day of a girl who was a hired companion just like you who ended by getting an offer of marriage from her mistress's son."

Once again, Emily's face was expressive. "In the case of the Honorable Ronald, I think it much more likely that I should merely get a carte blanche," she said bitterly. "He's hinted at it once or twice already, though I haven't encouraged him in the least."

Nell gave her a direct look. "Well, and why haven't you? To my way of thinking, it'd be a deal better to be Mr. Ronald's mistress than do the job you're doing now."

"You don't mean it!" said Emily, staring at her.

"I do mean it," said Nell firmly. "There's worse things than being a gentleman's mistress. It's not what you could call respectable or ladylike, but as far as I can see, being respectable and ladylike's nothing but a burden for a girl in your position. Only just look at the facts, Miss Emily. You work harder than any servant in the house and take more abuse than any of us, and for what? For a salary no higher than a kitchen maid's and the right to be called a lady! It's foolish, that's what it is."

Emily continued to regard the maid with amazement. "Nell, you must be joking," she said. "Are you seriously counseling me to be Mr. Ronald's mistress?"

Nell gave her a look of affectionate contempt. "No, for

it wouldn't do any good. It's plain to see you don't like
the notion, and so I'll say no more. But I can tell you this,
Miss Emily. If I thought Mr. Ronald'd look twice at me,
I'd be doing my best to cut you out with him, and so would
any other girl in the house. Why wouldn't we? He's an
openhanded gentleman with a real air about him, and as
handsome as a picture. I can't but think you're a fool to
jib at him as you do, and that's the truth.''

Emily made no reply to this. She merely followed Nell
in silence across the hall toward the drawing room, where
her mistress was waiting.

The insult contained in the maid's words had hardly
registered upon her. She disliked being called a fool, but
being called one was nothing new to her. There had been
many people to call her a fool during the last three of
her twenty-three years, and given the calamitous nature of
those years, it was beginning to seem to Emily that the
epithet might well be justified.

She had been born the only child of Mr. Theodore
Pearce, a gentleman of good birth but little fortune. He
had disappointed his friends and relations by refusing to
marry until late in life and then had disappointed them
further by taking to wife a lady whose birth and fortune
were a fit match for his own.

Despite the smallness of the Pearces' means, their marriage had been a happy one. Emily recalled her childhood
as a time of sunny days and unclouded prospects. At the
age of nineteen, however, her father had suddenly died,
slipping from life as gently and unobtrusively as he had
lived it. Her mother had lingered on for a time after him,
but so visible had been her decline that Emily had been
unsurprised when she had followed her husband into the
grave little more than a year later.

Orphaned at twenty, with an income inadequate to her
needs and no useful accomplishments whatever, Emily still

had not despaired. She had possessed all the optimism of youth, along with an independence of spirit that was generally called pride by those around her. In truth, "foolish pride" was how this trait of Emily's was most often described, and it was from this date that she had first grown used to hearing herself condemned as a fool. She had been a fool not to seek refuge in her Great-aunt Gertrude's home, where she might have spared that good lady the expense of a second housemaid. She had been equally foolish not to accept a place in the home of her cousin Eurydice, where she might have lent a much-needed hand with the children. Even Second cousin Phyllis's offer to go halves in a lodging at Harrogate had been most ungratefully refused by Emily, who knew all too well Second cousin Phyllis's uncertain temperament.

The fact was that Emily, surveying the matter with a clear and rational eye, could see nothing desirable about accepting a home with any one of her relatives. They were all good people in their way, but there were none of them with whom she really wished to live even had her situation not reduced her to an object of charity in their homes. And from that situation Emily frankly rebelled. One and all, her relatives had made it clear that in exchange for taking their impoverished kinswoman into their home, they expected her to make herself useful. Such was Emily's pride (or perversity, or foolishness, depending on who was describing it) that in the end she had chosen to take a position as hired companion to a stranger rather than make her home with one of her own blood relatives.

It had seemed a logical step to Emily. She did not wish to be an object of charity; therefore, it was necessary for her to find some kind of position whereby she might support herself. Unfortunately, there were very few ways in which a gentlewoman might decently earn a living. She might be a governess, or she might be a hired companion; anything else was outside the pale. A few interviews with ladies seeking governesses convinced Emily that she possessed neither education nor accomplishments enough to teach children. That being the case, companion was really all that was left.

Emily had therefore felt very fortunate to obtain a post with Miss Morris a few months after her mother's death. Of course, her relatives had roundly declared her a fool and predicted she would not last six months in her new position, but Emily had brushed such remarks aside. She did not suppose life with Miss Morris would be all delight, but she congratulated herself that at least she was maintaining her independence and self-respect.

It had not taken long for this illusion to be stripped away. As companion and general dogsbody to Miss Morris, she enjoyed precious little independence, and her self-respect had likewise suffered a steady decline in the face of her employer's constant criticism. It had not been so bad during the first year or two of her service with Miss Morris, when that lady had enjoyed good health. Of course, Miss Morris had still criticized Emily and frequently called her a fool, but this was something Emily was growing used to.

A year ago, however, Miss Morris's health had taken an abrupt turn for the worse. She had suffered a mild fit of apoplexy that had resulted in a partial paralysis. Great as the physical effects of this illness had been on Miss Morris, they were nothing compared to the emotional ones. Her temper, always quick, had grown until the smallest incident was enough to set it off. She would then fly into one of the uncontrolled rages that Nell referred to as "states" and which Miss Morris's doctor had cautioned the entire household against provoking.

Emily had heard the doctor's advice, and during the past year she had tried harder than ever to satisfy her employer's often unreasonable demands. But she had soon reached the despairing conclusion that Miss Morris was impossible to satisfy. To further complicate matters, it had been about this time that Ronald had appeared on the scene. His presence had served to make Emily's already difficult existence well-nigh impossible.

Ronald was the son of Miss Morris's younger sister. This sister had married a wealthy peer on her coming out and had since then lived in a fashionable bustle that left little time for dealings with her spinster relative. The two women had maintained a correspondence, however, and there had been a few visits back and forth through the years. Miss Morris had thus become early acquainted with her nephew Ronald and had conceived a fondness for him that was all out of proportion to his merits, in Emily's opinion at least.

The fact was that Emily had taken Ronald in dislike from the very beginning. He was, as Nell had said, an extremely good-looking young man, tall, dark, and handsome in the most approved romantic style. To Emily, however, his good looks were spoiled by his own obvious awareness of them. Likewise, the air that Nell had described with so much admiration seemed to her merely a combination of arrogance and impertinence. He took it for granted that everybody would find him charming, and Emily was obliged to admit that nearly everybody did. But to her, Ronald's charm was only a mask for a soul dominated by greedy self-interest.

In nowhere was this so apparent as in his dealings with his aunt. As long as Miss Morris had enjoyed good health, Ronald's visits to her had been few and far between. After she had fallen ill, however, his visits had become much more frequent. He had taken to spending weeks at a time in her house in Devon, waiting on her with smiling devotion and bringing her daily gifts of flowers and sweetmeats. Miss Morris was delighted by this behavior, seeing it as evidence of her nephew's love and concern, but to Emily it was a transparent display of calculating greed. Miss Morris had a handsome fortune in her own right and no children of her own to leave it to. It was obvious that Ronald wanted it left to him. And it *had* been left to him, as Emily knew for a fact. Only a few weeks before, Miss Morris had called in her attorney and arranged that the whole of her fortune be left to her nephew, apart from a few legacies to servants.

Even more disgusting to Emily than Ronald's greed was his behavior toward herself. Back in the days when his visits had been no more than a single night's stay or a brief afternoon call, he had shown clearly enough by his looks that he admired Emily, but she had found it easy to avoid any other expression of that admiration. Now that he was a virtual resident in the house, however, it was a different story. His attempt today to steal a kiss from her had not been the first such incident by any means. He seemed to take it for granted that Emily must find him irresistible. No doubt he had been encouraged by unbridled feminine admiration in the past and a long series of easy conquests. Emily had seen the silly way the maidservants simpered when he walked by, and Nell had probably not exaggerated when she declared that any one of them would have jumped at the chance to be his mistress. To Emily, however, Ronald was a monster of conceit and selfishness, and she found him no more attractive than she would have found any other monster.

Today's incident had seemed to her particularly monstrous. Not only had Ronald taken advantage of his position in the household and his greater physical strength to hold her hostage; he had also brought down the wrath of his aunt upon her head. And there was no way she could deflect that wrath to its proper object. Miss Morris was a lady of strict morals, and she would have condemned

Ronald's behavior in any other gentleman, but so greatly did she dote upon her nephew that any appeal to her on this score would have been worse than useless.

Even if she had believed Emily's story, it would only have taken a word from Ronald to convince her that he was blameless. And chances were she never would have believed Emily in the first place. The idea that her beloved nephew could behave in such a way would have been to her quite inconceivable. Besides, she would never have believed Emily attractive enough to tempt such a paragon of manhood.

"No man'll ever look twice at you with that ginger hair, my dear," she had often declared with a pitying shake of her head. "A great shame, but there it is. Besides that, you're away too tall for a girl and have no countenance to speak of. If you was rich, now, you might have a chance of getting a beau in spite of being so plain. As it is, though, I don't doubt you'll end up a spinster like me."

Emily, who had enjoyed little experience with beaux prior to coming to live with Miss Morris, believed unhesitatingly all her mistress had told her. It therefore seemed to her all the more perverse of Ronald to fix on her as an object of his attentions. Her heart was hot with resentment as she followed Nell into the drawing room and into the presence of Miss Morris.

"High time you got here!" were Miss Morris's opening words. Her voice held the throbbing note of rage that Emily and the other members of the household had come to dread. The old woman lay upon the sofa, a frail and pathetic figure beneath her cocoon of blankets and shawls, but there was nothing pathetic about her tight mouth, aggressive jaw, and furious eyes. She struggled to raise herself on one elbow, the better to fix Emily with a direful gaze. "You stupid girl, what the devil have you been doing all this while? I sent you for my drops half an hour ago!"

"I'm so sorry, Miss Morris," began Emily, though she knew how futile would be any attempt to apologize. Before she could say more, however, Nell spoke with calm authority.

"It weren't her fault, ma'am," she said. "She fetched the drops, all right. It was Mr. Ronald's doing that she didn't return with them directly like you told her to. He stopped her as she was coming through the parlor and wanted to know how you was. And he wouldn't let her go till she told him what kind of a night you'd passed and what the doctor said when he came to see you this morning."

"He did?" said Miss Morris. The anger in her voice gave way abruptly to a startling tenderness. "Dear boy! It was like him to be concerned." Once more she raised herself on her elbow to look at Emily. "So Ronald was asking about me, was he, my dear?"

"Oh, yes, he was," answered Nell before Emily could speak. "Wouldn't hardly let her go, he wouldn't—not till I told him you was waiting for your drops."

She dropped the eyelid nearest Emily in a sly wink. Emily gave her a grateful look. Miss Morris, meanwhile, was still taken up with pleasure at this evidence of her nephew's concern.

"Ronald is such a dear boy. Such a *good* boy," she told Emily and Nell. "I'm sure no one could have a more dutiful nephew. It must be dull work for the poor boy to spend all his time waiting on an invalid like me, but he never makes any complaint."

"No, he doesn't," said Nell solemnly. "Keeps himself occupied wonderfully well, he does." To Emily, she added, "You'd better let me have those drops, Miss Emily, and I'll see about giving them to Miss Morris. I've got a glass of water all handy for them."

Emily silently handed the drops to Nell and watched as she dissolved them in water and administered them to her mistress. The storm appeared to have been averted, but once again Ronald had come out bearing laurels to which he was not entitled. When he sauntered into the drawing room later that afternoon, an elegant figure in his green topcoat, fawn-colored inexpressibles, and shining Hessian boots, she eyed him with dislike and purposely busied herself with Miss Morris's medicine bottles so that she need not even look at him.

Miss Morris, by contrast, was delighted to see her nephew. "Dear boy! I heard you had been asking about me," she told him, stretching out a withered hand for him to salute. "I hope Miss Pearce succeeded in setting your fears at rest?"

"Er—yes," said Ronald cautiously. He threw a covert look in Emily's direction, but as Emily continued to be busy among the bottles, he decided there was nothing to fear in taking this credit for his own. "I am glad to see you looking so well, Auntie," he said, raising her hand gallantly to his lips. "When I heard the doctor had been waiting on you this morning, I feared the worst."

"The doctor! The doctor is an old woman," said Miss Morris, shaking her head with contempt. "Why, to hear him talk, you would think I was at death's door instead of being really quite well and strong."

Emily, shooting a quick glance at Ronald, was not surprised to see an avid gleam in his eye. It was gone almost as soon as it came, however, and his expression became merely one of smiling dismissal. "These medicos always take a dark view of one's condition," he said. "When I was down with a touch of influenza at Christmastime last year, I'm sure my doctor acted as though I had the smallpox or worse. But I pulled through, all right, as you see, and I'm not a penny the worse for it."

"But I think in your case he was quite justified in taking a serious view, Ronald. You always were rather delicate, you know. Do make certain you wrap up well while you are here, and if you need an additional comfort for your bed, I am sure Nell or Miss Pearce will be happy to fetch one for you."

"Let Miss Pearce do it, by all means. I am sure she can do all that is necessary for my comfort." Ronald's statement was a masterpiece of sly innuendo. Emily pretended not to hear, but she could not prevent a flush from rising to her cheeks.

"Very well, then. Miss Pearce, see to it that Mr. Ronald has another comfort to his bed if you please," said Miss Morris. She tried to smile at her nephew as she spoke, but her voice was suddenly weary, and her face had gone pinched and gray. Nell, who had been bustling about the room while she and Ronald were speaking, gave her a long look. She then advanced to her mistress's side, addressing Ronald with smiling firmness.

"I'm sorry, sir, but I think you'd better be letting your aunt rest now. She tires rather easily nowadays, you know."

"Tired, fiddlesticks! I'm not tired a bit. You're a fool, Nell," said Miss Morris. But her voice was even weaker than before, and when she tried again to smile at Ronald, the result was a ghastly parody of amusement. "Forgive me, my boy, but I suppose I must rest now," she told him. "Come and see me again after dinner. Miss Pearce, you'd better dine with him and see that Cook doesn't skimp on the dishes just because I'm not there to count them."

Emily looked up with consternation. "But I would rather stay with you, ma'am," she said. "Who will make your tea and read to you while you eat?"

"Nell can do it this once. Don't argue, girl." Weak as she was, there was a hint of anger in Miss Morris's voice that warned Emily not to push the issue further.

"Very well, ma'am," she said quietly. "I will dine with Mr. Bartholomew if you insist."

"Aye, see that you do. And put on something more cheerful than that old brown merino you've been wearing all this week. Gentlemen like to see a bit of color about them. Your green cambric's about the best. You don't look so gawky in that as in most things, though it does bring out your red hair." Miss Morris sank back on the sofa and closed her eyes, signaling that the conversation was over.

Emily managed to avoid catching Ronald's eye as she left the room. But there was foreboding in her heart as she went upstairs to dress for dinner.

Chapter 2

In the small and airless bedchamber that Miss Morris had allotted to her use, Emily set about changing her dress and tidying her hair with anxious haste. Her feeling of anxiety did not leave her even after she was attired in her best dress, a simple frock of dark green cambric with a modest round neckline and short sleeves.

"I cannot dine alone with Ronald. I simply can't," she told her reflection in the mirror above her dressing stand. Her reflection looked back at her glumly, a red-haired girl with anxious brown eyes and downturned lips. She knew only too well that her words were mere posturing. If Miss Morris said she must dine with Ronald, then she must do so. It was either that or lose her position.

"But perhaps it won't be so very bad," she told her reflection. "There will be servants in the dining room with us the whole time, or at least until the dessert course is served. I'll wait until dessert is brought in, then excuse myself on the grounds that I must see to Miss Morris. That will mean I won't get any dessert, of course, but I would gladly go without dessert—or dinner altogether—if it allowed me to escape a tête-à-tête with Ronald."

On the whole, these reflections encouraged Emily, so she was able to go downstairs in a tolerably composed frame of mind. When she reached the door of the dining room, she looked sharply to the left and right of her. If she could slip into the dining room by herself, she might avoid the ordeal of going in on Ronald's arm and of having him seat her formally at the table. She knew from experience that he was the kind of man to make an unprincipled use of these formalities. But just when she felt assured he was nowhere in sight, he suddenly stepped out from the doorway of the dining room itself.

"There you are, Miss Pearce," he said. "I thought I heard your step. Dinner is ready for us, and I've ordered Auntie's butler to bring us up something special from her cellar."

He smiled as he spoke and took Emily's arm in a possessive grasp. Her skin crawled at his touch, but there was nothing she could do but acquiesce to his unwanted assistance.

As she had feared, Ronald made the most of the small ceremony of escorting her to the table. His hand lingered unnecessarily long on her arm as he led her to her seat, and as he helped position her at the table, he allowed his fingers to brush against her neck as though by accident. Emily shuddered as though a spider had run across her skin and wished in her heart it had been so innocent a trespasser.

She was relieved when Ronald took his place at the head of the table and nodded to the butler to serve the wine. "None for me, thank you," she said as the butler approached with the decanter. "I want only water."

The butler would have followed these instructions without question, but Ronald intervened. "You must at least try the wine, Emily," he said. "It's something rather special, as I mentioned before. Give Miss Pearce some wine, please," he ordered the butler.

The butler obeyed, though the glance he threw Emily was a troubled one. Ronald waited till wine had been poured in both glasses, then spoke again with casual authority. "That will do very well, Carter. You and the others may go now. Miss Pearce and I can serve ourselves."

Emily gave a gasp of surprise at these words. She had been counting on the presence of the butler and his attendant footmen to help keep Ronald at bay. Now it appeared she would have to do it alone. She felt sure her own efforts in this direction would be as unavailing as usual. Instinctively, she threw a look of appeal at the butler. He looked more troubled than ever, but it was clear he did not dare disobey Ronald's orders. "Very good, sir," he said. "Of course, you may serve yourselves if you like. Only be sure to call if you need anything. I shall be within earshot if you do," he added, and looked directly at Emily.

His look conveyed a measure of reassurance. Emily's heart, which had been going nineteen to the dozen, began to settle down again.

Of course, Ronald would not dare to molest her with the servants in the next room. The dining room was not a likely venue for molestation in any case. Likely he only meant to try to flirt with her and wished the servants to be out of the room while he did so. She took a drink from her water glass, deliberately pushing her wineglass farther away as she drank. Looking up, she found Ronald regarding her with vexation.

"You *are* a tiresome girl, aren't you?" he said. "I am sure you would like that wine if you tried it."

"What I like more than anything is having my wishes

respected," said Emily, returning his gaze squarely. "I do not care for wine this evening."

"Very well, but you're missing a treat." Deliberately, Ronald drained his glass, then refilled it from the decanter. "What other wishes do you have this evening, Emily?"

His voice made the words unspeakably suggestive. Emily eyed him with dislike. "For one thing, I would prefer that you call me Miss Pearce rather than using my Christian name," she said coldly. "I know your aunt calls me Emily now and then, but I don't think it's appropriate that you should do so."

"You think not, do you?" Ronald appeared to be considering the matter as he filled a couple of soup plates from the tureen and passed one over to Emily. "I confess that I don't see the objection myself. You know how I feel about you, Emily. To my mind it would be foolish to keep on addressing you in formal terms when I've already declared my feelings for you."

Emily drew a deep breath. "But that presupposes I return your feelings, Mr. Bartholomew," she said.

"Yes, I expect it does," agreed Ronald. "But am I wrong in such a supposition? I don't think I am, Emily." He held Emily's eye a long moment.

Emily returned the look unwaveringly. "But you *are* wrong, Mr. Bartholomew," she said. "I assure you that you are wrong. I am sorry if it gives you pain, but the fact is I have no feeling for you at all." *Except contempt*, she added mentally.

Ronald merely looked amused. "I see," he said. "You are more a woman of the world than I took you for, Emily. Just how much would it take to inspire you with the proper feelings for me?"

"Nothing could inspire them," said Emily, and now she was unable to keep the contempt out of her voice. "You misunderstand me entirely, Mr. Bartholomew."

"I don't think I do." Ronald pushed aside his soup plate and got up from his chair. Emily was alarmed by the purpose in his face. She, too, got up and began backing away.

"Don't," she said. "Please don't, Mr. Bartholomew." As before, the words were so much wasted breath. Ronald caught her in his arms and lowered his lips purposefully to hers. At the last minute, Emily turned her face away, struggling meanwhile to free herself from his arms. "Don't!" she said again. "Let me be, Mr. Bartholomew! Let me be."

"I can't," he said, smiling down at her in a way she found infuriating. "You really are a delectable creature, Emily. That skin—and those eyes—and that glorious hair. It's simply too much to resist. Anything you want, Emily— I will give you whatever you ask if only you will come away with me. I'll rent you a house in town and get you your own carriage, and you may have carte blanche as to clothes and jewelry."

"I don't want it!" said Emily. "I tell you, nothing on earth would make me come away with you, Mr. Bartholomew."

"Nothing?" repeated Ronald. His voice still sounded amused rather than angry.

"No, nothing." Emily was on the verge of tears. "When have I ever encouraged you to make love to me? Why should you suppose me so lost to decency as to desire a carte blanche?"

Her words seemed to give Ronald pause. "I didn't suppose you a woman of the town, if that's what you mean," he said. "But you must know I cannot offer you marriage, Emily. Lord knows I'm crazy about you, but my family all expect me to marry out of the peerage."

"I don't want marriage, either," said Emily, but her words only made Ronald grin.

"What woman doesn't want marriage?" He gave her a knowing smile. "You're a tempting creature, Emily, and you've got me properly wrapped around your finger, but you won't get an offer of marriage out of me. You may as well give up hoping and be content with a carte blanche."

With these words, he attempted to kiss her once more. Emily saw there was no use reasoning with him. Looking around for another avenue of escape, she espied the bell-pull hanging not far off. Ronald was not expecting a show of resistance at this point, and by exerting all her strength, she was able to break from his hold. She ran to the rope, pulled it quickly three or four times, then stood regarding Ronald with defiance.

"What the devil did you do that for?" demanded Ronald, his brows drawing together.

Emily was spared answering by the appearance of the butler. He glanced from Ronald to Emily, taking in the former's scowl and the latter's faintly disheveled appearance. When he spoke, however, his voice was wooden. "You rang, Miss Pearce?"

"Yes, Mr. Bartholomew is ready for the fish now," she said. "Please excuse me." She swept Ronald a low curtsy. "I must go to your aunt, Mr. Bartholomew." Before he could give any answer, she had hurried out of the dining room.

She felt dizzy with relief at her narrow escape, but mingled with her relief was a nagging anxiety. Miss Morris would not be pleased to learn she had left Ronald to eat alone in defiance of her orders. What was worse, there was no way she could explain her disobedience in a way that would not rebound upon herself. She might well have lost her position by her show of defiance, but what else could she do? Emily went slowly down the hall, a worried frown creasing her forehead. But her thoughts were given a different turn by the sound of a bell ringing wildly somewhere near at hand and the sight of several housemaids huddled near the drawing-room door.

"Oh, Miss Emily, Nell was just asking for you!" cried one, catching sight of her. "Miss Morris has had another apoplexy. They've just sent a groom after the doctor, but Nell doesn't think he can get here in time. Poor missus, it looks like she's done for." The maid burst into tears.

These words wiped every other thought from Emily's mind. Hurrying past the housemaids, she entered the drawing room with a silent tread.

Nell was bending over Miss Morris's couch. She looked up as Emily came in, and her anxious expression changed to one of relief.

"Thank God it's you, miss," she said. "I was just about to send for you. Those silly girls are worse than useless, and we've a deal to do, though none of it likely to do much good, I'm afraid. Still, we may as well try our best until the doctor gets here."

From that moment on, Emily had no time to think twice of Ronald or of her own difficulties. She was too busy obeying Nell's orders and joining with her in ministering to their stricken mistress. Warming pans and additional blankets were piled on Miss Morris's couch; the paralyzed limbs were chafed and stimulated, and Nell sought repeatedly to introduce a few of the drops the doctor had prescribed between her lips. Nothing was to any avail, however. The doctor came at last, toward morning. He had been attending to a lying-in some miles away and had been unable to come sooner. He took one look at Miss Morris and shook his head.

"There's nothing to be done. Just make her as comfortable as you can and let nature take its course. The end shouldn't be long in coming."

The end came soon enough, as the doctor had predicted. With tears running down her cheeks, Nell gently closed Miss Morris's dead eyes and folded her hands atop her breast. As Emily watched Nell perform these final services, she discovered she was weeping, too. She had not loved Miss Morris, but the old lady had been a forceful character and a fair mistress, according to her lights. There was something indescribably awful in seeing her now lying silent and motionless, never to move or speak again.

"Do you—do you want me to sit with her, Nell?" she whispered. "It's almost morning, anyhow, and I don't think I could sleep."

Nell shook her head. "Thank you, Miss Emily, but I'd rather sit up with her myself." There was a touching dignity in her voice as she added, "I've served Miss Morris for twenty years now, and I'll serve her till the end. You go on to your room and lie down for a while. Even if you can't sleep, you ought to get some rest or we'll be having you as a patient next."

Seeing that Nell really did not want her, Emily was grateful enough to flee that grim chamber. Going to her room, she undressed and lay down upon her bed. She did not suppose she could sleep, but the fatigue of the night had been sufficient to overcome even the effects of stress and sorrow. She slept soundly and did not awake until the morning was far advanced.

With a sense of shame, Emily rose and began to dress. It was the first morning in three years that she had slept late. Miss Morris had been an early riser and had insisted that all her household rise early with her, and it seemed heartless to flout her rules the very day after her death. At the same time, however, Emily recognized that this was no time for indulging in misplaced sentimentality. Miss Morris was gone now, and her passing had left her, Emily, out of a position. She must lose no time finding another one or the small sum she had managed to save while in service would be quickly dissipated.

She began to gather together her belongings, all the while planning what her next steps should be. Her first, beyond doubt, must be to remove herself from Miss Morris's house. It was Ronald's house now, and that made it impossible for her to stay under its roof even for the few days remaining until the funeral. It would prejudice her prospective employers if they knew she had been staying alone in an unmarried man's household even had that man possessed a decent and respectable character. And Ronald's was not a decent and respectable character. Emily sighed wearily as she packed her brushes and combs in her old-fashioned morocco dressing case. Yet despite the uncertainty of her prospects, she felt her spirits rising. The worst had happened; she was out of a position and with no certainty of another; but at least she was rid of Ronald.

I will not even ask him for a recommendation, she told herself. *I can make do instead with one from Miss Morris's attorney. He will recommend me, I'm sure, and I expect Dr. and Mrs. Astley at the vicarage would speak for my character as well. That should be enough to go on with.* She was busily planning the advertisement she would insert in the local newspapers when the door opened and Ronald walked into her room.

For a moment, shock held Emily speechless. "You!" she exclaimed at last. "What are you doing here?"

"Celebrating," said Ronald with a grin. He was wearing the same garments he had worn at dinner the night before, though they looked somewhat the worse for wear. His dark hair hung in rakish disorder about his face, and taken altogether, his appearance suggested that he had not slept at all but had rather spent the night in close communion with the wine decanter. It struck Emily suddenly that she had not seen him since she had left him in the dining room early the previous evening. Through all the flurry of Miss Morris's last illness he had not set foot in her room, not even when Nell had sent a message suggesting he might like to look upon his aunt one last time before she died.

This fact, and his announcement that he was celebrating, inspired Emily with a disgust even greater than that which she usually felt for him. "Get out," she said, and her voice was so fierce that Ronald instinctively took several steps toward the door. The next moment, he recovered himself, however, and came forward again, still surveying her with that shameless smile.

"It's all right, Emily," he said. "Auntie's dead, and we don't have to play propriety anymore. I'm sure the servants won't tell tales."

"Get out of my room," said Emily, her voice rising. "Get out now."

Ronald stood surveying her with a triumphant leer. "But it's not your room," he said. "It's my room and my house— everything's mine that was Auntie's. And that makes you mine, too, Emily."

In two swift strides he was upon her. Emily tried to push him away, but he caught her hands and drew her to him. "Mine, Emily!" he whispered. She struggled furiously, but in a matter of seconds Ronald had forced her down atop her bed with him on top of her.

"No!" said Emily. Again she sought to free herself. Ronald was much stronger than she was, however, and merely laughed as he looked down at her.

"Don't fight it, Emily," he said. "I know you want me just as much as I want you."

"I don't!" said Emily, but her words were cut short by Ronald's mouth descending on hers.

If what had gone before had been bad, this was a nightmare. The mere physical proximity of him was repugnant, with his stale, wine-tainted breath and the disgusting wetness of his lips. Emily was overcome by revulsion, and when he sought to force his tongue into her mouth, it was the

final straw. She could not move; she could not free herself
of his weight, but Ronald had released her hands, no doubt
thinking his position secure enough without them. She
reached out frantically on either side of her, searching for
anything that might assist her in beating off Ronald's
attack. Her right hand found only empty air and bed-
clothes, but when she stretched out her left hand, her
fingers brushed the handle of her dressing case, which was
lying on the floor beside her bed.

It was not the weapon Emily would have chosen, but it
was the only one at hand. Gripping the morocco-bound
handle, Emily swung it for all she was worth.

She had chosen better than she knew. The case was
loaded with all her small personal possessions as well as
her toilet articles, and Emily wielded it with a strength
born of desperation. The blow struck Ronald squarely on
the side of the head. He gave a surprised grunt and went
suddenly still.

For a moment Emily lay there, still gripping the handle
of her case. She hardly dared hope her effort had been
successful. But after a full minute had gone by and Ronald
had not moved, she began cautiously to ease herself from
beneath him. This was no simple task, for Ronald's tall
form was a considerable weight upon her and just now it
was all dead weight. Indeed, once Emily had gained her
feet and was able to look at him closely, she realized with
a jolt of horror that it might not be only his weight that
was dead. His eyes were closed, his face was like marble,
and there was no sign that he was breathing.

"Oh, God," she whispered. Kneeling down, she grasped
his wrist and searched for a pulse. But her hands were
trembling and her own pulse was beating so loud that she
could not tell if he had one or not. She dropped his hand
and tried to recall what other tests doctors used to detect
the presence of life. If she had possessed a hand mirror,

she might have held it beneath his nostrils to see if he was breathing. But the only mirror in the room was the one attached to her washstand, and there was no way to bring it near Ronald's face without breaking it. Besides, she very much feared that any further tests would only confirm what she already suspected. Ronald was dead, and she, Emily Pearce, had killed him. She was a murderess, and the fact that she had murdered in self-defense was of surprisingly little comfort.

Emily buried her face in her hands, trying to think what to do. The proper action, of course, would be to alert the servants and have them send for the doctor. Naturally, they would all be shocked; they would ask how Ronald had come by his injuries and why. She would have to tell them the whole sordid story, then tell it over again when the doctor arrived. Later, she would probably have to tell it again to the local magistrate. And what if none of them believed her? She was a poor and nameless hired companion, while Ronald had been a man of position who was heir to a lofty title and estate. Her own relatives had disowned her, while behind him stood a wealthy and powerful family who would probably exert all their wealth and power to avenge his untimely death. She might end up imprisoned, transported, or even hanged.

Emily shuddered. She turned to look again at the still figure lying on the bed. Even in death, Ronald was able to hound her. If she stayed where she was and let matters take their course, his vengeance would close in upon her as surely as death itself.

The thought drove Emily to a kind of madness. Without pausing to think or even don her bonnet or shawl, she simply walked out of the room and closed the door behind her. With the same unhurried step, she passed down the hall, down the backstairs, and out through the side door of the house.

No one remarked at her going. There were only a few servants about, and those few did not notice her in the least, being intent on discussing their late mistress's death in sepulchral tones. Thus it was that Emily left the house that had been her home for three years and made her way into a world that seemed most unlikely to embrace her.

Chapter 3

Outside the house, Emily continued on her way at the
same unhurried pace. She passed through the gardens and
grounds of the big house and into the lane that ran behind
the garden.

The choice of the quiet lane instead of the busy high
road was purely instinctive on Emily's part. Her mind was
so numbed with shock that calculations of any kind were
impossible to her. Likewise, she did not choose to walk
away because running away would make her conspicuous
and lead quickly to exhaustion. She walked because it was
the normal and natural thing to do, and her numbed
senses fell back on the normal and natural by a kind of
default. She walked for the best part of two hours in a state
of shock so complete that when she finally awoke from it,
she had no recollection of how she had reached her present location. Looking from the hedge that bounded the
left-hand side of the lane to the open farmland on her

right, she began to reflect with consternation on her position.

If I had to run away—and I suppose I did have to, although I did nothing that was not justified—the least I could have done is bring my reticule with me, Emily told herself. *Now I have no money. How am I to live? I cannot get a position without a recommendation, and I cannot apply for any recommendations when I am a fugitive murderess. I don't have a change of clothes with me—why, I don't even have a hat.*

Considered rationally, her position could hardly have been worse. Emily walked on through the waning afternoon, growing more and more frightened as she went. She also found herself growing more and more hungry. She had eaten no breakfast that morning, and there appeared equally little prospect of getting any dinner. She had no money to buy food, and unless she could find some berries growing wild or an orchard where she might gather a few windfalls, it looked as though she would be obliged to go hungry.

So be it, Emily told herself grimly. *I can endure a little hunger if I must. Thank heavens it is June! There must be something growing wild hereabouts that I can eat. And at least I need not worry about freezing to death. What a fool I was to walk out without my money or shawl or hat!*

For the next hour or so, Emily trudged along the lane calling herself every species of fool she had been called before and some she had not. At last she came to a fork in the road. The left-hand fork bore a signpost with the legend "To Westhaven" on it. The right was unmarked and straggled off across a stretch of open heath in an easterly direction.

Emily stood and reflected doubtfully. She had only the vaguest idea of where she was. She had walked without thinking much of the way, and she was in any case little acquainted with the geography of Devonshire. Miss Morris had hired her in London, then brought her immediately to Devonshire, and since coming there she had been kept so busy that she had had no opportunity to do any exploring farther afield than the local village. "Westhaven" sounded familiar to her, but she did not know how big a town it was or what its character might be. On the whole, it seemed best to avoid towns and strike toward some more rural locale. So she took the right-hand fork and set off across the heath.

She was growing footsore and weary by this time. Hunger was a gnawing ache in her stomach, but even worse was her growing sense of thirst. There had been no water that she had seen along her way thus far, and she had not thought to drink anything before she left Miss Morris's house, any more than she had thought to bring her money or shawl or hat. Just when she thought she could bear it no longer, she came to a rough plank bridge that spanned a small brook. Emily had never drunk from a stream before and was dubious about doing it now, but the water looked clean enough, and she was too thirsty to be particular. So she drank and went on her way feeling a little heartened.

It was growing dark by this time. The sun setting over the heath threw long shadows on the bracken-carpeted earth around her. Emily began to turn her thoughts to the problem of where she was to spend the night. She had heard of tramps sleeping in haystacks, but there appeared to be no haystacks about, and so ignorant was she of agricultural matters that she did not even know if this was the proper season for them. Likewise, she supposed a barn or other outbuilding might offer a refuge, but there were none to be seen—no buildings at all, in fact. The only thing she could see for miles around her was rough hill pasture, broken here and there by outcroppings of stone.

Having no alternative, Emily continued across the heath. The sky grew darker and darker as she went. She found it increasingly difficult to pick her way along the path. Once, she stopped and sat down for a few minutes on a boulder to rest. But the loneliness of the landscape around her was beginning to get upon her nerves, and she soon got up and continued on her way, walking a little quicker in spite of her fatigue.

There must be someplace I can find shelter, Emily told herself. But it was so dark now that even if she chanced upon some potential shelter, she feared she would walk right past it. No moon had risen as yet, and the night was very dark, though thankfully clear and fair. "At least it's not raining," said Emily aloud. "I would be in sad straits if it were, with no hat or cloak or umbrella. If worst comes to worst, I can simply sleep on the ground."

But though sleeping on the ground might be an option, it was not one that appealed to Emily's sensibilities. She determined to go on as long as she possibly could in hopes she might yet find shelter.

"Besides, it would be better if I put as much distance as possible between me and Miss Morris's house before I think of stopping. I wonder—I wonder if they have found Ronald yet."

The idea made her feel sick, but she forced herself to consider it dispassionately. The servants would probably have discovered Ronald's body by this time. It was usual for the housemaids to make up the bedchambers soon after breakfast, although it might be that on this occasion things had not gone as usual. She was such an unimportant person in the household that her room was always one of the last to be dealt with, anyway, and in the confusion following on Miss Morris's death, it was quite possible that the housemaids had slighted that part of their duties altogether. That meant the discovery of what she had done might be delayed a few hours longer. But even given the best possible circumstances, it could not be postponed for long.

"In any case, I don't suppose they will begin looking for me all at once. They will have to send for the doctor first and determine what happened to Ronald. But his being in my bedchamber will certainly fix their suspicions on me, and when they find I have disappeared, their suspicions will become a certainty."

For the past eight hours or so, Emily had been regretting that she had run away with so little thought or preparation. Now she began to wonder whether she ought to have run away at all. Perhaps it would have been better to have stayed and faced the consequences. At least then she might have presented her side of the matter to the proper authorities. Besides, it was just possible that Ronald was not dead at all but merely stunned into temporary unconsciousness. Regarding that possibility, however, Emily would not allow herself to hope.

It doesn't much matter, anyway. Ronald would call it a murderous attack even if it didn't result in murder, she told herself bitterly. *It would only be my word against his that I was defending myself. And if it comes to my word against his, I am sure the authorities would believe him rather than me.*

Having settled the matter once and for all in her mind, Emily continued grimly on. But it was not long before she ran into difficulties. The path she had been following seemed to dwindle into a mere cattle path, very overgrown and difficult to negotiate in the darkness. By the time she had gone another mile or two, it seemed to disappear altogether.

Emily stood amid the waist-high tangle of gorse and bracken and considered her predicament with dismay. She suspected she had taken a wrong turning somewhere. But where it had happened and how she was to retrace her steps, she had no idea. Straining her eyes in the darkness, she tried to make out some landmark that might give her a clue. It was difficult to be certain, but in the distance she thought she could detect a denser patch of darkness that might be trees.

"I'll go that way," she decided. "Perhaps there are houses there as well as trees. Even if there aren't, a tree would offer more shelter than this dreadful moor." So she began pushing her way through the underbrush in the direction of the darker spot in the landscape.

This was weary work and took a dreadful toll on her clothing. Pulling her skirt free from a bramble bush for the hundredth time, Emily stopped to reconnoiter. She was close enough now to see that the patch of darkness ahead of her *was* trees—not merely a few trees but what appeared to be the beginnings of a forest. As she stood looking on, a light suddenly gleamed forth in the midst of the trees. It was as welcome to Emily's eyes as a lighthouse to a disoriented mariner. She began to make her way toward the light, forgetting that she was a fugitive who would do better to avoid the company of her fellow men.

Just as she reached the margin of the forest, the moon made a belated appearance. It was only a thin crescent moon, but it gave enough light for Emily to see a small cottage standing a few hundred yards ahead of her. The light she had seen was gleaming forth from one of its windows.

At this point, it occurred to Emily that she could scarcely walk up to the cottage door and demand shelter. The appearance of a strange young woman at that time of night—she reckoned it was nearly midnight—could only inspire the cottage's inhabitants with fear and distrust. But it might be that there was another, uninhabited cottage in the area or at least a woodshed or cow byre where she could rest a few hours without being seen.

As she stood there, searching amid the trees for some

sign of such a shelter, something came rushing at her out of the dark.

It was only a dog, and not an ill-disposed dog at that, but its appearance frightened Emily. She let out a shriek, turned, and began to run. The dog, surprised but gratified by this response, promptly followed her, barking loudly.

"What's that? Who's there? Come back, Brutus!" Emily heard the words shouted behind her, but she did not turn to look. She ran on and on, even after the dog had turned back in obedience to its master's call.

Before long, her breath was coming raggedly, and her heart within her breast felt as though it would burst. It was neither of these things that caused her to stop running, however. Rather, it was some sixth sense, a sharp awareness of imminent danger, that made her stop short and stand looking about her with fear and trembling.

The moon, making another of its shy, belated appearances, suddenly shone out, revealing a chasm in the ground almost at Emily's feet. It stretched away before her, a dense pit of blackness to which she could see no bottom. Emily started back with a gasp. As she did so, she noticed for the first time a rude sign posted nearby on which she could just make out the words Quarry and Danger. In the circumstances it struck her as funny. She gave a brief, hysterical gasp of laughter and began to retreat from the quarry step by cautious step, as though she feared it might still reach out and draw her down into its depths.

She had gone only a few steps when she realized she was on a path of sorts. It seemed to run along the brink of the quarry, disappearing into the night both to the right and to the left. There was no particular reason why Emily chose the right-hand way except that it promised to take her soonest from the vicinity of the quarry. She followed along it and soon found herself deep in the woods once more.

It was dark within the woods, but the darkness seemed safe and comfortable to Emily after her two recent scares. She continued on, and after a few minutes' walking, she came to a point where the path divided into two ways. Neither way was marked, but the left-hand path appeared narrower and less well traveled than the other. Nevertheless, it was the left-hand path that Emily chose. She continued on, and when this path in its turn branched into two ways, she once again chose the way to the left, even though it had by now dwindled to little more than a trail through the woods.

Something about it drew Emily on, however. She was weary now to the point of dropping with fatigue. Her feet felt as though they were a solid mass of blister, while her head ached and her thirst was once again mounting to unbearable proportions. Conscious thought was beyond her. It was instinct that was leading her once more, and that instinct proved remarkably sound. Emily had gone only a few hundred feet along the narrow trail when the woods suddenly opened into a clearing. Looking up, she found herself standing in front of a small building.

It seemed to be some sort of folly or summerhouse, an open pavilion standing on slender stone columns. Inside she could see several wicker chairs and a low wicker settee. In the midst of these furnishings stood something that looked like a well. Emily moved closer, stepping cautiously as though she feared the pavilion might vanish like a dream at her approach.

As she came closer, she saw she had been right. There *was* a well within the pavilion, and what was yet more important, there was water in it. It shone smooth and dark within the well's waist-high circle of stonework. This stonework was carved with curious designs worn indistinct with time, and a metal dipper was fastened to its lip by means of a chain and iron staple.

To Emily, it seemed a direct answer to a prayer. "Thank you!" she whispered, and lost no time in plunging the dipper into the water. It took several dipperfuls to satisfy her thirst, but when at last Emily laid down the dipper, she felt wonderfully restored. She began to look around the pavilion with a speculative eye, considering how it might serve her as a place of rest as well as refreshment.

"That settee will make a decent bed, I should think. It's a trifle narrow, but still it should be a great deal more comfortable than sleeping on the ground." Going over to the settee, she shook out its cushions thoroughly, then rearranged them as comfortably as she could along its length. She also grouped some of the chairs around it to make a kind of railing lest she should roll off in the night. No further preparations were necessary or even possible. Emily did not feel comfortable undressing to any extent, and she reckoned she would be chilled enough in the morning even with all her clothes on. *But it couldn't be worse than gaol,* she told herself with a shiver. Climbing atop her makeshift couch, she settled herself for sleep.

Weary as she was, sleep did not come to her immediately. Her limbs ached from her long day's unaccustomed exercise, and the cushions on which she lay smelled musty and felt much harder than her usual bed. She also felt strange and exposed lying in the open air. When sleep finally came, it was a light and restless slumber from which she awoke from time to time with her heart in her mouth and an indefinite fear paralyzing her senses.

She had just recovered from the fourth such episode and was composing herself to sleep once more when a noise caught her ears. It sounded like a woman's laugh, and it rang out startlingly loud within the still wood.

Emily leaped up and looked about her wildly. Away in the east, she could see a glow that signaled the approach of a new day. This amazed Emily, who felt she had hardly slept at all, but her amazement changed to consternation when she looked to the west. A light was approaching in the darkness—one that bobbed up and down, occasionally disappearing from view for an instant before reappearing closer at hand. Emily had no difficulty in recognizing it as a lantern being carried by someone walking through the woods. As though to confirm her recognition, the sound of laughter rang out again. It was not merely one woman's laugh this time but what sounded like several women laughing together.

Alarmed and bewildered, Emily dropped back upon her couch once more. She could not imagine why a party of women should be walking through the woods at such an hour. But her alarm quickly subsided when she realized their errand could hardly have anything to do with her. Probably they were farm women on their way to perform some rural chore. She need only remain where she was and they would pass her harmlessly by. So she settled herself amid her nest of chairs and cushions once more and listened curiously to the chatter that was now within clear earshot.

"Give over, Meg, do! You never suppose it'll be Harry Winston you see in the well, do you?"

"Why not?" returned the girl addressed as Meg with another bold laugh. "I suppose I've as good a chance of marrying him as any of *you*."

At the word "well," Emily started and nearly sat up again in consternation. She had not understood all the women had said, but the mention of wells made her fear they might be coming to the well within the little pavilion. *But that's ridiculous*, she assured herself. *There's no reason in the world for them to visit an old well like this one. And at this hour of the morning, too!*

Yet ridiculous or not, it soon became obvious that this was what the women intended to do. They swept into the

pavilion like a flock of chattering magpies and clustered
around the well in its center. Emily, crouching behind her
screen of chairs, felt sure they must catch sight of her at
any moment. She could see them plainly enough through
the wicker meshes of the chair backs: eight or nine girls
varying in age from their late teens to their early twenties.
They were country girls, to judge by their dress and speech,
and happily for Emily, they all seemed intent upon their
present task. One by one they stepped up to the well and
solemnly washed their faces while the other girls laughed
and joked around them.

This seemed a strange proceeding to Emily. After she
had watched three or four of the girls go through the same
routine, she began to notice something stranger yet. After
each girl had washed her face, she would stand looking
intently into the water for a moment or two. Then she
would laugh or shrug, step aside, and allow another girl
to take her place while her companions fluttered around
her, crying, "What did you see? What did you see?"

Eventually, the last girl had washed her face in the well.
One of them picked up the lantern, and they swept out
of the pavilion in a body, laughing and chattering as before.
Emily could hear the voice of Meg above them all asserting,
"I *did* see Harry Winston, and I *shall* marry him, whatever
you choose to think, Sarah Tate! Just you wait and see!"

As soon as their voices had faded from earshot, Emily
arose once more. Wincing a little at the pain of her
cramped muscles, she hobbled over to the well.

It looked exactly as it had the night before except that
there was a good deal of water splashed on the stone floor
around the well curb. The sight of it made Emily feel
suddenly thirsty once again. She felt a natural distaste for
drinking where others had just washed, but she reminded
herself that a fugitive murderess could not afford to be
too fastidious. Taking up the iron dipper, she filled it and

drank resolutely. The water was clear and cold, but she wished she had something more substantial with which to fill her stomach. Her whole midsection felt pinched and empty, and there was a curious swimming sensation in her head when she straightened up. Hoping to relieve this last symptom, Emily bent over the well again and splashed water on her face.

I wonder what those girls were looking at? she mused to herself. She looked down into the well intently. The sky had been steadily lightening all the while the party of girls had been at the well, and it was light enough now to see her own reflection looking dimly back at her. Look as she might, however, there was nothing else to be seen. She could not, for instance, see the well bottom or any sign that money had been thrown into it. Listening to the girls talk, it had occurred to her that this might be a wishing well, such as she had heard stories about as a child. It was well known that the west country abounded in wishing wells, and Devon must qualify as west country if any place did. But as far as she could tell, the girls had only washed their faces at the well, not thrown a penny in for luck.

"That's all to the good," she told her reflection. "I haven't a penny with me, and if I did, I couldn't spare it to a wishing well! But even if this isn't a wishing well, it will serve nicely as a looking glass. I have need of one, too. My hair looks as though I had been dragged backward through a bush, as my old nurse used to say."

Taking down her hair, she began to comb through it with one of her side combs. As she combed, she took a rueful survey of her appearance. The sober, plum-colored poplin that she had donned the day before out of respect for Miss Morris's death was now torn and bedraggled after her encounters with the bramble bushes on the heath. Her stockings and petticoat were likewise torn, not to mention streaked with grime, while her shoes were cracked and dusty.

I look a fright, but it can't be helped, she told herself. *I must go on just as soon as it is light enough to see.*

Yet she felt a marked disinclination to do any more walking that day. Even combing her hair was an exercise almost beyond her strength. She lay down the comb and gripped the well curb as a wave of dizziness swept over her. As soon as the wave had passed, she leaned down to splash more water on her face.

"How lovely it would be if I could just stay here in this pavilion all day and rest," she whispered. "But I must go on. If only I knew where I was to go to. I wish—I wish I could see what lay ahead of me and if it were any use going on."

She looked down into the well. Once more she could see her face reflected in the still water. As she watched, a change seemed to pass over the mirrored image, enveloping it in a kind of shimmering light. Emily blinked and bent closer, wondering if hunger and fatigue had combined to affect her vision. For even as she watched, another face had appeared beside her own in the water—a man's face, unknown to her but possessing a kind of haunting familiarity nevertheless.

"I beg your pardon," said a voice in her ear.

It was a very pleasant voice, a masculine baritone with a hint of music in it. To Emily, however, it was merely another shock. Coming upon everything that had already happened to her in the last twenty-four hours, it was one shock too many. Her knees crumpled beneath her; the world went suddenly black, and she knew no more.

Chapter 4

When Emily opened her eyes again, she found herself lying once more on the wicker settee. Her wrists were being chafed, and a man's face was hovering over her. With a sensation of surprise, Emily recognized it as the same face she had seen in the well.

"You!" she exclaimed. "You're real, then?"

The man's face, which had looked worried to the point of being frantic, now relaxed into a smile. "Yes, I'm real," he said. "Did you think I was a bogle creeping up behind you? I know I'm no Adonis, but up till now no one's ever fainted at the sight of me!"

Emily's gaze wandered critically over the man's face. He looked to be in his early thirties, with light brown hair worn long on his collar and a face that was more interesting than handsome. Yet taken altogether, his features possessed an attraction all out of proportion to the sum of their parts. His chin was strong, square, and clefted; his mouth was wide and humorous, and his eyes were a particularly bright, clear blue. He was certainly not an Adonis, but he was very good to look at, and Emily could not help smiling at the idea of any lady fainting at the sight of him.

"I didn't think you were a bogle," she said. "It was only that you surprised me. I didn't hear you come up." As an afterthought, she added, "Do I know you? Your face seems familiar to me."

The man shook his head slowly: almost, it seemed, regretfully. "I don't think so," he said. "I should have remembered you if I had ever met you before. Are you—do you—is it possible that you live in this neighborhood?"

The mixture of hope and diffidence with which he asked this question struck Emily as very charming. If she had been a conceited girl, she would have been tempted to believe that he had been as impressed by her appearance as she had been by his. But that was hardly possible. She looked down at herself as she lay on the settee: torn and draggled dress, cracked shoes, and (merciful heavens!) hair streaming loose over her shoulders. Blushing, she sought to gather her hair into a knot as she answered his question. "No, I don't live in this neighborhood," she said. "I am only visiting."

No sooner had she spoken than she cursed her own foolishness. Of course, the man would ask next at whose house she was visiting. She could hardly tell him that she was staying here at the pavilion, nor could she risk inventing a fictional address, for the man quite likely knew all the houses in the neighborhood if he himself were a resident here. But as she sought frantically for a way around this difficulty, the man set her fears to rest with his next speech.

"We are in the same situation, then. I am merely visiting in the neighborhood, too. It's a pretty place, isn't it?"

"Very pretty," said Emily, looking around her. The sun was just beginning to peep over the horizon, filling the pavilion and the woods surrounding it with soft, pearl-tinted light. After a minute's hesitation, she decided to risk asking the man a question in her turn. "What exactly is this place? Do you know?"

"Indeed I do, though I'm afraid I don't know much else. But on that question I can satisfy you most entirely. It would be a strange thing if I could not, seeing that I am leasing it." Laughter lit up the man's eyes. "This is Honeywell House. Or, rather, this is part of the Honeywell House estate. The house itself is off that way, just through the woods." He waved his hand in a southerly direction.

"I see," said Emily. The man's answer left her no wiser than before, for she had never heard of Honeywell House. Still, she found the name intriguing, and she was glad when the man went on with his explanation without waiting for further comment.

"If you look, you can see the site of the original Honeywell House through the trees there," he said, pointing to a ruin just visible to the east of the pavilion. "And of course the spot where we are standing now is the most important and historic part of the whole property. This, I am credibly informed, is none other than the well itself, from which the estate takes its name. At least I assume it is. It's the only well I've been able to find, and it answers to the housekeeper's description of it." The man lowered his voice. "I must admit I'd never heard of the well at Honeywell House before I came to this neighborhood. I didn't like to admit it to the housekeeper, however, for I could see she set great store by it. It was at her insistence that I was routed out of bed before dawn this morning so I could come and see the well in action, as it were."

"Oh, yes," said Emily. Noncommittal as her reply was, it seemed not to be the one the man had expected. He looked at her with something like suspicion in his eyes.

"Yes, of course. That is how I came to startle you just

now. I had heard it was the custom for girls to come here on Midsummer morning before dawn and wash their faces. According to my authority, the housekeeper, when one has performed this ritual, one is rewarded with a glimpse of one's future reflected in the well's waters. Did you see your future, or did my appearance interrupt you at the critical moment?''

Enlightenment came to Emily in a blinding flash. "So that is what they were doing!" she exclaimed. Seeing that the man was regarding her quizzically, she hurried to explain. "Some girls were here a little earlier washing their faces, and I heard them talking about their futures."

"So you weren't performing the ritual yourself?" said the man, regarding her more quizzically than ever.

"I—" began Emily, then stopped. Just in time, she had realized that the face-washing custom made a good excuse to justify her presence at the well. There was really no other way she could excuse her presence on a stranger's property at that hour of the morning. So she replied carefully, "Yes, I was washing my face. I didn't understand exactly what it was supposed to do, but I had heard enough about the well's powers to be interested. I didn't see anything in the water, though. Nothing but my own face— and then yours, of course, when you came up behind me."

As she spoke, she rose to her feet. She thought she had better make her escape before the man could ask any more questions. But the dizziness that had plagued her earlier was still with her, and she was forced to sit down again quickly.

"You're ill!" said the man with concern in his voice. "No, don't try to deny it. I can see you still look very pale. Are you feeling faint again? Shall I send for a doctor?"

"No!" said Emily. The idea threw her into such a panic that she tried to rise to her feet once more. But her limbs

simply would not support her. The man hurried forward
and caught her just as her knees collapsed.

"My dear, this won't do at all," he said. "You are obviously unwell. Let me take you back to the house and call
for a doctor. Did you come here on foot, or is there a
carriage waiting for you somewhere?"

"I came on foot." Emily panted. "But I don't need a
doctor, truly I don't. I will be well enough to go on in a
minute."

"But I cannot let you go while you are still so weak. If
you were to faint again and injure yourself, I would hold
myself responsible."

"I won't faint again," said Emily, almost sobbing in
frustration. "There's nothing wrong with me except—
except I am a little hungry. I was in too much of a hurry
this morning to have any breakfast."

"Then you must at least allow me to give you food and
drink before you return home," said the man. "Forgive
me for being so heavy-handed about my hospitality, but I
think the situation warrants it. You are obviously not fit to
go on."

Before Emily realized what he intended, he had picked
her up like a child and carried her out of the pavilion.
"No!" she said frantically, trying to free herself from his
grasp. "Put me down, please. I am well enough to walk."

He regarded her with a mixture of amusement and exasperation. "You're not, you know," he said. "And if you
do not stop thrashing about like that, you will be in even
worse case. I shall certainly drop you if you don't lie still
like a good girl and let me take you to the house."

"I don't want to go to the house!" said Emily. She had
stopped trying to struggle, but her voice was panic-stricken
as she went on speaking. "It's very kind of you to take me
in charge, but I would not be a burden to you."

"You aren't a burden," asserted the man, not pausing

in his progress through the woods. His breath was coming rather fast, and there was a flush of exertion on his face, but he repeated the words stoutly. "You aren't a burden. No burden at all, I assure you."

In spite of her panic, Emily could not help smiling a little. "Nonsense! I am persuaded you feel otherwise, sir, though you are chivalrous enough to say so. But I am a tolerably well grown woman and no small weight to be carried over such rough ground."

A flicker of an answering smile appeared in the man's eyes. "Yes, you are certainly a well-grown woman," he said. "I noticed it particularly the moment I saw you. As for your weight, however, it is nothing, or ought not to be if I were in proper training. It will do me good to get a little exercise." He paused to hoist Emily a little more securely in his arms, then continued on doggedly through the woods.

"But you must not!" said Emily, her panic returning in a rush. "Indeed you must not! Please put me down— please, please!" She could see disaster looming plainly ahead of her. In spite of all her walking the day before, she could not be much more than a dozen miles from Miss Morris's house. Such a distance was not nearly enough for safety. Word traveled fast in the country, carried from house to house by servants and tradespeople, and such a sensational piece of news as Ronald's death and her own suspicious disappearance would spread with twice the usual speed. The Honeywell House servants had probably already heard of it, and if they had not, there was always the doctor to contend with. He might well be the same one who had waited on Miss Morris: the same doctor who would have been called in to verify Ronald's death. In that case, her fate would be sealed beyond doubt. And she was helpless to do anything about it, too weak and dizzy to even argue with her captor, let alone escape him. Try though she might, a despairing sob escaped her lips.

The man stopped as suddenly as though he had been shot. "What is it?" he asked, looking anxiously down at Emily. "What's wrong?"

"Please put me down! Do not take me back to your house! Please, do not!"

The man looked down at her a long moment. When he spoke at last, his voice was slightly hurt. "I am a gentleman, you know. I hope you don't think—you must know I don't intend you any *harm* by bringing you to my house."

"No, no," Emily assured him, but her voice broke in spite of herself . "It's only that—Oh, you must not take me to your house. If you do, I shall be quite undone."

"You look rather as though you will be undone if I don't," he said, regarding her fixedly. "Why should you not come to my house? It seems to me the most sensible proceeding under the circumstances. And it would not be in the least improper, if that is what concerns you. I have an elderly aunt who is staying with me at present, and my housekeeper, too, is a very good and respectable woman. Between them, they will know just what is best to be done for you."

"It's not that," said Emily in desperation. "But I cannot come to your house. I simply cannot."

"Why not?" said the man. "I assure you it would be quite respectable."

"But you see, I am not," said Emily with a fresh burst of tears. "If you knew what I had done, you would not want me in your house."

She had not meant to say so much and was fearful as soon as she had said it. The man gave her a look that traveled from the top of her disheveled red-gold head to the dusty shoes upon her feet. When he spoke at last, his voice was calm and decided. "I don't believe it," he said.

"But it's true," said Emily. Terrified as she was of committing any further indiscretion, she still possessed enough natural stubbornness to resent the man's contradiction. "I assure you it's true, sir."

Again he looked at her, then shook his head. "No," he said. "You may have made mistakes in your life—I don't doubt it. Nobody who is alive and human can avoid making a mistake now and then. But if you did wrong things, I am sure you did them with a right intention."

"But you cannot know that!" said Emily, regarding him with astonishment.

The man looked back at her steadily. "But I do know it. It's true, isn't it? As soon as I looked in your eyes, I thought to myself, *There's a woman with a conscience.* I felt instinctively that if I were ever compelled to put my life and affairs in your hands, I might trust you to care for them as conscientiously as your own."

This was so much what Emily had been thinking about him that she could only regard him in open-mouthed silence. The man went on, a note of persuasion in his voice. "I believe you'd better tell me the whole story. What you've already said has made me very curious, you know, and now the only way you can satisfy my curiosity is to make a round tale of it. I need hardly say you can trust me not to betray you no matter what you may have done. You have my word as a gentleman, upon my honor."

Looking into his eyes, Emily found herself sorely tempted. As though reading her mind, the man went on, his voice more persuasive than ever. "I'll tell you what we'll do. The first place we come to that looks reasonably comfortable, I'll put you down and go find something to eat. I know you said you hadn't any breakfast this morning, and something tells me you hadn't any dinner last night, either." He smiled at Emily, and she gave him a wan smile in return. "Then, once you've eaten and are feeling stronger, you can tell me how it is you come to be in difficulties. Who knows? Perhaps there is some way I can help you. Even if there is not, I am sure it must make you feel better to confide your problems to someone. 'A trouble shared is a trouble halved,' as the country people say. Does that sound like a fair proposition?"

It sounded like heaven to Emily. To be sure, there was a part of her mind that urged her not to trust a stranger with her secret, but she turned a deaf ear to its urgings. She had already told the man enough to rouse his curiosity, as he himself had pointed out. It would be safer to tell him the whole story rather than leave him to make inquiries on his own. He had promised not to betray her, giving her his word as a gentleman that he would not, and Emily was inclined to trust him. Why she was so certain he was trustworthy, she could not have said, but if he had proposed putting her in a wheelbarrow and trundling off with her across country, she would have felt that this was the best thing to do.

So she said, "Yes, I will tell you the whole story if you insist. But I warn you that it's a sordid tale, and the ending is not likely to be a happy one."

"But I insist the ending shall be happy," returned the man cheerfully. "All stories should have happy endings. That is the rule I abide by—at least it has been up till now."

He looked suddenly thoughtful as he added these last words. Emily looked at him curiously, but he made no effort to explain them. Instead, he nodded toward a clearing in the trees ahead of them. "The Italian garden is just through those trees. That will be a pleasant place for you to eat your breakfast—and for me to eat mine, too, if you have no objection. I'll deposit you here and go find something for us to eat."

As he spoke, he placed Emily on a stone bench overlooking the Italian garden. "You can sit and admire the view while I'm gone," he told her with a smile. "But please

don't try to do anything else. I'm convinced you're not fit
for it, and I don't want to return and find you've gone off
in a swoon again.''

Emily sat watching as he crossed the garden and disappeared behind the hedge that bounded its farther side.
Her heart glowed with gratitude toward this perfect
stranger who had taken her under his wing. But just as
she was reflecting warmly on all he had done and promised
to do for her, the suspicious part of her mind broke in
with another whispered doubt.

''What if his kindness is merely a take-in? You don't
know a thing about him except that he has a pleasant voice
and the appearance of a gentleman. He might be the
greatest rogue under the sun, for all you know to the
contrary. And even if he is as honest as he looks, his honesty
might not work in your favor. It may be that he has heard
the news of Ronald's death and guessed who you are. In
that case, he might not have gone to get breakfast but
rather to summon the local constable. If you are fool
enough to wait here for him to return, you will soon find
yourself arrested and thrown into gaol for murdering
Ronald.''

It was an alarming thought, and for a moment Emily
seriously considered getting up and making good her
escape. But sanity soon reasserted itself. She was so weak
that any attempt to run away would be doomed at the
outset. If the man had really gone to summon the authorities, they would have no difficulty tracking her down even
if she ran like a deer. It would be much more comfortable
and dignified to be arrested here in the Italian garden
rather than be tracked through the woods like a beast.
Besides, Emily had another motive that kept her seated
firmly on the bench. The man had believed that she was
honest and well-intentioned. He had said as much during
their brief conversation and showed he meant it by leaving

her alone while he went off to fetch breakfast. He had
trusted her to keep her part of the bargain, and she meant
not to betray his trust even if it meant being betrayed in
her turn.

Having made up her mind on this point, Emily put aside
all notion of running away and resigned herself to whatever
fate might hold in store for her. In the meantime, she was
content to survey the Italian garden along with the rest of
the prospect spread out before her.

The Italian garden was large and rectangular and sunk
several feet beneath the surface of the surrounding earth.
Near Emily's bench was a set of marble steps that led down
into it, with another set of steps leading out the other side.
In the center was a fountain flanked by formal beds of
flowers. The sides were bounded by high hedges against
which were ranged classical statues, interspersed by large
marble urns on pedestals.

Through the gap in the hedge opposite, Emily could
see more gardens and on their farther side a handsome
terrace. Beyond this she could not see much, for trees
obscured her view, but there were glimpses of a large, slate-
colored building that must be Honeywell House. Emily
was considering it with curiosity when the man suddenly
appeared beside her, bearing a napkin-wrapped bundle in
one hand and his hat in the other.

"Do you like strawberries?" he asked, thrusting the hat
toward her. "I hope so, for that's what I brought you—
that and some bread." He unwrapped the bundle to reveal
a cottage loaf still steaming from the oven. " I would have
liked to bring you something more sustaining, but for now
I thought it best merely to help myself to what was most
readily available and not say anything to the servants. They
would ask questions if I were to demand a picnic breakfast
for two, and I think it's better not to arouse anybody's

curiosity until we've decided what is best to be done about you. Don't you agree?"

"Yes," Emily agreed fervently. The smell of the bread and berries together made her feel nearly ill with hunger. Her hand trembled as she reached out to break a piece from the loaf the man offered her. It tasted delicious, better than any food she could remember, and the berries were like nectar and ambrosia. It took all her self-control to eat with proper attention to manners rather than wolfing the food down like a famished animal. Even with proper attention to manners she managed to eat a great deal in a very short time, and the man smiled as he handed her the last of the berries.

"You need them more than I do, I think. I can see I was right when I guessed you had no dinner yesterday."

"No, nor luncheon or breakfast, either," said Emily frankly. "This is the first I have eaten since—Gracious, when did I eat last?" she considered as she nibbled the last strawberry. "It has been nearly forty-eight hours, I believe. I had nothing at all yesterday and no dinner the night before that." Her face darkened as she recalled the dinner with Ronald and how she had been forced to leave the table without eating. The man, who was watching her face, cleared his throat.

"Do you think you feel well enough to tell me about it now?" he inquired diffidently. "You look and sound much better, and there is color in your cheeks."

"Yes, I feel quite well now. Food was all I needed." The flush of color in Emily's cheeks grew darker as she glanced at the man. "As for telling you what happened, however— well, I hardly know where to begin."

"Begin at the beginning, of course," he said promptly. "But I appreciate your reservations. Perhaps it would be easier if we were formally introduced. Of course, we have no one to perform an introduction between us, but if you are willing to overlook that nicety, we can make shift to achieve some degree of social acquaintance." Rising to his feet, the man swept her a bow. "May I present to you Sir Terrence O'Reilly? He is a very pleasant, well-intentioned fellow, I assure you, and admirably discreet. Even the housekeeper here at Honeywell House admits that I am tolerably well-behaved, for all I *am* an Irishman."

Emily looked at him with surprise. "Irishman?" she said. "Are you indeed? You don't *sound* Irish."

"Sure, and I am, though," protested Sir Terrence in such a broad Irish brogue that Emily could not help laughing. Reverting to his normal voice, he added, "I am Irish on my father's side but English on my mother's. And by her wish I have spent as much of my life in England as in my native country. I went to school here and spent three years at Cambridge, so I suppose it is no wonder that I don't sound particularly Irish."

Emily nodded. "Now I think of it, you do have just a trace of accent," she said. "I noticed the first time you spoke that there was something not quite English about your voice. But I couldn't think what it was."

"Well, I hope you do not find it displeasing. Sure, and I'll talk as broad as old Mick O'Halloran back home if it will please your ladyship better."

Emily giggled. "If you do that, I won't be able to talk at all for laughing," she said. "Your everyday voice will do very well." Privately she thought she had never heard a more attractive voice than Sir Terrence's mellow baritone, but this was hardly something she could say to him. He smiled at her, his blue eyes merry.

"Just as you wish, ma'am. That's one-half of our introduction performed; now what about the other half? To whom have I the pleasure of introducing my friend Sir Terrence?"

Emily hesitated, a troubled frown puckering her brow.

Sir Terrence stood watching her, the merriment gradually fading from his face. "You need not tell me if you do not like," he said gently. "I thought it would make you more comfortable if you knew to whom you were confiding your secrets, but you need not return the favor if you prefer not to."

Emily looked into his face, with its strong features, square jaw, and frank blue eyes. She took a sudden decision. "No, I will tell you. But I must beg you to keep your promise about not telling it to anyone. My name is Emily Pearce."

She waited fearfully for his reaction. He gave no start of shock or revulsion, however, such as one might expect in making the acquaintance of a renowned murderess. "Emily Pearce," he repeated thoughtfully. "A very pretty name."

"You have never heard it, then?" said Emily, still regarding him fearfully.

Sir Terrence shook his head, his face surprised. "No, I think not. Should I have?"

"I had fancied everyone must know it by this time," said Emily. Squaring her shoulders, she added resolutely, "I am a murderer, you see."

Sir Terrence's eyes opened wide. "A murderer!" he said. He looked Emily up and down, then shook his head again. "I don't believe it. Forgive me, but I simply can't believe it. There is no way in the world you could ever have purposely committed a murder."

"But I did," insisted Emily. "At least—I'm not sure whether it might really have been manslaughter. But it comes to the same thing. I am sure Ronald's family will call it murder if they ever succeed in tracking me down."

Sir Terrence shook his head in a bewildered manner. "Ronald's family?" he said. "This is not beginning at the beginning, Miss Pearce! Perhaps you had better start your story over and explain the murder or manslaughter or whatever it was at the point where it comes in."

Emily obligingly did so, describing her background and how she had come to take a position as Miss Morris's companion. It was harder to explain when she got to the part about Ronald's persecution of her, but Sir Terrence made it easy for her by understanding immediately what kind of man Ronald had been.

"I know the type," he said. "Overbearing, conceited, and sure that anything he wants is his by divine right. A natural bully, in fact. And like all bullies, he would naturally choose his victims among those unable to defend themselves."

"Exactly," said Emily, nodding vigorously. "That's exactly what Ronald was like. I didn't wish to lose my position, and Miss Morris would have blamed me if she had known he was—he was making advances to me. As long as Miss Morris was alive, it was all right, for he was too much afraid of offending her to behave very badly. But two nights ago she died very suddenly and unexpectedly. And the very morning after she died, he came to my room and tried to—tried to—"

She stopped, unable to go on. Sir Terrence looked at her a moment, and into his eyes crept a look of indignation that made them blaze up like blue fire. "Are you saying this brute tried to *force* himself upon you?" he demanded.

"Yes," said Emily, bowing her head.

"On you, who were dependent on him and his goodwill for your livelihood! While his aunt was yet lying dead in the same house! Good God! I never heard of such infamy." Sir Terrence began to walk up and down in front of the bench, seeming hardly conscious of Emily's presence. "The man deserves to be beaten like the dog he is— though I'm thinking that same remark's an insult to honest dogs. Cur is more like it. It's not thinkable that he should

be allowed to go scatheless after such behavior. By the
saints, I wouldn't mind a share in the chastising myself."

In his indignation, the Irish flavor had crept more
strongly into his voice, and Emily could not help smiling
a little. When she spoke, however, her voice was filled with
despair. "It's very kind of you, but you needn't have a
share of anything," she told Sir Terrence. "I am afraid I
have done all that is needful toward chastising Ronald,
and a great deal more besides."

Sir Terrence gave her a startled look. "You mean you—
Oh, I see." He was silent a moment, then repeated in a
stronger tone, "I see. Very unfortunate, but it sounds as
though you were justified. How did you—how did it
happen?"

"I hit him in the head with my dressing case. It was the
only weapon I could find when I—when Ronald attacked
me. I didn't mean to kill him, only to make him stop. But
the case was full and very heavy, and I swung it very hard.
He just grunted and went still, and after that I couldn't
see him breathing."

Sir Terrence was silent several minutes, absorbing this
information. "I see," he said again. "Very unfortunate,
but I don't see how you could have done anything else. I
expect the law will take the same view."

Emily shook her head dismally. "I don't believe it will.
Ronald's father is a lord, you see—Lord Bartholomew. He
will be furious when he learns what has happened. I am
sure he will spare no pains to see I am punished."

"Yes, but his son was trying to rape you, for God's sake!"
said Sir Terrence. "He would not have a leg to stand on
in court."

"Do you think not? I think otherwise," said Emily with
the calm of despair. "There weren't any witnesses, you
know. Some of the other servants knew Ronald was pursu-
ing me, but I don't believe their word would count for

much if Lord Bartholomew chose to make an issue of it. Besides, he wouldn't need to. The mere fact that I ran away after it happened will be proof enough against me if the matter ever comes to court."

Sir Terrence was silent for several more minutes, then shook his head. "It's very unfortunate," he said. "I still think you were justified in what you did, mind you. But I'm afraid you are right in saying it might be difficult to prove in the circumstances. Unless—" He looked at Emily hopefully. "Tell me, are you certain Ronald was dead? The human frame can take an amazing amount of abuse, you know. I've seen men get knocked out completely, then get up again a few minutes later and be right as a trivet."

Emily shook her head. "I'm afraid it was more serious than that with Ronald. He was so very still and white, and I couldn't find a pulse at all."

"Nevertheless, I think it ought to be investigated before we do anything else," said Sir Terrence briskly. "Once we have made sure of Ronald's condition, we can decide what your next step should be."

Emily looked at him in amazement. "*We* can decide?" she repeated. "But this is nothing to do with you, Sir Terrence. It's kind of you to wish to help me, but you know I could not allow you to involve yourself in my affairs even if you wanted to."

"I do want to," said Sir Terrence. "In fact, I'm involved already. What you've told me has given me a great dislike for this Ronald character, and I'm determined to see he doesn't plague you anymore, alive or dead."

"But it's nothing to do with you," repeated Emily. "And it's such an ugly business! I thank you, but really I think I shall have to go this alone."

"Pardon me, but I don't think you can," said Sir Terrence calmly. "You were near dropping with hunger and fatigue when I found you an hour ago. I don't blame you for wishing to keep your problems to yourself—in fact, I admire you for it. But in this case, your problem is too great for one person alone. I have already helped you in some small measure, have I not?"

"Yes," admitted Emily, looking down at the empty napkin and pile of strawberry hulls on the bench between them. "I don't know where I would have been if you had not brought me this food."

"Then why will you not allow me to assist you further?"

"But I cannot allow you, a stranger, to become embroiled in my business," protested Emily. "Doubtless you have affairs of your own to manage."

She was looking at Sir Terrence as she spoke and observed a strange look flash across his face at these words. "Yes, I have affairs of my own, to be sure," he said. "But they are neither so numerous nor so involving as to keep me from taking a hand in yours. Indeed, helping you deal with your affairs would be a welcome respite from dealing with my own."

Emily looked at him doubtfully. He appeared to be perfectly serious. In a hesitating voice, she gave expression to her second doubt. "But what could you do? I have wracked my brain for hours, and yet I don't see that there's anything anyone can do. I have committed myself by running away, and now I must either keep running or resign myself to standing trial for murder."

"Well, and I could assist you in both those things if necessary. But I hope it won't come to that. The more I think on it, the more certain I feel that Ronald's injuries cannot have been as serious as you imagine. I have heard no word of any attack taking place in the neighborhood, and there would be no end of public furor if a person in Ronald's position had been injured, let alone murdered."

"Do you think so?" said Emily wistfully. "I would like to believe you're right, Sir Terrence. But what if you aren't?

I have no way of investigating the matter without betraying myself in the process."

"Ah, that's where I can help you. As a stranger in the neighborhood, it's perfectly in order for me to ask questions about everything. I'll make a few discreet inquiries about this Ronald and find out just how badly you and your dressing case damaged him."

"That would be wonderful," said Emily with heartfelt sincerity. "But it will mean a great deal of trouble for you, I'm afraid. And I don't know what I should do with myself in the meantime."

"As to that, I have another idea," said Sir Terrence. He eyed Emily speculatively. "You are a companion by trade, are you not? Why, then, should I not employ you in that capacity in my own household?"

"You employ me?" exclaimed Emily. "But I cannot be *your* companion!"

She spoke incredulously, and there was suspicion in the look she cast at Sir Terrence. He met the look squarely, however, with just a hint of hurt in his eyes.

"No, not my companion, but my aunt's," he said. "I mentioned earlier that my aunt was staying with me, if you will remember. I don't blame you for being suspicious in the circumstances, Miss Pearce, but do please believe my intention is not to seduce you. Not all men are like Ronald Bartholomew."

"I beg your pardon," said Emily in a low voice. After a moment, she went on, still struggling with shame and embarrassment. "But this aunt of yours—what will she say when you tell her you have hired a companion for her sight unseen? She might not take to me, you know. And even if she does take to me, will it not be very awkward to bring me into your household before we know for certain whether Ronald is dead? Did you envision my going under

a false name to her and the servants? I should dislike that
very much!"

"And so should I," said Sir Terrence. "If we start out
by introducing you under a false name, we should soon
find ourselves entangled in a mesh of lies. Much better to
simply tell the truth."

"But I cannot tell the truth!" said Emily, staring at him.
"I can hardly go giving my real name and history to your
aunt and all the servants! Not until I know whether Ronald
is alive or dead, at any rate."

"No, we cannot tell the servants, certainly," agreed Sir
Terrence. "They seem a reasonably discreet lot, but even
so I would rather not make them accessories after the fact.
My aunt, however, is a different story." Sir Terrence's lips
curled in a reminiscent smile. "Aunt Katie is a most reliable
confidante. You can trust her neither to turn a hair at
your most appalling secrets nor to betray a word of them
afterward. She possesses the art of discretion in fuller measure than any person I ever knew."

Emily eyed him in amazement. "You seriously propose
to hire me as your aunt's companion without my ever
having met her, without her even knowing you mean to
hire a companion, then introduce me to her casually as a
young woman who may or may not have killed a man?
Discretion or not, I think that is asking rather a lot of the
poor woman!"

Sir Terrence laughed. "You don't know Aunt Katie! She
will take it all in her stride. Besides, I don't see how we
are to manage this business without the aid of another
woman. You must stay somewhere while I am making
inquiries about Ronald, and Aunt Katie's rooms will be
ideal. She never lets servants into them, preferring to do
for herself like the independent body she is. Between us,
we can keep you hidden from the rest of the household

until we find just how serious this business of yours is likely
to turn out."

Emily considered. She could see any number of potential
weaknesses in Sir Terrence's plan, the chief one being the
unknown and possibly uncooperative Aunt Katie. But there
was no gainsaying that his plan also possessed certain obvious advantages. Living incognito in his aunt's rooms, she
would be a fugitive still, but a safe, well-fed, and comfortable fugitive rather than a weary, hungry, and footsore one.
Considered in this light, Aunt Katie's possible opposition
dwindled to a small risk compared to the prospect of hostile
dogs, uncomfortable nights, and uncertain provender.
"You're sure?" Emily asked urgently. "You're sure you can
trust your aunt to help and not betray me, Sir Terrence?"

"Sure as I am I won't betray you myself," he returned
promptly. "You'll just have to trust me about that." He
looked into her eyes. "I know it seems a gamble. But I
don't see that we really have any alternative in this situation
but to trust each other, do you? I never saw you before
today—don't know a single thing about you other than
what you have told me—but I am going to trust that you
are what you appear to be and will not betray me down
the road. And I would be greatly honored if you would
extend the same trust to me."

Emily, looking back at him, found her mind suddenly
made up. "Yes, I will trust you," she said. "Take me to
your Aunt Katie, if you will. I only hope she will be half as
understanding as you are!"

Chapter 5

Emily was nervous as she accompanied Sir Terrence toward Honeywell House. The prospect of meeting the unknown Aunt Katie was weighing upon her, and as they approached the house, she was struck by another concern.

"What if one of the servants sees me?" she inquired nervously as they threaded their way amid fountains and flower beds. "If they see me entering the house, they will wonder who I am and what I am doing with you."

"Yes, they will," agreed Sir Terrence. "That had already occurred to me, and so I am keeping a sharp eye out for the gardening staff. We don't want any of them to see you, but once we're inside the house, there shouldn't be any difficulty. I have a plan that should allow you to pass unremarked."

Emily hoped he did. As they went along, she cast unhappy glances at her torn and rumpled dress, wishing she had some way of changing, or at least mending, it.

When they were only a few rods from the house, Sir Terrence stopped.

"Forgive me, but I'm going to ask you to wait here while I slip into the house and explain to my aunt what we're doing. While I'm there, I'll see if I can borrow her old red cloak. That should disguise you nicely from a distance, and we'll take care no one gets a close look at you. If any of the servants notice you with me, they'll merely think you are Aunt Katie returning from a walk."

Following Sir Terrence's suggestion, Emily concealed herself amid a little copse of elms and stood waiting anxiously as he set off toward the house. While he was gone, she had plenty of time to worry about Aunt Katie's probable reaction to her nephew's plans and her own folly in consenting to them.

I must have been mad, she marveled to herself. *To put such trust in a stranger, a man I know nothing about! If I had any sense, I'd run away now while I still can.* But sensible though this counsel might have been, Emily did not choose to follow it. She was still waiting in the copse when Sir Terrence rejoined her a few minutes later. There was a smile on his face and a red garment slung over his arm.

"It's all settled," he said. "Aunt Katie is perfectly willing to join in our conspiracy. She begs you to make use of her cloak and lose no time in conveying yourself to her rooms, where she will endeavor to make you as comfortable as possible."

Emily wondered with amazement how he had gained his aunt's consent to such a radical plan in such a short time. But she was too relieved to question him about it. She allowed him to help her into the red cloak, and with the hood pulled well down over her face, she accompanied him up the steps of the terrace and into the house.

"No servants about. That's all to the good," whispered Sir Terrence, leading her quickly through an elegant draw-

ing room furnished with crimson and gold hangings.
"Hold hard, here's a housemaid on her way up the stairs.
No, it's all right; she's merely glanced at us and gone on
her way. We'll give her a minute to get where she's going,
then go up ourselves."

Their progress through the house required a good deal
of such strategic maneuvering, reminding Emily of a children's game of hide-and-go-seek. Sir Terrence seemed to
be enjoying it, and despite her worries, Emily found herself
entering into the spirit of the game, too. She felt triumphant when they finally reached Aunt Katie's rooms without having been betrayed. But she was nervous as well as
triumphant, and as Sir Terrence pushed open the door
and beckoned her toward it, she hung back.

"Are you quite, quite sure your aunt does not mind
putting me up for a few days?" she whispered.

"Certain sure, my dear," answered a voice behind Sir
Terrence. Emily looked and beheld her first glimpse of
Sir Terrence's Aunt Katie.

Aunt Katie was a slender, elderly woman with iron-gray
hair coiled neatly beneath a monumental frilled cap. She
wore a frilled apron, too, and a soft Kashmir shawl of
magnificent weave was draped over her slim shoulders.
Despite her age and slenderness, however, she gave the
most concentrated impression of strength and energy of
anyone Emily had ever seen. Her blue eyes appraised Emily
in one swift glance, then turned to her nephew.

"Terry, bid the young lady come in, won't you," she
said, her clear voice colored with a charming brogue. "She
mustn't stand in the hall where she can be seen by a
gossiping pack of servants."

It was Aunt Katie herself who drew Emily into the room,
however, and helped her out of the red cloak. "Ah, what
pretty hair!" she exclaimed as Emily's red-gold head was
revealed. "Me own mither's hair was just the same when

she was a girl. 'Twas much admired in the county, and we girls all hoped our hair would be like to hers, but to no avail. One and all, we turned out dark like our fayther.''

"Indeed?" said Emily faintly. She was a trifle stunned by Aunt Katie's flow of small talk, the more so as it had not prevented that lady from making a very searching examination of her person while it was going on. Flushing, she addressed Aunt Katie in an apologetic voice. "Do forgive me for foisting myself on you and your nephew in this way, ma'am. I don't know what you must think of me. I assure you, if I had had any other alternative—"

" 'Deed, but you didn't, my dear, did you?" said Aunt Katie, briskly interrupting this speech. "You needn't make any apologies on my account. Terry told me how it was with you, and I'm quite willing to do my part to help. 'Tis a wicked world, and no mistake—a wicked world, and wicked men aplenty in it, and a pretty girl alone ever a target for wickedness. Your story's not a new one, my dear; I'm sure I've heard it a dozen times in me life. Still, you're the first girl I've met who stopped a rake's advances by whacking him on the head, and that's something!" She surveyed Emily with approval in her blue eyes. "If more girls did the same, there might be less of that particular kind of wickedness in the world."

"Perhaps there might be," said Emily, smiling wanly. "But I am not sure I would recommend other girls doing what I have done, ma'am. My actions have landed me in a fearful pickle, as your nephew has no doubt told you."

"Aye, that he has," said Aunt Katie with a sage nod. "But never you mind, my dear. Even if it turns out you have killed this good-for-nothing young man (and good riddance to him, I'd say!), Terry will see you get justice. Now he's taken a hand in the affair, you've nothing more to worry about."

Emily was both amazed and amused by Aunt Katie's

confidence. She glanced at Sir Terrence, who threw her a deprecating smile. "Now Auntie, it will not do to be too sanguine," he told her. "I'll certainly do my best for Miss Pearce, but there may be complications arising from this affair that we cannot anticipate."

"Yes, and I do not expect either of you to involve yourselves in my affairs as much as that," said Emily quickly. "All I need is a place to stay for a few days while I obtain news about Ronald. Once I have done that, I need trouble you no longer."

"Sure, and it's no trouble, my dear," said Aunt Katie, giving her an indulgent smile. "I'm not overburdened just now with things to do. Terrence brought me here to keep house for him, but the servants all know their work well enough without my trying to teach it to them. I just tend my own rooms and do a bit of needlework, and it's dull work putting in the days, I can tell you that. 'Twould be a godsend to have a bit of excitement about the place."

"You are very kind to say so, ma'am," said Emily. "But Sir Terrence—?"

She left the question unfinished, but Aunt Katie seemed to understand what she was asking. "Never you worry your mind about Sir Terrence, my dear," she said, patting Emily's arm. " 'Twill do him good to think of someone's affairs besides his own for a change."

There was an almost acid note in her voice that surprised Emily. Glancing at Sir Terrence, she saw a flush appear on his cheeks. "For all his talk of needing a quiet place to write his new book, he hasn't done a bit of writing that I can see," Aunt Katie went on remorselessly. "Might as well have stayed in Ireland and mooned about there as here."

"That will be enough, Auntie," said Sir Terrence.

His flush had darkened, but he spoke with a ring of steel in his voice that made his aunt subside with a muttered

"Your pardon, Terry, I'm sure. But it's no more than the truth, as all the saints can attest."

Sir Terrence appeared not to notice this aside. He turned to Emily and addressed her with formal courtesy. "Please do not distress yourself with concern for me, Miss Pearce. It shall be my pleasure to do what I can for you. Now I will leave you, for I feel the sooner I ride over to Wybolt and make inquiries into Ronald's condition, the better it will be. My aunt will make you comfortable, I trust, and perhaps when I return this evening, I will have news for you." Bowing first to Emily and then to Aunt Katie, he turned and left the room.

"Ah, I've offended him again," said Aunt Katie with a sigh as the door shut behind him. "He didn't used to be so quick to fly into the boughs. But ever since that sad business with Moira Flanaghan this spring, he hasn't been like himself. And that business about his book, too—I didn't ought to have spoken of it. It's by way of being a secret, my dear, and I beg you'll forget I ever mentioned it to you."

Emily promised to do so, but she could not help being intrigued by Aunt Katie's words. What book could she be talking about, and how did it affect Sir Terrence? Emily abandoned these questions as insoluble mysteries, but the mention of Moira Flanaghan and a "sad business" was more comprehensible to her. Of course, it must have been a love affair of some kind—one that had ended unhappily, to judge from Aunt Katie's tone. Emily wondered why the idea was so disturbing to her. Such an attractive man as Sir Terrence must have had dealings with women in the past.

It's none of my affair, she told herself firmly. *I had better put the whole thing out of my mind.* But she found herself wondering all the same whether Sir Terrence had been very fond of Moira Flanaghan and whether it was at her instigation or his that their relationship had devolved into "a sad business."

She had little time for such reflections, however, for Aunt Katie had taken charge of her once more in her usual brisk fashion. "You look a trifle pinched to me, my dear," she said. "And I'm sure it's no wonder if you were traveling on foot much of the night, as Terry tells me. Would you like to lie down for a while? This bed's not a bad one (though none so good as my own back home), and I'm not using it myself at the moment. There's no danger of the servants interrupting you, for I tend my own rooms myself and never let a servant set foot in them. It's been a habit of mine all my life, and I don't intend to change it now, whatever the fashion may be."

Emily did feel very weary, and the tester bed with its eiderdown and plump pillows appeared very attractive. "But I cannot like to take your bed, ma'am," she protested. "You might want it yourself, and I would feel I was putting you out."

Aunt Katie declared this nonsense, but Emily stood firm, and after a certain amount of polite argument, they compromised by making up a bed for Emily on Aunt Katie's sitting-room sofa. "Just slip off your dress there, and while you sleep, I'll see if I can't do something toward making it more presentable. You've ripped it something terrible, I'm thinking." Aunt Katie surveyed the plum-colored fabric with a regretful eye. "A pity to treat good stuff in such a manner, but I don't suppose you could help it."

Emily said meekly that she could not and allowed Aunt Katie to take charge of the misused dress. She supposed she ought to insist on mending it herself, but she had already sustained one argument with Aunt Katie that morning and carried her point only with the greatest difficulty. This time, it was easier to give way than make an issue of it. So she lay down on the sofa while Aunt Katie got out her workbasket, and before long she was fast asleep.

She awoke a few hours later to find that morning had given way to afternoon. Her dress, brushed, sponged, and neatly mended, lay on a nearby chair, and Aunt Katie was looking down at her with an indecisive eye. "Ah, you're awake, my dear!" she said, her indecision giving way to a look of satisfaction. "I was just wondering whether I ought not to wake you. I'm going down to nuncheon, and I didn't want you to wake and wonder where I'd gone." With a hint of apology in her voice, she added, "I'd have ordered the servants to serve nuncheon up here, but I'm not in the habit of taking meals in my rooms, you see. I thought it better not to risk any remark by changing my ways. But never fear, my dear: I'll bring you up a bite and sup. I hope you won't mind waiting for it."

Emily assured her she would not, and Aunt Katie left, having promised to return as soon as humanly possible. Once she was gone, Emily got up, tidied her hair, and resumed her dress. It still retained signs of abuse, but Aunt Katie had done an exquisite job of mending its many rents and tears. Emily marveled at the fineness of her stitches. *Truly, my lot has fallen in a goodly place,* she told herself happily. *I wish there was something I might do in return to show my gratitude.*

There seemed to be nothing just at present, however. Aunt Katie's rooms were admirably clean and as neat as a pin. Emily, having straightened her couch, found nothing else to do and so picked up the first volume of a novel that was lying on Aunt Katie's bedside table. She was deeply engrossed in it when Aunt Katie slipped back into the room, bearing a cup of tea in her hand. Her other was concealed beneath her apron, in the manner of a child smuggling contraband cakes. It was not cakes that she presently gave to Emily, however, but rather a ripe nectarine and some cold meat and cheese wrapped in a napkin.

"There you are, my dear," she said cheerily. Then her eye took in Emily's occupation, and her manner underwent a sudden change. She stiffened, and her mouth opened as though to protest. But no protest came, and the next instant she seemed herself again, though Emily noticed her expression was more reserved than before. "It's reading you are, is it?" she said. "I am glad you found something to occupy yourself while I was gone."

"Yes, I hope you don't mind," said Emily. She was puzzled by Aunt Katie's manner and worried lest she had inadvertently committed some faux pas. "I found this book lying on your table," she went on apologetically. "Perhaps I ought not to have looked at it, but when I saw it was a new Patrick Fitzpatrick novel, I couldn't resist."

"You like Fitzpatrick's novels, do you?" said Aunt Katie. Her manner was still cautious, but it seemed to Emily that she also looked gratified.

"Certainly; who does not? My former employer was quite mad for them. She used to send me to the bookseller's every time a new one came out. I thought she had them all, but this seems to be a new one."

"Aye, so it is," said Aunt Katie, then closed her lips tightly as though determining to say no more. But curiosity seemed to get the better of her, for after a moment she inquired casually, "What did you think of it? The book there, I mean? D'you think it's up to his usual standard?"

"Yes, as much as I can judge from the little I have read. It seems very entertaining. But then all of Fitzpatrick's novels are that. People call him the Irish Scott, you know, but to my mind his books are much better than Scott's."

"Indeed?" said Aunt Katie encouragingly. "And why would you be saying that?"

"There's more humor in them—and more heart, too,

I think. His characters seem like real people. One fancies one knows them by the end of the book. His descriptions of places, too, are very fine." Emily gave Aunt Katie a deprecating look. "But of course his books are set mainly in Ireland, so I can't really judge as to that. Would you say they are true to life?"

"Aye, that I would," said Aunt Katie warmly. "But then I'm partial, of course. Knowing the dear boy as I do—"

She broke off with a guilty look, but Emily caught eagerly at the words. "Knowing him? Do you mean to say you know Patrick Fitzpatrick?"

Aunt Katie's lips parted, then closed. She looked so guilty, and at the same time so confused, that Emily was driven to the unavoidable conclusion. Her eyes widened.

"My dear ma'am, you do not mean to say that—It cannot be! But yes, I had always heard Patrick Fitzpatrick was merely a nom de plume. And so it is really your nephew who writes those delightful books? How proud you must be!"

"Aye, that I am," said Aunt Katie. She still appeared slightly embarrassed, but when she spoke again, her tone was more pleased than abashed. "Terry was always a clever lad. It's no surprise to me that he should succeed in anything he put his mind to. His first book was published when he was still at Cambridge, and since then he's sold near a dozen of them. Very popular they've become, too. That one there"—she nodded with pride toward the volume in Emily's hands—"you'll notice 'tis dedicated to the regent himself. His Royal Highness begged the privilege of it in a letter he wrote to Terry by his own hand, saying how much he enjoyed Terry's books and a deal of other pleasant things besides. Terry just laughed—he's a small opinion of the lot of the royal family—but his publisher wanted him to do it, and I told him I didn't see any harm in it myself.

" 'It's all very well to disapprove of His Highness as a man,' I said, 'and very natural, too, considering the way he goes on. But he *is* regent now, and like to be king one of these days, and it can't hurt you any to pay him your respects in what you might call a purely professional way.' And he said, 'Well, Aunt Katie, if you think I ought to, then I'll go ahead and dedicate the blasted book to him. But the gesture will be purely professional, as you say— and I intend to dedicate my next book to the dustman on the corner, just to even things up!' "

Emily laughed. "And does he really intend to?" she asked.

Aunt Katie had been laughing, too, but her brow clouded at this question. "As to that, my dear, the Lord only knows," she said with a sigh. "I thought it only a joke when he said it and supposed that by the time the book got written he'd have thought of somebody more suitable to dedicate it to. But now I don't know. If ever the book gets written, I believe I'd be happy to see Terry dedicate it to a dustman or a street sweeper or any other body who does an honest day's work for his bread. They'd be a deal more deserving than some I could name."

Emily found most of this speech incomprehensible, but it was plain from Aunt Katie's expression that she was laboring under a grievance. "I suppose there are many people who seek to take advantage of Sir Terrence's position?" she said. "But of course there must be. I might be accused of doing it myself, in a manner of speaking."

Aunt Katie waved this aside, however. "No, my dear, that's not what I meant at all. Terry may be helping you just at present, but it's his way to help anyone in need, and assuming the need's genuine, I don't begrudge it them. A pretty hypocrite I'd be if I did, for he helps me more than anybody, giving me a home and pretending I do something useful to earn my keep in it."

Here Aunt Katie paused for breath, and Emily essayed another cautious question. "But there are people not in need who take advantage of his generosity?"

"That's about the size of it, my dear," said Aunt Katie, and folded her lips tightly once again. Emily was beginning to understand her ways, however, and so was not wholly surprised when Aunt Katie went on again after a moment's pause.

"To my mind, Terry's the finest young man that ever drew breath. There's precious few girls I'd consider a fit match for him, but a man doesn't commonly take his opinions from his aunt on such matters, and so I wasn't altogether surprised when he took up with Moira Flanaghan."

Again she paused, and Emily nodded, confirmed in her suspicion that Moira Flanaghan and Sir Terrence had been lovers. Although she was interested in hearing Aunt Katie's remarks on the subject, at the same time she found herself almost shrinking from them, too, as from a source of pain. "Had Sir Terrence been acquainted with Miss Flanaghan for long?" she ventured.

Aunt Katie shook her head. "Not Miss Flanaghan, my dear—Lady Moira. That's her proper title, though I don't often give it to her. A lady she is not and never has been, to my way of thinking. But you ask how long Terry has been acquainted with her? Well, that depends on what you mean by being acquainted. He's known her all his life in one manner of speaking and not at all in another."

Emily thought this over. "You think he was deceived in Lady Moira's character?" she said.

"Aye, that I do," said Aunt Katie emphatically. "So does everyone else who knows the two of 'em—except for Terry himself. *He* thinks he was not worthy of *her*, if you please! And after the way she treated him, too! It's a shame to see a man so deluded, but he won't bear hearing the truth about Moira. The Lord knows I've tried to tell it to him, but he's got it fixed in his mind that she's an angel from heaven, and there's no convincing him he's mistaken." Aunt Katie shook her head over the folly of men in general and her nephew in particular.

"I suppose Lady Moira is very pretty?" inquired Emily diffidently.

"Aye, that she is, my dear. There's the mischief of it, for she does look like an angel even if she don't act like one."

"But what did she do that was so dreadful? Sir Terrence seems like an intelligent man. Surely his eyes must have been opened to her true character if she had done anything really wrong?"

Aunt Katie sighed. "You'd think so, wouldn't you? But it's not such a simple matter as that. It's not Moira's actions themselves that was so wrong, you see, as the motives behind them. Any young lady might change her mind and decide she prefers one man to another, and presuming she's not stood at the altar yet with the first one, I wouldn't consider it my place to criticize her. But to abandon a man when she was as good as engaged to him only because she'd a chance of snaring a richer one—well, that's not the conduct of a lady, to say no worse of it."

"I see," said Emily slowly. "So Lady Moira jilted Sir Terrence for another man?"

"That she did, my dear. Mind you, they wasn't engaged yet, but it was spoken of as an understood thing all through the county. Cut Terry to the heart it did, though he never made any complaint about it."

Emily was silent a moment. "But perhaps Lady Moira really did care for this other suitor of hers," she said. "If she found she no longer loved Sir Terrence—"

"Ah, but she did love him, my dear. At least she told him so, though I'm thinking that any woman who could behave as she has doesn't know the meaning of the word. But Terry thinks she loves him, and it's that which is eating away at him now.''

Emily was bewildered. "But he must know she does not love him—or at least that she is unworthy of him. How could she possibly justify her conduct in his eyes?"

"You don't know the brazenness of her. She convinced Terry it was her duty to marry Lord Duncannon because he was so very rich!"

Emily blinked. "But—Sir Terrence isn't a poor man, is he?"

"Nay, he's not a poor man," said Aunt Katie, smiling a little at this question. "Most folk would consider him very well off. He's a deal of property both in England and Ireland, leaving aside what he earns from his books. But even so, he's not half so rich a man as Lord Duncannon."

Emily shook her head. "That may be, but I still don't see how Sir Terrence could be deluded by Lady Moira's motives. For her to reject a man she claimed to love and who possessed a good income for another man merely because he was richer—and, perhaps, because he possessed a higher title—that must strike even a man in love as unworthy conduct."

Aunt Katie sighed. "You and I would see it that way, my dear, but I'm obliged to say that Terry saw it different. It's not surprising when you consider it. Moira's not what you'd call a clever woman, but there's no doubt that where managing men is concerned, she's got all her wits about her."

"But even so, I don't see how Sir Terrence could help seeing her conduct as anything but mercenary," said Emily stubbornly.

"But she put it on the grounds of duty, you see. It was her duty to marry Lord Duncannon because he was a powerful man whose purse was deeper than Terry's and who could better aid her family. The Flanaghans are a large family, as you may know, well-born but poor as church mice. There's six daughters besides Moira yet to be provided for, and near as many sons. Since Terry's got a powerful sense of duty himself where family's concerned, he saw what she meant, or thought he saw. But I'd be surprised if the Flanaghans get much help from Moira, even in spite of her marrying Lord Duncannon. She's a deal better at taking than giving, as the way she treated Terry shows."

"Jilting him for a richer man, you mean?"

"Aye, and worse besides." Aunt Katie sunk her voice to a whisper. "You'll hardly credit it, my dear, but before Moira married Lord Duncannon, she was brazen enough to come to Terry and borrow money of him to buy her bride clothes. A thousand pounds she borrowed, and she'd have been sore put if he'd refused, for there's nary a creditor in Ireland would advance her so much."

Emily regarded Aunt Katie with fixed attention. "Are you saying Lady Moira borrowed money from her unsuccessful suitor to buy bride clothes to marry her successful one?" she demanded.

Aunt Katie nodded mournfully. "You wouldn't think it possible, would you? But that's just what she did. And never a penny has she paid back, though she's money enough now by all accounts. You'd think such a debt would chafe any woman past bearing, and with any woman of decency and feeling, I've no doubt it would. But Moira seems not to feel it at all."

Emily drew a deep breath. "She must be quite a woman," she said. "To get money out of a man for such a purpose under such circumstances seems hardly creditable. And having met and talked with Sir Terrence, I would not have thought he could be such a—"

She broke off in some confusion, but Aunt Katie completed the sentence for her. "Fool?" she said. "Aye, he's behaved foolishly in the matter, I can't deny. Though I can see better than you how it came to happen. Terry's got such a fine, noble nature, you see. It's natural to him to think the best of people, and in Moira's case he was already convinced she was a little too fine for him (though the Lord knows how she convinced him of that!). So when he couldn't marry her himself, he just made up his mind that it was his duty to help her however he could to fulfill *her* duty and take the high place she was called to."

"I suppose I can see that," said Emily slowly. "Although it sounds too much like knight errantry to be true in this day and age!"

Aunt Katie smiled. "Ah, there's a good bit of romantic in Terry, though you wouldn't know it to look at him," she said. "It comes of writing novels, I suppose." She was silent a moment, brooding. "But for all it sounds like something out of a book, I'm afraid Terry really did care for Moira," she added with a sigh. "And being the kind of man he is, I don't suppose he'll get over it soon. That's the mischief of it. I wouldn't begrudge Moira the money if only it had opened his eyes to her, but now it seems as though his eyes have been shut tighter than ever where she's concerned. He doesn't say much, but it's plain to see the matter's still weighing heavy on his heart. I don't think he's taken up a pen since Moira was married, though his publisher's been writing and writing of him and asking when he'll have a new book ready."

"When was Lady Moira's marriage?" asked Emily.

"In April, my dear, just after Easter. Terry didn't think it right to attend the ceremony, for which I was grateful, you may be sure! But as long as he stayed in Ireland, he couldn't help but be reminded of Moira at every turn. So when I saw how it was going to be, I just up and said, 'Terry, I've taken a fancy to spend some time in England. You've been talking about it ever since you was a little lad, and I'd like to see it for myself.' "

"And what did he say then?"

"It was easy to see he didn't like the notion. But he answered politely enough, 'Of course, I'll take you to London if you like, Aunt Katie.' Well, that didn't suit my book at all. There's a deal of folk who divide their time between Dublin and London, and I reckoned one place would be near as bad as t'other when it came to gossip about Moira and her new husband. So I said, 'Thank you kindly, but if I wanted to stay in a noisy, smoky city, I might as well bide right here in Dublin. If I'm going to England, it's the country I'd like to see—someplace where it's green and quiet and a body can get a little peace.' He looked at me shrewdlike, and I could see he guessed what I was about, but he only said, 'Very well. I'll consult an agent and see about finding a place in the country I can lease for a few months.' And that's how we came to be staying here at Honeywell House."

"I see," said Emily. "It does seem like a quiet, pleasant place. I would imagine Sir Terrence would find it very conducive to writing books."

Aunt Katie shook her head dolefully. "Ah, but he hasn't. I've kept an eye on him ever since we got here, but I haven't seen him write anything aside from a note or two."

"But you haven't been here very long, have you?" said Emily. "When I met Sir Terrence at the well this morning, he mentioned he had only been in the neighborhood a week or two. It will probably take longer than that to see any improvement. Indeed, ma'am, if I were you, I wouldn't despair. Time is commonly held to be a sure cure in such affairs, though perhaps a rather slow one. I daresay Sir Terrence will recover his spirits if left to himself a while longer."

Still, Aunt Katie shook her head. "Maybe that would be so with other men, my dear," she said. "But for a man like Terry, being left to himself is only likely to make him more melancholy than ever. I see it now, and that's why I was so glad to have you come and stay with us.'' She patted Emily's arm. "Terry's taken a wonderful interest in you and your affairs. I admit I was a bit taken aback when he first told me about you, but then it struck me that it'd be all to the good that he should dwell on somebody's troubles besides his own for a while. So I encouraged him to bring you here—and now that I've seen you for myself, why, I think it a better notion than ever. If you could see your way clear to staying here at Honeywell House a while, you'd be doing us both a great favor.''

"That's very kind of you, ma'am," said Emily, greatly touched by the old woman's words. "I must say I am relieved by what you say. Despite Sir Terrence's assurances, I could not rid myself of a fear that I was thrusting myself in where I was not wanted. As to staying, however, I'm afraid that may not be in my power.''

"It will be quite within your power," asserted a calm voice behind her. Turning with surprise, Emily saw Sir Terrence standing in the doorway.

Chapter 6

Sir Terrence was pleased with himself as he strode along the hall toward his aunt's rooms. It had been a long and wearisome day, but his industry had been rewarded in a most satisfactory manner.

He was looking forward to making his discoveries known to Emily. Emily! His heart warmed as he thought of her. Of course, it was not love that warmed his heart, or even admiration. *Though it would not be wonderful if I did admire her*, he told himself, *she is a very lovely girl.*

He had admitted as much to himself when he had first beheld Emily there by the well, tall, slim, and with her bright hair streaming over her shoulders. But only for one instant had he yielded to her charm before wrenching his thoughts away with a feeling of self-disgust. Lovely she was, but his ideal of feminine beauty was a different one—an altogether different one and one that was now lost to him forever.

The thought of Moira brought pain with it, as it always

did. But the pain was brief and less bitter tonight, for he had other thoughts that occupied him even to the exclusion of his all-encompassing sorrow. He was thinking of Emily now, not with love or admiration but with satisfaction nonetheless.

She had been proven to be exactly what she had claimed. Her story had been accounted for in every particular. He had interviewed everyone connected with the case, from Miss Morris's butler to the serving woman, Nell, to Ronald himself. For far from being dead, Ronald had proved to be both alive and well, though he bore the scar of his last encounter with Emily in the form of a lurid black eye and a bump on the head that even a careful arrangement of his romantic black locks could not entirely conceal. He had not seemed eager to publicize the cause of his injuries, saying, when pressed, that he had been thrown from his horse. But his manner was proof enough of Emily's accusation even if his words were not, and Sir Terrence had been satisfied.

He was glad to know she had told him the truth. Unconsciously, he had been fearing to find she had deceived him in some wise. He had been convinced of her integrity all the time he was in her company, but as soon as he had left to make his inquiries, doubts had assailed him. He began to feel he might have done an unwise thing in taking her into his home. Rather than a beleaguered innocent, she might be an adventuress or even a criminal.

Although the idea had nagged at him as he made his inquiries, the result of those inquiries had soon quieted his apprehensions. Emily was exactly who and what she had claimed to be. He felt pleased with her and with himself for having correctly estimated her character. Even more was he pleased to have the privilege of delivering to her the good news about Ronald. He was smiling as he threw open the door to his aunt's sitting room.

Both Emily and his aunt were there, although they did not immediately see him. They both stood some feet away, plunged in what appeared to be deep conversation. As Sir Terrence came a step farther into the room, he heard Emily say in a constrained voice, "I must say I am relieved by what you say, ma'am. Despite Sir Terrence's assurances, I could not rid myself of a fear that I was thrusting myself in where I was not wanted. As to staying, however, I'm afraid that may not be in my power."

"It will be quite within your power," said Sir Terrence.

Emily swung round with a cry. Her hand was pressed to her breast, and her eyes were wide with fear. Overcome with remorse, Sir Terrence went to her, taking her hands in his and pressing them warmly. "Forgive me," he said. "I ought not to have been so abrupt. I am afraid I have given you a shock."

"It's nothing," said Emily, but she spoke a bit breathlessly. Sir Terrence, looking down at her, was startled by what he saw. When he had left her, she had been *en déshabillé*, with torn dress and muddy shoes and her face pinched with weariness. None of these things could hide the fact that she was an attractive girl, of course, but they had tended to obscure it, and once his first, instinctual reaction had passed, Sir Terrence had fallen into the way of thinking of her more as an object of pity than a woman. Now he was suddenly aware of her as a woman once more. The curves of her figure were very evident beneath the plum-colored dress, freshly brushed and newly mended. The red-gold hair was brushed and combed and pinned in a cluster of curls atop her head, and it shone like copper in the late-afternoon sun. And though her face had been pale with fear and apprehension when she had first turned around, relief had transformed it to the opposite extreme, flushing her cheeks with color and bringing a shy smile to her lips.

"It's nothing," she said again. "I beg you won't think of it anymore, Sir Terrence. I was only surprised."

Sir Terrence shook his head. "I ought to have been more careful," he said. "If I had been thinking, I would have known you would be nervous. But I wasn't thinking at all, unfortunately. I was in too great a hurry to talk to you."

As he spoke, he caught his aunt's eyes resting upon him. Something in their expression made him aware that he was still gripping Emily's hands. He let go of them quickly, with a sensation of annoyance. It was just like his aunt, he reflected, to read more into the situation than had been imagined either by him or Emily. Aunt Katie would be fancying next that he was on the verge of letting Moira's place in his heart be taken over by this girl. Nothing could have been more ridiculous. His voice was perceptibly cooler when he spoke again. "I have some rather startling news," he said. "May I sit down for a minute? I think it would be best if we all sat down so we might discuss it in full and decide what is best to do."

"Sure, and I've been keeping you standing here like a great noddy," said Aunt Katie penitently. "Sit down, both of you, and let's hear what Terry has to say."

Emily sat down obediently, but her expression had become apprehensive once more. Sir Terrence forgot his momentary irritation in his hurry to reassure her. "First, let me say my news is good," he said, smiling at her. "In fact, it is very good indeed. Ronald is not dead at all. He is, on the contrary, very much alive and as near to well as makes no difference."

"Saints be praised!" Aunt Katie exclaimed. Emily merely stared at him, and he could read her doubts as plainly as though she had spoken them.

"You need not doubt it," he said in a gentle voice. "I spoke with Ronald myself only a few hours ago. He looked to be in good health, though it does appear you battered him a bit! But he spoke of going to a party tonight, so I think we can take it that no serious injury was done."

"I don't believe it," said Emily in a faint voice. Then, as though realizing that her words sounded ungracious, she flushed again charmingly. "Forgive me, Sir Terrence. I will believe Ronald is alive and well if you say so, but indeed I can hardly credit it. It seems like a miracle, an answer to a prayer."

"Sure, and aren't prayers answered all the time?" demanded Aunt Katie. "For my part, I never supposed the young sinner was dead for a minute. It's only the good that die young, as they say, while the devil's mortal certain to take care of his own."

Emily gave a weak laugh. "It appears so," she said. Turning to Sir Terrence again, she went on with a hint of appeal in her voice. "Did Ronald seem very angry with me when you talked to him? I am sure he could still make trouble for me if he wanted to. I dare not drop my guard against him until I am sure he does not mean to prosecute."

"He doesn't," said Sir Terrence firmly. "When I tested him on the subject, asking him how he came by the bump on his head, he said only that he had fallen off his horse. There was a servant in the room when he said it, too, so there would be two witnesses to testify to his statement if necessary. But I am perfectly sure he means to let the matter drop just where it is."

Emily drew a deep sigh. "It seems like a miracle," she said again. "I don't know how to thank you, Sir Terrence. But I'll send for my things at Miss Morris's house at once so at least you and your aunt need not be troubled with my affairs any longer."

Sir Terrence hesitated. Once more he was aware of his aunt's eye on him, and it made him bite back his first, impetuous protest. "That isn't necessary, you know," he said. "You needn't be in such a hurry to leave Honeywell House. And certainly there is no need for you to send for your things. I took the liberty of calling for them while I was at Miss Morris's house today, and they're out in my carriage right now. Oh, yes, and I also have your last quarter's salary here in my pocket. Considering the nature of your departure, I was pretty sure you had not thought to collect it!"

Emily looked with amazement at the slip of paper Sir Terrence had just handed her. "Good heavens!" she said. "Do you mean to say Ronald was willing to pay me the salary that was owing me even in spite of what I did to him?"

"I think he is eager to put the whole matter behind him regardless of the cost," said Sir Terrence, smiling.

"But what did he say? About your calling for my things, I mean, and asking for my salary? He must have thought it very odd."

"No, not at all. He merely assumed I was your new employer—as I took care that he should. I told him you were acting as companion to my aunt. You don't mind, do you?" Sir Terrence looked at Emily intently.

Slowly, she shook her head. "No," she said. "It is a good story, as far as it goes."

"I did not think it was a story." Sir Terrence continued to look at her steadily. "We spoke earlier today of your staying here as companion to my aunt. You haven't changed your mind, have you?"

Again she shook her head. "No," she said. "Only I cannot like to impose on you any further. And on your aunt, too." She glanced at Aunt Katie. "You have both done so much for me already."

"Sure, and we wouldn't mind doing a deal more," said Aunt Katie heartily. "You'd be very welcome if you decided to stay."

"But do you *need* a companion?" The question was addressed to Aunt Katie, but Emily's eyes were on Sir Terrence. "You know I could not consent to stay here unless I was able to make myself useful. Work is one thing, but charity quite another."

"I doubt not we could find something for you to do," said Aunt Katie comfortably. "Terry's got a deal of interests both here and in Ireland, and I keep busy enough in me own way. There's a dozen things a clever girl like you could help with if you had a mind to."

"Is that true?" Emily's eyes continued to search Sir Terrence's face.

Sir Terrence was conscious that his aunt was looking at him, too, and that her face bore the same speculative expression it had worn earlier. In an effort to throw off the embarrassment it aroused in him, his response to Emily's question came out both more brusque and more emphatic than he had intended.

"My dear Miss Pearce, please believe I have no intention of offering you charity," he said. "My aunt is quite right in saying I am a busy man. I haven't as much time to spend with her as I would like, and I am sure you might make yourself useful to her in a hundred ways if you would. For that I would pay you a reasonable salary, but there would be no question of charity."

He was sorry as soon as this speech was out of his mouth, for in his haste to prove he had no personal interest in Emily, he felt he had been rather rude to her. But Emily merely replied quietly, "I see. In that case, Sir Terrence, I shall have no compunction about accepting your kind offer. It comes at a most opportune time for me, as you must know. I shall try to show how grateful I am for your assistance by endeavoring to give satisfaction to both you and your aunt."

"And I'm sure you will, my dear," said Aunt Katie with

a reproachful look at Sir Terrence. "We'll all get on fine together, I don't doubt."

Sir Terrence thought it best to ignore this remark along with the reproach in his aunt's eyes. He turned again to Emily. "Why don't you look about the house and see which room you would like for your own? One of the bedrooms on this floor would be best, for that would put you closer to my aunt. Just let her know which you choose and she'll have the servants make it up for you later. Most of them are at dinner right now, which is a fortunate thing, for there was no one to see that I was alone when I came in a few minutes ago. They'll simply assume you accompanied me over from Miss Morris's this afternoon along with your baggage, and we shan't tell them any differently."

Although he had begun this speech in a voice calm and impersonal, he could not help finishing it by giving Emily a conspiratorial smile. Emily returned it, but her voice was as calm and impersonal as his as she replied, "I thank you, Sir Terrence. I shall do as you say and try to get settled as soon as possible so I may not keep you longer from your own affairs."

There being no answer to this, Sir Terrence bowed and left the room. He felt guilty about his treatment of Emily but assured himself that such guilt was irrational. Their relationship was now one of employee and employer, and it was vital that it should be kept on a strictly businesslike level. No one must be allowed to get wrong ideas: not Emily, not his aunt, not even himself. Of course, he himself was in the least danger of such a mistake. His heart and hopes were in the grave, figuratively if not literally, and he had no intention of resurrecting them. Yet he was obliged to admit that he had been bothered by the reserve he had detected in Emily's manner a few minutes ago. She had been so frank and open with him that morning, so willing to speak her mind and lay her problems before him. He recalled the comfortable way they had laughed and chatted together as they had eaten their breakfast. It was depressing to think that he himself had destroyed this delightful camaraderie.

Or had he? It suddenly occurred to Sir Terrence that the new reserve in Emily's manner might have a different cause altogether. He was her employer now and of necessity held a certain power over her. Based on her previous experiences with men in positions of power, she might well think it best to keep her distance from him now that he had taken her into his employ. The past stood as an awful warning to her, and it would not be wonderful if she saw him as another potential Ronald.

The thought made Sir Terrence frown. His mind flew back to the conversation he had had with Ronald that afternoon. Ronald had been smiling and urbane at the outset, though his smile had disappeared rather quickly once Emily's name was mentioned. Still, he had recovered his composure well enough and had gone on to speak of her intelligence and industry in glowing terms. Sir Terrence was obliged to admit that this was generous conduct on his part, considering that he still bore the marks of Emily's wrath upon his face. Yet obvious as those marks were, they had disfigured him remarkably little. He was an indecently handsome man even in spite of a blackened eye and a bump on his head.

Sir Terrence's frown deepened. He had disliked Ronald quite as much as he had been prepared to dislike him, but it irked him to find that his dislike was tinged with something very like jealousy. No woman could look at Ronald without admiration, he was quite convinced. It followed, therefore, that Emily must admire Ronald even if she also despised him. This thought troubled him quite as much as the idea that she thought him likely to behave like Ronald in a similar situation.

She needn't trouble herself. I will admit she is a handsome girl, but her type is not one I admire, he told himself. Still, he felt in his heart that this statement smacked of sour grapes. The situation was absurd, as Sir Terrence acknowledged to himself, he had known Emily for less than twelve hours now. Although he had no romantic feelings for her at all and would have been greatly alarmed had she shown any such feelings toward him, he could still resent her for a detachment that was, in the circumstances, exactly what he desired!

I can't imagine what's wrong with me, he told himself as he went along the corridor to his room. *One would think I was quite deranged.*

For the past two months he had been accustomed to blame every mental weakness, every want of reason and rationality, on Moira's marriage and the blow it had dealt to his hopes. It did not occur to him to do this now, however. He went to his room to change for dinner, quite perplexed at his own mental state but entirely free for once of the burden of despair that had weighed on him so long.

Chapter 7

As the day wore into evening, Emily, like Sir Terrence, found herself perplexed by her own contradictory feelings.

She was no longer a fugitive plagued by doubt and fear. She had a home, she had all her clothing and personal possessions once more, and she had a bank draft for a quarter's salary that she had only partly earned. She had a new job situated amid pleasant people and surroundings. Best of all, she never need see or speak to Ronald again. What more could she wish for?

I don't wish for anything, Emily told herself stoutly. All the same, she could not help feeling there was a fly in the ointment somewhere. And as she sat at the dinner table that evening with Sir Terrence and his aunt, the sense that something was amiss grew more and more strongly upon her.

It was certainly not the meal. A delicate crawfish soup was succeeded by stuffed lobsters and then by a leg of lamb with mint sauce, served with peas and new potatoes. The second course was equally delectable, including a pair of roast ducklings, a rabbit pie, and some artichokes braised in white wine. Dessert was a whole selection of creams, jellies, and pastries rather than the single stolid tart or pudding that had closed Miss Morris's more frugal banquets.

Emily's luncheon of meat, cheese, and fruit had worn off hours ago, and she was able to do full justice to this splendid array of viands. Sir Terrence helped her politely to all the dishes on the table, and she caught the shadow of a grin on his face when she accepted a second helping of strawberries and cream.

"You are fond of strawberries, Miss Pearce?" he said.

"Yes, I am," she said. "I could eat them morning, noon, and night quite happily."

"You have managed two of the three today, at any rate," he said, and a smile flashed between them. The next instant it was gone, however, and Sir Terrence's manner was stiff and formal as he offered her sugar with her berries.

So it went throughout the rest of the meal. After dinner, Sir Terrence joined her and his aunt in the drawing room, but he spoke hardly at all during the time he was there. Emily felt constrained by his silence, and so it was Aunt Katie who bore the lion's share of the conversation. This burden she was perfectly willing to bear, but still, there were long silences and moments of desperate awkwardness.

"Terry, you'll be wanting the head of me when you hear what I've been doing," said Aunt Katie, breaking into one of these pauses with an apologetic smile. "I don't know what you'll say, but the mischief's done, and there's no undoing it."

"What have you been doing?" said Sir Terrence. He did not look particularly alarmed, as Emily observed, but his expression was wary.

"Why, I've gone and let slip to Miss Pearce, here, about

your writing," said Aunt Katie. She regarded her nephew
with trepidation. "She got to reading your new book this
afternoon while she was waiting in my room. And when
she started admiring it and saying how good it was, I was
just so pleased and proud that the truth slipped right out
of me. Don't look at me like that, Terry, my boy! I know
I promised, but it's proud of you I am, and I don't see
why you're so set against having people know you're Patrick
Fitzpatrick. Heaven knows it's nothing of which you need
be ashamed."

Emily, glancing at Sir Terrence, thought he looked not
so much ashamed as exasperated. "I might have known
it," he said. Glancing at Emily and then away again, he
repeated, "I might have known it. And to think I was just
praising your discretion to Miss Pearce this morning! Why
don't you just put an advertisement in all the papers saying,
'My nephew, Sir Terrence O'Reilly, is Patrick Fitzpatrick?'
It would save you the trouble of telling it over to every soul
you meet."

"Sure, and I don't tell every soul I meet that you're
Patrick Fitzpatrick," protested Aunt Katie. "Miss Pearce is
the only one I've ever told. And she won't repeat what I
told her, will you, my dear?"

"Of course not," said Emily. Looking directly at Sir
Terrence, she added, "You may depend on my discretion,
Sir Terrence. It's the least I can do to keep your secret,
considering all you have done for me."

Once more Sir Terrence glanced at her, then away again.
"Very well," he said. Although his manner was still stiff,
Emily observed that much of the exasperation had gone
out of it. There was even a rueful smile on his face as he
surveyed Aunt Katie. "You must know my aunt has many
good qualities, Miss Pearce," he said. "But along with them
she possesses a certainty that her judgment is superior to
everyone else's. She would never betray a confidence that

would harm one, but when it comes to keeping a secret she thinks would be better made public—well, in that case the secret is liable to escape her in spite of her best intentions."

" 'Deed, and if that was the case, I'd have told everyone long ago that you're Patrick Fitzpatrick," said Aunt Katie good-humoredly. "There isn't a reason on earth why I shouldn't, as far as I can tell."

"Except that I would rather you did not," said Sir Terrence. "But I will trust you and Miss Pearce to keep the secret between you from now on." Looking at Emily, he added, "Perhaps now that you have someone to share it with, the pressure to confide will not be so great."

"Faith, and I shouldn't wonder if you weren't right," said Aunt Katie. With seeming naïveté, she added, "And I shouldn't wonder if you didn't end up being glad I've told Miss Pearce about your writing, Terry. She'll be someone maybe you can talk to if you get in difficulties about your new book. And perhaps she can help you write out the fair copy, too, when it's time to send it off to your publisher."

Sir Terrence looked sharply at his aunt, but her expression was innocent. "Maybe," he said shortly. "But I'm a long way from needing the services of a copyist yet." Rising abruptly, he wished Emily and his aunt a good night and left the room.

Reflecting on this incident later, Emily had no difficulty interpreting Sir Terrence's behavior. He was still so immersed in grief over losing Lady Moira that he was unable to write. Emily could not help sympathizing with his sorrow, though she thought it a misplaced one. From what Aunt Katie had told her about Lady Moira, it sounded rather as though he had had a miraculous escape. Still, he obviously did not see it that way, and Emily was fair enough to admit that the situation might appear different to him than to her, an outsider hearing about it from a third party. At any rate, this was the only way she could reconcile Aunt Katie's account of her nephew's love affair with the man Sir Terrence seemed to be. He simply did not seem the type to be taken in by a vulgar adventuress.

Lady Moira must be more clever than Aunt Katie gave her credit for. It would take an uncommonly clever woman to jilt a man like Sir Terrence for another and still retain enough of his devotion to convince him to pay for the bride clothes to marry his successor, Emily told herself. *But then, Aunt Katie said Lady Moira was very pretty.* She felt something like a pang of envy at the thought. No man had ever thought her pretty—no man except Ronald, and he clearly had debauched tastes. *But I am a fool to fret about that now when I have so much else to be thankful for,* she reflected. *I will try to put my own and Sir Terrence's affairs out of my mind and enjoy the good fortune that has fallen to my lot.*

In the weeks that followed, it did seem as though good fortune were hers at last. Daily she presented herself in Aunt Katie's room, but only rarely was she given anything to do. Aunt Katie was an independent old lady who preferred to do things for herself, and she let Emily know this right from the start. Almost the only tasks she would allow Emily to perform for her were to read aloud while she sewed, to accompany her on her walks, and to gather flowers for the rooms.

"Indeed, ma'am, I feel the uttermost fraud," Emily told her one day, watching as Aunt Katie dusted and swept her own rooms. "I am supposed to be your companion, and yet you will let me do nothing for you except the merest trifles."

"On the contrary, my dear," said Aunt Katie, sweeping briskly. "You're keeping me company, aren't you? And isn't that the chief thing a companion's supposed to do? I may not have Terry's command of language, but even I can tell you that, for 'tis plain from the word itself." Laying aside the broom, she added firmly, "Now 'tis time to dust, and I haven't any need of company while I do that. Why don't you run along and take a walk, my dear? 'Tis a lovely day, and you look as though you could use some fresh air."

Nothing loath and yet feeling as though she were shirking her duty, Emily put on her hat and shawl and went outside. She walked about the grounds and gardens for an hour or so, admiring what seemed to be endless miles of close-clipped hedges, whole museums of classical statuary, and nurseries filled with rare trees, shrubs, and flowers. At length, her eye grew weary of formal symmetry, and she felt a desire to see nature in its more natural form. The thought of the well pavilion occurred to her. She knew it lay beyond the Italian garden, and so she turned her steps in that direction. Presently, she found the narrow trail that led from the garden's farther end through the woods. A few minutes' walking brought her again to the little stone pavilion within the circle of trees.

She was at the very entrance to the pavilion before she realized it was already occupied. On the same settee she had used as a bed that fateful night weeks ago sat Sir Terrence, frowning down at a sheaf of papers in his hand.

Emily halted, embarrassed at having discovered him thus. He did not seem aware of her presence, however. He went on staring at the papers in his hand. So great was his absorption that it flitted across her mind that the papers might be letters—love letters from Lady Moira, perhaps—that he had brought there to read over in private. Stealthily, she began to retrace her steps. But as luck would have it, she had gone only a few steps when a raven began to call loudly in the woods beyond the clearing. Sir Terrence looked up and saw her standing there.

"Miss Pearce!" he said. Emily remarked with surprise that he looked as much pleased as startled to see her. His manner toward her had been so unvaryingly distant during the past few weeks that she had come to believe him incapable of being anything else. Now here he was, looking as though he were actually glad to see her. Yet even as she watched, his face changed, assuming the distant expression she had grown accustomed to during the last few weeks.

Emily was nettled. Sir Terrence himself had insisted she come to Honeywell House; had insisted she take a job as companion to his aunt; and had insisted on paying her a very generous salary considering how little she did to earn it. But now he was behaving as though she were some encroaching pest whom only the most discouraging treatment would serve to keep in line. The thought angered her, and she spoke with cold formality. "Forgive me. I did not mean to intrude, Sir Terrence. Only wait one moment and I will take myself away."

"No, no," protested Sir Terrence, the distant expression on his face giving way to one of discomfiture. He rose to his feet as though to further protest Emily's words. In doing so, he became aware that he still held the sheaf of papers in his hand. He made a move as though to thrust them behind him, then restrained himself. But the look of discomfiture on his face had deepened, and there was a faint color in his cheeks as he glanced down at his hand. "No, no, please don't think of going, Miss Pearce. You are not intruding in the least."

Emily gave him a searching look. "I think I am," she said. "But you need not disturb yourself, Sir Terrence. I will be gone very soon, only there is something I would like to say to you first if you can spare me a moment."

"Certainly, certainly," said Sir Terrence, once again glancing involuntarily at the papers in his hand. "I can spare you as many minutes as you like, Miss Pearce. Do sit down." He gestured toward a wicker chair opposite.

"No, thank you. I prefer to stand. A moment of your

time is really all I need. I only wished to inform you that as of today I am tendering my resignation."

"I beg your pardon?" If Sir Terrence had looked discomfited before, he looked positively flabbergasted now. "You say you are tendering your—You are resigning your position?"

"Yes, that is my intention. I would like to leave Honeywell House as soon as possible. Of course, if you need time to make other arrangements, I would be willing to stay on a few more weeks. I have no other position in view as yet, and so my time is quite my own."

Sir Terrence continued to stare at her with uncomprehending eyes. "I don't understand," he said. "Why do you wish to leave Honeywell House, Miss Pearce? I thought you and my aunt were getting along very well."

"Yes, we are, Sir Terrence. Your aunt is a delightful woman, and I enjoy her company very much."

"Well, then!" said Sir Terrence, looking relieved. "There is no reason to talk of leaving if that is the case, Miss Pearce. I am sure my aunt enjoys your company quite as much as you do hers. She was saying as much to me only last night."

"I am honored by her sentiments, Sir Terrence. But much as I enjoy your aunt's company, I cannot delude myself that I am the least use to her. If I were a family friend or relative, that would not matter so much, but as a hired companion I cannot but feel myself a sad failure."

"Nonsense!" said Sir Terrence firmly. "I am sure my aunt feels otherwise. You must not think of throwing up your position for such a trivial reason as that."

Emily thought she detected an air of patronage in these last words. Her chin went up immediately. "It does not seem a trivial reason to me," she said. "I cannot think it right to accept money for a job I do not perform. You will have to respect my scruples in this matter, Sir Terrence.

May I be released from my position immediately, or would you prefer I stay a little longer?"

"If you really wish to leave," began Sir Terrence, then stopped with a shake of his head. "But this is ridiculous, Miss Pearce! Surely you cannot be serious about leaving? I never heard of anyone throwing over a position because they were not made to work hard enough!"

"Then you have heard of it now," said Emily. "I assure you I am quite serious, Sir Terrence."

A glance at her face showed Sir Terrence that she was. He said nothing for a minute or two, then spoke in an altered tone. "Very well. I will accept that you are a woman of principle who insists on giving full measure for her pay. But surely we can think of some way to adjust the matter so that it is not necessary for you to leave! Perhaps we could find some additional duties you might perform."

"I cannot think what they could be," said Emily. Her eyes were skeptical as she regarded Sir Terrence. "I am already doing everything for your aunt that she will allow me to do, and that takes no more than two or three hours a day. And I doubt there is anything I could do about the house, either. The servants run it perfectly as it is, and any attempt to meddle in their routine would be more likely to hinder than help. There is nothing I am qualified to do here at Honeywell House that someone else cannot do as well or better."

"There is one thing," said Sir Terrence with sudden determination. "You can help me with this." He waved the sheaf of papers in his hand.

"Indeed?" said Emily. It was her turn to be dumbfounded. She was still imagining that the papers must be love letters, and the idea that she might help Sir Terrence in any way with such missives was so inconceivable as to boggle the mind. "You want me to help you with your—with your correspondence?"

Sir Terrence gave her a look of surprise. "No, I need you to help me with my new book," he said. "Or rather I should say I need *someone* to help me. And since I strongly suspect all help will be futile, anyway, you may as well have the job as anybody."

This was not a flattering speech, but Emily was too intrigued by Sir Terrence's words to take offense. "So you *are* writing a new book!" she said. "Your aunt spoke of it, but she did not seem to think you had done any work on it as yet."

"There's a great deal my aunt doesn't know about me," said Sir Terrence. He spoke with asperity, but the next moment a rueful grin had appeared on his face. "As it happens, however, Auntie is more right in this case than I care to admit. I haven't done very much on the blasted book as yet, and what I have done seems dry as dust."

"And you think I can help?" said Emily. "You know I haven't any experience in such things, Sir Terrence."

"I don't know that it needs experience. All I want is an intelligent person to discuss ideas with and to give me an unbiased opinion on what I have already written. And if you write a clear hand, you can help me later on, when it is time to get the book in order for publication. Although as I said before, I doubt whether this particular book will ever see publication."

"Yes, I write a clear hand," Emily assured him. "But do you really think I can help? Wouldn't your aunt be the more natural person to ask?"

"Lord, no!" said Sir Terrence with some force. "Not on *this* book. Not that I intend to disparage Auntie in any way," he added hastily. "She has been good enough to help me in the past when I wished to read her some part of a manuscript that I wanted an opinion on, but I haven't found she had many useful suggestions to make. Though

come to think of it, she did make one useful suggestion."
Sir Terrence's eyes rested on Emily speculatively.

"And what suggestion was that?" asked Emily.

"That I should enlist you to help me." Sir Terrence's
eyes continued to regard Emily thoughtfully. "Don't you
remember her making some such suggestion that first
night we were together at dinner? Well, I've decided to
take her advice. I'm offering you a position as my amanuen-
sis—if you want it. But I warn you ahead of time it is likely
to prove a thankless job and most likely futile as well."

"I don't care for that," said Emily. "As long as I can
feel I am doing something useful, that would make all the
difference. I hope you understand, Sir Terrence. I do not
want to leave here."

"Yes, I understand," said Sir Terrence. "I don't want
you to leave, either."

A brief silence followed this statement. The words
seemed to hang in the air between them. Though Emily
was sure he had not meant them as more than a friendly
reassurance, she experienced a sudden difficulty in looking
Sir Terrence in the eye. He seemed to be experiencing
the same difficulty. Before he spoke again, he cleared his
throat a couple of times as though finding it hard to continue. "Well," he said at last, "well, I suppose—I suppose
I had better let you read what I have written thus far."

"Yes, that would be a good idea," agreed Emily.

She held out her hand for the sheaf of papers. He
released them to her almost reluctantly. "I'm afraid you
shan't find the manuscript very readable," he told her.
"It's a good deal written over, and some of it is mere
synopsis, which I intend to enlarge on later."

"I understand," said Emily, scanning the topmost paper.

"And it's only a first draft in any case. I always do a good
deal of rewriting before I'm done with a book. You must
make allowances if it isn't very coherent."

"I understand," repeated Emily. "Of course, I should not expect it to be like one of your finished books."

"No, you mustn't. As a matter of fact, it is likely to be very different from any of my other books even when it is finished."

Emily glanced curiously at Sir Terrence. He was looking at her anxiously, as though there were more he wanted to say without knowing quite how to go about it. But when her eyes met his, he turned away. "I'll leave you to read in peace, then," he said. "As the manuscript is in such bad shape, I am sure it will take you a long time to get through it, although there isn't much of it there. Shall we agree to meet at the same time tomorrow to discuss it? Or would that be too soon?"

"I am sure I shall have finished it by then," said Emily. "Tomorrow will do very well."

"It's settled, then. Tomorrow at this time, here at the pavilion," said Sir Terrence. For a moment he stood looking at Emily and at the manuscript in her hand. There was still indecision in his eyes, and Emily felt sure he meant to say something else, but in the end he merely tipped his hat to her and hurried out of the pavilion as though pursued by Furies.

Chapter 8

For the rest of that afternoon, as Sir Terrence tried to busy himself with some neglected correspondence, his thoughts kept turning to Emily. He could not decide whether he had done a wise or foolish thing in entrusting her with his manuscript.

I don't know what came over me, he told himself. Never before had he allowed anyone to read one of his books in such a rough state. And certainly never such a book as this one, a serious work that revealed more of his own thoughts, feelings, and life experiences than any of the light comedies that he had written before.

I ought not to have done it. Indeed, I don't know why I did do it except that I had reached such an impasse that I felt I simply had to have help.

Sir Terrence admitted this reason grudgingly, acknowledging to himself that it was no more than simple fact. But that brought him to a question even more perplexing. Why had he asked Emily, of all people, to look at the manuscript? His editor in London, his aunt, or a close personal friend would have been more natural choices. But to ask a young lady with whom he was so little acquainted to read what was, at bottom, a most intimate and revealing document was a gesture he could not understand at all.

Of course, she was asking for something to do. She would have left Honeywell House if I had not found her some real employment, Sir Terrence reminded himself. But it seemed to him an inadequate excuse, and it also gave rise to another perplexing question. Why did it seem so important that Emily should not leave Honeywell House? He might have felt it his duty, in the beginning, to take her in, straighten her tangled affairs, and find her a position. So much he had done, and so much he might have done for any unfortunate who had crossed his path.

But it clearly went beyond the line of duty to go to such lengths to pacify a dissatisfied employee. *If she wants to go, I should have let her,* he told himself. *If I were to judge the matter impartially, I would say I have already done my duty by her and then some.*

But though duty had not demanded it, some impulse had caused him to offer Emily his embryonic manuscript to read and criticize. It was a ridiculous situation, Sir Terrence acknowledged to himself. He had been going out of his way to avoid Emily for the past few weeks for reasons he did not care to examine too closely. Yet now he had purposely entrusted her with a task that must, of necessity, bring them into close contact.

But of course it need not do so for any length of time. She can read the manuscript and tell me what she thinks of it, and then I need trouble her no longer, Sir Terrence told himself. *Considering what an awkward book it is turning out to be, I doubt I shall be going on with it in any case.*

This reasoning did much to satisfy his conscience, and he was able to leave unanswered the larger question of why he was so reluctant to let Emily quit Honeywell House. Indeed, he had no real answer to that question. He only knew that he liked the idea of having her there, though he resolutely denied himself much contact with her, and that the mere thought of her leaving filled him with dismay.

But he had pacified her for the time being, perhaps at the cost of exposing his heart and soul to her scrutiny. Indeed, he felt quite uncomfortable when he remembered how completely he had exposed himself on certain points. *Still, she likely will not realize that the book is largely autobiographical,* he comforted himself. *She can hardly know anything of my personal affairs. I wonder what she will make of it?*

What Emily was making of it was very heavy weather indeed. She had sat down and read the manuscript through as soon as Sir Terrence had left the pavilion. She had read it through again in bed that night before going to sleep and a third time upon awakening. It was not the easiest literature to read, being (as Sir Terrence had warned her) much amended, with many passages marked through, over-written, or appended in the margins. But once Emily had worked her way through these small faults, she discovered they paled in comparison to the larger ones contained within the narrative itself. Indeed, her first reaction on reading it was disbelief that it could have been written by the same Patrick Fitzpatrick whose writings had often reduced her to helpless laughter and had even been known to raise a smile on the grim visage of Miss Morris. She would have almost thought Sir Terrence guilty of some strange, humorless joke had not there now and again occurred in the book some characteristic turn of speech that called to mind his earlier writings.

There was no gainsaying it. The book was dull—dreadfully, earnestly dull. There was not a glimmer of humor in it, from its contrived beginning to its abrupt finish midway through the fourth chapter. Nor was there a character in it whom Emily felt she would have liked to know or could even believe in as a real person. This was all the more amazing because the main character was so clearly modeled on Sir Terrence himself.

And I can guess who the heroine must be, Emily told herself grimly. After plowing through endless repetitive descriptions of that character's beauty and virtue, she could not doubt Sir Terrence had modeled his heroine on his lost love, Lady Moira. *But she's not much of a heroine at that. Even such a fool as the hero ought to be able to see through her protestations of virtue.*

It struck Emily as amazing that Sir Terrence could have written what appeared to be a full and factual account of his dealings with Lady Moira and yet missed entirely the implications of her behavior. But so it appeared to be. The general tenor of the narrative was to admire and even glory in the heroine's self-sacrificing conduct—conduct that to Emily appeared definitely self-serving rather than self-sacrificing. Having finished her third reading of the heroine's address to the hero on the eve of her marriage in which she thanked him prettily for giving her money so she might appear at the altar in a fashion that would not disgrace her before her noble husband-to-be, Emily pushed the manuscript away from her with an exclamation of disgust.

"It's dreadful," she said, looking down at the pile of blotted and scribbled papers lying on her table. "Simply dreadful."

She wondered what she could possibly say to Sir Terrence when he asked for her opinion of the manuscript. She disliked criticizing his work, but there was almost nothing good she could say about it unless she were to lie outright.

Well, perhaps he won't ask me about it, Emily told herself hopefully. *Perhaps he will confine himself to asking me specific questions about plot and characters rather than my overall opinion of the book. But even so, I hardly know what I would say to him. In my opinion he would do well to destroy the whole manuscript and begin again. It can do him no good to have such a work as this published. I'm no literary critic, but even I can see it is vastly inferior to his other books.*

She worried the rest of that morning what she would say to Sir Terrence when they met that afternoon. When Aunt Katie rallied her gently on her abstracted mood, she came close to confiding her difficulties to the old lady, but something held her back. Sir Terrence had entrusted the manuscript to her, not to Aunt Katie. It seemed likely he did not wish his aunt to know anything about it.

Considering this behavior in light of Aunt Katie's remarks about Lady Moira, Emily could hardly blame him. It was clear that Sir Terrence's aunt had undertaken on several occasions to open her nephew's eyes regarding Lady Moira's character. And even though his eyes had remained firmly shut, he still must know she could not be very sympathetic toward a character modeled on a young lady whom she openly denounced as a scheming hussy.

But she is *a scheming hussy,* Emily told herself. *I'd bet five pounds it's so. I almost wish I could meet her simply to prove I am right.*

This being impossible, she prepared instead to meet Sir Terrence. At two o'clock that afternoon, she presented herself at the pavilion bearing the manuscript in a pasteboard box beneath her arm. Sir Terrence was already there, and Emily saw at once that he was ill at ease. He jumped up when he saw her, uttered a constrained greeting, and then came forward to take the box from her hand with a haste that was almost ill-mannered. "This is my book?"

"Yes, it is," said Emily. She, too, was nervous, as she

seated herself on a wicker chair and waited for Sir Terrence to ask her opinion of the manuscript. He did not do this for some minutes, however, being apparently engrossed in opening the box of the manuscript and counting over its pages.

"Yes, it is all here," he announced presently. A brief silence ensued during which Sir Terrence leafed through the pages of manuscript once more. At last, he shot a look at Emily. "I have been regretting that I bequeathed you such a thankless task," he said. "I am afraid untangling this labyrinth of words must have given you a great deal of trouble and was little to your taste."

"Not at all. I found it very interesting to see how an author sets about writing a book," said Emily. This was true as far as it went, but she feared Sir Terrence's next question would be less easy to answer honestly. She waited with trepidation to hear what it might be.

Sir Terrence was looking through the manuscript once more. "It is kind of you to say so," he said. "But the manuscript is in such dreadful shape. I don't suppose you could even get through it."

He sounded as though he hoped this were the case. Emily shook her head. "Oh, no, I got through it well enough. In fact, I read it three times."

"Three times!" said Sir Terrence, giving her another quick look. "I hardly dare ask what you thought of it."

This was the moment Emily had been dreading. She tried to be tactful as she sought for words. "Oh, as to that, I am scarcely competent to judge your work, Sir Terrence. Especially since there are only four or five chapters here. It's difficult to form an opinion from such a small sample."

Sir Terrence was looking at her closely. Emily feared he could see right through this polite evasion. "It's true I have not gotten farther than the opening chapters," he said. "It is proving rather a difficult book to write. You have probably noticed it is somewhat different in style from my other books."

"Yes, I noticed that," said Emily with what she immediately felt to be unfortunate emphasis.

Sir Terrence gave her another searching look. "I envision it being more in the tragic than comic vein," he said. "You can see the situation between the hero and heroine precludes any easy or happy ending."

"Yes, I can see that," said Emily dryly. But Sir Terrence's words had made her curious, and she could not help asking him, "What kind of an ending did you envisage?"

"I hadn't quite made up my mind," said Sir Terrence. He spoke the words reluctantly, and there was wariness in the look he threw Emily. "As you know from reading the manuscript, the heroine marries someone other than the hero. From that point on, the plot could diverge in several different directions."

"Yes?" said Emily encouragingly.

Sir Terrence looked down at the manuscript again. "Well, in the first place, the hero might continue to hang about the heroine even after her marriage. He might devote his life to serving her as a—well—as a kind of *cavalier servente*. But I didn't see that as being quite in his character, somehow."

"No, I should think not," said Emily in what she endeavored to make an innocent voice. "Of course, I only know his character from the little I read, but he seemed to me to have more sense than that."

This brought Sir Terrence's eyes on her immediately, a hint of suspicion in their depths. "What do you mean by that?" he demanded.

"Why, only that it does not seem reasonable for him to go on hanging about the heroine once he realizes the situation is hopeless," said Emily, meeting his gaze limpidly. "It does not seem sensible conduct, and I do not

think it would be very moral conduct, either. If his love
for the heroine is as powerful as you would have me believe,
it would be a great temptation to be close to her and yet
not give in to his feelings. And you have made a great
point of stressing that he is a man of principle."

"So I did," agreed Sir Terrence in a not entirely natural
sounding voice. "Well, that seems to let out that alternative. My next thought was that I might have the hero go
into a kind of self-imposed exile after the heroine's marriage. He might leave the country and travel in foreign
lands—or he might simply remove to someplace out of
her immediate neighborhood, where he would not be continually reminded of her."

"Very sensible," approved Emily. "Once he is away from
her, he should be able to put the matter in its proper
perspective. And as soon as he has recovered from his
infatuation, he might go on to do something worthwhile
with his life."

There was a moment of silence. Emily glanced at Sir
Terrence. He was staring at her as though hardly believing
his ears. "Infatuation!" he said. "The hero's feelings for
the heroine are not *infatuation*. And he does not *recover*
from them, as you put it! His love for her is eternal, change-
less."

"Why?" asked Emily.

This simple inquiry seemed to fluster Sir Terrence
greatly. "Why? Why? Because—because she is that kind of
woman. And he is that kind of man. Their love for each
other is inalterable."

"Indeed!" said Emily, not bothering to keep the disbelief out of her voice. "I can accept that they may have
fancied themselves in love once. I can even accept that
the hero may have truly loved the heroine and fancied she
returned his love. But he must have begun to recover from
that when he realized her true character."

There was an awful silence. At last Sir Terrence spoke, his voice barely restrained. "What do you mean by that?" he said. "What do you mean, 'when he realized her true character'?"

"Why, when she jilted him for another man," said Emily, opening her eyes very wide. "I should think it would have become obvious at that point that she was not worthy of him."

"She did not jilt him for another man!" said Sir Terrence. "She was forced to marry another man in order to assist her importunate family."

"But how can that be?" said Emily with seeming bewilderment. "You have made it clear the hero was not a rich man, yet he evidently possesses enough money to keep the curricle and four in which he drives madly away from his and the heroine's last interview. And he has money enough to 'fill her room with flowers' as a gesture of chivalrous renunciation. Indeed, from what I gathered from your narrative, he seems to enjoy a very comfortable income."

"Yes, but nothing like his rival's," said Sir Terrence. "I also said *that* in the narrative, if you will recall."

"Of course you did," agreed Emily. "And you said also that the heroine reluctantly 'surrendered her hopes of happiness in order to benefit her struggling family.' But if you will pardon me for saying so, I thought you were straining your readers' credulity at that point. For you said specifically, earlier in the book, that 'everybody in the county thought it a suitable match' when the hero and heroine first became engaged. And would not 'everybody,' of necessity, include the heroine's family?"

There was another long silence. "Yes," said Sir Terrence reluctantly. "Yes, I suppose it would."

"Then that shows they were satisfied with whatever settlement the hero was going to make initially, does it not? Well, then, this business of the heroine's marrying a wealthy lord 'for her family's sake' begins to sound like a thin excuse."

Emily looked triumphantly at Sir Terrence. He looked back at her, his lips set in a thin line. "That does not necessarily follow," he said. "Likely there was pressure brought to bear on her to abandon her first engagement once her family realized that a more eligible *parti* was disposed to admire her. Indeed, I am sure that was the way of it."

"Then it would have been more commendable of her to resist such unreasonable pressure," said Emily. "What could her family do, after all? They had already approved of her engaging herself to the hero. She might have married him at that point even without their consent, and I daresay most people would have thought she was justified. There's an idea! Why don't you have her elope with the hero on the eve of her marriage to the wealthy lord? That would leave the plot open to all kinds of interesting complications."

"That isn't the way the book goes," said Sir Terrence. He sounded as though he were speaking through gritted teeth. "The heroine marries her lord and nobody else. I have quite made up my mind on that point."

"Then do not try to pretend she married out of motives of self-sacrifice! For you know it can only have been greed that caused her to jilt a perfectly respectable, well-off young man for an elderly lord."

Sir Terrence looked at Emily. He looked at her so long that she began to grow rather nervous. "Indeed?" he said at last. "And have you any other reasons for making such a sweeping assertion, Miss Pearce?"

"Yes," said Emily at once. "There is her conduct about her bride clothes, for one thing."

"Her bride clothes!" said Sir Terrence, looking at Emily very hard. "To be sure, that was rather unconventional.

But I thought it understandable, given the circumstances. I explained how it all came about in the book.''

"Yes, you did. But I am afraid your explanation did not quite answer, Sir Terrence. For your female readers, at least, you will have to take that incident out if you expect them to have any sympathy for her.''

Once again Sir Terrence was staring at her. "I should think my female readers would have sympathy with her if anyone did!'' he said. "Surely any woman can understand that a girl would not like to go to her marriage dressed like a pauper?''

"They would understand that she would not like to, but they would hardly approve the measures she took to avoid it. Only think of it, Sir Terrence! She has jilted her first love for motives we have agreed can only be based on self-interest—''

"We have agreed nothing of the sort!'' put in Sir Terrence hotly.

Emily ignored him and went on in a smooth voice. "—And having engaged herself to a wealthy lord, she then has the gall to go to her first love and beg him to help pay for her bride clothes 'so she may not be disgraced before her new husband's family!' Indeed, it will not answer, Sir Terrence. Especially since you have taken pains to stress that she is always beautifully and fashionably dressed from the first chapter on.''

There was another long silence. "But do you not think— do you not think that her youth and inexperience excuse her?'' said Sir Terrence. His voice was almost pleading as he went on. "Remember, she has never been out of Ireland. Indeed, she has hardly been out of her home county apart from one Season in Dublin. And then she finds herself suddenly engaged to a nobleman of distinction! Is it not natural that she would want to appear well before him and his relations? And is it not also natural that she would turn to the man who cares for her as a source of help?"

"If you ask me, it's the most unnatural thing in the book," said Emily. "No woman would behave in such a way—no woman with any decency or principle, at least. Indeed, after the way your heroine has treated the hero, he ought to be the last man she would approach for financial help."

Sir Terrence was looking mulish. "But put yourself in her position," he argued. "You are young, your family is struggling on the verge of bankruptcy, and you are on the eve of a grand marriage—"

"If I were in that position, I would rather go to the altar in rags than wear clothing my ex-lover had paid for," said Emily uncompromisingly. "And I would rather not be married at all if I could do so only by abasing myself in such a manner."

Another long silence ensued. Emily risked a glance at Sir Terrence and saw he was looking at her queerly. "That is how you feel, is it, Miss Pearce?" he said.

"Yes, that is how I feel," said Emily.

Sir Terrence said nothing. He merely sat and looked at Emily. After a while she began to feel uncomfortable once more. "Of course, that is only my opinion, Sir Terrence," she said. "But I believe most women would feel the same way. You will have to take that scene out, or at least deal with it differently, if you expect your readers to care for your heroine."

"Is there anything else?" said Sir Terrence. Emily fancied there was barely controlled irritation in his voice. She was moved to reply in kind.

"Yes, you might also tone down your descriptions of your heroine. We know from the start that she is a paragon of feminine grace and loveliness, for you have taken care to tell us so on the very first page. It is therefore not

necessary when referring to her eyes to *always* describe
them as 'her beautiful eyes of cerulean blue' or when
mentioning her hands to *always* say they are 'small, finely
formed, and white as snow.' Indeed, if you would give her
a flaw or two, she would be very much more likable.''

"According to you, she already has a flaw," said Sir
Terrence tightly. "She has two flaws, in fact. She is greedy
and without feminine delicacy."

Something in the way he spoke alarmed Emily. "I mean
a human flaw—a *likable* flaw," she said. Sir Terrence did
not answer. Instead, he rose and began to gather up the
pages of the manuscript. Emily rose, too, overcome with
contrition. "I'm sorry, Sir Terrence," she said. "I did not
mean to be so critical of your work. You know I am no
judge of literature. What I have said is only my own opinion,
and it is quite possible I am mistaken."

Sir Terrence glanced at her, then returned to his task
of ordering the manuscript. "No, I think you are probably
right," he said. "The book is flawed. I am much obliged
to you for taking the time to read it and give me your
opinion."

Though his voice and manner were mild, Emily felt
reproached. "I'm sorry," she said again. Sir Terrence did
not answer. Unable to stand his silence any longer, Emily
turned and ran out of the pavilion.

Chapter 9

Sir Terrence left the pavilion a few minutes after Emily. He walked slowly along the path toward the house with the manuscript beneath his arm. Upon reaching the house, he entered by the side door, avoiding the drawing and reception rooms on the ground floor. The library was his goal, and once he had reached it, he seated himself in a chair that stood before the fireplace and began to read the manuscript. He read it through slowly, giving attention to each individual word and sentence. When he was done, he remained a moment or two with the mass of papers in his hands, then cast it away from him with a gesture of despair.

"Good God, she's right," he said. "How did I miss seeing it before?"

He felt as though someone had just hit him over the head with a cudgel. The blow had been an emotional rather than a physical one, but the results were exactly the same as far as Sir Terrence was concerned. He sat for some

minutes, looking blankly into the fireplace. At first he was
too dazed even to think, but soon his writer's imagination
awoke, and he found himself trying to describe his own
feelings, as though he were a character in one of his books.

*It's as though the prop that had been supporting me for months
were suddenly removed and I had gone sprawling onto the floor.
No, that's not it. It's more humiliating and painful than simply
falling on my face. It's as though I had spent weeks toiling on a
sonnet to celebrate the beauty of my mistress, then found her using
it to light the kitchen fire! Yes, that's a much better analogy. The
element of self-sacrifice is there, made ludicrous because what I
thought was a sacrifice turns out to have not been worth sacrificing
for in the first place.*

The thought made Sir Terrence wince and turn his head
away as though trying to escape so painful a realization.
The sight of the manuscript lying on the floor was an
additional source of pain to him. "Trash, pure trash," he
said aloud. "What a fool I was to write it—a credulous,
self-deluded fool! I'll burn it this minute. Then at least
there will be one less thing in this world of which I need
be ashamed."

Springing up, he began to gather the leaves of the manuscript together. But when he went to put them in the
fireplace, he realized the shortcomings of his plan. It was
a warm July day, and no fire was lighted or even laid within
the grate. To obtain a fire, it would be necessary to call a
servant. And though this would have been easy enough to
do, something within him shrank from all contact with his
fellow men.

Never mind, I can burn it or tear it up later, he told himself,
dropping the manuscript onto the library table. *That's the
least of my concerns right now. Instead of worrying about this
drivel, I had better devote myself to deciding what I am going to
do about Moira.*

But when he considered it, he realized there was even

less to be done in that matter than with the manuscript. Moira was married to Lord Duncannon. Of course, she had extracted a thousand pounds from his pocket first, but he had willingly permitted her to do so, and it did not seem to him that he had any grounds for complaint on that score.

It was true that the money had been given her in the guise of a loan. And it was also true that she had made no effort to repay so much as a penny of it in the three months that had passed since her marriage. But despite those two undeniable truths, Sir Terrence was reluctant to begin dunning her. It would have been a cheap and ignoble sort of revenge, and he felt as though he had already had his fill of cheapness and ignobility where Moira was concerned. Besides, he found he also shrank from the idea of holding any communication with her even on such unexception-able grounds as these. Having discovered, belatedly, what she was, he felt he would rather never see or speak to her again even if it meant writing off his thousand pounds as a bad debt.

Which I might as well have done at the outset, he told himself wryly. *How could I have been such a fool?* Over and over he asked that question of himself without getting any satisfac-tory answer. He was still asking it when one of the servants came to the library to inform him that dinner was ready.

"I'm not hungry," he said. "Please tender my apologies to my aunt and Miss Pearce and tell them they may begin without me."

He still felt disinclined for company, and the thought of sitting down to dinner with his aunt made him even more so. She would be sure to notice his mood and remark upon it. Then, too, there was Emily. He did not feel pre-cisely resentful toward Emily, but there was no denying that her remarks that afternoon had caused him a good deal of pain. In a few pithy sentences she had stripped the

scales from his eyes, turned him toward a mental glass,
and made him see himself as he really was—a credulous,
self-deluding fool who had been fancying himself a romantic hero. It had been a mortifying experience, and though
Sir Terrence suspected he might one day be the better for
it, just at present he was reluctant to face the author of
his mortification.

*There is no reason why I need see her tonight, or my aunt,
either,* he told himself. *I can stay here all evening, and all
night, too, if I like. I don't suppose I will care to sleep any more
than I care to eat.*

Toward nine o'clock that evening, however, he found
he was growing both tired and hungry. He struggled
against both sensations a long time, feeling that they were
unworthy of a man who had suffered heartache and disillu-
sionment on such a grand scale; then he awoke to what
he was doing and laughed at himself. Once again he was
trying to play the part of a Hamlet or Othello when his
role more closely resembled that of Bottom with his ass's
head.

*And since I must needs play an ass, there is no reason why I
must starve myself,* he told himself, reaching for the bellpull.
A servant soon appeared in answer to the summons, and Sir
Terrence requested tea and sandwiches. He ate hungrily of
the food when it arrived, and when the servant reappeared
to take the empty plates and cup, he requested that a fire
be lit in the fireplace. The servant looked a little surprised
at this request, for the night was a warm one. But he
obeyed it nonetheless, and before long a cheerful blaze
was crackling in the library grate.

As soon as the servant had taken himself off again, Sir
Terrence took the manuscript from the library table. His
intention had been to put it in the fire without further
ado, but as he carried it toward the fireplace, the words
"dazzling eyes of cerulean blue" caught his eye. He

stopped, stood reflecting a moment, then laughed aloud. Sitting down at the table, he took up a pencil and scored through the offending words. He then went through the manuscript removing every other reference to cerulean blue eyes, white, finely formed hands, a fairylike figure, and luxuriant curls of spun gold.

When this was done, he went back to the beginning and started to rewrite his initial description of Lady Moira's character. "Her looks were striking enough at first glance, encompassing the conventional prettiness of the blue-eyed blonde," he wrote. "But a second glance might have shown that her eyes were set too close together and that some part of the golden ringlets ornamenting her small head were not of her own growth."

"Which is true enough," he said aloud, surveying the words with a grin. "I remember at that race meeting a year ago when the wind blew off her hat and half her back hair went with it. Of course, I pretended not to notice, but it was plain enough in all conscience. And her eyes *are* too close together. I knew it, of course, but I never let myself admit it before now."

Sir Terrence was amazed to find how much therapeutic value was to be found in describing accurately the flaws in his former love. He felt much better when he had rewritten the offending paragraphs, but he also felt tremendously sleepy.

"It's this damned warm room," he grumbled. "What was I thinking of, asking for a fire on such a sultry night?" Walking over to the fireplace, he took up the poker and pulled the fire apart. Then he took the rewritten manuscript and put it carefully away in the drawer in the library table. Finally, he took up a candle, extinguished the other lights in the room, and went to his bedchamber. Having washed and undressed, he lay down in his bed and fell instantly into a deep and tranquil sleep.

*   *   *

Emily, by contrast, was experiencing the very reverse of deep and tranquil sleep. She tossed restlessly from side to side, tormented by the thoughts that revolved endlessly inside her head.

How could I have behaved so foolishly? she asked herself. *Criticizing his book as I did, just as though I were in any position to judge its demerits! What must he think of me?*

In her memory she relived over and over everything she had said to Sir Terrence and everything Sir Terrence had said to her. The memory of it was enough to turn her stomach.

How could I have been so petty—so spiteful? she asked herself. *It's as though I set out to make a thoroughgoing fool of myself. Of course he was disgusted with me, and I can't blame him. I am disgusted with myself.*

She could not imagine what impulse had led her to heap such scathing contempt on the conduct of Sir Terrence's hero, especially since she knew that the hero was modeled on himself. But bad as her criticism of his hero had been, Emily felt even worse when she recalled the way she had criticized his heroine.

And I don't have to wonder what led me to do that, she admitted ruefully. *I know perfectly well. It was jealousy, plain and simple.* Nor was it mere jealousy of an idealized character in a book. That would have been bad enough, but the truth was even worse. It was not the fictionalized heroine in Sir Terrence's novel of whom she was jealous; rather, the living woman who had inspired the character. Emily found the admission a difficult one, but she could not deny it. Reading the paeans of praise Sir Terrence had heaped on Lady Moira had made her feel sick with jealousy toward the other woman. And she had responded by making those childish remarks to Sir Terrence about his heroine's appearance—remarks whose motivation must have been perfectly obvious to him.

"In fact, I have disgraced myself," Emily said aloud, staring up at the canopy of bed curtains above her. "He can never have any respect for me after the way I have behaved. I daresay he will avoid me completely from now on." Gloomily, she recalled the way Sir Terrence had failed to appear at dinner. Of course, that had been her doing. He had preferred not to sit down with a foolish, jealous, petty woman, and it would be no wonder if he avoided doing so for the rest of her stay at Honeywell House.

Which will no doubt be a short one, she told herself unhappily. *I shouldn't wonder if he decided to discharge me after the way I behaved today. Perhaps I had better give him my notice before he does so.*

She shrank from handing in her notice a second time. It had been only two days since she had tried to do so, and Sir Terrence had assured her then that he wanted her to stay at Honeywell House. Likely he had changed his mind since then, of course, but in that case it would be for him to say so.

I have made a fool of myself, and now I must take the consequences, she reasoned to herself. *And if that means I must endure the disgrace of losing my position, then so be it.*

But though Emily was fully resigned to endure such disgrace, she did not find the prospect conducive to sleep. She tossed and turned for several hours more before finally dozing off toward morning. It seemed only seconds later that she was awakened by the sound of the maidservant rattling open the window curtains and depositing a jug of hot water on her washstand. With a dismal heart and repeated yawns, Emily crept out of bed and began to prepare for the day she was sure must end in disgrace and unemployment.

She dressed rapidly, choosing a dress at random and

arranging her hair into a simple knot at the back of her head. Since disgrace was imminent, she felt she would rather get it over with as soon as possible. When she went downstairs to the dining room, however, she found only Aunt Katie seated there. "Terry's up betimes this morning, seemingly," said the old lady cheerfully as she poured Emily a cup of tea. "The servants tell me he ate his breakfast an hour ago and rode off somewhere, saying he wouldn't be back till nuncheontime or thereabouts."

"Indeed?" said Emily. As she drank her tea and made a pretense of eating a buttered roll, she considered what this information might mean. On the one hand, Sir Terrence's behavior seemed to show that discharging her from her position was not his first priority. If it had been, he need only have waited in the dining room until she appeared and then told her that her services were no longer required. Yet Emily could not obtain too much comfort from this stay of sentence. Perhaps Sir Terrence had more important affairs to attend to and considered he might postpone such a small matter as discharging her until later in the day. Or it might be that the delay was owing to Sir Terrence's softheartedness. He might find the duty of discharging an employee an uncongenial one even when the employee was as unsatisfactory as she was.

On the whole, Emily judged this last explanation to be the most likely. She felt intuitively that Sir Terrence would dislike the job of discharging employees, just as she herself had shrunk from the task of delivering Miss Morris's strictures to her staff. *But though he may dislike such duties, I doubt not he discharges them conscientiously nonetheless,* she told herself unhappily. *One can tell simply by looking at him that he is that sort of man. He may be softhearted, but nobody in their right mind could call him soft—except where Lady Moira is concerned, of course.*

The thought of Lady Moira plunged Emily into an even

deeper gloom. She could only pick at the porridge, bacon, and eggs Aunt Katie insisted she take in addition to her roll in order to "keep her strength up." After breakfast, she assisted Aunt Katie in writing some letters, an occupation that helped to divert her thoughts a little, but all the while she was keeping a nervous ear cocked for Sir Terrence's return. When he entered his aunt's rooms a little before the hour of eleven, Emily was certain the moment had come.

"Good morning, Auntie," he said. "And good morning, Miss Pearce." He bestowed a smile on both ladies, but Emily noticed his eyes lingered longest on her. She was not surprised when he turned to his aunt a moment later. "I wonder, ma'am, if I might borrow Miss Pearce for a time? I am doing some work in the library and could use her assistance."

"Sure, and you may," said Aunt Katie heartily. Emily could tell she was curious, but she made no further comment, and neither did Sir Terrence. He merely stood looking expectantly at Emily. Nervously, Emily rose from her chair and accompanied him out of the sitting room and down the hall to the library.

The library was, in Emily's opinion, one of the nicest rooms at Honeywell House. It was a large, rectangular apartment, wood-paneled and parquet-floored, with a row of windows ranged along its longer side. These windows overlooked the terrace, and each was provided with a window seat set deep within the embrasure of the wall. The cushions of the seats were of moss-green velvet trimmed in gold, as were the looped and festooned curtains that draped the windows themselves. Comfortable armchairs were scattered about; tables and bookstands stood ready for use; and the great fireplace that stood on the wall facing the windows was surrounded by quaint and curious carved figures that might have been children, elves, or imps.

Even more than these items, however, the main furnishing of the room was books. Every available inch of wall space not devoted to fireplace, doors, or windows was covered with them, right up to the ceiling. This made necessary a stout set of rolling steps to reach the topmost shelves.

Since coming to Honeywell House, Emily had spent several pleasant hours in the library, reading, inspecting the curios in their cabinets, and poking about among the drawers of maps, folios, and charts. But today the room held no charm for her. As she followed Sir Terrence through its dual-paneled doors, her heart seemed to sink deeper and deeper into her slippers.

When Sir Terrence reached the central table beneath the chandelier, he stopped. A stack of papers was lying on the table's polished surface. Emily recognized it as the manuscript of the book that she had criticized so savagely the day before. Her heart seemed to sink yet deeper within her. Of course, the end must be near now, and she waited with trepidation for the ax to fall. It seemed a long time in falling, however, and at last she could not resist glancing in Sir Terrence's direction.

"You are quite free, are you not?" he asked. "I hope there was nothing else you were planning to do this morning?"

Emily shook her head. She was puzzled by Sir Terrence's words and manner, both of which seemed inappropriate to the occasion. He either possessed a hitherto-unexpected streak of cruelty or was being amazingly obtuse. "No," she said faintly. "No, there is nothing else I had planned to do."

"Well, then, shall we begin? I have been thinking about what you said yesterday afternoon, and I have come to the conclusion that you are perfectly right. The book as it now stands is a mass of contradictions. The greater part of it will have to be completely rewritten before I can continue with it."

Emily stared at him a full minute before she could find words to reply to this speech. "Do you mean," she said at last, "do you mean you want me to help you with your book?"

Sir Terrence gave her a surprised look. "Of course," he said. "That was our understanding, was it not? You said you would leave if I did not find you some additional work to do, and so I said you might help me with my writing."

"But after the things I said!" Emily was so amazed and relieved that she found herself stuttering as she sought to explain herself. "I was dreadfully rude, I know. Indeed, I have been regretting that I—that I spoke so warmly. I had no right to criticize your book."

"On the contrary, you had every right," said Sir Terrence. "I asked you to criticize frankly, if you remember. You were quite within your rights to do so."

"But I am not a literary critic!" said Emily. "And some of my criticisms might not be valid ones."

"On the contrary," returned Sir Terrence, smiling. "Your criticisms were, as I believe, both valid and uncommonly pithy."

"But they were not!" said Emily desperately. "Not all of them, at any rate. Those remarks I made about your heroine, for instance." Averting her eyes from Sir Terrence, she went on in a halting voice. "I am quite ashamed when I think what I said about her. Judged by English standards, of course, her behavior is unconventional—but then she is not English. I daresay in Ireland her behavior might be quite acceptable."

"No, it would not be," said Sir Terrence with emphasis. "You have a strange opinion of Ireland and Irish manners if you think her conduct could ever be considered accept-able."

He looked and sounded so grim that Emily felt she had made an additional blunder. "But I did not mean to speak against Irish manners, Sir Terrence! I only meant that the customs of the two countries no doubt differ from each other in many particulars."

"They differ less than you would think, Miss Pearce. And I do not hesitate to say that behavior condemned as grasping and unladylike in one country would likewise be condemned in the other." While Emily was still groping for an answer to this speech, Sir Terrence went on briskly. "However, we need not concern ourselves with the heroine just at present. I have already done some rewriting of her character, but it is the character of the hero that most needs clarification. I spent several hours last night considering different ideas. The easiest thing, of course, would be to simply make him poor rather than well-to-do. That would make both his and the heroine's behavior quite straightfor-ward."

"Yes, I suppose it would," said Emily. Her embarrass-ment was fading, so she was able to consider the possibili-ties of this new idea with interest. "It would solve some of your difficulties, Sir Terrence, but I'm afraid it would only create others. For if the hero was poor, the heroine's family would not have been likely to have given their consent to his suit in the first place. That would mean that he and the heroine could not be engaged—or if they were, it would have to be a clandestine engagement. And since he is supposed to be a man of honor, that seems rather out of character."

Sir Terrence acknowledged that the hero's sense of honor presented a difficulty. "Well, then, let us say he is *not* a man of honor," he said after a few minutes of frowning

cogitation. "We shall rid him of his uncomfortable conscience and leave him free to act in any way he sees fit."

"In that case, he would simply run away with the heroine
instead of engaging himself to her," Emily pointed out.
"It is his sense of honor that ties his hands in the matter.
Unless you were willing to make him the villain rather than
the hero?"

"No, I don't see him as a villain somehow," said Sir
Terrence with a shake of his head. He considered a
moment longer, then laughed suddenly. "No, there is
nothing for it. I shall have to give up my vision of him as
a tragic hero. The fact is that he behaves more like a fool
than a hero—and so a fool he must be. Don't you think
so?"

There was a curious smile on his face as he regarded
Emily. "I don't know," she said cautiously. "It would solve
most of your difficulties of plot and character, certainly.
But it would also change the whole tone of the book. And
I thought you envisioned it as a serious work."

"Yes, but I find serious works do not agree with me,"
said Sir Terrence. He looked down at the pile of manuscript with an expression half-smiling, half-pensive. "The
truth is that I have no talent for serious writing. Comedy
is my forte, and I would do better to stick to that."

Emily heartily agreed with this statement but thought it
more diplomatic not to say so. "I prefer comedy myself,"
she said. "That is why I always enjoyed your other novels
so much."

"Then we shall make this one a comedy, too. It will, of
course, take a good deal of rewriting. But it has possibili-
ties—yes, definitely it has possibilities. Think of the heroine's grand renunciation scene in chapter three! There is
plenty of comedy to be mined out of that now that we
have discovered her true motivation. And the scenes with

her mother, too. I always thought her mother was a character ripe for parody, but I never let myself admit it."

Emily cocked an eye at him, but he seemed not to be aware that he was betraying himself. He was leaning over the library table, turning through the pages of the manuscript and smiling to himself. Presently, he laughed aloud, took up a pen, and began to write. "Yes, that should do it," he said. "That should do very nicely. And here—definitely I must change this."

He scribbled rapidly for a minute or two while Emily watched him, not daring to speak or move lest she interrupt him and be ordered to leave. At last he stopped, frowning down at what he had written. "Is something wrong?" she ventured to ask.

"Not exactly," said Sir Terrence, still frowning down at the manuscript. "It is only that the manuscript is so marked over that I can scarcely make out what I have written."

"Yes, it is rather confusing," agreed Emily. "Would you—would you like me to copy it over? I would be glad to do so, and it would give you a clear place to start with your revisions."

She made this offer with a certain amount of trepidation, being unsure if Sir Terrence would care for her assistance now that he seemed to have found inspiration once more. But he seized on the offer gratefully. "Oh, yes! If you would do that, Miss Pearce, it would make the whole business much simpler. I can be planning out the subsequent chapters of the book while you recopy what I have already written."

Within minutes, Emily was seated at the library table with pen, ink bottle, blotter, and a fresh ream of foolscap in front of her, recopying the blotted manuscript. Sir Terrence, seated across from her at the table, had the same equipment but seemed to be doing little with it. Emily, stealing glances at him from time to time, saw him write something on the paper now and then, but more often than not he immediately scored through what he had written. From time to time he let out a sigh.

Emily worked on as long as she could without disturbing him, but finally she was forced to speak. "I'm afraid I can't quite make this bit out, Sir Terrence," she said apologetically. "Is it 'she sat quiet on the sofa,' or 'she sat quietly on the sofa'?"

Sir Terrence rose from his chair and came around the table to look over her shoulder. "It's 'she sat quietly on the sofa,' " he said. "At least that is what I intended it to be. But now I consider it, I'm not sure it doesn't sound better the other way around. What do you think?"

"I don't know," said Emily. She was surprised to have Sir Terrence consult her in this manner, but flattered, too. He spoke as though he really wanted her opinion, as though she were a person of eminence like himself rather than a simple hired companion. "If I had to state a preference, I would say 'she sat quiet on the sofa' sounds better," she said. "But that is only my opinion."

"Your opinion is exactly what I want," said Sir Terrence. He considered the page of manuscript a moment longer, then nodded with decision. "You are quite right, Miss Pearce. The second reading is better. Let it stand as 'she sat quiet on the sofa.' "

"Very well," said Emily. She tried to keep her voice and manner matter-of-fact, but inside she was deeply gratified. It was a new and heady experience to be treated like this. Her previous employer had never consulted her opinion on any matter, let alone deferred to it as Sir Terrence had just done. She was smiling as her pen flew over the paper, reducing the blotted and scribbled lines of the manuscript into smooth and flowing order. But her smile changed to a look of surprise when she came to the altered paragraphs describing Sir Terrence's heroine. She read through them once, then a second time, hardly able to believe she had read them correctly. Having assured herself that they were exactly what they seemed to be, she glanced across the table at Sir Terrence.

He was looking straight at her. There was a smile on his lips, and Emily had the strangest impression that he knew what she was thinking. Of course, that could hardly be, for he had no way of knowing her thoughts or even what part of the manuscript she was working on unless he was able to read upside down. Given the manuscript's present condition, that seemed most unlikely. When he spoke, however, his words were direct and to the point.

"You see I took your advice in other matters as well," he said. "Having given the matter a thorough reconsideration, I discovered my heroine was endowed with a few human faults, after all."

"Yes," said Emily. She did not dare say more. The way Sir Terrence was looking at her made her slightly uncomfortable.

"I am much obliged to you for the discovery, Miss Pearce," he went on, still regarding her with that strange, knowing gaze. "Now we must put our heads together and see what we can do with the poor girl."

"Do with her?" said Emily. "You mean, to make her a proper heroine?"

Sir Terrence shook his head. "No, not that. It is becoming clearer and clearer to me that she is not the stuff of which heroines are made. She may be more real and human now we have given her some faults, but she still has not the sympathy that a proper heroine should have."

"No," agreed Emily. She was confused by Sir Terrence's manner, which seemed to give to his words a meaning beyond their surface one. And she was confused even more by the way he was looking at her, still with that direct and penetrating gaze. But even in a state of advanced confusion, she could not deny the truth of his assertion. "I agree with you, Sir Terrence," she said. "As she is written now, your heroine could never be entirely successful."

"Then let her play her part, and then we will be done with her." Sir Terrence made a gesture as of sweeping something away. "That leaves us free to do whatever we like with our story—and with our sadly unheroic hero. What shall he do, poor fellow, once he finally awakens to his Dulcinea's true nature? Shall he join a monastery, enlist as a foot soldier in the army or pursue some other mad, romantic course?"

Emily laughed. "Send him to the Continent," she suggested. "He can recover the tone of his mind while fighting *banditi*, enduring fires and floods, and dallying with kings' daughters."

Sir Terrence gave this suggestion a serious consideration. "I don't know that he's a heroic enough hero to cope with *banditi* and floods," he said, "but he could certainly dally with kings' daughters."

"Well, then, let dalliance be his occupation. He can spend a year or two traveling about the Continent, flirting with a succession of German margravesses, Russian czarinas, and Italian *principessas*."

"That should keep him busy for a year or two," agreed Sir Terrence. "But what will he do when the charms of the royal ladies of Europe begin to pall upon him?"

"Why, then he need only go south to Africa. I daresay the Hottentot princesses and the sultanesses of Arabia would provide him with distraction for a time. Or let him find entrance to the sultan's harem! That would occupy him for a good many months, I daresay."

"I daresay," agreed Sir Terrence. His mouth was twitching, but his voice was admirably composed as he added, "I see that you envision making a regular epic tale of this, Miss Pearce. The book shall have to be much more than the usual three volumes to include all the adventures you have outlined."

"We can pare them down a good deal if need be," Emily assured him. "Limit your hero to—say—three love affairs per continent and the thing is done."

Sir Terrence gravely wrote down "Three Love Affairs Per Continent" upon the page in front of him. Emily then set about suggesting appropriate examples of female royalty to represent each continent. They were still arguing over whether there were princesses among the tribes of the Esquimau of the Americas when the bell rang for nuncheon.

"We have been so busy fooling that I am afraid I have done very little to help you on your book," said Emily penitently.

Sir Terrence, who was putting the pages of the manuscript carefully back in the drawer, turned to look at her. "On the contrary," he said. "You have helped me a good deal."

"I have?" said Emily incredulously. "How? Apart from copying barely three pages of manuscript, I have done nothing but make a number of perfectly ridiculous suggestions. And you cannot really mean to use those!"

Sir Terrence merely shook his head. Having disposed of the manuscript neatly in the drawer, he offered Emily his arm. She accepted it, and together they left the library. As they went down the stairs to the dining room, however, she could not forbear one last protest. "Oh, but it is too absurd, Sir Terrence! You do not really mean to use those suggestions, do you?"

Sir Terrence gave her an inscrutable smile. "I might," he said. And together they went into the dining room.

Chapter 10

Emily had been unable to decide whether Sir Terrence had been in earnest about using her suggestions regarding his book. He had sounded serious when he said it, but his demeanor during dinner and for the rest of that evening was the very reverse of serious. He kept Emily and his aunt laughing with a series of witticisms, and his high spirits continued even after the party had removed to the drawing room.

"You must have a glass of wine instead of tea, Miss Pearce," he told Emily. "After your heroic exertions this afternoon, I am sure you are in need of a restorative."

Aunt Katie, who had been pouring herself a cup of tea, looked up sharply at these words. "What's that?" she said. "What's Miss Pearce been doing that she needs restoring?"

This question, and the look that accompanied it, made Emily color. She glanced at Sir Terrence uncertainly. Although Aunt Katie's question could hardly be left unanswered, to answer it would involve explaining about his book, a matter that he had previously shown himself loath to discuss with his aunt. She was very surprised when he answered quite readily, "Why, you must know she has been helping me with my book, ma'am. We were laboring on it most of the afternoon."

"Hardly laboring," Emily managed to say, but her voice was feeble. In any case, Aunt Katie did not hear her. She was regarding her nephew with astonishment.

"You say Miss Pearce is helping you with your book?" she questioned. "What book might that be?"

"Why, the new one I have just begun. I started writing it a few weeks ago but had lately reached a standstill. It was then that I recalled your suggestion that Miss Pearce might be of assistance to me."

This artful speech caused Aunt Katie's suspicious look to change to one of gratification. "So you decided to take my advice, did you?" she said. "It's not often you'll be doing that or admitting it when you do."

"I freely admit it in this case," said Sir Terrence. "Your advice was not only sound but positively inspired." Smiling a little, he turned to look at Emily. "Miss Pearce has been a great help to me. I expect now the book will go on swimmingly."

Aunt Katie also looked at Emily, who colored again. "Upon my word, I have done very little, ma'am," she protested. "Sir Terrence is kind enough to say I have helped him, but apart from copying a few pages of manuscript, I cannot conceive how."

Aunt Katie threw a keen look at her nephew. All she said, however, was, "It's glad enough I am to see him working again, my dear. If you're helping him in any way, I beg you'll keep right on doing it and not hesitate on my account."

Having received this blessing from Aunt Katie, Emily felt a good deal easier in her mind. Of course, there had been

nothing wrong in helping Sir Terrence with his book; even
the nonsense they had indulged in that afternoon about
kings' daughters and royal harems had been innocent
enough in all conscience. Yet Emily found there was something in the memory of her last two conversations with Sir
Terrence that disturbed her on some underlying level.

She supposed it must be because of the secretive nature
of both encounters. No one else had known about them
apart from her and Sir Terrence. It was true that nothing
improper had passed between them on these occasions,
but any clandestine meeting between a man and woman
must always carry a strong flavor of the questionable. However, the secret was out now. Aunt Katie knew of their
meetings, and not only had she expressed no disapproval
of them, she had given her consent to their continuing in
the future.

This thought was a great satisfaction to Emily. She had
much enjoyed working with Sir Terrence that afternoon
and was glad she might do so again without feeling guilty
about it. The only guilt she felt now was when she remembered how little work she had really done. She would have
to labor much harder after this if she were to earn her salary
and be a help rather than a distraction to Sir Terrence. But
in the meantime, her position was given official sanction,
and she was very happy indeed.

She continued happy in the days that followed. It was
true that she did less work than she would have liked. She
and Sir Terrence met regularly each afternoon for the
purpose of discussing the manuscript, but in practice their
discussions often veered off the subject of Sir Terrence's
plot and characters and became general conversations on
such diverse subjects as history, philosophy, and politics.
Emily always felt a trifle guilty afterward about such digres-
sions, but Sir Terrence insisted so earnestly that they were

of help to him in his writing that she could not feel too badly.

"I think many people have the idea that an author's work must be executed in silence and solitude," he told Emily. "I will allow that those things are helpful when I am actually writing, but between times I find outside stimulation to be very helpful. That is where you come in, Miss Pearce. With you, I can enjoy an hour or two of intelligent conversation, explore fresh ideas and opinions, and come in contact with a mind and personality other than my own. I can't tell you how helpful that is. After talking with you, I always return to my labors rested and refreshed."

After this flattering speech, Emily made no further demur about the hours they spent discussing Napoleon, the Elgin marbles, and Lord Byron. To be sure, it did not seem to her that Sir Terrence's book was coming along very fast despite the inspiration of her fresh ideas and opinions. She had recopied the first chapters of the manuscript in her best copperplate handwriting, but when she inquired after further chapters, Sir Terrence always had some excuse why they were not yet ready to be copied. And when she tried to question him about what direction he meant to take his plot, he would propose various absurdities that set her laughing and offering similar ones while distracting her entirely from the subject at hand.

This was very bad, of course, and not at all what Emily had intended. But though she deplored her own inability to do anything truly useful, she could not find it in her heart to deny Sir Terrence "intelligent conversation" and the benefit of her mind and personality.

In the meantime, she was becoming better acquainted with Sir Terrence's own mind and personality. Not only did she see him during their work sessions; more often than not she also saw him in the evening, after dinner.

Instead of coming to the drawing room, drinking a single cup of tea, and then excusing himself, as had been his habit during Emily's first weeks at Honeywell House, he now seemed inclined to spend the whole evening there with Emily and his aunt.

There could be no doubt that this did a great deal to enliven their evening hours. Oftentimes they merely spent the whole evening talking. This was an amusement not to be scorned, for both Sir Terrence and his aunt could talk amusingly on almost any subject, and Emily was often reduced to whoops of helpless laughter as the repartee flew between them in the form of good-natured jokes, innuendos, and insults. At other times, the three of them played games or took turns reading aloud. The works they read on these occasions varied widely according to the reader's choice, but Sir Terrence was always firm in his insistence that they should not be novels.

"Not that I regard novels as morally objectionable," he told Emily. "That would be a hypocritical attitude, seeing that I write them! But since I've become an author myself, I find I don't enjoy reading novels so much as I used to. Either I find myself smugly congratulating myself because the author's technique is inferior to my own, or I fall into a black despair because it's better than anything I'm able to do! So let us stick to plays or poetry or history or even sermons and leave the novels for those who can read them with impunity."

Emily had always been an enthusiastic novel reader, but she endured no pangs at renouncing them on these occasions. To hear Sir Terrence read plays, poetry, or history was, she thought, enjoyment enough for anyone. And though they never got around to reading any sermons, it seemed to her that his beautiful voice and finely nuanced reading could have rendered even those dry works enjoyable.

All their evenings were not given up to such quiet pursuits as reading and conversation. Soon after Emily had begun to assist Sir Terrence with his novel, several neighborhood ladies came to call. Their avowed purpose was to meet the new tenants of Honeywell House and welcome them to the neighborhood, although Aunt Katie observed afterward that to inquire into the newcomers' birth, breeding, and antecedents appeared to be their main objective. Whatever the case, the result of their inquiry seemed to be satisfactory, for a dinner invitation to the home of one of the ladies, a Mrs. Winslow, came shortly on the heels of their visit.

"Shall we go, Terry?" asked Aunt Katie, showing the slip of pasteboard to her nephew.

"What is it?" said Sir Terrence, surveying the invitation. "Dinner at the Winslows', eh? I don't think I know the family."

"You wouldn't know Mrs. Winslow, for she called that afternoon you were gone to Wybolt. But you've met Mr. Winslow, or so his wife says. She made a great deal of his encountering you a week or two ago in the village and being introduced to you."

"Yes, I remember now—a stout, red-faced gentleman with a painfully firm handclasp. I had trouble using my right hand for a week afterward. On the whole, the handclasp stays best in my mind, but I do seem to recall his muttering something about asking me to take potluck at his house on some future occasion. This is the threat fulfilled, I suppose."

"It doesn't sound as though you're overeager to go," observed Aunt Katie, raising her brows.

Sir Terrence laughed. "I admit I am not. A dinner party where I'm not even on nodding acquaintance with most of the guests is likely to be an awful bore. But I suppose I must go all the same. It doesn't do to offend one's neighbors in a place like this."

"Well, if you go, then I must go likewise," said Aunt Katie, regarding the invitation with resignation. "Though I can't say I took to Mrs. Winslow overmuch. A peering, prying kind of woman with no shame about asking what the gown on my back cost me or how much income you had a year, Terry. Still, I liked her a deal better than that Mrs. Wrexford. A disagreeable old biddy *she* was, and no mistake. As my old uncle would have said, she acted as though it was an honor for us to have her wearing our cushions with her backside and soiling our carpets with her feet. Didn't she, Miss Pearce?"

"Yes, she did," agreed Emily. She could clearly remember Mrs. Wrexford's face as she had sat on the sofa, looking about the room as though she suspected it and its occupants of harboring some scandalous secret. She had taken no part in the conversation, confining her remarks to a frigid greeting to Aunt Katie at the beginning and ending of the call. Initially, she had extended the same courtesy toward Emily, but when Aunt Katie had referred to her in the course of conversation as "my companion, Miss Pearce," Mrs. Wrexford had given her one contemptuous glance and ignored her entirely thereafter, as if any person as negligible as a hired companion simply did not exist as far as she was concerned.

Emily had been irritated by this treatment, but she had endured too many similar slights during her career to be surprised by it. Indeed, it was a mild rebuff of its kind. The chief of its sting lay in the fact that for the past few weeks she had been treated with so much kindness, consideration, and courtesy. But of course the rest of the world was not like the O'Reillys, and she could not expect to be treated as an equal outside Honeywell House.

It was very likely, for instance, that the Winslows had

not included her in their dinner invitation. Emily wished
very much to be assured on this point but felt delicate about
asking. She was surprised and pleased when Sir Terrence
turned to her a moment later, saying, "And of course you
mean to go to this dinner party with us, don't you, Miss
Pearce? Do say you will. Auntie and I cannot let you off
at any price."

"I shall certainly go if you wish me to," said Emily. "But
I was not sure whether Mrs. Winslow had included me in
the invitation."

"Of course she did," said Sir Terrence, looking surprised. "Why would she not?"

Emily did not like to answer this question, so she merely
smiled and said, "I shall be very pleased to accompany you
and your aunt to the Winslows' party, Sir Terrence. But I
shall take warning from your experience and avoid shaking
hands with Mr. Winslow if I possibly can. It would be inconvenient to lose the use of my hand for a week!"

Sir Terrence said that he, too, hoped to avoid a repeti-
tion of this incident and asked Emily to help him think of
some strategy whereby he might avoid being crushed by
Mr. Winslow's too-fervent handshake. They got a good deal
of fun out of this during the next week and a half, Emily
suggesting such extreme measures as getting the doctor to
put a plaster cast on Sir Terrence's right arm or, alternately,
inducing Mr. Winslow to kiss his hand rather than shake
it as though Sir Terrence had been an archbishop.

On the evening of the party, however, Emily found herself in a less exhilarated mood. She had taken care to dress
herself in her best green cambric, and she had also taken
unusual pains with her hair, dressing it in curls around
her face rather than merely pulling it back into a simple
knot. Nonetheless, she was very conscious of the flaws in
her appearance. Her dress might be only a year old, but
it was a simple thing with a modest round neckline and

short sleeves, and Emily knew from the ladies' fashion
column in the local paper that low square necks and long
sleeves were the style for dinner dresses right now. She
had not even any jewelry to distract her fellow guests' eyes
from her unfashionable neckline and sleeves. And though
the paper had assured her that green was still an unexcep-
tionable color for young ladies' toilettes, when Emily surveyed her appearance in the glass, she could not be
confident that even this detail was right.

For one thing, the deep green of her dress seemed to
intensify the color of her hair. It looked even redder than
it usually did—*and heaven knows it was red enough already*,
Emily reflected with chagrin. She wished it were possible
to change the color of her hair, or if not that, at least to
exchange her dress for some garment that would subdue
rather than accentuate the flaming hue of her tresses. But
even had that been possible, there was no color that would
deaccentuate her unfashionable height. Here she stood,
five feet nine in her stocking feet, red-haired, and dressed
like a dowd. Miss Morris had been right: she *was* an unattractive girl, and no amount of care in dressing could
disguise it.

Well, what does it matter? Emily told herself impatiently.
I have looked the way I look for a good many years now. But
though she told herself it could not matter if she looked
an unattractive dowd tonight more than any other night,
she found it did matter. She was going among strangers
tonight—men and women whom she had never seen
before. Just as she would look at them and judge them
first of all by their appearance, so would they judge her.

The thought of being adjudged an unattractive dowd
by a dozen strangers was a dismaying enough prospect to
Emily. But when she probed deeper within her heart, she
found yet another reason why she shrank from showing
herself in her present array. It stood to reason that at least

half the guests tonight would be women. It was likewise reasonable to suppose that some of them would be young women. Mrs. Winslow had spoken of a daughter, and so had Mrs. Wrexford, during one of the very few utterances she had made during the ladies' call. It was natural, then, to suppose that these and other young ladies should be at the party tonight.

And since the party was being held in honor of a handsome bachelor baronet, it was likewise natural to suppose that the young ladies attending the party would take great pains with their appearance. They would have spent hours beforehand primping and preparing. Given that they possessed any personal advantages at all, they could hardly help outshining a too-tall, red-haired girl in an unfashionably cut green cambric. Emily could see it all in her mind's eye: a bevy of beautiful girls in fashionable array sweeping down on Sir Terrence and dazzling him so that he could not even see the girl with whom he had spent so many hours in the library discussing impossible plots for impossible novels.

Good heavens, I'm jealous! The discovery came to Emily like a bolt out of the blue. She stared at her reflection in the glass. It stared back at her. She, Emily Pearce, was jealous of any other woman usurping her place in Sir Terrence's eyes. Once she had recognized this fact, it took no time at all to understand why. If she were not already in love with her employer, she was well on her way to being so. And she had proceeded far enough along that dangerous road to resent any woman who showed signs of diverting Sir Terrence's attention.

"Good heavens," said Emily again. She could have spent hours pondering the consequences of her discovery, but at that moment Aunt Katie tapped on her door.

"Are you ready, my dear?" she called. "Terry says the carriage has just been brought around."

Emily pulled herself together with a snap. "Yes, I'm ready," she said. She snatched up her cloak and reticule and hurried downstairs to where Sir Terrence and the carriage were waiting.

Chapter 11

Sir Terrence found Emily strangely uncommunicative on the drive to the Winslows'.

In truth, he was not feeling very communicative himself. The prospect of a formal meal taken largely in the company of strangers was not one that appealed to him. Though possessing a social nature, he preferred his society familiar and comfortable, like a pair of boots that had been thoroughly broken in and could be depended on not to pinch. He smiled as he expanded this analogy in his mind. Of course, there would be pinches that evening, uncomfortable, embarrassing, or merely tiresome moments such as were inevitable when one was spending the evening with a dozen or more unknown personalities. It might be that there would even be a blister as a result of some particularly uncomfortable encounter, though there would scarcely be time in the space of a single evening to form a callous.

Sir Terrence smiled again and glanced at Emily, wishing he could share his thoughts with her. Between them, they might have expanded the analogy to ridiculous lengths, finding social parallels for bunions and corns and every other foot ailment under the sun. But Emily did not seem in the mood to appreciate an analogy between footwear and society tonight. When he had remarked a few minutes ago what a beautiful sight the sun was, sinking slowly over the horizon, she had merely nodded without even glancing toward the west. And an effort to reengage her in their game of how best to avoid shaking hands with Mr. Winslow had fallen quite flat.

Sir Terrence looked again at Emily as she sat on the banquette beside his aunt. He was disappointed by her silence and frustrated by it, too. The companionship that had grown between them the last few weeks had been very enjoyable to him. It was refreshing to find someone who enjoyed the same pursuits as he, someone who could argue passionately about the aptness of a word or the motivation of a fictional character, someone who could throw herself enthusiastically into thinking up all manner of absurd and creative nonsense.

Now it was obvious that Emily's thoughts were a thousand miles away. She sat with her hands folded in her lap, her eyes fixed straight ahead. Sir Terrence was able to study her quite openly, for she seemed unaware that he was looking at her. She wore a green dress, he noted, with a darker green cloak thrown over her shoulders. Against its dull color, her hair rioted in a mass of bright curls caught back with a ribbon that matched her dress.

He was struck suddenly by the discovery of how lovely she was. Of course, he had thought her a pretty girl even in the beginning, when he had first seen her that morning beside the well. But ever since that morning he had been resolutely trying not to notice or respond to her physical attractions. There had been times lately when he had been so filled with admiration for her intelligence and imagination that his earlier and more elemental admiration for her face and figure had been almost pushed aside. Now it was as though the two kinds of admiration came suddenly together in his new eyes. He saw Emily as she really was: a woman both physically desirable and mentally stimulating, strong in wit, humor, and integrity—a woman in a million, in fact. As he sat staring at her, stunned by his discovery, she looked up suddenly and met his eyes.

For a long moment they looked at each other. Then Emily looked away again, but in that moment it seemed to Sir Terrence that everything was changed. The setting sun glowed brighter; the birds in the hedgerow by which they were passing sang sweeter; and his blood pulsed faster in his veins. He sat staring at Emily until the carriage came to a stop in front of the Winslows' house.

At that point, Sir Terrence was forced to put away his thoughts and concentrate on doing his social duty. It ought to have been terribly hard, given his state of emotional turmoil, but strangely enough it was not. He felt like a man in the most exhilarating phase of intoxication. Everything was beautiful, everything was interesting, and he was prepared to welcome the whole world as a friend.

He won Mrs. Winslow's heart straightaway by praising her house in the warmest terms. He allowed Mr. Winslow to shake his hand without even wincing at the strength of that gentleman's grasp. When he was introduced to Mr. Winslow's son, Ben, he said he was glad to make Ben's acquaintance in a voice that admitted no doubt that he was speaking the sincere truth. As for the seventeen-year-old Miss Sophia Winslow, she was so dazzled by the smile and bow he bestowed upon her that she devoted a whole page in her diary that night to describing the incident.

The other guests at the dinner likewise came under the glow of Sir Terrence's liking and approval. To be sure, there were a few to whom he did not take so warmly. When he was introduced to Mrs. Wrexford, for instance, he found himself secretly sharing his aunt's opinion of her as a very disagreeable woman.

"Sir Terrence," said that lady, bowing stiffly and flexing her thin lips in a chilly smile. "I am glad to make your acquaintance. I had the pleasure of making your aunt's acquaintance just last week."

"Yes, so she told me," returned Sir Terrence. He supposed he ought to say something about his aunt's having taken pleasure in the meeting, too, but could not bring himself to utter such a blatant falsehood.

Mrs. Wrexford did not wait for any further remark from him, but went on speaking in her cold, precise voice. "Allow me to make you known to my daughter, Sir Terrence," she said. "Isabel, this is Sir Terrence O'Reilly. You know he is living at Honeywell House now."

"Of course I know that, Mama," said Isabel. Smiling, she gave Sir Terrence her hand. Sir Terrence, politely saluting it, thought he had never seen such an awful illustration of the power of heredity. Isabel's hair was fair, not gray, and she was taller than her mother, but in every other detail they were the same: the same narrow face, the same thin lips and cold blue eyes, the same angular figure. This last feature Isabel had sought to disguise beneath a ruched and ruffled dress of celestial blue. The results were less than happy to Sir Terrence's eyes, but it was obvious Isabel was pleased with her appearance. She drew Sir Terrence's attention to it several times during the course of the ensuing conversation.

"I do like this new style of dinner dresses, don't you? Square necks are so vastly becoming. Scarcely anyone wears round necks anymore, and I am so glad, for I think them very dowdy."

"Do you?" said Sir Terrence. He was seeking for a way to end the conversation and abandon Isabel and her mother for more congenial company, but he did not wish to be rude about it.

Isabel nodded vigorously. "Yes, to be sure. Of course, not everyone is fortunate enough to be able to keep up with the fashions. I quite understand that, and you must not be thinking I am criticizing the young lady in any way."

She paused, looking expectantly at Sir Terrence. He stared back at her, bewildered. "Young lady?" he repeated. "What young lady?"

"Why, the young lady who came in with you. Your aunt's companion, is she not? I am sure it is quite understandable if she chooses to disregard fashion, and very appropriate, too. One does not like to see persons of her station aping their betters."

Sir Terrence stared at Isabel so long that she began to think she had made a conquest of him. "Miss Wrexford," he said at last. "Are you referring by any chance to *Miss Pearce*?"

"Is that her name? I didn't know it. Mama merely mentioned that there was a companion hanging about when she called on your aunt the other day, a youngish woman with red hair. I assumed it might be the same."

"It is," said Sir Terrence concisely. There were many other things he would have liked to say to Isabel—so many that to choose between them was impossible. He merely bowed, turned, and walked away without saying another word.

It did not take him long to locate Emily. She was standing at the far end of the room, listening to an elderly gentleman with a clerical collar who appeared to be holding forth on some absorbing subject. Sir Terrence started toward her, but he had not gone three steps before the drawing-room door opened and a liveried manservant appeared to announce that the dinner was served.

At that point Sir Terrence was forced to abandon his

intention of speaking with Emily and give his arm to Mrs. Winslow. At the table, he found himself seated between her and Lady Mabberly, an elderly dame who appeared to be cut from much the same kind of cloth as Mrs. Wrexford. She unbent a little as the meal progressed, however, telling Sir Terrence that it was good to have persons of breeding like him and his aunt staying at Honeywell House.

"I am afraid that in general we have a very limited society in this neighborhood," she told him with a flash of wintry smile. "There are very few persons of any distinction living hereabouts."

"I wouldn't say that, ma'am," protested Mrs. Winslow. "There are yourself and dear Sir Thomas, of course—"

"Of course," said Lady Mabberly, acknowledging the compliment with a complacent nod.

"And the Percys, too, are a very old and distinguished family. And then there are Lord and Lady Meredith at the Abbey."

"Lord and Lady Meredith!" exclaimed Lady Mabberly. Her heavy face bore a frown as she regarded Mrs. Winslow. "No doubt the Merediths must be counted the aristocrats of the neighborhood, but I say frankly that it goes much against the grain with me to acknowledge them as such. The conduct of the present Lord Meredith was never of a kind I could approve. As for his wife's conduct, the less said about that, the better."

With this statement, however, she had obviously gone further than Mrs. Winslow would follow. "I never saw anything wrong with Catherine's conduct," she protested. "Not while she was living here in Langton Abbots, at any rate. Oh, of course, I know that old story about her and the dancing master, but I cannot think there was much in it, myself. And now that she is married to Lord Meredith, I for one have no hesitation about receiving her."

Lady Mabberly shook her head darkly. "You may say

that she and Lord Meredith are married," she said. "I have my doubts about it. It was a very strange and hasty business, to say no worse of it."

"There can be no doubt they are married," said Mrs. Winslow firmly. "The announcement was in all the papers. And so I have no hesitation about inviting them here. I actually had invited them to this dinner party, you must know, so that they, too, might become acquainted with Sir Terrence." She gave Sir Terrence a shy smile. "Unfortunately, they already had a previous engagement. But Catherine—Lady Meredith, I mean—said she and Lord Meredith would try to drop by later in the evening if they had time."

Lady Mabberly said sourly that she was just as glad the Merediths had seen fit to decline Mrs. Winslow's invitation, as she would as lief not sit down to dinner with people of such dubious respectability. Sir Terrence listened to this talk with only half an ear. Being unacquainted with the Merediths, he had very little interest in their doings, respectable or otherwise. He was more interested in watching Emily at the other end of the table. She was seated between the elderly, clerical-looking gentleman and another younger gentleman with fair hair and a vaguely sporting appearance. He wondered if she found either of them congenial company. The thought did not make him jealous, merely envious. He wished he might have been seated beside her so that he could have had the pleasure of talking to her himself.

Emily was wishing much the same thing, though for different reasons. The dinner party had been nothing but an ordeal for her so far. Glancing around the table in despair, she could see no signs that it would get any easier as the evening wore on.

The meal itself was good enough. Mrs. Winslow had

given her guests two full courses, beginning with turtle soup and working through a series of joints and saddles accompanied by vegetables and light "made" dishes. The dessert course was equally expansive, encompassing cakes, tarts, trifles, creams, jellies, and every other variety of sweet thing. Emily could find no fault with it, and neither could she complain about the way she had been received by her hostess. Mrs. Winslow had been the soul of kindness, welcoming her warmly and introducing her to several of the other guests. But as soon as Mrs. Winslow had left her to her own devices, the trouble had begun.

Emily already knew Mrs. Wrexford from that lady's call the previous week, and it seemed only right that she should smile and say a word of greeting to her. But Mrs. Wrexford had behaved as though this were the grossest impertinence, and Emily had been snubbed roundly for her pains. Mrs. Wrexford's daughter, Isabel, had also snubbed her, and though she was more politely treated by the other young lady guests, still she was not received into their circle with any enthusiasm.

"*She* is to be here tonight, you know," one of the young ladies was saying in a lowered voice as Emily came over to join them. She broke off with an embarrassed look at Emily, and Emily, already made sensitive by her previous snubs, felt sure they had been talking about her. She stood in silent humiliation, pretending to listen to their talk but really wishing she might plead sickness and excuse herself from the gathering.

Of course, that was out of the question. Either Aunt Katie or Sir Terrence would have to accompany her if she left, and both of them seemed to be enjoying themselves. Sir Terrence, indeed, seemed to be in the highest of high spirits, and as Emily watched him circulate among the guests, she felt a sensation of dissatisfaction—almost one of disappointment. It was not so much the fact that he was having a good time that disturbed her, she decided, but that he was having a good time without her. That was ridiculous, of course, for she was nothing to him except his aunt's hired companion and—occasionally—a friend with whom he might discuss his literary endeavors.

She knew, however, that though she might be only a friend and employee to Sir Terrence, he was far more than that to her. And there had been a moment that evening when she had felt as though he might feel the same way. It had happened when they were on their way to the Winslows' party. She had been sitting in the carriage, engrossed in her thoughts, when she had happened to look up and found Sir Terrence's eyes upon her. There had been an expression in his eyes that had filled her with an odd compound of hope, fear, and excitement.

But it seemed now as though she must have been mistaken. It was evident from Sir Terrence's behavior that he could get along quite happily without her. In desperation, Emily had turned her back both on him and the group of young ladies and gone in search of something to distract her unhappy thoughts. Mrs. Winslow had caught sight of her in her wanderings, taken her under her wing once more, and made her known to several other guests, including Mr. Hamthorpe, the parish vicar. A pleasant, elderly gentleman, he had kindly drawn her into conversation, and so she had passed the remaining moments until it was time to go in to dinner.

At dinner she had found herself again paired with Mr. Hamthorpe, which was as good a situation as she would have dared hope for. Her other dinner partner, a Mr. Woodward, was less satisfactory. Upon being introduced to Emily, he stared at her so hard as to give her a very bad opinion of his manners, and when he found she would not flirt with him, he ignored her to carry on a lively exchange with the young lady across the table. They did this so loudly that Emily was able to pick up a great deal of local gossip and tittle-tattle. Most of it was incomprehensible to her, but there was one item that made her prick up her ears.

"Tell me, Susan, is it true that Meredith and his wife are to be here tonight?" asked the gentleman of the young lady. "I heard a rumor that they had been invited."

The young lady nodded eagerly. "Yes, so did I. Some of the girls were talking about it earlier. I hope the Merediths do come, but it will be just my luck if they do not. I am dying to see if Lady Meredith is as scandalous as everyone says."

The gentleman laughed. "Aye, you've never seen her, have you? Nor Meredith, either, now I think of it. The two of them have been over on the Continent for the past year or two."

"Yes, and I only moved to Langton Abbots a year ago. But Isabel has told me all about them, and I am terribly eager to see them both. Is it true Lady Meredith once ran away with a dancing master?"

Again the gentleman laughed. "So the story goes, but I couldn't say if it's true or not. Indeed, I'm afraid you'll be disappointed in our scarlet woman, Susan. I remember Lady Meredith when she was Catherine Summerfield, and I assure you that to look at her you would never have guessed she had it in her to run away with a dancing master or anybody else. Not that she wasn't a handsome girl, mind you. I don't say she wasn't, but she always seemed a bit standoffish to me."

"Was she indeed?" said the young lady in disappointment. "I would never have thought it after the things Isabel said. According to her, Lady Meredith was quite scandalous before she married. And wasn't there even some scandal about her marrying Lord Meredith? Isabel said he was engaged, or going to be engaged, to marry another girl, and then suddenly he married Miss Summerfield."

The gentleman grinned. "You won't make anything out of that! There was a lot of talk at the time, but it's been two years since Lord and Lady Meredith married, and no heir has appeared on the scene as yet."

"I didn't mean *that*," said the girl, blushing. "I only meant it seemed strange they married so suddenly. And if Lord Meredith was actually engaged to another girl—"

"He wasn't," said the gentleman with authority. "My sister was bosom-bows with Laura Lindsay, the girl he was supposed to be engaged to. And Laura told her in confidence that not only were she and Lord Meredith not engaged but that she personally approved of his marrying Miss Summerfield."

"Oh," said the young lady, looking disappointed. "I made sure from what Isabel said there was some scandal about it."

"There was plenty of scandal, but it wasn't anything to do with Miss Summerfield. You'll have to ask Isabel about that. But don't expect her to be unprejudiced where Catherine Summerfield is concerned. Isabel always had her knife into her, even back in the old days." The gentleman glanced at Isabel, sitting cold and aloof farther down the table. "I always suspected it was jealousy, myself. Isabel's nothing much to look at, and she's getting older and sourer by the minute. Unless Sir Terrence takes pity on her, she's like to end up an old maid."

The young lady laughed at this and said Sir Terrence was a charming man whom she wouldn't mind marrying herself. The gentleman immediately offered to stand groomsman at the wedding, and the conversation degenerated once more into mere flirtation.

Emily, who had listened to their conversation with equal parts of disgust and amusement, now settled down to eat her dessert. But in spite of her contempt for the two scandalmongers, she had been intrigued by what they had said concerning Lady Meredith. It occurred to her that the remark she had overheard earlier, "*She* is to be here tonight," had probably been referring to Lady Meredith rather than herself. This made her feel better, but it also made her curious to meet the lady who had been the cause of so much conjecture. She found herself sharing the hope, expressed by her dinner companions, that Lady Meredith would honor her half-promise to drop by the Winslows' party later in the evening.

As the evening wore on, however, Emily found herself in difficulties that made her forget the subject of scandalous peers and peeresses. After dessert had been eaten, Mrs. Winslow gave the signal, and the ladies arose to return to the drawing room. Emily clung close to Aunt Katie, feeling she would be less likely to endure any more snubs if she stayed with that redoubtable lady. But her hostess thwarted her efforts by insisting she sit with the other young ladies. "You will find that more interesting than listening to us old women chatter," she told Emily with a smile.

More interesting it might have been, but it was also far from comfortable. Mrs. Winslow's daughter, Sophia, smiled at her shyly, and another young lady wished her good evening, but the others more or less ignored her. Isabel Wrexford was one of those others, but while refusing to openly acknowledge Emily's presence, she yet managed to direct a few jabs in her direction.

"I must say that Sir Terrence seems a very genteel, well-bred man," she told her companions. "Knowing that he was Irish, I came here tonight expecting the worst. But one would hardly know he was an Irishman by his way of speaking."

"Yes, he seems quite English," agreed one of the other girls.

"His aunt is Irish enough for both of them," put in a third girl with a laugh. "Such a quaint way of speaking she has! I must say I thought her very charming."

"Yes, she is charming enough," agreed Isabel in a dry voice. "But I prefer Sir Terrence's manners to those of the females in his household."

She did not look at Emily as she spoke, but her tone made it obvious to whom she was referring. One or two of the girls gasped or giggled, and there was a brief, highly charged silence. Sophia Winslow, with the idea perhaps of easing the situation, turned to address Emily. "Are you Irish, too, Miss Pearce?" she asked in her soft little voice.

"No, I am not," said Emily. That was the extent of their exchange, for Isabel had gone on speaking without seeming to notice the interruption.

"A very delightful party tonight," she said, addressing the group generally. "There are very few persons present whom one would prefer not to meet. Of course, one understands your mama's dilemma, Sophia. One cannot invite some members of a household while excluding others. Yet one would think that such persons would have delicacy enough to excuse themselves from gatherings where they must know they are not really wanted."

Emily felt this to be too pointed a slur to allow it to pass unchallenged. She turned to Sophia Winslow. "I hope you will tell your mother how grateful I am that she invited me to your party," she said loudly. "I have met so many interesting and pleasant people this evening! Of course, there are always people whom one would rather not meet, but I am sure it is difficult in a restricted neighborhood like this one to exclude any of one's near neighbors." Looking directly at Isabel, she asked, "Are you a near neighbor of the Winslows', Miss Wrexford?"

There were gasps all around at this speech. Isabel, looking as though her nostrils had just been afflicted by a very

bad odor, said coldly, "Not very near, no," and turned
her back upon Emily. Sophia Winslow, looking flustered,
began to talk in a desperate way about the weather. One
or two of the other girls joined in, but they were careful
not to look at Emily. After a minute, Emily pushed back
her chair and got to her feet. Still nobody looked at her,
so she went over to the window, pulled back the curtain,
and stood gazing out at the garden with unseeing eyes.

She stood there for what seemed a very long time. By
the time she heard the gentlemen coming back into the
drawing room, the fire of anger had died out of her heart,
and she felt only hurt and humiliation. Even then she did
not turn around but only stood and waited. Would Sir
Terrence come to her? It seemed a test, somehow. If he
cared at all, he must notice her standing there alone. Even
in the midst of his own good time, he must notice that
she was lonely and come speak with her for a few minutes.

She could hear his voice now, picking out his musical
baritone among the other gentlemen's voices. Evidently,
he was narrating some humorous story, for there was laughter from those around him. Now he was saying something
else, and someone—it sounded like Mrs. Winslow—protested, "Oh, no, you must come and talk to Mrs. Percy for
a moment, Sir Terrence. She is most eager to become
better acquainted with you."

There was an acquiescent murmur from Sir Terrence.
Emily waited, but she already knew the verdict. He did not
intend to come. It was, in fact, Aunt Katie who finally
joined her at the window, saying, "My dear, is everything
well with you? Why do you not join the others?"

"I felt a little unwell and thought I could use some
fresh air," said Emily. This was certainly true, though her
indisposition was more an emotional than a physical one.
Aunt Katie scrutinized her closely.

"I'm thinking you do look a bit peaked. Shall I order out the carriage?"

There was nothing Emily would have liked more than to say, "Yes." But her pride would not allow her to take such a coward's way out. As long as she was here, she was resolved to stay and plumb the full depths of misery that the evening held in store for her. Then she would go home, and after this she would have the delicacy to excuse herself from gatherings where she was not really wanted.

"No, I'm sure I will be quite all right," she told Aunt Katie. "You go back to the others. I'll join you as soon as I am feeling better."

She would have felt better immediately if she had known what Sir Terrence was thinking. His first act, on entering the room, was to look around for her. He spied her immediately standing by the window, and as soon as he finished the story he was relating, he had made an effort to go to her. But his high spirits had been such that everyone was eager to see and hear more of "that amusing Sir Terrence," and every time he tried to excuse himself to go speak to Emily, he found himself thwarted.

He was surprised and a little worried to see her standing alone at the window. At last, he had sent Aunt Katie to see if she was well. Aunt Katie had returned, saying Emily was merely feeling a trifle indisposed. Rather than allaying Sir Terrence's worries, this report only intensified them. He decided he must speak to Emily at all costs and find out if she was really unwell. Firmly excusing himself to his fellow guests, he had just risen to his feet when the drawing room door opened and the butler's stentorian voice boomed out triumphantly, "Lord and Lady Meredith!"

Chapter 12

Like everyone else in the room, Emily looked around when the butler made his announcement.

There was a brief pause, breathless with expectation. Then Lord and Lady Meredith came into the room. Though they entered quietly, even decorously, Emily felt she would have known they were no ordinary couple even if she had not previously heard the gossip of her dinner partners.

Lord Meredith was a tall, dark gentleman in his middle thirties. His figure was admirable; his face handsome; and his clothes embodied the austere elegance espoused by Brummell. In spite of these qualities, he was clearly no languid and world-weary beau. There was real interest in the look he cast around the room, a real smile on his face as he greeted his hostess, and a kind of suppressed energy about his movements that made him fascinating to watch.

Lady Meredith was just as fascinating to watch, if much more difficult to define. As Emily watched her make her greetings to Mrs. Winslow, she was struck chiefly by her composure. If Lady Meredith knew that she was being watched by every other person in the room, she did not show it by her manner. Emily, surveying her critically, decided it was quite true that she did not look the part of a scarlet woman. Yet there could be no doubt that she was beautiful, with her glossy chestnut hair, heart-shaped face, and slim, graceful figure. And there was certainly nothing prudish about the way she was dressed. Her bronze-colored taffeta gown had a square neckline like Isabel's, but unlike Isabel's, it bared not merely her neck and collarbones but a generous portion of her décolletage as well. Topazes sparkled on her breast and in her ears, and when she turned her head, Emily glimpsed the flash of more gems set above the chignon at the nape of her neck.

She's lovely, Emily admitted to herself. *No wonder Lord Meredith is wild about her.*

Emily could not doubt that this was the case. She had already noticed the way Lord Meredith's eyes followed his wife as she moved around the room. Lady Meredith, on the other hand, seemed unaware of, if not actually indifferent to, her husband's adoration. Emily was just marveling at her insensibility when she saw Lord Meredith, in the course of conversation, casually reach out and put his arm about his wife's shoulders. Lady Meredith glanced up at him, and in that glance Emily read emotions the very reverse of indifference and insensibility. So powerful was the impression that Emily turned away in embarrassment, feeling she had seen something not meant for the eyes of others.

Her embarrassment was the greater because she was sure that Lady Meredith had noticed her staring. Even as she had turned away, the other woman's eyes had flickered toward her. Emily had been careful not to look at her after that, but she had several times been aware that Lady

Meredith was looking in her direction. And even though
the peeress's face was so naturally inexpressive that it was
difficult to tell what she was thinking, Emily thought she
read curiosity in those looks. She kept her own face turned
toward the window, however, and refused to meet the other
woman's eye.

Yet so interested was she in all that was passing in the
drawing room that she could not help being aware of it,
even with her back to the other guests. She knew, for
example, the exact moment that Sir Terrence was introduced to the Merediths. From that distance she could
not catch the actual words being exchanged or see the
expressions on their faces, but her imagination could sup-
ply all that well enough. Of course, Sir Terrence must be
struck by Lady Meredith's beauty. She in turn must be
struck by his wit and charm, though Emily was not so
disturbed by this reflection as she might have been if she
had not caught Lady Meredith looking at her husband
unawares. Any woman who could look at a man like that
was not likely to dally with another man, however witty
and charming he might be.

Nonetheless, Emily was relieved when the Merediths
passed on from Sir Terrence to the other guests. She was
amused to hear the same young ladies she had heard speaking in such a bold way about Lady Meredith now greet her
with shy voices and stammered compliments. Only Isabel
stood aloof, saying coldly, "Lady Meredith and I are already
acquainted," when one of the other girls sought to introduce them.

"Yes, we are already acquainted," agreed Lady Meredith
in a calm voice. She added something in a lower voice that
Emily could not hear. Isabel's reply came to her ears,
however, with disastrous clarity.

"Her? Oh, that's only the companion. You needn't worry
about *her*."

Again Lady Meredith spoke, and again her voice was too low for Emily to hear. The context of her words was obvious, however, for Isabel presently said, in an ungracious voice, "Oh, very well, since you insist. But kindly let one of the other girls perform the introductions, if you please. I have nothing to say to the creature, and she was quite rude to me earlier when I was seeking only to give her a hint about how to go on. I would as lief not speak to her again."

Emily went stiff at this speech, but it prepared her in some measure for what happened next. She felt a touch on her arm, and turning, found Miss Winslow and Lady Meredith standing beside her. Poor Miss Winslow was looking even shyer than usual, but Lady Meredith's lovely face was perfectly calm and self-possessed as she regarded Emily.

Miss Winslow was the first to speak. "Miss Pearce," she said with a little gasp. "I would like to present you to Lady Meredith. Lady Meredith, this is Miss Pearce."

Emily might have been staggered at this turn of events, but she was not too shocked to remember her manners. "Lady Meredith," she said, curtsying.

As she curtsied, she observed several things about Lady Meredith that she had not had a chance to notice before. The first was that the peeress was only a little less tall than herself. The second was that Lady Meredith's eyes, which she had taken for blue or gray, were really a curiously light and luminous golden brown; and the third was that Lady Meredith's mouth, for all its seeming demureness, had about it a slight quirk—a quirk suggestive of humor.

The quirk was very noticeable as Lady Meredith returned Emily's curtsy. "I am very pleased to meet you, Miss Pearce," she said. "Forgive me for intruding, but I was anxious to make your acquaintance. I believe we have some friends in common."

Emily looked at her doubtfully. One heavy-lidded golden

eye closed momentarily, then opened again in an unmistakable wink. Turning to Miss Winslow, Lady Meredith bestowed a casual nod upon her. "Thank you, Miss Winslow," she said. It was clearly a dismissal, and Miss Winslow took it as such, retiring precipitately to the group of other young ladies. Emily and Lady Meredith were left facing each other beside the window.

As soon as she had gone, Emily spoke. "Do we really have friends in common, ma'am?" she asked.

"Of course," said Lady Meredith. "Surely I am correct in supposing you have made the acquaintance of Miss Wrexford? You must know she is a very old friend of mine, and I am sure you join with me in finding her perfectly charming."

She spoke so gravely that Emily was almost deluded into taking her seriously. Then she observed the sparkle in the golden eyes, and a laugh escaped her. "Oh! No, I am afraid I do not, Lady Meredith."

"You surprise me," said Lady Meredith, more gravely still. Lowering her voice, she added, "I see a comfortable-looking sofa over there which no one seems to be using. Shall we go sit down and discuss the matter?"

"Certainly," said Emily. Together, the two of them went over and sat down on the sofa. As soon as they were comfortably situated, Lady Meredith drew a deep sigh and smiled at Emily.

"You must think me a very strange sort of woman," she observed.

"On the contrary, I think you a very kind one," said Emily. "But you must not be laboring under a delusion, Lady Meredith. Isabel Wrexford was quite right in saying I am 'only a companion.' I am sure I do not warrant such a distinguishing degree of attention."

"I should say you deserve it more than any of them," returned Lady Meredith. "Certainly more than Isabel

Wrexford. I am sure no one would ever voluntarily pick *her* to be one's companion."

Again Emily laughed. "One would hope not! Oh, I ought not to say such things, but indeed I found her very disagreeable."

Lady Meredith nodded sagely. "You would, of course. She cannot resist the temptation to torment anyone whose position is the least vulnerable." She flashed another smile at Emily. "I should know, for I was once in that position. Happily I am beyond her touch now."

"I wish I were," said Emily with a sigh.

"You will be." There was perfect assurance in Lady Meredith's voice as she regarded Emily. "I could tell it as soon as I looked at you, Miss Pearce. There's a quality about you that sets you head and shoulders above Isabel Wrexford, even if you *are* 'only a companion.' Whose companion are you exactly? No doubt someone has already told me, but I did not catch it."

Emily pointed out Aunt Katie and went on to explain her situation at Honeywell House. "Honeywell House," repeated Lady Meredith with an inscrutable expression. "Yes, I had heard it had been leased again. And so you are living there with Miss O'Reilly and Sir Terrence? That sounds as though it would be an agreeable situation. Miss O'Reilly seems a lady in the best sense of the word, and as for Sir Terrence, Jonathan and I both found him very charming."

"He *is* very charming," agreed Emily with a certain reserve. "I have been very happy living at Honeywell House."

Lady Meredith's golden eyes studied Emily curiously, but all she said was, "I am very glad to hear it. I only wish you could be as happy when you go out in public. It seems a shame that the residents of Langton Abbots are inclined to take such a small-minded view of a woman who must work for her living."

"Some of them are not so bad. Mrs. Winslow and her daughter, for instance, have been the soul of kindness. And of course you, too, Lady Meredith. I cannot be grateful enough for your singling me out in this way. Believe me, I am very much honored."

Lady Meredith shook her head, smiling. "As to that, you must know that most of the people hereabouts consider me quite a scandalous person, Miss Pearce. If you have lived here any length of time, I am sure you must have heard some of the rumors. I tell you fairly that it may do your reputation untold harm if you sit with me much longer."

She smiled at Emily, and Emily returned the smile. "I am willing to risk it, my lady," she said.

"Then let us go get some tea and settle ourselves for a comfortable coze. I can think of no one I would rather spend the evening with—always setting Jonathan out of the question, of course!"

For the rest of the evening, Emily sat on the sofa with Lady Meredith, talking and drinking innumerable cups of tea. They spoke of Honeywell House, which Lady Meredith seemed to know well, and of the Abbey, the ancient house where she and Lord Meredith lived. Lady Meredith told Emily something of her history and that of the neighborhood, while Emily countered with a little about her own history. They were deep in a discussion of several neighborhood residents when a voice rang out suddenly above them.

"Here they are, O'Reilly! Wallowing in the iniquity of tea and gossip, as I live."

Emily looked up. There, standing behind the sofa, were Sir Terrence and Lord Meredith. Lord Meredith shook his head at his wife, saying reproachfully, "She swore most faithfully to stand beside me in sickness and in health, for richer or poorer, etc., etc. But let her come to a party and she abandons me without a thought."

"Not without a thought, Jonathan," said Lady Meredith, rising to her feet. "But certainly without guilt. I thought you quite capable of fending for yourself for the space of an hour or two."

Lord Meredith shook his head at this, saying he had never expected to be so cruelly abandoned by the woman to whom he had entrusted his heart and happiness. Sir Terrence, meanwhile, was looking down at Emily. So concentrated was his expression that she could not help asking shyly, "Why are you looking at me like that, Sir Terrence?"

He gave a little start, then smiled. "Was I staring? I was merely thinking to myself, *Found! Found! Found!* like the goblin page boy in Scott's poem we were reading the other night. Only my discovery causes me jubilation rather than horror and dismay. Do you know, I have been trying to talk to you all evening, Miss Pearce? But always something has arisen to thwart me."

"Has it?" said Emily. She felt a sudden soaring in her spirits. The evening that had started out as a humiliating ordeal was miraculously turning out to be one of the best in her life. She had spent over an hour talking with Lady Meredith, who had not only treated her with the most distinguishing consideration but with whom she had found many opinions in common. Now here was Sir Terrence saying he had been wanting to talk to her and expressing his regrets because he had been thwarted in this desire. That might have been mere politeness, of course, but Emily felt somehow that it was the truth. There was a look in Sir Terrence's eyes that bore out all he said and more besides.

But Emily shied away from analyzing the look in Sir Terrence's eyes. Her cup of happiness was already filled to overflowing, and she felt it would be greedy to desire any more. Yet more was to come all the same. Lady Meredith, having quieted her husband's complaints by the simple expedient of kissing him, turned again to Emily. "You have not yet met my husband, Miss Pearce," she said, and proceeded to make introductions. Emily, as she exchanged greetings with Lord Meredith, was able to ascertain that he was fully as good-looking close-up as he had appeared at a distance. He, for his part, seemed perfectly willing to accept Emily as a friend on his wife's recommendation, for he told her she would have to attend the ball he and his wife were giving in a few weeks.

"Ball?" exclaimed Lady Meredith, looking mystified. "Whatever do you mean, Jonathan? We are not giving a ball to *my* knowledge."

Lord Meredith looked guilty as a small boy caught out in some misdeed. "Lord, yes, I ought to have told you first! Upon my word, Catherine, I hope you won't be offended with me. But you must know it's your fault for going off and leaving my flank exposed. Mrs. Percy launched an immediate assault on me with all battalions and wouldn't let up until I promised to give a ball for the county. 'It is the *least* you can do to honor your lovely bride,' she told me. I did point out that since we were married slightly more than two years ago, a ball given in honor of my bride might be held to be rather overdue. But she said that was only the more reason to give one now and not wait any longer. On my soul, she beat me hollow on all points."

He looked so rueful that Emily and Sir Terrence could not help laughing. Lady Meredith laughed, too, with an air of resignation. "I suppose I shall have to see about giving a ball, then," she said. "Of course I shall send out cards to you and your aunt, Sir Terrence. And to Miss Pearce." She smiled at Emily. "Promise me you will come, Miss Pearce. Now I have met you, I should think the evening sadly flat if you were not among the guests."

Emily stammered out that she was greatly flattered. Lady Meredith laughed, pressed her hand, and told her not to be a ninny. "Never mind being flattered, but only come and support me at my ball. I assure you, I shall need support if I am to successfully sustain the onslaught of such critics as the Wrexfords."

"I will come if I can," said Emily, and took leave of Lady Meredith with a happy heart. She took leave of the Winslows next, in company with Sir Terrence and his aunt, the latter of whom was visibly fighting back yawns.

"A very pleasant party, but it doesn't agree with me to stay up till all hours," she told Emily as they left the house. "Did you have a nice time, my dear?"

"Wonderful," said Emily with enthusiasm. "It was a wonderful party."

On the drive home, she and Sir Terrence discussed the party, talking, praising, and criticizing its arrangements freely. Aunt Katie was too busy yawning to take much part in this conversation. When they reached home, she lost no time excusing herself and going upstairs to her room. "I suppose I ought to be going up, too," Emily told Sir Terrence. "Though I don't feel a bit tired. It's all that tea I drank after dinner, I suppose. Or perhaps it is merely that the conversation was so stimulating!"

"Yes, it was a stimulating party," agreed Sir Terrence. Rather diffidently, he added, "Should you like to come to the library and have a glass of sherry with me? That might do something toward settling both of us down."

If Emily had stopped to think, she might have realized that drinking sherry at midnight, unchaperoned and in company with a man for whom she cherished romantic feelings, was an imprudent proceeding at the very best. Something of the sort did cross her mind, but when Sir Terrence added, "I will not keep you long, Miss Pearce," and followed it up with a smile, she impulsively agreed. The evening had been such a pleasant one that she welcomed any excuse to prolong it. She quieted her conscience by reflecting that Sir Terrence could be counted on to behave like a gentleman, whatever the situation. As for whether this last point was an advantage or a disadvantage, Emily simply refused to consider it.

Together they went into the library, and Sir Terrence poured out a couple of glasses of sherry. "It has certainly been a memorable evening," he said as he handed one to Emily. "For me, at least—and it sounded as though you found it enjoyable, too, Miss Pearce."

"Yes, I certainly did," agreed Emily. With a rueful laugh, she added, "Though I do not know how enjoyable I would have found it had not Lady Meredith come to my rescue!"

"To your rescue?" repeated Sir Terrence, looking at her oddly. "What do you mean? What did she rescue you from?"

As Emily had not felt it necessary to tell either Sir Terrence or his aunt about the snubs she had suffered early in the evening, she was embarrassed by this question. "Perhaps rescue is too dramatic a word," she said with an attempted laugh. "I was only feeling a little awkward and out-of-place before she arrived. But she insisted on being introduced to me and then made me sit down with her and started asking me questions as though she were really interested in finding out all about me. It was kind of her to pretend an interest in a perfect stranger."

Here Emily stopped, for Sir Terrence was looking at her more oddly than ever. "What makes you think she was pretending an interest in you?" he said. "Why should she not find you as genuinely interesting as you seem to have found her?"

Emily found this as difficult to answer as his previous question. "Why—because Lady Meredith is a wealthy noblewoman," she faltered. "She has traveled widely, by all accounts, and has seen a great many things—"

"And so you think a wealthy, titled, worldly person who

showed interest in you must necessarily be feigning that interest?"

"Not feigning it, no." Emily thought there was an implied criticism in Sir Terrence's question, and she thought she knew the cause of it. He had obviously been so captivated by Lady Meredith's charms that he resented hearing her disparaged in any way. She hastened to correct his mistaken impression. "I did not mean to imply any criticism of Lady Meredith," she told him earnestly. "Indeed, I thought her a delightful woman. She is witty and generous, and very lovely, too."

"She is an attractive woman," agreed Sir Terrence.

Emily looked at him in amazement. It had been no stretch of the imagination to suppose him enthralled by Lady Meredith's charms. She herself had been captivated by them, and no wonder, for Lady Meredith had seemed to her the very epitome of feminine loveliness. Yet here Sir Terrence was now describing the peeress as attractive in the same calm, dispassionate voice he might have used to describe an indifferent landscape or a vapid poem. It was too much for Emily. "Attractive!" she said. "Yes, I should say she is attractive! I wish I were one-tenth as attractive myself."

Sir Terrence tilted his head. "I should say myself you are more attractive," he said. "I thought so several times this evening when I saw the two of you together."

He spoke as before, in the same calm, dispassionate voice. Emily stared at him. "Surely you are not serious?" she said. "You cannot really think me as attractive as Lady Meredith?"

Sir Terrence shook his head. "Not *as* attractive," he said. "*More* attractive. In fact, to state the matter bluntly, I think you are beautiful. There wasn't another woman there tonight who could touch you, in my estimation. What are you doing?"

"Taking away your sherry glass," said Emily. "Because it is obvious you have had more than enough to drink already."

Sir Terrence made no effort to resist as she removed the glass from his hand. But when she had set it on the table beside the other one and corked the decanter, he spoke again in a voice suddenly vibrant with emotion.

"You know I am not intoxicated, Emily," he said. "What I said was in simple earnest. Why will you not believe me?"

Something within Emily snapped at that moment. She walked over to Sir Terrence and stood facing him with her hands on her hips. "Do you remember last week when we were arguing about the existence of ghosts? You said then that no wise person believes anything without firsthand proof. Very well: I give you the chance to prove what you have said. Prove that you think me beautiful."

In the silence that followed this speech, Emily felt she could hear her own heart beating like a trip-hammer. Then Sir Terrence spoke. "By God, I will," he said, and the words were a solemn vow rather than an irreverent oath. The next thing Emily knew, she was enfolded in Sir Terrence's arms and being kissed with a passion that left no doubt of his sincerity.

After the first shock of surprise, it seemed to Emily she had been waiting all her life for that kiss. Her body seemed to fit against Sir Terrence's in the most natural way, while her mouth opened to his like a flower to the sun. She had a dizzy sense of being caught up in a maelstrom or some other natural force just as impossible to resist. She could not think, but could only feel, and what she felt was so overwhelming that she gave up even trying to think and abandoned herself to the swelling tide of feeling. Sir Terrence's arms, his mouth, the warm intimacy of his body against hers, all combined to create a growing pressure within her, a sensation of mingled love and desire and longing that was at once exquisite and intolerable. A noise like a sigh escaped her. Sir Terrence ceased kissing her for an instant to gather her more closely in his arms.

"Emily!" he whispered. "Emily."

"Yes," said Emily, and lifted her lips to him again. And in the stillness that followed, they both heard someone cough.

In an instant, Emily and Sir Terrence had sprung apart. They stood staring at each other, breathing hard. A million thoughts flashed through Emily's mind in that instant. She opened her lips to speak. Before she could do so, however, there came a second cough, accompanied by a faint scratching at the door.

"Quick, behind the sofa," Sir Terrence hissed. "You mustn't be seen here." He gestured toward the large sofa that was placed at a right angle to the fireplace. Emily darted quickly behind its bulk, and an instant later she heard Sir Terrence's voice, raised to a normal tone, inquire, "Who is it?"

"It is Haywood, Sir Terrence." The butler's voice came clearly to Emily behind the sofa. "I wondered if you were done downstairs so that I might lock the doors and extinguish the lights for the night."

"Yes, I am quite finished downstairs. I shall probably stay here in the library a little longer, then go to bed."

"Very good, sir. Shall I take those glasses for you?"

"Glasses?" Emily could hear the consternation in Sir Terrence's voice. She imagined him looking to where the sherry glasses sat, on the table beside the sofa. From where she was crouched, she could have reached out and touched them. "Oh, yes, the sherry glasses. No, never mind about those now, Haywood. I'll take them downstairs myself later on. Or better yet, I'll just fetch them now and take them down to the kitchen while you're locking up."

"If you insist, sir." The butler's voice sounded dubious.

"I do insist," said Sir Terrence.

Emily, behind the sofa, heard his footsteps approaching where she sat. She ducked her head, feeling suddenly shy. There was a rattle as Sir Terrence picked up the glasses, then a slight pause. Emily felt he was looking down at her, but she kept her eyes fixed on the floor. After a minute, she heard him say, "I'm coming, Haywood," and the sound of his footsteps going away. Then there was only silence, profound and absolute.

Chapter 13

Emily continued kneeling behind the sofa for several minutes until she was sure both Sir Terrence and the butler were gone. Then she rose to her feet, went to the door, and looked cautiously up and down the hall. No one was about, so she left the library, hurried down the hall, and was soon safely within her own bedchamber.

Once in her bedchamber, she sank down, trembling, in a chair. She felt weak in all her limbs, and her heart was pounding. When she shut her eyes, the events of the last hour sprang to life once more, passing slowly before her in inexorable detail.

How could I have behaved as I did? Emily demanded of herself. *How could I have stood before Sir Terrence and virtually demanded that he kiss me?*

The answer came readily to hand: because she had wanted him to kiss her. She had been wanting him to kiss her all evening with a hopeless desire that had no expectation of being fulfilled. Now her desires had been fulfilled beyond her wildest expectations, and instead of feeling satisfied, she only found they had been elevated to a whole new level that both frightened and appalled her.

"I cannot seriously wish that—that Sir Terrence would make love to me?" she whispered. But the question had already been answered for her back in the library, when Sir Terrence had first taken her in his arms. And if she had had any doubts remaining after that, her present state of mental and bodily agitation would have laid them to rest. Emily knew in her heart that if Sir Terrence had sought to do more than kiss her that evening, she would have had no will to oppose him.

The idea came as a shock to her. As a gently bred, nicely brought up girl, she felt she had no business harboring such unladylike feelings. Up till now she had been fairly successful in keeping herself free of them, though of course her association with Ronald had gained her firsthand acquaintance with the concept of lust. But even while enduring Ronald's lecherous attacks, she had never felt the slightest vestige of desire in return. The only feelings she had ever harbored for Ronald were anger and disgust.

By contrast, her feelings for Sir Terrence were entirely different. It seemed to Emily almost obscene to compare him with Ronald in any way. However, when she considered the matter, she realized there was a superficial similarity in her situation regarding both men. Both had been her employer or had exercised the authority of one; by both she had been employed in a more or less menial position, as companion to an elderly female relative. And to both she must ever be considered utterly ineligible for any attentions more serious than dalliance.

But despite these similarities, Emily balked at classing Sir Terrence with Ronald. In her mind, no gulf could have been wider than the one separating the two men. Of course, they had both performed roughly the same actions, but there had been a world of difference between Ronald's kisses and Sir Terrence's. Ronald had forced himself upon her against her wishes and even against her will, while Sir Terrence had kissed her only after she had challenged him to do so. That was what her words had amounted to, after all. She had challenged him to prove his feelings for her, and she had no one to blame but herself if she did not like the outcome.

"I don't blame him," she whispered to herself. "Indeed, I don't." Emily felt assured that this was true. There was no blame for Sir Terrence amid the turmoil in her heart, but there was a great deal of blame for herself. She obviously possessed serious flaws of character if she could wantonly encourage a man who was both her employer and far above her in social station to make love to her. What was worse, the mere fact of recognizing her own wantonness did not seem to be any help in controlling it. If Sir Terrence had knocked on the door that minute, she would have flown to let him in, even knowing what must be the inevitable consequences.

But of course Sir Terrence would not knock. Emily was as certain on that score as she was convinced of her own moral depravity. When the butler had interrupted them in the library, Sir Terrence had acted quickly to protect her. He had then considerately absented himself from the library so that she might make her way to her own room without the embarrassment of a final interview between them. For this, Emily was deeply grateful. She had already realized such an interview could never bring her anything but shame or sadness. What, after all, could Sir Terrence say? He might say that he had enjoyed kissing her, or alternately, that he regretted kissing her. He might promise to forget the incident and resume their previous relationship, or he might make her a dishonorable proposal on the strength of it. What was practically certain was that he would not say what Emily wanted him to say: namely, that he loved her madly; that he had never cared for any woman as he now cared for her; and that he wanted her by his side forever, or at least until death did them part

I don't want much, do I? Emily told herself with a grim smile. The impossibility of ever hearing Sir Terrence speak such words struck her with a sense of melancholy. But she told herself she was being foolish. Of course, the situation had been hopeless from the beginning. Indeed, when she tried to look at the matter dispassionately, she realized that she was much better off than she had any right to be. She had heard Sir Terrence call her beautiful, and she had the memory of his kiss to treasure in her heart. It might be morally wrong to treasure the memory of an illicit kiss, but Emily was not striving for very high moral ground just then. Being an ordinary, weak human being, she felt justified in taking her comfort where she could find it.

After all, she reasoned, Sir Terrence must have some feelings for her if he could speak and behave as he had done. Even if his feelings did not fully echo her own, he had at least betrayed some small partiality. Emily supposed she should fear such partiality, for it might lead her and Sir Terrence to act on their feelings a second time if an opportunity arose. But she could not think such an event at all likely. Sir Terrence was too much a gentleman to take advantage of her weakness even if she wished him to do so.

Still, Emily felt strongly that she must not tempt either fate or Sir Terrence too far. That would be unprincipled as well as immoral. The best thing to do, of course, would be to resign her position and put herself out of the way of temptation altogether. But Emily felt this would be asking too much of flesh and blood. She not only loved Sir Terrence, she liked him—liked his intelligence, his sense of humor, his easygoing ways. She liked living with him and his aunt and the happy routine of their days. She simply could not bear the thought of going back to a life of dreary servitude such as she had endured at Miss Morris's.

Even so, however, she knew that if she stayed on at Honeywell House there must be changes. She and Sir Terrence could never again be on quite the same footing as before. She must take care in everything she said and did around him from now on, and there must be no more dangerous tête-à-têtes. Of course, this meant she could no longer spend her afternoons working with him on his book. Emily felt a dreadful sense of loss at this idea. It was not likely that Sir Terrence would feel the loss as she did, for really their sessions had not been very productive as far as any actual writing was concerned. But they had been tremendously enjoyable, and Emily mourned the loss of that enjoyment with jealous dismay.

Still, it's a small price to pay if it means I can stay on at Honeywell House, she comforted herself. *And I daresay Sir Terrence has already come to the same conclusion I have. We were wrong in letting our relations become so friendly and informal— though it certainly did not feel wrong at the time. However, I expect the same thing could be said of a great many other wrong things.*

Having made up her mind on this matter, Emily set about preparing herself for bed. But as she lay in her bed that night, reflecting in a chastened way on her own folly, she was conscious of a spirit distinctly unchastened running beneath the current of those thoughts. Sir Terrence had thought her beautiful. He had thought her so attractive that he had forgotten Lady Moira, overlooked her own excessive height, red hair, and dowdy dress, and kissed her with a passion that had made her forget and overlook those things herself. Whatever the cost of that kiss might be,

Emily felt she would gladly pay it rather than forgo such
a transcendent experience.

It had been a transcendent experience for Sir Terrence,
too.

He had been annoyed when he had been forced to
relinquish Emily because of the butler's untimely appearance. Almost immediately, however, he had realized that
it was probably for the best. Only that evening had he
realized the full depth of his feelings for Emily. It was
neither proper nor prudent to give way to those feelings
on impulse no matter how tempting it might be. The
proper and prudent thing to do was to sit down and analyze
his feelings and then decide exactly what he meant to do
about them.

However, Sir Terrence found that propriety and pru-
dence held small attractions for him after the exhilaration
of kissing Emily. Having escorted the butler downstairs,
he hurried upstairs to the library again to see if she might
still be waiting for him there. Of course, she was not. He
had expected her to take advantage of the diversion he
had provided to escape to her room unseen, and it
appeared that she had done so. Sir Terrence was relieved
for her sake, but he could not help being disappointed
for his own. He would have liked to see her again for just
a minute or two before she went to bed. It would have
taken no longer to settle the whole matter, assuming Emily
shared something of his feelings. And Sir Terrence did
not think he was being unduly presumptuous in supposing
that she did.

As he went down the hall to his room, Sir Terrence
marveled at himself. In the space of an evening, he had
gone from a man calm and objective to a one wholeheartedly in love. How had it happened? Of course, he had felt

attracted to Emily from the very beginning. But after his
disappointment with Moira, he had supposed his heart
incapable of any second essay at love. It might be that he
was mistaken and this was not love, after all, but if it was
not, it looked and felt remarkably like the real thing.
Indeed, when he examined his feelings, he began to wonder if his mistake had not been in supposing himself in
love with Moira rather than with Emily.

This was an eye-opening revelation to Sir Terrence. He
had always taken it for granted that he had been madly in
love with Moira. Now, however, he began to see that pride
rather than love had played a dominant role in that ill-
fated affair. The plain fact was that Moira had never been
the woman he had wanted her to be. She had merely been
a shallow, self-centered woman with a handsome appearance.

And though he had not realized it at the time, he saw
now that his own behavior had been equally shallow and
self-centered. If Moira had not been the handsomest
woman in the county, would he ever have wanted her for
his wife? Of course not. But he had been so taken with
the idea of winning this much-courted Helen that he had
purposely closed his eyes to the many glaring faults in her
personality. And even when those faults had resulted in
her jilting him for another man, his pride had been such
that he could not admit his mistake. He had invented a
fairy-tale story of doomed love and noble sacrifice to
account for his disappointment, and if it had not been for
Emily, he might be clinging to it still with the obstinacy of
thwarted pride.

But Emily had made short work of his illusions. Not only
had she pointed out the fallacies in the Moira-as-ideal myth,
she had done him a greater service in showing him how
his ideal really looked when embodied in a living woman.
And it was a source of pride to him that, whatever follies

his pride had led him to commit in the past, he had at least had discernment enough to recognize Emily's true worth when it had been properly presented to him.

Having examined and admitted his feelings for Emily, it only remained for Sir Terrence to decide what to do about them. He found this question as easily settled as the previous one. There was only one course he could take as an honorable man, and happily it was the same one that he longed to take above all others. He must declare his feelings to Emily without delay and find out whether she returned them. If she did, then nothing could be simpler. They would become engaged and in due course married; and after that there would be nothing for them to do but live happily ever after in perfect conjugal love for the rest of their lives.

Sir Terrence hoped it would all be that easy. But he had lived long enough to instinctively distrust anything that appeared too simple and straightforward, and when he reflected on the matter, he foresaw several possible areas where trouble might arise.

To begin with, there was always the possibility that Emily's family might object to her marrying him. It was true that Emily had told him she was estranged from her family, but experience had taught Sir Terrence that family estrangements were odd and transient affairs, capable of shifting or even disappearing altogether when outside pressures were brought to bear on them. The relatives who had disowned Emily for taking a position as a hired companion might own her again in a hurry if they found she was to be married, particularly if they discovered she was marrying an obscure Irish baronet of whom none of them had ever heard.

Sir Terrence was not greatly worried by this possibility, for he trusted he could convince Emily's relatives of his respectability if given a reasonable chance. What worried him more was the attitude Emily herself might take to the idea of marrying him. By this time she knew him very well—much better, he felt sure, than anyone else in the world. And she must have been a much less intelligent and discerning woman than he knew her to be if she had not gathered that there had been another love affair in his past. It was not a new heart he was offering her but a poor, patched-up thing that had already been rejected by one woman. Might not Emily reject it, too? Although they had both maintained the pretense that his book was fictional, he did not doubt she had long ago tumbled to the fact that there was autobiographical material in it. She knew, then, what a fool he had been and was capable of being. It seemed to him entirely possible that knowing the extent of his past folly, she might on that account hesitate to marry him.

On the positive side, she had not demurred in any way when he had kissed her that evening. Sir Terrence thought this a very positive sign indeed, for he was fully acquainted with the measures Emily had taken in the past to discourage unwanted attentions. Seeing that he had escaped without so much as a slap in the face, let alone a concussion, he was encouraged to hope that she must like him reasonably well. But he feared lest he would appear fickle if he told her he loved her now when only weeks before he had been languishing in literary form at the feet of another woman. Still, he had gone so far as to kiss her, and that was behavior that needed explaining if it was not to be misunderstood.

Of course, Emily ought not to misunderstand if she knew him as well as he thought she did. But where matters of the heart were concerned, Sir Terrence was convinced that it was better to be safe than sorry. He felt he would rather lay his cards on the table, even if he ran the risk of being presumptuous or premature, than run a risk of misunderstanding. That being the case, he made up his mind to speak to Emily tomorrow morning as soon as he could get a moment alone with her.

As he lay in his bed that night, he could not help planning out the exact words with which he would reveal his feelings for Emily. He knew this to be a waste of time, for though in a book one could count on the heroine's making the right responses to the hero's speeches and never interrupting when she ought to be silent or being silent when she ought to speak, in life it would undoubtedly be different. He really had no idea what Emily would say or do.

It struck him as ominous that this should be so. In general, he felt fairly well assured what Emily thought and felt on any given occasion. Very often he was thinking and feeling the same thing. But he was far from sure that it would be the same on this occasion. He could not help remembering her as he had last seen her in the library, crouching behind the sofa with rigid figure and downcast eyes.

She had refused to look at him then, though he had tried his best to catch her eye. Perhaps she was angry with him for putting her in such an awkward position. Sir Terrence could not blame her if this were so. But he hoped she would accept his apologies—and perhaps, in time, his offer of marriage as well. In that case, he would be in the happy position of never having to apologize for wanting to kiss her again.

With so much excitement and uncertainty to look forward to on the morrow, Sir Terrence experienced no little difficulty getting to sleep. But he was awake with the first cockcrow and half-dressed by the time his valet arrived to assist him with his toilette. That business he completed at all speed and then hurried downstairs to the dining room. He knew his hurry was probably unnecessary, for in general Emily breakfasted later than he. But he wished to take no risk of missing her if she should for some reason come downstairs early.

Emily was not in the dining room, however, so Sir Terrence settled down to wait. He could not eat much, but drank several cups of coffee and flipped through the London newspaper that had reached him through the previous day's mail. Usually he cast at least a casual eye over the news, but today the list of engagements and marriages was the only thing that really held his attention. With luck, his own name might soon be among them. He was reading the announcement of a betrothal between a Lord Edward Stacey, widower, and a Miss Eustacia Miller, spinster, when Emily finally appeared.

Her appearance was not so fortunately timed as he could have wished, for his aunt had just taken her seat at the table. Sir Terrence greeted Emily with as much warmth as he dared, but a reserved "Good morning" was all he got in return. This made him more certain than ever that Emily must be angry with him.

The idea distressed him, but he comforted himself with the thought that her anger could not be of long duration. Soon he would explain to her what had motivated him to act as he had the previous night, and then all would be well between them. He waited impatiently for his aunt to finish her breakfast in hopes of catching Emily alone for a moment. Unfortunately, as soon as his aunt rose to go, Emily, too, was on her feet. Sir Terrence was forced to make his bid for her attention more openly than he would have liked.

"I hope you are not busy this morning, Miss Pearce," he said with a smile that he hoped was pleasant. "I would very much appreciate it if you could give me a few minutes of your time."

Emily surveyed him gravely. "I don't think that will be

possible, Sir Terrence," she said. "It happens that I *am* rather busy this morning."

There was a chill in her manner that daunted Sir Terrence. Still, he persevered. "Well, then, if you are busy this morning, I shall simply have to wait until this afternoon to speak with you. You will be assisting me in the library as usual, I hope?"

Emily's eyes flickered—with what emotion, Sir Terrence could not tell. When she spoke, her voice was constrained. "No, I think I shall have to forgo that pleasure, Sir Terrence. Do please excuse me."

Sir Terrence was beginning to be seriously alarmed. Both by her words and by her manner, she seemed to be trying to distance herself from him. As he stood trying to think what to say, Emily made a move as though to follow Aunt Katie out the door. Instinctively, Sir Terrence put out an arm to stop her. "Don't!" he said. "Please don't go, Emily."

The name "Emily" came to his lips as naturally as though he had been using it all his life. It was not until Emily turned a look of amazement upon him that Sir Terrence realized what he had done. His face grew hot, and he hurriedly removed the hand that was still resting on her arm. "Forgive me, Miss Pearce," he said. "I did not mean to presume. But I really do wish to talk to you. Cannot you spare me one moment?"

Emily hesitated and looked around before speaking. Sir Terrence thought he understood her dilemma. It was hardly a private venue for a tête-à-tête. Aunt Katie had gone, but the butler was washing knives at the sideboard, and a pair of footmen were busy clearing the breakfast dishes. "What is it?" she asked in a low voice.

"I cannot tell you here." Sir Terrence threw an expressive look at the servants. "Cannot you come to the library for a few minutes?"

"I don't think that is a good idea, Sir Terrence." Emily spoke the words calmly enough, but Sir Terrence saw a faint color rise in her cheeks. "It would, I think, be better if we curtailed any further private sessions in the library."

"But I must talk to you!" In his perturbation, Sir Terrence spoke more loudly than he intended. One of the footmen stopped clearing and turned to look at him curiously. Lowering his voice, he repeated, "I must talk to you, Emily—Miss Pearce. Indeed, I must."

"Of course, you may talk to me if you choose, Sir Terrence. But—forgive me—I would rather you did not say anything to me that cannot be said in front of a third party."

Sir Terrence stared at her. The pink in her cheeks had deepened as she spoke, but her eyes met his unwaveringly. He could not doubt that she was in earnest. She looked at him a long moment, then turned again to go. Sir Terrence half-raised his hand to stop her, then let his hand drop to his side again. What was the use of persevering? She had made her feelings very clear. All he could think to say, lamely, was, "You do not wish to help me with my book anymore?"

Emily stopped and turned again to look at him. "I am perfectly willing to help you with your book, Sir Terrence. But I think we had better limit my assistance to the original terms of our agreement. If you have any manuscript that needs copying, I would be very pleased to do it for you. I can write it out in my spare time and return it to you at your convenience."

"Very well," said Sir Terrence, and with those two words he felt the curtain ring down on his hopes and dreams. Emily waited a moment, as if to make sure he had nothing more to say, then turned and left the room.

Chapter 14

The next few weeks seemed to Emily to pass at a funereal pace. Not that she put it that way herself, but if the idea had been suggested to her, she would have instantly approved its aptness. "Funereal" seemed the proper word to express her whole outlook on life about this time. Like a surgeon amputating a diseased limb, she had given up her private hours with Sir Terrence, hoping by this sacrifice to salvage some remainder of the peace and happiness she had enjoyed before the Winslows' party. But now she found that discontent and longing were spreading like an infection in every quarter and threatening to prove, if not actually fatal to the patient, at least sadly debilitating.

It was hard to say wherein the change lay. Apart from spending her afternoons with Aunt Katie rather than Sir Terrence, Emily's days went on in much the same way as before. Sir Terrence still ate his meals with her and his aunt, and he still spent his evenings with them in the drawing room. Together, they still read books, played

games, and discussed current events. But to Emily, everything seemed changed.

Or perhaps it was merely that Sir Terrence himself
seemed changed. This, too, was an alteration not easily
defined. He still talked as much, or nearly as much as
before; he still teased his aunt and responded good-
humoredly when she teased him back. To Emily, he was
as unfailingly polite and attentive as ever, and he seemed
to be making every effort to revive the camaraderie they
had enjoyed previous to the Winslows' party. But it only
too clearly *was* an effort. All that had been natural and
spontaneous before had now become unnatural and
stilted. Emily could not help feeling that it was all her fault,
and she mourned the change.

She had gone over that evening at the Winslows' countless times in her memory, wishing that she could somehow
go back and live it differently. She told herself that if only
she had gone to her room immediately after returning
home from the Winslows', that scene between her and Sir
Terrence might never have taken place. But she knew in
her heart this was false reasoning. The kiss Sir Terrence
had given her was the natural outcome of a series of events
that had been set in motion long before that particular
evening. In her more superstitious moments, Emily even
found herself wondering whether that kiss might not have
been predestined to take place: whether it might have
been a test of character devised by the Almighty or perhaps
by some more mischievous power. Whatever the case, she
had done her best to remedy the situation in the only way
she decently could, and she assured herself there was no
reason to feel guilty.

These assurances were of little comfort, however, as the
days went by and the world seemed to grow darker and
colder around her. Things were at their very darkest and

coldest one afternoon about two weeks after the Winslows' party when she received the card for Lady Meredith's ball.

Aunt Katie, who had brought the card into her room, lingered to say cheerfully that it looked as though they were destined to do a deal of raking now that they were acquainted with their neighbors. "Terry seems to think we might as well go as not, and I don't doubt you'll like to go, Miss Pearce. I well remember how you and Lady Meredith got on at the Winslows' party the other night."

"Yes, Lady Meredith was very kind," said Emily. She studied the engraved card, wondering whether it might be another test of character. Did conscience oblige her to give up Lady Meredith's ball as well as her private hours with Sir Terrence? On the whole, she felt that on this occasion conscience was less an obstacle than wardrobe. She had never owned a ball dress in her life, and the only way to get one now would be to disgorge a large chunk of her small savings. Emily doubted whether she could justify spending her hard-won earnings in such a way.

By evening, she had made up her mind that she must decline Lady Meredith's invitation. It was a decision made not merely with regret but with a degree of regret Emily had never supposed she would feel for such a trivial thing as forgoing a party. It was, in fact, reminiscent of how she felt when she thought of Sir Terrence and the way their friendship had been spoiled.

So strong did her regret become that Emily was forced to the conclusion that there must be a link between these two regrettable incidents. And when she subjected her own heart to a merciless scrutiny, she found she was right. In the back of her mind had lingered a hope—inexpressibly foolish—that she would somehow win Sir Terrence's love at the ball.

She saw herself in her mind's eye, splendidly attired and magically made beautiful, dancing with Sir Terrence and reducing him to a state of hopeless adoration. Of course, it was a ridiculous fantasy. Emily told herself she was better off not going to the Merediths' ball if she could cherish such unrealistic expectations about what was likely to result from it. She kept this stern and pious attitude through most of the evening, right up until the package arrived from Lady Meredith. At that point, Emily suddenly found all her good resolutions and pious aspirations under heavy siege.

She received the package unsuspectingly from the butler, who said merely that one of the Abbey servants had delivered it with Lady Meredith's compliments. By good fortune Emily was alone in the drawing room when it was delivered. She lost no time tearing it open, being consumed with curiosity to know what Lady Meredith could be sending her.

"Oh," said Emily as the parcel's strings yielded to her eager fingers. "Oh, my!"

Before her, shrouded in folds of tissue paper, was the most beautiful dress she had ever seen. She sank back in her chair, regarding the rich silken folds with awe and confusion. As she did so, a slip of paper that had been enclosed with the dress floated down to the floor. Emily stooped to retrieve it and read:

The Abbey, Devon

Dear Miss Pearce,

When you open this package, you may quite possibly think its contents a presumption. If so, you are justified in returning it to me with a stinging message saying you do not accept personal gifts from near-strangers. But it is my hope that you will accept my gift not as an act of presumption but as a trifling favor from one woman to another.

Please let me explain. You will by now have received your invitation to our ball. You know, I hope, that I sincerely desire your presence there. I greatly enjoyed talking to you the other night and look forward to improving our acquaintance. But it occurred to me that in light of certain personal revelations you made during our conversation, you might find it difficult or even impossible to secure a dress suitable for such a formal affair.

Of course, I am well aware that our wisest philosophers declare that "fine feathers do not make fine birds" and other words to that effect. No doubt that is true, but I suspect it is also leaving something out of the equation. My experience has been that it is impossible to enjoy oneself at any social occasion if one feels self-conscious about one's appearance. And so, not wanting you to be faced with a dilemma between attending our party in a state of self-consciousness or not attending it at all, I have ventured to send you the enclosed dress.

It may be, of course, that you already have a suitable dress prepared for the occasion. In that case I can only apologize for my presumption and beg you to dispose of my offering as you see fit. But please believe it kindly meant, and please, please let neither this nor any other consideration keep you from attending my party. It may merely be further presumption on my part, but I felt the other night that we had a common bond of understanding and sympathy between us. If that is so, you will readily understand the urgency of my appeal. I may be skeptical about the philosophy that states, "Fine feathers make fine birds," but I have complete reliance in that which says, "In union is strength." And in our united strength, I trust we may succeed in having an enjoyable evening in spite of certain ladies whose names begin with a "W."

Yours in friendship,

Catherine Meredith

Emily read through this letter several times with increasing wonderment. At last she put down the letter and looked again at the silky folds of the dress spread out in front of her.

"Of course, I ought not to accept such an expensive gift," she told the dress. "It would not be at all proper. And it wouldn't be at all necessary, either. I have already made up my mind not to go to the ball. I therefore have no need for a ball dress—even if my conscience allowed me to accept one as a gift."

But these were merely words, and empty ones, too, as Emily already knew. She had given up the idea of going to the ball with the utmost reluctance, and then only because the state of her wardrobe made it impractical. Now, with Lady Meredith's gift, all impracticality had been drained out of the venture, and it was laid before her as a tempting prize that she only had to reach out her hand to claim. Caution and common sense could do nothing against so fierce a temptation.

There were, in fact, several temptations involved. She wanted to go to the ball, the first she had ever been invited to. She wanted to oblige Lady Meredith, who had been so kind as to send the dress, and to do it in a way that implied that Emily would be doing her a favor to wear it rather than the other way around. And she wanted to be with Sir Terrence—to arrive as one of his party, to dance with him if he asked her, and to spend some small part of the evening in his company.

"That's all I want," Emily assured herself as she looked down at the dress. "Only that and I will be satisfied."

She knew, even as she spoke the words, that they were untrue. What she wanted from Sir Terrence went far beyond a dance and a few minutes of conversation. By attending the ball, she was purposely putting herself in the way of yet another sort of temptation: one that she had narrowly escaped in the library only a couple of weeks before. But she purposely closed her mind to all such considerations. She had decided to attend the ball, and whatever consequences might result she resolved to deal with when the time came.

In the short term, at least, the consequences were all favorable. Having the ball to look forward to improved Emily's spirits tremendously, and the days no longer dragged by with such intolerable slowness. This would probably not have been the case had Emily been looking forward to the ball with unalloyed eagerness, but in fact her enthusiasm was alloyed with anxiety. This point was driven forcibly home to her on the night of the ball as she stood before the glass in her bedchamber putting the finishing touches on her toilette.

The dress Lady Meredith had given her was an open robe of white lace, closed with pearl buttons and worn over a white satin petticoat. Only the smallest of alterations had been necessary to make it fit Emily like a glove. She had washed her hair that afternoon, so that it gleamed like copper gold in the candlelight. She had dressed the waves and curls loosely around her face, with the back hair twisted high and held in place with the wreath of white lace trimmed in pearls that had been included with the dress. When she looked at her own reflection in the glass, she came close to not recognizing herself. It was not only the splendor of her dress but a new radiance that seemed to glow forth from every feature, investing her face with an unfamiliar glamour. Emily did not go so far as to think she looked beautiful, but she could not help seeing that she looked strikingly well. If Sir Terrence could consider her attractive in the simple green dress she had worn to the Winslows' party, how would he regard her tonight?

I mustn't dwell on that, Emily told herself. *I mustn't.* Yet the question of what Sir Terrence would think of her was still in her mind when she left her room and started downstairs to the drawing room. And when, halfway down the stairs, she heard a low exclamation and looked up to see Sir Terrence standing at the foot of the stairs, she had all the answer she wanted in his eyes.

"Emily," he said. "You look . . . beautiful."

"Thank you," she said. All at once she felt not nervous at all but rather exultantly happy. A little laugh escaped her, and she descended the last steps in a rush. Sir Terrence came forward to meet her. When he reached her, Emily expected him to say something more, but he did not. He simply took her in his arms and kissed her with a passion that spoke more eloquently than any words could have done.

And Emily, at that moment, did not need words. She had seen the look in Sir Terrence's eyes as she came toward him. She felt the beating of his heart against hers as he held her in his arms, and she knew with utter certainty that she had realized her heart's desire. She knew that Sir Terrence loved her, just as she loved him. When he finally did speak, his words were only confirmation of what she had already felt.

"Emily," he whispered. "Emily—you *do* care for me, don't you?"

"Yes," said Emily simply.

Sir Terrence's arms around her tightened. "Oh, Emily, I was afraid you didn't," he said. "I've been so miserable, Emily—and now I am the happiest man on earth."

"And I am the happiest woman," said Emily, and laughed aloud with sheer delight. Sir Terrence's arms tightened around her.

"Emily, if we had time, I would like to try to tell you what this means to me—what *you* mean to me. Devil take this party tonight! I've half a mind to send Aunt Katie to the Abbey with my excuses and stay home with you."

Again Emily laughed. With every word Sir Terrence spoke, she felt she was attaining a new peak of euphoria. "That would not serve, Sir Terrence," she said. "Your aunt would only feel obliged to stay home and keep us company!"

"You're right, of course. And I would feel guilty about crying off from the Merediths' at this late date. Although I am sure they will have such a crowd that we would hardly be missed."

"I would not like to disappoint the Merediths," said Emily with a secret smile down at her dress. "Lady Meredith has been extraordinarily kind to me."

"Then I suppose I must let go of you and try to behave with propriety for the rest of the evening. If I *can* behave with propriety. I shall secretly be wanting to kiss you all the time we are at the Abbey." Letting go of Emily, he smiled down at her ruefully. "My only comfort will be that I can at least look at you, even if I cannot kiss you. And I can dance with you, too, if you are generous enough to grant me that boon."

"I am. I will," said Emily. She gave him her arm, and together they went into the drawing room, where Aunt Katie was awaiting them.

Aunt Katie threw a shrewd look at her nephew as he came in and then a look equally shrewd at Emily. Her only remark, however, was a commonplace one about its being high time they left for the Abbey. Sir Terrence agreed, and together they went out to the carriage.

Emily found the ride to the Abbey equal parts frustration and exhilaration. She continually caught Sir Terrence's eye and as constantly experienced a rush of happiness at what she saw there. It was a communication as eloquent as words, though it still left her feeling dissatisfied. But then words would not have satisfied her, either. What she really wanted was a private interview with Sir Terrence, and she was hoping that before the evening was over such a private interview might be arranged.

Strong as her hopes were, Emily felt she could bear it with equanimity if they were disappointed. It would be pleasant to have a full and complete understanding threshed out between her and Sir Terrence, but he had already said and done enough to secure her present happiness. As for the future, Emily was content to leave it to itself. Perhaps there was, in the back of her mind, an awareness that the course of true love was never known to run smooth, but she firmly and purposely shut her eyes to it. She had already received so much that to wish for any more seemed downright greedy.

After a short drive, they arrived at the Abbey, a gray stone mansion that still bore traces of its monastic origins. Only a handful of carriages preceded them up the drive, for they were among those elite guests whom Lady Meredith had invited to dine at the Abbey before the ball. Lady Meredith herself received them in the Abbey's elegant drawing room, and when she saw Emily, her golden eyes lit up with mingled satisfaction and triumph.

"My dear Miss Pearce!" she said, giving Emily her hand in the most democratic way. "I am so glad that you could come. You look magnificent." Lowering her voice, she added, "I cannot take all the credit for myself, but at least I may plume myself on having provided a suitable setting for the jewel. Indeed, now I look at you, I am disposed to think my taste even better than I supposed it. That dress was made for you."

"And I cannot thank you enough for giving it to me, ma'am," said Emily, squeezing the proffered hand. "Your generosity is as worthy of praise as your taste."

Lady Meredith shook her head, smiling. "Please don't thank me. That you condescended to accept my gift is thanks enough."

"You are very kind to say so. But I should like to do more if I could," said Emily. "If there is ever any way I can repay you, Lady Meredith, I beg you will let me know."

"You can repay me best by enjoying yourself this evening," said Lady Meredith. "Indeed, I feel in my bones that it will be a memorable night. Jonathan called me an egoist for saying so earlier, but I can take no credit for it. No more than I can take credit for your looking like an angel this evening." She smiled at Emily. "It has been my experience that there is a fate in these things. Having played my role by providing an appropriate background for my guests, all I can do is stand back and watch."

Notwithstanding this modest speech, Emily observed that Lady Meredith did a great deal in an unobtrusive way to ensure the success of her party. The dinner that she and the other guests sat down to presently was a masterpiece of its kind, perfectly cooked, faultlessly served, and eaten in that happy atmosphere of conviviality that is the outcome of a well-chosen gathering. Conversation flowed as freely as the wine throughout the meal, and raillery was the seasoning to every dish. Even Emily, who did not fancy herself a wit, made several remarks that earned a general laugh, and as for Sir Terrence, he was the life and soul of the party.

Emily, laughing helplessly at one of his stories, felt a warm glow of love and pride as she regarded him from across the table. He might not be as handsome as Lord Meredith, but there could be no doubt that he was the better raconteur, as that gentleman freely admitted. "Sir Terrence, I will leave it to you to propose a fitting salute to the ladies before they leave the table," he told Sir Terrence. "Any man who can talk as you do should have no difficulty in melting even the hardest feminine heart to a mood of tender compliance." He winked shamelessly at his wife, who tried to frown him down but could not conceal a self-conscious smile.

"My lord, I fear you do me too much credit," said Sir Terrence as he got to his feet. "But I'll do my best. To the ladies! May they accord us this evening their admiration for our virtues—their forbearance for our failings—and their kisses as encouragement for both."

Everyone laughed and drank willingly to this proposal—everyone except Sir Terrence himself. He turned instead to look at Emily and, having caught her eye, smiled and lifted his glass to her. Emily returned the gesture, smiling back at him.

A moment later, Lady Meredith gave the signal to rise. Emily set down her wineglass, accorded Sir Terrence a final, quick smile, and left the drawing room with the other ladies.

Chapter 15

In the dining room with the other gentlemen, Sir Terrence stole frequent looks at his watch. Although he did his best to pretend a polite interest in the conversation, all his energies and interest were now directed toward the moment when he could see Emily again.

It appeared to him that the other gentlemen dawdled unspeakably over their port and Madeira, though in fact the time allotted for the consumption of these beverages was much less than usual at dinner parties. But it seemed aeons to Sir Terrence before Lord Meredith finally put down his wineglass with a genial, "Well, gentlemen, shall we go and join the ladies?" and received an affirmative murmur in response.

In the ballroom, Sir Terrence had no trouble locating Emily. Her height and bearing, bright head and dazzling gown, made her easily the most striking woman there. She was standing with Lady Meredith near the little bower where the orchestra was stationed. The two of them appeared deep in conversation, but they turned to him with welcoming smiles as he approached. "It's just on nine o'clock. I must go prepare to receive my other guests," Lady Meredith told Emily as Sir Terrence joined them. "You will excuse me, I know, now you have Sir Terrence to take my place." She flashed a smile at them both, then glided off in the direction of the ballroom doors.

"Tactful woman," said Sir Terrence. Looking at Emily, he added, "I have had a revelation."

"About Lady Meredith?" asked Emily, looking a little startled.

"No, about Helen of Troy. Most scholars believe Helen was blond, you know—hence Homer's quotation about her being 'divinely tall, and most divinely fair.' But it has suddenly become clear to me that she was actually red-haired."

Emily laughed, blushed, and shook her head. "Sir Terrence, that is ridiculous," she said. "You must have been drinking too much wine if you can believe such nonsense as that."

"I am certainly drunk, but not on wine." He dropped his voice. "Emily, I do love you. Did I dream it, or is it possible you really love me, too?"

Emily's cheeks flamed to a gorgeous scarlet. "Yes, of course I do," she whispered. "Sir Terrence—"

"Terrence," said Sir Terrence firmly. "Or Terry, if you like. But you cannot keep calling me Sir Terrence if you mean to encourage me to make love to you. It's a point I'm very sensitive about."

Emily laughed and blushed deeper. "Terrence, then. Oh, Terrence, I cannot believe this is not a dream. It seems as though it isn't right to be this happy."

"I know exactly what you mean," he agreed. "But never mind, Emily. We'll defy fate together and be happy nonetheless, just you wait and see."

Their tête-à-tête was cut short at this point by the entry of a party of guests into the ballroom. Among them was Mrs. Winslow, who recognized Sir Terrence with a cry of delight and came over at once to speak to him. Also among these new guests was Isabel Wrexford, looking striking, if not attractive, in a dress of lilac and primrose sarcenet. She, too, joined the party around Sir Terrence. As she did so, she noticed Emily and stopped dead, staring as if she could not believe her eyes.

Emily felt there had never been a moment sweeter than that one—except, of course, for the moment Sir Terrence had told her he loved her. This was a less exalted sensation but satisfying nonetheless. Isabel's eyes narrowed, and she looked Emily up and down with jealous incredulity. Emily smiled and inclined her head slightly toward Isabel. "Good evening, Miss Wrexford," she said.

"Miss Pearce," said Isabel, and gave her a brief nod in return. She said nothing more for the rest of the time she was standing there, but a little later in the evening, as Emily was passing the refreshment room, she overheard Isabel speaking to one of the other girls who had been at the Winslows' party.

"Did you ever see anything so inappropriate? The idea of her getting herself up in such a fashion and coming here as though she were a lady of the *tôn* instead of a hired companion! Of course, it's perfectly obvious what she is about. She means to get Sir Terrence by hook or by crook, and I shouldn't be surprised if she succeeded. Oh, yes, she looks quite handsome tonight, I don't deny it. But nothing can change the fact that she is a servant, or the next thing to one. Poor Sir Terrence, let us hope he has sense enough to evade her clutches. He seems a very agreeable man, though he *is* Irish."

This speech left a disagreeable impression on Emily, though she tried to laugh it off. It helped when Lady

Meredith came over to speak to her a few minutes later, just as the dancing was getting ready to start.

"You must know you are making quite a sensation tonight, Miss Pearce," she told Emily with a smile. "I have had fully a dozen young men begging me to make them known to you and as many ladies wanting to know who you are and why they have never heard of you before now. And I have heard Isabel Wrexford being catty about you, which is the surest proof of all that you are a success."

"Is it?" said Emily, trying to smile. "But she was catty to me before, when I had not the advantage of this lovely dress to make me look more like the other girls."

Lady Meredith regarded her quizzically. "For myself, I should say the dress had nothing to do with it. My dear Miss Pearce, are you really unaware of what a beautiful woman you are? I assure you I am half jealous myself whenever I look at you. Isabel, of course, is wholly so; that is why she needles you so relentlessly. If you were plain and gauche, she would simply ignore you as beneath her notice."

Emily's lips parted, but no sound came out. Lady Meredith stood regarding her, still with a quizzical smile on her lips.

"Don't tell me I am the first person to call you beautiful?" she said. "I must tell you I refuse to believe it. You cannot possibly have lived this long without some man or other having remarked favorably on your looks!"

"No," said Emily faintly. "My looks, as you call them, have been favorably remarked on by—by one or two men. But I didn't believe they were telling the truth."

Lady Meredith laughed. "Well, that is not a bad policy," she said. "It is probably wise to disbelieve men's compliments, at least until their motivation can be established! But it can do you no harm to have an accurate idea of your own attractions, Miss Pearce. Having too modest an opinion of one's looks can be as dangerous as having an inflated one, in my opinion."

This was a new idea to Emily, but she was obliged to admit it seemed reasonable. Lady Meredith glanced at the tiny diamond-studded watch at her waist. "Almost ten o'clock. The dancing is to begin at ten. Have you a partner for the first set?" she asked Emily.

"Yes," said Emily with more fervor than she intended. Lady Meredith surveyed her again with a quizzical smile.

"Perhaps you put more credence in those compliments than you will admit!" she said, and laughed at Emily's confusion. "No, don't blush, Miss Pearce. I shan't embarrass you with any more impertinent suppositions. Instead, I shall entrust you to Jonathan (whom I see approaching even as we speak) and tell him to help you find your partner. For myself, I must go find Lord Alderston. He drove all the way from London to attend tonight, so I am obliged to stand up with him for the first set, but I tell you in confidence that I would rather stand up with Jonathan. It is not merely that Lord Alderston is elderly, fat, and incapable of keeping time on the dance floor. Most unfortunately, he also fancies himself a killing Lothario."

"You're not talking about me, by any chance?" inquired Lord Meredith, coming up in time to hear the last part of this speech. "Because I was assured only this afternoon, by a lady who ought to know—"

"That's enough, Jonathan," said Lady Meredith, biting back a smile. "I was just telling Miss Pearce that I must go find Lord Alderston. Will you please take charge of her for me and see that she finds her partner in time for the first dance?"

"With pleasure," said Lord Meredith. Giving Emily his arm, he asked her who her partner was. Emily told him she was engaged to dance with Sir Terrence, and Lord Meredith steered her through the crowd to Sir Terrence's side after first securing a promise from her that she would stand up with him for the second set of dances.

At any other time the prospect of dancing two dances with a handsome, rakish, sophisticated nobleman like Lord Meredith would have flustered Emily greatly. Tonight, however, all her thoughts were centered on Sir Terrence. When he smiled at her, offering his arm and saying, "I believe this is our dance, Miss Pearce?" she felt as though life had nothing more to offer her.

It was enough to simply be with him, to feel the fleeting touch of his hand as he maneuvered her through the dance and be greeted by his smile when the figures brought them together. Emily talked scarcely at all, and Sir Terrence, too, was uncharacteristically silent. "It's a strange thing," he observed as they went down the line of dancers. "There are so many things I want to say to you. But when I try to say them, all the words wind up sounding trite and futile. One would think I would make a better job of it, seeing that I am a writer." He smiled at Emily. "But I think you understand what I want to say without my saying it. Don't you, Emily?"

"Yes, I think I do," said Emily.

Those first two dances were over far too soon for Emily's taste. Sir Terrence looked at her regretfully as he led her off the dance floor.

"I don't suppose I'll be able to dance with you again, will I? No doubt you are booked for the rest of the night."

"No, not the whole night," said Emily, smiling. "Perhaps I may be able to dance with you again later in the evening, if you think it would not be indiscreet."

"I don't believe it would be. At any rate, discretion appeals to me as an overrated virtue just now. What I would like most to do, if untrammeled by social restrictions, would be to kiss you right here on the dance floor. And I'd do

it, too, if I didn't think it would encourage others to follow
my example!''

Emily laughed and shook her head. Lord Meredith came
up just then, inquiring whether it was not their dance.
"Yes, it is, my lord," said Emily, and bade Sir Terrence a
wistful farewell. As she turned away, she noticed a pair of
young ladies avidly watching her. They turned away when
they caught her eye and began to talk vivaciously among
themselves. As Emily went to take her place on the floor
with Lord Meredith, however, she was conscious of several
other pairs of curious and speculative eyes turned in her
direction.

Well, let them look, Emily told herself. *It won't hurt me,
and it might entertain them.* But she could not feel quite so
insouciant as she pretended. The idea that others were
watching her and perhaps criticizing her conduct in regard
to Sir Terrence was one that both angered and embarrassed her. She remembered once again Isabel's spiteful
comment, "She means to get Sir Terrence by hook or by
crook."

It's not true, Emily argued to herself. *I did nothing to "get"
Terrence—not until this evening, at any rate. Well, perhaps I
did encourage him a little the night of the Winslows' party, but
I don't think that ought to be counted against me. He started the
whole business by saying I was beautiful. Besides, would it be so
wrong if I had tried to encourage him? The attraction seems to
be mutual now, so I don't see that it matters who started it.*

Having reached this indefinite conclusion, Emily made
an effort to put the whole matter out of her mind. She
smiled at Lord Meredith and at Miss Winslow, who was
standing in the set beside her. But as she stood with the
others, waiting for the music to start, she began to feel a
sense of unease. It grew stronger and stronger within her
until at last it resolved itself into a definite impression.

Someone was looking at her—not merely looking at her but staring at her with a fixed attention.

Curious but unsuspecting, Emily turned to see who it was. And in that instant, the evening that had gotten off to such a promising start suddenly dissolved into a nightmare.

Ronald was standing at the edge of the dance floor barely twelve feet away. His arms were folded across his chest, and he was staring at her with smoldering eyes.

It was only for a moment that Emily looked back at him, but in that instant she registered a thousand details both important and unimportant. Ronald was wearing a blue evening coat, pearl-colored satin knee breeches, and a waistcoat embroidered with fleurs-de-lis. He was standing with a pretty, dark-haired young lady whom she recognized as the daughter of a wealthy merchant in the village where Miss Morris had lived. Ronald's face was pale—much paler than she remembered it—but his eyes were dark with emotion. Emily recoiled from them as from a physical danger. Quickly she turned away, and as she did so, the music started. Emily knew she could not dance. Her whole body felt frozen with shock and dismay.

"My lord!" she said, addressing Lord Meredith with urgency. "My lord, would you mind if we did not dance this set, after all? I—I feel unwell." She could barely force the words from between her lips, and she felt she must look very queer and alarming. However she looked, it must have been queer and alarming enough for Lord Meredith, who did not even bother to reply but quickly caught her arm in a strong grasp and half-led, half-carried her off the dance floor.

Fortunately, he had chosen to lead her away from Ronald rather than toward him. This was a relief to Emily, and she felt doubly relieved when she saw Lady Meredith hurrying toward her with a look of concern on her face.

"My dear Miss Pearce, are you unwell?" she exclaimed.

"You look white as a sheet!" Like her husband, she apparently found Emily's looks sufficient testimony to her condition, for without further speech she seized Emily's other arm and helped him bear Emily out of the ballroom.

"Let us take her to the green parlor, away from the crowd," she instructed her husband. "Now, let us lay her down on the sofa. Yes, Miss Pearce, I must insist that you lie down for a while. I cannot have you fainting away while you are a guest in my house. Just lie still and close your eyes. Jonathan, will you tell one of the servants to ride into the village and fetch Dr. Edwards?"

"I don't need a doctor," said Emily, opening her eyes quickly. "Indeed, I am not actually unwell, ma'am. It is only that I have had a—a shock."

"It must have been a considerable shock," Lady Meredith observed dryly.

Involuntarily, Emily shuddered. Lady Meredith's eyes grew narrow, but when she spoke again, her voice was light. "You quite frightened me for a moment, but I see now your color is coming back," she said. "Never mind the doctor, Jonathan. But if you will, please ask one of the servants to bring us some sal volatile before you go back to the ballroom."

When Lord Meredith had departed on this errand, Lady Meredith drew Emily's hand into hers and squeezed it. "My poor Miss Pearce," she said. "When I saw you only a few minutes ago, you looked the happiest woman in the room. And now I find you in a state of collapse!"

Emily said nothing, but shut her eyes again. Despite this effort at self-control, she could not keep a tear or two from trickling beneath the closed lids. Lady Meredith evidently saw them, for her voice sharpened. "Is there anything I can do?" she asked. "Did someone say something hurtful to you? If they did—"

"No, it's nothing like that," said Emily. "I—I merely

saw someone I did not expect to see here tonight." Again she shuddered.

Lady Meredith was quiet a long time. When she finally spoke, her voice was hesitant. "Please believe I do not mean to pry, Miss Pearce," she said. "You need say nothing more if you would rather not. But if you would like to talk about whatever is troubling you—well, I assure you I am capable of keeping a secret. Anything you told me would be held in the strictest confidence."

"I am sure it would be," said Emily. She thought a minute. "Yes—yes, I think I would like to tell you the whole story, if you are willing to listen. But I am afraid you will be disgusted."

"I am not easily disgusted by human nature," said Lady Meredith, patting her hand. "Tell me, and let us lay it to rest, whatever it is."

"If only it could be laid to rest!" Emily said unhappily. "But I don't think that is possible. Still, if you will only listen to me, I think I will at least find it easier to bear, Lady Meredith."

"Catherine," said Lady Meredith firmly. "If we are to the point of exchanging confidences, then it is high time we started using each other's Christian names."

She smiled at Emily. Emily gave her a wan smile in return. "Very well," she said. "I will call you Catherine, and you may call me Emily. Now listen, and try not to judge me too harshly, if you will."

Speaking slowly and choosing her words with care, she described how she had come to be acquainted with Ronald. Lady Meredith listened intently, nodding now and then to show she understood the circumstances. But when Emily began to describe Ronald's harassment and how it had finally forced her to flee Miss Morris's house, Lady Meredith sat up straight and looked at Emily incredulously.

"Emily, do you mean to say that is what you thought would disgust me?" she demanded.

"Yes," said Emily. "Doesn't it? Of course, I never said or did anything to encourage Ronald to think I desired those kind of advances, but—"

"Of course you did not! Good God, did you think I supposed it? I know well enough how it was, none better."

Lady Meredith spoke the words with a passion that made Emily look at her wide-eyed. Lady Meredith saw the look and gave Emily a quick, apologetic smile. "Forgive me, Emily. I did not mean to sound so fierce. Only it happens that I had a similar experience years ago, and it left a disagreeable impression on me." She patted Emily's arm. "Go on and tell me the rest of your story, and do not fear that I will think less of you. If I cannot understand and sympathize with you, then no one can."

Emily went on to narrate how she had taken refuge at Honeywell House and how Sir Terrence had helped her verify that Ronald was not dead or severely injured. "A pity he wasn't, if you ask me," was Lady Meredith's acid comment. "But of course it would have made matters worse for you if he had been, Emily. I quite see that." She said nothing more until Emily came to the account of how she had seen Ronald at the ball that night. Then she sat up straight once again, turned her eyes full upon Emily, and inquired in a deadly voice, "Do you mean to say that man is actually in my house? In my house now, even as we speak?"

"Yes, unless he has already gone," said Emily. "I hope he has, but knowing Ronald, I doubt it."

"If he has not left, then he soon will," said Lady Meredith, rising to her feet with energy. "I will see to that. Not another minute shall he remain under my roof. If he will not leave at my request, I'll have the servants throw him out."

She would have left immediately on this errand, but Emily sprang to her feet and caught her by the arm. "Indeed, you must not, ma'am," she said urgently. "Only think what a scandal it would make. There is no reason why you should be embroiled in my affairs—"

"I am glad to be embroiled in your affairs, scandalous or otherwise," interrupted Lady Meredith. "But to my mind it would be more scandalous to allow a man of that sort to remain in my house rather than to throw him out."

"Yes, but Lady Meredith—" argued Emily.

"Catherine," said Lady Meredith.

"Catherine," amended Emily. "Yes, but Catherine, I would rather you did nothing in this matter, at least not tonight. Indeed, I would dislike extremely to be the cause of such a scene as must result if you are obliged to put Ronald out by force. And there would be no point in it. Even if he left, I could not go back to the party. I am not fit for it."

"Oh, Emily," said Lady Meredith sadly. "And I had hoped you would enjoy yourself tonight!"

"I did enjoy myself, up until a few minutes ago," said Emily. "And even though I hated seeing Ronald again, I don't mind it so much now I have told you about it. But I believe it would be better if I went home." With a twisted smile she added, "The only thing I regret more than leaving your wonderful party myself is making Sir Terrence and Aunt Katie leave it. It seems so unfair that their pleasure must be cut short as well as mine. But I know they will insist on accompanying me if they learn I am leaving."

"Then we must not let them learn it until it is too late for them to accompany you," said Lady Meredith. "I'll fetch your things for you, and you can leave in my carriage. Once you are gone, I'll tell Sir Terrence and Miss O'Reilly that you were called away. I'll say that you were not feeling well but that your indisposition was so slight that you saw no reason why they should not stay and enjoy the party. Will that serve?"

"It would serve wonderfully!" said Emily with gratitude. "But I'm afraid it only puts me more in your debt than ever, Lady Meredith."

"Do not think of it as a debt," said Lady Meredith, kissing her. "I consider it a privilege to assist you, and I only wish I could do more. Still, I shall do what I can." And having embraced Emily and recommended her to lie down again until she returned, Lady Meredith bustled off to see about ordering her carriage.

Chapter 16

A short time later, Emily was seated in Lady Meredith's luxurious chaise on her way home to Honeywell House.

The chaise, sped by four fast horses, quickly traversed the few miles between the Abbey and Sir Terrence's home. As soon as it arrived, Emily got out, thanked the footman, who opened the door to her, and begged him to carry her thanks back to his mistress. She then entered Honeywell House, hardly noticing the surprise of the butler and other servants at her early and solitary return. Unthinkingly, she made her way upstairs to her room. At the door to her room, however, she hesitated. She felt not at all sleepy. Quite the contrary, the events of the evening had so keyed her up that she felt as though it would be hours before she could sleep.

I'll get a book from the library and read for a while, she decided. *Perhaps that will settle my nerves.* So instead of going into her room, she went down the hall to the library.

The library was in darkness, but Emily soon remedied

that by touching a taper to the branches of candles set around the room. A fire was laid in the hearth, and she set that alight, too, for the evening was chilly enough to justify it. *I'll sit and read in here instead of my room*, she told herself. *The chairs are more comfortable.*

This was true, but Emily had an additional reason for choosing to do her reading in the library. It was just possible that Sir Terrence, too, might decide to come home from the party early. It was his nightly custom to visit the library for at least a few minutes before retiring, and by staying in the library, Emily hoped she might be able to see and talk to him one last time that night. The same reasoning prompted her to leave on her ball dress instead of changing to a simpler costume. Like her, the dress had been cut short of its natural career; it seemed only right that it, too, should have one more chance with Sir Terrence before the two of them would be forced to retire.

Choosing a book from the shelves, Emily curled up on the sofa, arranging her shawl over her shoulders until such time as the fire should have taken effect. It was the sheerest chance that her choice should have alighted on *Pamela*, out of all the thousands of books in the library.

She knew *Pamela* by repute, naturally. It had been a very popular book during the previous century, although its popularity had waned a good deal in recent years. When she was a girl, she had once overheard a gentleman describe it as "a deucedly dull book and deucedly long-winded." Yet Miss Morris had frequently denounced it as an obscene work that no decent woman would allow in her home. It seemed to Emily that any book that could inspire such widely varying opinions ought to be worth reading. So she settled down to read with the idea of judging it for herself.

* * *

Hours passed. Bit by bit the shawl slipped from Emily's shoulders. The logs in the fireplace blazed up, then settled down to the slow process of dying into embers. The candles burned lower in their sockets. The clock over the mantel marked off the progress of time with silvery notes on the quarter-hour. But Emily noticed none of these things. She read on and on, her lips pursed and her brow furrowed into an expression of growing indignation.

It was three o'clock in the morning when Sir Terrence arrived back at Honeywell House. He was in a state of anxiety that was the more pronounced because he had been obliged to repress it for so many hours.

His anxiety had begun the moment Emily had left him after the second dance. He had stood watching as she had gone with Lord Meredith to take her place on the floor. Of course, his anxiety was not motivated by jealousy—or at least not enough to count. He did feel a certain inferiority when he contrasted his own person with Lord Meredith's, but he had too much to be happy about to allow such thoughts more than a fleeting harborage. Emily had said she cared for him. She had looked and spoken to him in such a way that he had no doubt she was speaking the truth. Therefore, he had nothing to fear in her sharing a dance even with such a *bel homme* as Lord Meredith. He watched her, admiring the lines of her statuesque figure and the red-gold glory of her hair against the snowy white of her robes.

And then suddenly, without warning, a change had come over Emily. One moment, she was standing in a relaxed and graceful attitude, glancing around the room with mild interest; the next, her figure had gone stiff and her eyes wide with shock. Even as Sir Terrence watched, he saw the color drain out of her face.

Often, in writing, he had used such expressions as "her face went white with shock," but the words had been only a literary formula to him. Now he was observing the phenomenon firsthand, and it was a disturbing experience. Seeing it take place on the face of the woman he loved made it even more disturbing. Involuntarily, he started forward, but before he had gone more than a step or two, he saw Lord Meredith seize Emily's arm and hurry her off the floor.

By now seriously alarmed, Sir Terrence followed after the two of them as quickly as he could. But the crowd around the dance floor impeded his progress, and when he finally reached the other side of the room, both Emily and Lord Meredith had vanished.

Sir Terrence stood looking about him, wondering where they had gone. He did not like to ask, for that would only draw attention to Emily's departure, and he felt sure she would wish to avoid such attention. He decided to look around a little, keeping his search purposefully casual, to see if she might be in one of the parlors or drawing rooms. Here again, however, the crowd hindered him. He could not go three steps without someone recognizing him, hailing him as a friend, and asking him how he did. Even the briefest response to these inquiries took time. It was nearly an hour later when, entering a parlor that had been set aside for cardplayers, Lady Meredith appeared in the doorway opposite.

She saw him at the same moment he saw her. Her eyes flickered as though she were pleased or relieved; Sir Terrence could not tell which. But she came across the room to him and tucked her arm beneath his, leading him deliberately away from the cardplayers. "Sir Terrence," she said. "This is a fortunate meeting. I have a message for you from Miss Pearce."

"Thank God," said Sir Terrence with relief. "I am happy to have any news of her. I saw her leave the dance floor some time ago with your husband, but then I lost track of her."

It occurred to him after these words were spoken that he might have phrased them more happily, but Lady Meredith merely nodded. "Yes, she was feeling unwell, and Jonathan helped her off the floor. We thought it best to get her away from the crowd and into a private room where she could lie down for a while."

"Then she *is* unwell? I thought so when I saw the way she was looking out on the dance floor. May I see her?"

Lady Meredith hesitated, and it occurred to Sir Terrence that she was deciding how much to tell him. "I am afraid not," she said at last. "Miss Pearce has already gone home, as it happens. We agreed it would be best for her to do so, and I insisted she take my carriage so as not to disturb you and Miss O'Reilly."

"But she should have disturbed us!" said Sir Terrence. "Good God! If she is really unwell—"

Lady Meredith shook her head. "I beg you will calm yourself, Sir Terrence. Miss Pearce assured me she was not really unwell. Of course, such assurances are often merely a form, but I am confident that in this case she was speaking the truth. Indeed, she appeared all but recovered by the time she left."

"Then why was it necessary for her to leave at all? There's something you're not telling me." Sir Terrence looked angrily at Lady Meredith. "I saw her face, out on the dance floor. I saw how distressed she was. Why was she so distressed? What did she see? You know, don't you?"

Again Lady Meredith hesitated, and her golden-brown eyes flickered. "Yes, I know," she said at last. "But I think it would be better if Miss Pearce told you that herself, Sir Terrence."

"Then I'll ask her," said Sir Terrence, turning toward the door. "Thank you very much for giving me her message, Lady Meredith. If you will please excuse me—"

Instead of excusing him, however, Lady Meredith moved to bar the way. "Indeed, Sir Terrence, I think you had better reconsider," she said. "I know you mean well, but frankly you would do better to let Miss Pearce alone for a few hours before you try to ask her any questions. Without betraying the confidences she made me, I can at least say she has suffered a very distressing shock. What she needs now more than anything else is peace and quiet. To question her now would only distress her the more."

"But if she is truly in distress, I would think—" Sir Terrence stopped, then started again rather awkwardly. "I do not mean to question your judgment, Lady Meredith. But I give you my word that I do think I might be able to help her. Besides, it's hard lines to have to idle my time away at a party while I know she is in distress—"

Again he stopped, looking with embarrassment at Lady Meredith. Something like a smile flickered on that lady's lips.

"I understand you, Sir Terrence," she said gravely. "Naturally, you would have little interest in balls while you are concerned about Miss Pearce's welfare. But since you ask me, I do think you would do better to stay here rather than returning immediately to Honeywell House. If nothing else, it would be obeying Miss Pearce's expressed wishes, and that must count for something with you."

It did count for something, though Sir Terrence was loath to admit it. In the end, however, he assented to Lady Meredith's suggestion that he return to the ballroom and try to get what amusement he could out of the rest of the evening.

As he had anticipated, it was very heavy going. It was all the more so because, after his high spirits at dinner, people were expecting him to be witty, and wit did not come easily to him in his present mood. It was some comfort to see that his aunt, at least, was having a good time. When he took her aside and told her about Emily's indisposition, however, she reacted much as he had done.

"And to think I never even noticed her leaving! By all that's wonderful, Terry, I begin to think I'm not fit to chaperone a goat, let alone a young lady. Order around the carriage, if you will, and I'll be ready to go in two shakes. I've been having that fine a time, talking to Miss Payne—did you meet Miss Payne yet, Terry? And did you know she was Lady Meredith's aunt? I just found out this evening. We haven't met her before because she just got back from visiting Montenegro. She was telling me all about it, and she does have some very interesting stories to tell about folk and customs there. But interesting or not, I ought not to have let Montenegro distract me from my duty to Miss Pearce."

Sir Terrence, however, felt it his duty to dissuade his aunt from flying to Emily's side, just as Lady Meredith had dissuaded him. If Emily truly needed peace and quiet and respite from questions, then she would be more likely to get all three if neither he nor Aunt Katie were around. So he assured his aunt that Emily had no need of her and even stretched the truth a bit by saying she had merely been fatigued and was probably even now in her bed asleep.

Privately, he hoped this was not the case. He had a burning desire to talk to Emily one last time that evening. Even setting aside the issue of her mysterious departure from the ball, he had plenty to say to her. He kept an eye on the clock, wishing he might hurry events along, but the ball proceeded in the time-honored way of all balls without reference to his wishes. He was introduced to Miss Payne,

Lady Meredith's aunt, and to various other people with whom he made conversation and strove to be agreeable. He ate lobster patties and blancmange at midnight and drank champagne punch. But he did not dance anymore, either before or after supper, much to the disappointment of several damsels who had been hoping for an invitation to stand up with "that charming Sir Terrence." If he could not dance with Emily, then he did not wish to dance at all.

He had made up his mind to stay until Aunt Katie expressed a wish to leave. He reckoned that would be long enough to give Emily an ample interval of peace and quiet. But it proved a longer interval than he had bargained for. Aunt Katie had found several kindred spirits among the guests and was having such a splendid time talking to them that she did not grow tired nearly so early as she usually did. In fact, it was Sir Terrence who finally broke down and suggested, around three in the morning, that it was time they took their departure. Both he and his aunt thanked the Merediths for their hospitality, then started home for Honeywell House.

Once back at Honeywell House, Aunt Katie insisted on stopping by Emily's room to see if all was well with her. But her soft tap on Emily's door brought no answer, so she told Sir Terrence that Emily was sleeping soundly and gave it as her opinion that they ought not to disturb her. Sir Terrence agreed, but he was disappointed. He went slowly down the hall, reflecting with chagrin on the way the evening had turned out. It seemed to him he might as well go to bed now that all chance of seeing Emily was over for the night. But at the last minute he was drawn to stop by the library for a few minutes. There was no real reason for doing so, for he felt too tired and dispirited to read or work. It was merely an impulse, one of those trifling decisions on which life-altering events sometimes hinge.

Sir Terrence swung open the library door. He was unprepared for the blaze of light that greeted him. All the candelabra were lit, and a fire burned in the fireplace. This surprised him, for the servants did not usually leave lights and fires burning in the library unless he had ordered them in advance. Or, of course, unless someone else was using the room. Yet there appeared to be no one there. Sir Terrence advanced a few steps, then stopped. He had just caught sight of Emily lying on the sofa in front of the fire.

At the sound of his entrance, she looked up. She was still wearing her white ball dress, and Sir Terrence noticed that she was holding a book in her hand. If he had not been so overcome by the surprise of finding her there at that hour, he might have noticed also that her lips were tightly compressed and her eyes ablaze with emotion.

"Emily!" said Sir Terrence. She rose to her feet, and he hurried forward, his heart rejoicing with happiness. He had intended to take her in his arms, but something in her expression brought him up short. Emily seemed to be looking at him but not seeing him—or rather, seeing him as something besides the lover whom she might have been expected to welcome.

"This book," she said, holding out the book so he could see it. "Have you ever read this book?"

Sir Terrence looked and saw it was a volume of Richardson's *Pamela*. "Yes, certainly," he said. "I read *Pamela* years ago. Emily, I—"

Emily did not allow him to continue. "This book," she said, shaking the book in her hand as a terrier might shake a rat, "this book is vile! I never read such wicked nonsense in all my life."

"Indeed," said Sir Terrence. He was puzzled by Emily's

indignation, which seemed all out of proportion to the subject they were discussing. "I'm afraid I don't remember the book very well, after all these years. Of course, I know the general plot—"

"Then you know how wicked it is! I never could have believed anyone could write such wickedness. Even in a novel, it is wrong to let people believe such things."

Sir Terrence's puzzlement increased. He still could not understand what Emily was so indignant about. It was obvious she was intent on discussing *Pamela* rather than putting the time to better use, however, so he obligingly fell in with her wishes. "I beg your pardon, but I believe the events in *Pamela* really did happen," he said diffidently. "As I recall, Richardson based the book on a true story— or so he gave his readers to understand."

"But the events could never have happened the way he has written them! No woman could behave in such a way— such a base and foolish and mercenary way all at the same time."

By this time Sir Terrence was frantically wracking his brain to recall the plot of *Pamela*. "You think not?" he said. "As I said, I don't recall the story very well, but didn't it have to do with a maidservant who falls in love with her employer's son?"

"Yes, after he has tried to rape her! And yet she prates of her love for him in the most sickening way and practically jumps at the chance to marry him. It is a pernicious book! You can tell a man must have written it, for no woman could entertain for a moment the likelihood of such a thing happening."

This speech naturally stung Sir Terrence. "I don't see that there's anything so intrinsically unbelievable about it," he said. "Pamela's behavior may seem contradictory, but you must remember that she is, as she is always telling us, a virtuous woman. She might wish to respond to Mr. B.'s advances but be restrained by a sense of morality."

"Morality!" There was not merely anger but outrage in Emily's voice. "Do you call her behavior moral? I should call it immoral in the extreme."

"But surely not," protested Sir Terrence. "I don't claim to recall the book perfectly, but I cannot be mistaken on that score. *Pamela* does not surrender her virtue to Mr. B. until after they are properly married."

"Yes, and that is exactly what I call immoral!" said Emily. "A man might be taken in by such behavior, but no woman would be deceived for a moment. It is nonsense to say she might have been tempted to respond to Mr. B.'s advances. They were not advances! They were attempts at rape, pure and simple. How could any woman love a man who would treat her that way? Tell me that, if you will!"

Light began to dawn in Sir Terrence's mind. He perceived that he was treading on dangerous ground. "Taking that fact into consideration, Pamela's behavior does seem a little difficult to reconcile," he admitted. "But she had cherished an admiration for Mr. B. previous to his attempts on her virtue, you know."

"If she had, it would have vanished the moment he attempted to rape her," said Emily with flat assurance. "After that, she could only have despised him."

"But does he not try to win her first without force? Not that I am trying to justify his conduct, mind you—"

"Yes, he does try to win her without force. And to me that is the most immoral thing of all. Not that he should have tried to win her but that she should have refused him. If she indeed felt the way about him that she says, then she never would have refused him in the first place."

"Indeed?" said Sir Terrence, confused. "But I thought—didn't you just say she should despise him?"

"Yes, of course. But they're two separate issues—or,

rather, two sides of the same issue. The truth, which is obvious from the start, is that Pamela wants to marry Mr. B. That is what all her fine talk about virtue and morality come down to, and that is the only way to reconcile her behavior."

Sir Terrence stared at her. "I don't see it," he said.

"It seems quite obvious to me," said Emily. "Only consider her behavior! During the first part of the book she prates of how far beneath Mr. B. she is. Yet it's perfectly obvious she wants to respond to his advances. Well, why doesn't she? Because, unworthy or not, she hopes to entice him into marriage! And that has nothing to do with love, whatever she may pretend. If she really loved him, she would not wish him to marry beneath him. She might or might not give in to his advances, depending on how strong her feelings for him were, but she would never do anything that would injure him. Don't you agree?"

Sir Terrence merely nodded. He was staring at Emily, mesmerized by the passion of her rhetoric. She went on, warming to her theme.

"Then when Mr. B. tries to rape Pamela and proves beyond doubt that it is he who is unworthy of her and not the other way around, does she cast him off like a rational woman? No, she keeps bleating about her love for him. She keeps angling and angling for marriage, like a fisherman trying for a trout, and in the end she gets it. Mr. B. marries her, and she has the gall to talk about 'Providence rewarding her for treading the paths of innocence!' Can you deny that is wicked, immoral, mercenary behavior?"

Put like this, Sir Terrence was not likely to deny anything of the kind. "Of course, you are not the first person to find Pamela's behavior hypocritical," he ventured. "Fielding wrote a rather scathing parody of the book, as I recall. But I still think you might be judging poor Pamela too harshly.

She might love Mr. B. and yet wish to keep her virtue intact."

"Not if she really cared for him," said Emily. "I am quite sure of that. If she loved Mr. B. as I love you, such considerations would go by the board."

Sir Terrence began to feel a little dizzy. There was something in the way Emily was looking at him that was very compelling.

"Emily," he said, and then stopped. Emily came a step nearer, still regarding him with that compelling gaze. Again he spoke, and this time the words flowed freely, as from a pent-up reserve.

"Oh, Emily! You know I love you, too, with all my heart. I've been thinking of you all night—"

"And I have been thinking of you, too," said Emily.

Sir Terrence held out his arms to her, but she did not come to them. Instead, holding his eyes with her own, she began to unbutton the pearl buttons that fastened her bodice.

Sir Terrence watched with fascinated eyes. "What are you doing?" he asked in a weak voice. He thought, however, that he had a very fair idea what she was doing.

Emily did not bother to answer. She only went on unbuttoning buttons until the ball dress slipped to the floor in a shimmering heap. Her petticoat followed. As she began untying the ribbon at the neck of her chemise, Sir Terrence forced himself to speak.

"Emily!" he said. "Do you know what you are doing?"

"I know exactly what I am doing. And so do you," said Emily. The chemise slipped to the floor, and Sir Terrence shut his eyes for an instant, momentarily blinded by the vision appearing before him. When he opened them again, Emily was completely naked. There was nothing timid or shrinking in her nudity. She stood straight and tall, confronting Sir Terrence in all the strength of her untrammeled femininity. And it seemed to him that he had never seen anything more lovely. She had loosened her hair, and it tumbled over her bare shoulders in wanton curls and ringlets of auburn gold. Her skin was pale and smooth as marble; her eyes were a reflection of the firelight, dark but with a fiery glow in their depths.

"I want you to make love to me," she said. She looked at that moment like a goddess to Sir Terrence—a goddess infinitely beautiful and desirable. And since it was clearly impossible to refuse a goddess anything, Sir Terrence did as he was told.

He went to her, taking her in his arms. She wrapped her own arms tightly around him and raised her lips to his. The feel of her body against his and her mouth yielding to his kiss would have been enough to fire his desire for her, if such desire had not already been burning at full flame.

As it was, he lost his head completely. He forgot that Emily was a young woman of quality and also his employee. He forgot that it was his duty, under both those circumstances, to safeguard her both physically and emotionally. He even forgot that she was almost certainly a virgin and that the very least he could have done, assuming his personal code of conduct had allowed for the deflowering of virgins, was to proceed with gentleness and caution. Neither gentleness nor caution was anywhere in the picture as far as Sir Terrence was concerned. He kissed her as though he were starving for her, and the passion of her response only increased his hunger.

Emily, for her part, felt something of the same intoxication she had experienced when she had come downstairs earlier that evening and seen the light of love in Sir Terrence's eyes. But this was a much more heady kind of intoxication. She felt caught up in a tide of events, although in control of them, too. For the first time, she glimpsed

the power she held over Sir Terrence: the force her body
had over his and the desire it inspired in him. And she
reveled in that desire. When he kissed her, she kissed him
back with a passion equaling his own. When he ran his
hands over her back, seeking to draw her into a closer
embrace, she wantonly pressed her body against his and
felt his quickening desire with a triumph that was pure
exultation.

There was no fear or apprehension in her mind over
what was to come. She felt secure in her power and secure
in Sir Terrence's love for her; the two together seemed to
render everything he did natural and enjoyable. Not only
that; they also inspired in her a desire to reciprocate the
pleasure he was giving her. She found herself kissing not
merely his lips but his face and ears and throat, just as he
was doing to her. Somehow in the process a good deal of
his clothing slipped away, and soon he was nearly as naked
as herself. The sensation of his bare skin against hers was
more exciting than anything she had felt yet, and it
occurred to her she could feel it much better lying down
than standing up.

The same thought had apparently occurred to Sir Terrence. He caught her in his arms and carried her toward
the sofa. Emily was glad to submit to this whim as to all
his others. The warmth and weight of his body atop hers
was both incredibly intimate and incredibly exciting.
Desire, which had been present in her up till now as a
vague and indefinite longing, sharpened suddenly into a
very definite longing indeed. She found herself making
little noises when he kissed her, which was hardly a dignified proceeding, but dignity seemed of secondary importance just then.

Strangely enough, having got her in this promising position, Sir Terrence seemed in no hurry to take advantage

of it. He kissed her over and over, letting his lips stray
from her lips to her neck, from her neck to her breasts.

At the first touch of his mouth on her breast, Emily drew
in her breath sharply. She had never supposed sensations
of that sort could be aroused in so unlikely a manner. And
as he continued to kiss and caress and lavish his attentions
upon her bosom, she began to feel a pleasure such as she
had never imagined, one she had never even imagined
possible. She felt flooded with pleasure, tormented with
pleasure, and she ached for a release that she only dimly
understood.

"Terrence," she said in a wavering voice. "Oh, Terrence!"

"Emily," he said, and murmured something in a low
voice. Emily thought she could distinguish the word "goddess" among the others, but she was in no condition to
pay much heed to mere words. All her attentions were
focused on the progress of Sir Terrence's mouth. Having
spent an incredible amount of time on her breasts, he had
moved lower to kiss her waist and hips—and then lower
yet. Emily's eyes, which had closed of their own accord,
opened wide. She looked down at him with disbelief .

"Terrence?" she whispered.

"Emily," he whispered back, and proceeded to kiss her
in the place that most burned for his attention. Emily drew
in her breath sharply.

"Terrence!" she said again urgently. Then, in a different
voice, "Oh, Terrence! Oh, God! You mustn't—I can't bear
it."

In truth, she thought she could not bear it. The feel of
his mouth on her most intimate parts was painful in its
sublimity. She began to sob aloud, conscious of an intolerable pressure building within her. And then, when she was
sure she could not bear it another moment, the delicate,
insistent caress of Sir Terrence's mouth, the touch of his

hands, the feel of his body on hers, blurred together suddenly into a pleasure so overwhelming that it buoyed her right out of herself. She felt afire with pleasure, burning with a mixture of love and exultation and pure physical release that was like a revelation of the divine. There was no irreverence in the thought nor in Emily's mind when she called out God's name and Sir Terrence's with impartial fervor. She then sank back shuddering on the sofa, overcome with what she had just experienced.

As though from far away she heard Sir Terrence saying something. Once again she thought she distinguished the word "goddess" among the others; it struck her as slightly unreal, but then everything seemed dreamlike at that moment. Then she caught sight of Sir Terrence, and everything was tangible and immediate once again. She stretched out her arms to him. He came to her, embracing her almost fiercely. He did not speak now, but merely looked at her. Looking into his eyes, Emily thought she had never seen anything so brilliantly blue. "Terrence," she whispered again, and reached up to touch his face.

He did not speak but buried his face in her neck. Emily stroked his face again, letting her hand slide down his neck to his chest. He raised his head to look at her again. Once again Emily felt that strange sense of power, the feeling that all hinged on her actions. Deliberately she slid her hand lower, to where she could feel the hard pressure of his sex against her.

At the touch of her fingers, Sir Terrence trembled slightly. The light in his eyes seem to darken to an ardent glow. Emily felt herself trembling, too, as she tentatively explored that part of his body that was so foreign to her. He felt hard to the touch but silky smooth; aggressively masculine and yet strangely vulnerable. She could hear Sir Terrence's breath grow ragged as she caressed him and see the quickening rise and fall of his chest. She could see that what she was doing gave pleasure to him, exactly like the pleasure he had given her. An impulse struck her, one that was at once shocking and exciting. Emily drew a deep breath. Then, half rising from where she lay, she bent until her lips touched his sex. A shudder went through him, and his sex rose, responsive to her kiss. Emily laughed, feeling a surge of power stronger than anything she had yet felt before.

"Emily!" said Sir Terrence. There was urgency in his tone. Emily looked up at him. "Emily?" he said again, and this time the words were a question. For answer, Emily lay back on the sofa. Then again she took his sex in her hand and this time guided the masculine hardness of him toward the feminine softness between her legs.

"Emily!" said Sir Terrence again.

"Yes," said Emily. She looked full into his eyes. They caught and held hers, and then she felt him entering her. The pain was more than she had expected, and she was conscious of tears squeezing from her eyes, but at the same time she was conscious of triumph. "Terrence," she said. "Oh, Terrence!"

He did not speak but only looked down at her. Emily caught her breath, released it, then caught it again as he thrust into her. The look in his eyes, the feel of him inside her, even the pain that accompanied his every thrust, began to arouse in her some of the strange, exalted sensation she had felt before. Again she felt that mounting urgency and the sense of being lifted out of herself. She knew Sir Terrence was experiencing the same thing. It was reflected in his eyes and in the strange, half-formed sentences that began to spill from his lips as his lovemaking grew more frenzied.

"Emily! Goddess! Oh, Emily," he said over and over. Emily found nothing ludicrous in being addressed thus.

"Yes," she whispered. "Yes, oh, yes." She was only dimly

aware of pain now. Presently she forgot it altogether and was conscious of nothing but him—of him and of herself, now joined into one. As one they were moving toward the same inescapable goal, and she felt it approach with that same sense of pleasure verging on the intolerable. Then she felt him tense and shudder in her arms; saw his eyes dilate and his lips part, even as her own body was wafted upward on a piercingly sweet wave of pleasure. "Oh! Terrence!" she whispered.

"Emily!" he whispered back. His voice sounded as though he were near to weeping. Emily knew exactly how he felt. There were tears in her own eyes as she looked up at him.

"Terrence—" she said.

"I love you," he whispered. "God, but I love you! I cannot bear it, Emily. I love you so much."

"I love you, too," said Emily. "And I will never stop loving you, Terrence. Never, as long as I live."

Chapter 17

The room was very quiet after Emily spoke. She had the sense of having just pronounced a solemn vow. It seemed to her that the great shadowy room with its dying fire and flickering candles was witness to the vow—one she was bound to keep as long as she lived.

Sir Terrence bent to kiss her on the brow. "And I will love you always, too," he said.

He, too, spoke as though he were pronouncing a vow. Emily looked at him and spoke impulsively in a low voice.

"Oh, Terrence," she said. "I wish I could die! I am so happy right now. I am sure I will never be so happy again."

His arms around her tightened. "Don't say that," he said urgently. "Emily, don't speak of dying. Do you think I could stand to lose you now?" He bent his head to her and kissed her again. "Emily, my love, my only love."

"Terrence," she said, and reached up to touch his face. He kissed her hand, then lay his head on her breast and closed his eyes. Emily put her arms around him.

"I can hear your heart," he said.

Emily started to speak, then paused. The clock on the library mantel had begun to strike the hour. It chimed five times and then was silent. Sir Terrence raised his head from Emily's breast with a sharp intake of breath.

"Five o'clock," he said. "I didn't know it was so late. Why, it's almost morning. And the servants will be coming soon. Good God!" In a single athletic spring he was on his feet and gathering up his clothes. "They mustn't find you here."

He had stopped and was staring at the sofa where he and Emily had been lying. Emily, who had half-risen at his first words, looked, too.

"It's only—" she said, then hesitated.

"Only!" said Sir Terrence. "My God!"

He looked stricken to the heart. Emily, looking at him, felt a strange, cold creeping over her own heart.

"The sofa is leather," she said. "I don't suppose it has taken any permanent harm." Snatching up her chemise, she bent to wipe off the darker stains that lay here and there atop the moss-green leather.

"But the servants!" said Sir Terrence. "If they see the blood on your clothing, they will think—they will know—"

"They will think only that my monthly flow came unexpectedly," said Emily crisply.

"Oh—yes. Yes, of course," said Sir Terrence. But there was a distraught look on his face as he turned away and began drawing on his clothing.

Emily did the same, but the chill in her heart was growing colder. If ever regret had been plain in anyone's voice and manner, they had been plain in Sir Terrence's. She did not bother with her chemise, stockings, or petticoat, but merely put on her dress and slippers and gathered up her other belongings. *Pamela* lay where it had fallen. Emily was careful not to look at it as she picked up the combs and hairpins that were scattered on the hearth.

Proceeding in this fashion, she was ready to leave before Sir Terrence. He looked up in surprise when he saw her standing there with the bundle of her other belongings in her hand.

"That was quick work," he said. "You'd better not wait for me, but go now just in case the servants come in early to clean the room. If they find me alone, they'll only think I had too much wine last night and fell asleep on the library sofa!"

He smiled as he spoke, but it was a strained smile. "Yes," said Emily. She turned to go. Before she could reach the door, however, Sir Terrence came to her. He caught her hand in his, so she was forced to turn and look at him.

"Emily!" he said, and kissed her hand. "Emily, my love, what have I done?"

"You didn't do anything that I didn't want you to do," said Emily very clearly and distinctly. "Don't worry, Terrence. I shall not hold it against you." Gently, she removed her hand from his, then turned again to go. He gave her a startled look.

"Emily!" he said, then hesitated as she turned to look at him. "No, never mind. You'd better get to your room now. We can talk later. But Emily—I do love you."

"I love you, too," said Emily gravely. "Good night, Terrence." Turning, she hurried from the room.

She was lucky enough to gain her own room without being seen by anyone. Once there, she set about removing her ball dress again, wincing a little at the memories it evoked. Nor were they the only painful thing she was conscious of. Her body felt stiff and sore, and she smiled grimly at her reflection in the glass as she brushed out her hair.

How strange, she told herself. *I look the same, but I feel completely different.*

In truth, she felt several centuries older. That evening alone had seemed to encompass at least a century by itself. She traced the whole course of the evening in her memory, from its promising beginning to Ronald's appearance; from her hasty departure from the Abbey to her arrival in the library at Honeywell House; from her seduction of Sir Terrence to the painfully anticlimactic scene that had just taken place between them.

Anyone could tell he regrets it, she told herself. *I must have seemed very forward—very brazen.* She shuddered at the memory of how forward and brazen she had been. But instead of feeling properly shamed, she actually found herself becoming inflamed all over again when she remembered what she had done and how Sir Terrence had responded. It seemed strange that in the midst of all the complex and unhappy emotions the evening had stirred within her, such a simple one as lust could have survived intact. But in spite of the promptings of her mind and conscience, she longed with an elemental hunger for Sir Terrence's touch and presence and the warmth of his body next to hers.

"But that's no good," Emily said aloud. "It isn't just his body I want. I want all of him."

She had never analyzed the nature of true love before. The depth of its desires filled her with dismay. What she wanted from Sir Terrence went far beyond the pleasures of the flesh to include the pleasures of the mind and something that Emily could only call communion of soul. She had glimpsed it in those transcendent moments in Sir Terrence's arms, when he and she had seemed to become one in some mysterious fashion. Every act, every word, had acquired a significance shared only by the two of them.

Yet such a sense must be an illusion—or worse yet, a snare. She and Sir Terrence were not one person, but on the contrary, two very different people. One was a wealthy baronet who was author of a dozen popular and critically

acclaimed novels and whose charm won him friends and
admirers wherever he went. The other was a girl of modest
birth, no means, and scanty accomplishments—a girl who
was actually employed as a hired companion to his aunt.
There could be no comparison between their two worldly
stations. Emily knew that if a union between two such
people had been described to her as a hypothetical case,
she would have denounced the unknown young woman
as an opportunist and fortune hunter, just as she had
denounced the fictional Pamela.

Because what I told him last night is the truth, she told
herself. *Any woman who really loved a man would take care to
do nothing that might harm him, even if it meant doing violence
to her own feelings. I claim to love Terrence—I do love him, and
he loves me. But it's not enough. If he were to*—Emily drew a
deep breath, then went on resolutely: *If he were to propose
marriage to me, I should have to decline it. Marriage ought to be
between two equals, and we are not equals. I could never be happy
knowing he had condescended to marry me.*

The idea of marriage was one Emily had been avoiding
for some time. Now she forced herself to look it squarely
in the face. Did Sir Terrence intend to offer her marriage?
She thought he might have been intending to, at least up
till the scene in the library. Even if he had had no thought
of marriage before, he would feel obliged to offer for her
after what had happened between them.

I know him, Emily told herself. *I know how he will react.*
She felt a poignant sadness when she reflected how well
known to her were Sir Terrence's mental and moral pro-
cesses. Of course, he had felt guilty for taking advantage
of her last night, though in truth the boot had been quite
upon the other foot. But he would not see it that way. He
would think he had been wrong in taking her maidenhead
even when it had been freely offered him. And he would
feel compelled to offer her marriage as compensation.

If I were an unprincipled woman, how easily I might take advantage of him! Emily told herself. But she was not an unprincipled woman. She knew it, and in some strange, paradoxical way, what she had done last night proved rather than disproved it. She could give her body to Sir Terrence, but she could not become his wife without sacrificing her own principles of what was right and wrong.

On this point Emily had no doubts. But when she tried to carry her reasoning further and decide what her future conduct should be toward Sir Terrence, the issue became more complex. She felt in her bones that having once known Sir Terrence in a physical sense, she could never be content to let their relationship lapse once more into the platonic. But the alternative was to become his mistress, and somehow her mind shrank from the thought. It was one thing to tear off one's clothes and proclaim one's superiority to conventional morality in the heat of passion, but it was another to systematically renounce the principles one had been raised with. Yet Emily knew her only other choice was to renounce Sir Terrence forever as her lover. She was almost certain that she would find this impossible. Even now she longed for him, and would not the longing be a hundred times worse in his actual presence? Emily groaned and leaned her head on her hand.

"I am damned either way, it seems," she said softly. "Therefore, it shouldn't matter what I do." But she felt it did matter. It mattered intensely, but it was quite beyond her to make a rational decision at the moment.

I'm tired, of course, having been up all night, she told herself. *I daresay I ought to try to get some sleep. Perhaps when I wake, I will find the decision clear in my mind.* As Emily got into bed, however, and disposed herself for sleep, it occurred to her that the decision was not hers alone to make. Sir Terrence, too, might have opinions on the subject. Anything she chose to do in reference to him would be naturally affected by those opinions. Emily's last thought, as she drifted off to sleep, was to hope she had the strength to face whatever lay ahead of her that day.

She slept late, but not too late. It was only ten o'clock when she roused herself from her bed and began to make her toilette for the day. As she hastily washed her face and arranged her hair, she reflected with guilt that she would be late in performing her usual morning duties. Sir Terrence might now be her lover, but she was still a hired companion, and she still had duties that her conscience felt badly about shirking. Then she recalled the ball the night before and was reassured. Aunt Katie had returned home even later than she had (though she had probably gone earlier to bed), and it was almost certain that she would rise later this morning than usual.

The thought comforted Emily, and she ceased to rush about her toilette quite so frantically. But there was still a flavor of guilt in her thoughts as she buttoned her cambric morning dress and put the finishing touches on her hair. What would Aunt Katie think if she knew what had passed between Emily and her nephew the previous night? Undoubtedly, she would be disgusted. Probably she would assume greed and ambition had been Emily's motivation and that her actions had been merely a ploy to gain Sir Terrence's title and fortune. Remembering Aunt Katie's comments on Lady Moira, Emily could only shudder when she imagined the comments the old lady might apply toward her own behavior.

I must be very careful to seem just as usual, she told herself. *I must not presume one iota on what happened last night. And I must do it as much for Terrence's sake as for Aunt Katie's. He must not imagine that I expect him to propose marriage simply because we made love.* It was Emily's hope that if Sir Terrence intended to make any such proposal, she might be able to head him off before he could actually speak. She had found it difficult enough to resist the temptation of simply being around him during the last few weeks; avoiding the temptation of being married to him might prove too much for her to resist.

She was fortunate in missing both Sir Terrence and his aunt at the breakfast table—or so at least she assured herself. But in reality their absence merely served to key her already tense nerves a little higher. As she picked at toast and cold ham, she found herself wishing she had gotten that first meeting over with no matter how awkward it might have been. As it was now, the awkwardness was only postponed to some future date that she could not help anticipating with keen anxiety.

She encountered Aunt Katie first, immediately after quitting the dining room. "There you are, my dear!" said Aunt Katie, laying a hand on her arm and surveying her with surprised pleasure. "I did not look for you to be up and about so early this morning."

"Nor I you," said Emily, "considering it was so late when you and Sir Terrence got home."

She broke off in confusion, realizing belatedly that she ought not to have known at what hour they had returned. But she need not have worried. Aunt Katie attributed her knowledge to a different and more innocent source than that from which it had actually come.

"So you heard me look in on you last night? I did not like to wake you, but I could not help being a bit worried when Terry said you had gone home early."

"Yes," said Emily noncommittally. "I am sorry you were worried."

"Ah, but indeed I couldn't help it, my dear." Aunt Katie looked at her closely. "If I may ask, what was the nature of your indisposition? Terry didn't seem to know any of the details, and no more did Lady Meredith when I asked her."

"Oh! Why, as a matter of fact there was no indisposition. It was only Ronald." Emily gave a shaky laugh. "You will think me an idiot, but I had almost forgotten."

"Ronald?" Aunt Katie was regarding her incredulously now. "You're not meaning that rascally fellow that plagued you in your last position? What did he have to do with it?"

"Why, he was at the party last night," said Emily. "He—"

"You say *Ronald* was at the party last night?"

This question, spoken in an explosive voice, made both Emily and Aunt Katie jump. "Terrence!" said Aunt Katie with pleasure. "I didn't know you were down yet."

Sir Terrence did not acknowledge this remark. He merely went on looking at Emily from where he stood just a few feet away. "Is this true?" he asked her. "Was Ronald at the party last night?"

"Yes, he was," said Emily. She felt herself blushing but endeavored to speak with dignity. "I noticed him there soon after we had finished dancing the second dance."

"So that is why you insisted on going home early! I wondered but could not guess what the trouble was. Why did you not tell me, Emily? You did not mention it even after I—You never mentioned a thing. You ought to have told me."

Emily had to admit he had done a fair job of disguising his near-slip, but still she was alarmed. In his heat against Ronald, Sir Terrence seemed likely to reveal more about the evening's events than she was comfortable revealing at this point. Even as it was, his manner held more both of indignation and reproach than were proportional to Emily's offense. Aunt Katie was looking at him with surprise, and a maidservant who was passing in the hall had caught the tone of his voice and turned to regard him with surprise also. Emily drew herself up, fixing him with a warning gaze.

"Indeed, I think you attach overmuch importance to

the incident, Sir Terrence," she said. "I did not mention it to you or your aunt last night simply because I did not think it worth mentioning."

"But you thought it sufficiently important to leave the party on account of it! Indeed, Emily, this will not do. You ought to have told me. If I had known Ronald was there—"

"If you had known he was there, you would have overreacted, just as you are doing now," said Emily. Her voice as well as her face held a warning now. Sir Terrence seemed to become aware of it, for when he spoke again, his own voice and manner were more restrained.

"Perhaps I would have overreacted. I confess I do not know exactly how one *should* react when a young woman of one's party encounters a blackguard who once assaulted her. But whatever I would have done or not done, I would not have permitted Ronald to harass you, Emily. And I certainly would not have allowed him to drive you away from the party. It is that fact that rankles most with me. He is the one who committed the offense, and yet it is you who suffer the penalty."

"I don't suffer," said Emily in a tight voice. "Indeed, you make too much of it, Terrence—*Sir* Terrence." Turning away, she added, "I beg you will say no more on the subject. I must go gather new flowers for the rooms, and I am late enough getting started as it is."

Out of the corner of her eye, she could see that this snub had had its effect. Sir Terrence started as though he had been stung, then turned on his heel and strode off in the direction of the library.

Emily felt badly about having to deal with him so roughly. But what could she do? He must be made to understand that he could not behave as though he were responsible for her and her affairs, at least not in front of his aunt. But her heart was heavy as she went out to the garden with her basket and scissors. She had so been looking forward to seeing him again; she had been wondering how he would greet her, look at her, and speak to her after what had happened the previous night. And somehow things had gone wrong. Given the circumstances, she did not know what she could have done differently, but she found herself with a new grudge against Ronald as the morning dragged into afternoon without Sir Terrence approaching her again.

An hour before dinner, however, he appeared just as she was putting on her shawl and hat to go out for a walk. "You are going out?" he asked. "Will you allow me to accompany you? There are some matters I think we need to discuss."

Emily assented. She could not help doing so, though she suspected a fierce ordeal lay ahead of her. Sir Terrence's face was resolute, as though he had made up his mind to some difficult course of action. Her knowledge of him made it easy to guess what this course of action must be; she only hoped she would have strength to refuse if he persisted in making the offer she wanted so badly to accept.

He started in abruptly when they were only a few yards from the house. "Emily, are you angry with me? Do you regret what happened last night?"

"No," said Emily quickly. "No, I don't regret it, Terrence. And I am not angry with you. If I seemed so this morning, it was only because—because I was not comfortable with the way you were talking to me. I could see your aunt was wondering at it, and I would rather not have her suspect that we—that we—"

"That we are lovers," finished Sir Terrence. "Yes, I thought it might be that." He did not speak again until they had reached the Italian garden. "I have been thinking a good deal about what happened, Emily. You must know

I do not regret what happened, either, but at the same time I cannot help feeling that I—well, that I ended up putting the cart before the horse, as it were. I love you, Emily. I had meant to ask you to marry me last night. And now—well, after what happened last night, I feel most definitely we ought to be married! But you—"

He stopped short, looking at Emily. "But I?" she prompted.

A wry smile appeared on his face. "But I have a suspicion you feel otherwise. I would be very glad to be proved wrong, however. Emily, will you marry me?"

There it was, the question she had been both hoping and dreading to hear. Emily forced herself to speak quickly, before the appeal in Sir Terrence's eyes could weaken her resolve.

"No, Terrence," she said. "Your suspicion is perfectly correct. I meant what I said last night—all of it. I could not marry you without feeling I had been false to my principles."

Sir Terrence shook his head. "Emily, this is madness," he said. "You have said you love me, and I believe you do. I know you, you see. I know you are a strong-minded and principled woman who would never knowingly commit an injustice. But in this case I believe you are committing a very grave injustice. I believe that what you are calling principle is really pride."

Emily raised her chin. "Call it what you will," she said. "In any case, I will not marry you, Terrence. No one will ever be able to say of me that I set my cap at you and got you 'by hook or by crook.' "

She smiled bitterly as she quoted Isabel's words. Sir Terrence struck one hand against the other with exasperation.

"Emily, you know it is not like that with us! Don't you see how foolish it is to let such considerations stand in the way of our happiness?"

Emily shook her head. "First I am proud, now I am foolish," she said. "I wonder you even want to marry me, Terrence."

Sir Terrence looked for a moment on the verge of exploding. Then suddenly he laughed. "You will not divert me that way, Emily," he said. "Proud, foolish, or not, I do want to marry you. And I begin to think I should simply carry you off to Gretna Green and marry you over the anvil like a fortune-hunting blackguard!"

"You wouldn't!" said Emily, taking a step backward.

"No, I wouldn't," agreed Sir Terrence. "Unhappily, I have principles, too. But I cannot help feeling there must be some way our principles can coexist. Tell me, Emily, if I were to renounce my title and give away all my money, how would that affect your position? Would you still refuse to marry me?"

"Now it is you who are being foolish," said Emily, avoiding this home question. "What I should do in such a contingency is entirely beside the point."

"I don't think it is," said Sir Terrence. With startling suddenness, he caught Emily round the waist. "Will you kiss me, Emily?"

"Yes," said Emily. The affirmative slipped out without even thinking. Sir Terrence kissed her, a slow, deliberate kiss that sent a trickle of fire coursing through Emily's veins.

"Will you let me make love to you?" he whispered. "Will you, Emily? As I did last night?"

"Here?" said Emily, opening her eyes. "You mean— here in the Italian garden?"

Sir Terrence laughed. "Here or another place. Will you, Emily?" He resumed kissing her, letting his lips stray from her mouth to her ear, where they lingered with devastating effect.

"I don't—I suppose—oh, Terrence!" Emily drew a shuddering breath. "How can I say no?"

"You said no quickly enough when I asked you to marry me," pointed out Sir Terrence between kisses.

"That was different," said Emily weakly.

As suddenly as he had begun, Sir Terrence ceased kissing her. He took a step back, regarding her with his arms folded over his chest.

"So you will not marry me? You will allow me to make love to you but nothing more?"

Emily regarded him with bewilderment. "No, nothing more. But isn't it enough, Terrence? It was enough last night—or so I thought."

"Yes, it was enough at the time," said Sir Terrence. He regarded her gravely. "But then I had to let you go. And that was almost worse than never having had you. I cannot do it, Emily. I want you to be mine always—to know you belong to me and I belong to you."

"But that's ridiculous," said Emily. She felt on the verge of tears and so had refuge to anger. "No one can really belong to anyone else. That is merely words—an idea invented by poets and novel writers."

Sir Terrence regarded her with an odd smile. "Well, but I *am* a novel writer, you know," he said. "As a member of that brotherhood, I suppose I am obliged to keep up the fiction." Turning, he started back toward the house.

"Where are you going?" demanded Emily.

Sir Terrence did not stop but addressed her over his shoulder. "To work on a novel, of course. I don't suppose you care to help me?"

"No," said Emily angrily. "No, I do not!"

Sir Terrence nodded with apparent unconcern and continued across the grounds toward the house. Emily, watching him, was moved to a most unladylike frustration. "Damn," she said. "Damn, damn, damn!"

Chapter 18

After Sir Terrence had left, Emily walked once or twice around the Italian garden. She was not observing any of its beauties, however. Her mind was in such turmoil that she was deaf and blind to everything outside herself. No unease assailed her as on the previous evening, even when she heard footsteps approaching from behind.

Supposing it to be Sir Terrence, she turned around eagerly. The visitor was not Sir Terrence, however. It was Ronald.

Emily's first reaction on seeing him was surprise rather than indignation. "What are you doing here?" she demanded. "This is private property, you know."

"I know," said Ronald. Planting himself aggressively in front of her, he stood looking down at her with a lowering brow. "I know perfectly well it is private property. I know also to whom it belongs. And I tell you plainly I don't give a damn about him or his property."

"I see," said Emily. Scorn was taking the place of surprise

now, and both her face and voice were heavy with it as she added, "You are entitled to care or not as you choose, I suppose. But I do not see that I am under any compulsion to stay and listen to you. Kindly excuse me. I am expected back at the house."

She attempted to go around Ronald, but he stepped sideways, blocking her way as before. "Don't go yet, Emily. I came here to talk to you, and I'm not leaving until I do."

Emily was furious at being made to accept such an ultimatum. It appeared that she had no choice, however. A quick glance around showed there was no one else in view, and Ronald's greater size and strength made it impossible to physically remove him from her path without assistance. "Then do it quickly and get it over with," she said through her teeth. "But you would do better to save your breath, Mr. Bartholomew. I am not likely to hear favorably anything you might say after the way you have behaved."

"After the way *I* have behaved?" Ronald's voice was thunderstruck. "You're a fine one to be talking about that! It was you who hit me a whacking great blow on the head, then went off and left me for dead!"

"*After* you had tried to rape me," said Emily, still through her teeth. "Kindly do not forget that point, Mr. Bartholomew. I think you will find it key to the whole situation."

Instead of abashing Ronald in any way, this speech only seemed to amuse him. He laughed. "Well, then, I'll forgive you if you forgive me," he said. "It sounds as though we're quits, doesn't it? I'm sure I couldn't be blamed for trying."

Emily regarded him with incredulity, then turned on her heel and started toward the house. Ronald caught her easily, however, and swung her around to face him. "Help!" shouted Emily at the top of her lungs. "Help!"

"Be quiet," said Ronald furiously. "Damn it, I'm not going to hurt you. I just want to talk to you."

For answer, Emily shouted the louder. Ronald swore and

clapped a hand over her mouth. "By God, I'm tempted to wring your neck despite your being such a tempting piece," he said. "There's not a reason in the world we can't be friends. I've already apologized for the way I behaved before, and I don't know what more you want."

The hand over her mouth kept Emily from answering, but her eyes were eloquent. Ronald seemed to feel her disgust, for his own eyes grew hard. Then suddenly they softened. "Damn it, Emily, it doesn't have to be like this," he said. "I'm prepared to behave handsomely by you. You know I'm crazy about you, even after all these weeks. Did you think I'd forgotten you? I hadn't, not by a long chalk. When I saw you last night, looking so beautiful—damme, I never saw you looking as beautiful as you looked last night. And then you ran away before I could even talk to you."

Once more, Emily's eyes said unspeakable things. Ronald studied her with frustration. "I don't understand you. Anybody'd think you'd be flattered to have a man like me head over heels in love with you. Instead, you act as though I'd insulted you."

Emily received this remark in silence, perforce. "I'm going to take my hand away," Ronald told her. "But don't you go yelling anymore or I'll have to—"

"Help," shouted Emily the instant her mouth was free. Again Ronald swore and clapped his hand over her mouth.

"That's it," he said through his teeth. "I'm done trying to reason with you. You contrary, cross-spirited jade!"

As he spoke, he lifted Emily in his arms and set off across the garden. Since he was using one hand to keep her from shouting and the other to hold her against him, he had none free to restrain her arms and legs. Emily made the most of this. Her feet rained blows on his shins, while her hands and nails tore at his face, neck, and other unprotected parts of his body. She also bit one of his fingers, which he had unwarily allowed too close to her mouth. Ronald swore savagely but stumbled on.

Emily supposed he was carrying her to some place of privacy to ravish her. But instead he took a more or less straight course through the grounds, cutting through the woods that surrounded them until he reached the lane that formed the western boundary of the Honeywell House property.

A carriage was waiting in the lane, with a groom lounging lazily on the perch. He sprang to attention as soon as he saw Ronald. Then he noticed Ronald's burden, and his jaw dropped.

"Mr. Bartholomew!" he gasped. "Whatever are you— why, it's Miss Pearce!" He looked with blank astonishment from Emily to Ronald. "What are you doing with Miss Pearce?"

"Shut up, you fool," snapped Ronald. "Help me get her into the carriage."

"But what are you doing?" repeated the man. "You can't mean to say you—a young lady like that! It wouldn't be right, sir."

Ronald merely ordered the groom a second time to shut up and help get Emily into the carriage. "And if you've a handkerchief, give it to me," he told the man. "She's already bitten me twice."

The groom surrendered his handkerchief unwillingly. "I don't like it, sir," he told Ronald. "I tell you I don't like it. I'd never have been party to such a thing if I'd known that was what you'd come here for."

"Well, you're a party to it now, so you'd better shut up and help me," growled Ronald, who was attempting to tie the handkerchief around Emily's mouth while at the same time restraining her hands and feet. "Come here and hold her feet for me, will you? And mind she doesn't kick you."

The groom obeyed this order, but it was evident he was

still very unwilling. He threw frequent looks of pitying horror at Emily and continued to expostulate with Ronald all the while Ronald was binding Emily's hands and feet with strips torn from his neckcloth. "I tell you, I don't like it, sir. You can't go abducting young ladies like this, not without there being the very devil to pay."

"There's already the devil to pay," said Ronald angrily as he deposited Emily's trussed form inside the carriage. "Don't you see, I couldn't turn her loose now without her lodging a complaint against me? So you might as well stop croaking and help me get her away from here."

The groom only repeated, "You didn't ought to have done it, sir. I don't doubt you'll be sorry you ever thought of this business before you're done."

"Shut up," said Ronald, and slammed the carriage door so hard that the window shattered. "Drive back to Wybolt now and don't spare the horses. She yelled bloody murder when I first grabbed her. For all we know, that Irishman or some of his servants might have heard her. The last thing we need is for him to pick up our trail this early on. Once we're well away from here, there'll be nothing to connect us with her disappearance, and we can go a little easier."

The thought of being connected with Emily's disappearance evidently fired the groom with fear. He certainly did not spare the horses on the drive back to Wybolt. Emily, lying bound and gagged on the floor of the carriage, found it a most uncomfortable ride. Every bump sent her jouncing into the air, and her hands and feet were bound so tightly that there was little she could do to cushion her fall.

Ronald, seated in a corner of the carriage, hung on to the strap, cursing at every bounce and sway. Emily noticed that he avoided looking at her. She supposed he must be feeling guilty or regretful about having abducted her. But she could not obtain much comfort from this circumstance. His words to the groom seemed to show he was committed to the enterprise, and she knew from previous experience that she could expect small mercy at his hands.

After what seemed a very long time, the carriage finally slowed and came to a stop. Looking out the window, Emily could see the familiar peaked roof of Miss Morris's house. Ronald jumped up as soon as the carriage slowed and had the door open before it was fully stopped. "Put the carriage in the stable," he told the groom. "Right away, before anyone comes along and sees it."

"Not with *her* in it, sir?" said the groom, sounding shocked.

"Yes, with her in it! Leave her in the carriage for now and put the carriage in the stable. I'll come get her as soon as I've got rid of the servants."

"But young Harry's due back from Langton Abbots at any time now, sir. And if he looks in the carriage and sees her—"

"Then for God's sake don't let him look in the carriage. Send him away on another errand when he comes or tell him he can have the rest of the day off. I'll have to take her through the stable yard when I bring her into the house, and I don't want anyone hanging about."

The groom said gloomily that it was his funeral, and Emily, lying on the floor of the carriage, heard Ronald's footsteps retreating as he went into the house. Soon after this, the carriage began to move again. Emily surmised that the groom was following Ronald's instructions about putting it in the carriage house, and when the trees and sky outside the windows were replaced by a dim, horsy-smelling darkness, she knew this was the case.

Lying inside the gloom of the carriage house, Emily had time to think of a great many things. First and foremost, she thought of Ronald and how, if she had only used a little more force escaping from him the last time, she would not be lying here now. She spent some time inspecting her bonds and trying to loosen them, but this proved to be as futile as her previous exercise. Finally, having exhausted herself trying to think of ways and means of escape when she did not yet know exactly what her prison would consist of, she began to think of Sir Terrence. Did he know she had left Honeywell House, and not of her own volition?

He might know, Emily told herself hopefully. *I yelled loudly enough that somebody ought to have heard. Of course, they might not know who was yelling and why.* This was a depressing thought, but Emily cheered again when she reflected that she was sure to be missed when she did not appear at dinner. But would that be soon enough? And would her absence be enough to stimulate Sir Terrence into making inquiries if by some chance her calls for help had not been heard? Emily thought with chagrin of her interview with Sir Terrence that afternoon and of the way it had ended. It was possible that if she were missing at dinner, he would merely think she was staying away owing to pique or wounded pride or some other trivial cause.

"Please let him be worried about me," she prayed. "Let him look for me—and oh, let him find me. And let him find me soon," she added with a shiver. It seemed to her that if Sir Terrence did not come soon, it might be better if he did not come at all.

The thought tormented her as she lay in the gloom for what seemed several hours, shifting from time to time in an effort to ease the pressure on her bound wrists and ankles. At last, she heard a door creak and footsteps approaching the carriage. With all her heart she hoped it would be Sir Terrence or a neighbor or young Harry the errand boy—anyone but Ronald.

But it was Ronald. His face was grim as he opened the door, picked Emily up, and threw her over his shoulder.

Emily struggled fiercely and even managed to get in a few more kicks despite her bound ankles. But it was of no use. Ronald did not even bother to swear at her as he hauled her across the stable yard and into the house. Having carried her into his bedchamber, he laid her down upon the bed and pulled off the handkerchief that bound her mouth.

"There you go," he told her. "But don't bother shouting. I told all the servants they could have the rest of the day off. There's no one in the house but you and me."

Emily was sure this was true. She had seen no sign of any servants as Ronald had carried her up the stairs, and the house was pervaded with silence. So she contented herself with saying, once the gag was removed from her mouth, "Do you call yourself a man?"

Ronald's jaw tightened. "I call myself a man who's been put to a devil of a lot of trouble," he said. "Why couldn't you be reasonable? I didn't want to do it this way, but you left me no choice."

"It seems to me that I am the one left with no choice," said Emily bitterly.

"You did have a choice," Ronald shot back angrily. "I told you dozens of times while you were living here that I'd be glad to set you up in a house of your own, with carte blanche as to clothes or furnishings. And what do you do? You hit me over the head and run off to live with a scrawny, smooth-talking Irishman! An *Irishman!*" Ronald's voice was vibrant with scorn. "Don't you see what an insult that was? It's as though you were telling everyone you preferred him to me!"

"I do prefer him to you," said Emily. "That Irishman, as you call him, is as much your superior as you would pretend you are his. But you are mistaken in saying I ran off with him. Sir Terrence was good enough to employ me when I was looking for a position—"

"Yes, and it's obvious what position he gave you!" said
Ronald, his voice even more scornful than before. "I saw
him dancing with you last night. I saw the way he looked
at you. And I saw him kissing you in the garden this afternoon. I was following behind you when you left the house
and saw the whole thing." He looked down at Emily with
compressed lips. "You *let* him kiss you. You never let me
kiss you, but you were happy to let him. Well, this time
you're going to let me, too."

Shrugging out of his jacket, Ronald began to unbutton
his shirt. Emily wrenched desperately at her bonds, but
they held as firmly as ever. "Don't bother to struggle," he
told her. "You'd better just make up your mind to it and
have done. I'm not about to be cut out by any Irishman."
Matter-of-factly, he added, "You're mine, Emily. I saw you
first, and I'm going to keep you."

"I'm not yours. I will never be yours," said Emily. She
was trembling with fear and disgust at the prospect of what
lay ahead, but at the same time she was conscious of a
fierce satisfaction. Whatever Ronald might take from her,
he could never take what she had already given to Sir
Terrence. "I will *never* be yours," she repeated fiercely.
"Because like it or not, Mr. Bartholomew, I already belong
to someone. I belong to Sir Terrence. And nothing you
do or say can ever change that."

Ronald parted his lips to reply, but at that moment there
came a fusillade of knocking on the front door. He paused
for an instant with a look of alarm on his face. Then his
expression relaxed.

"Probably just a trademan," he told Emily. "Or one of
the servants might have come back early. Whoever it is,
he can't get in. I locked the door."

But in spite of these self-assurances, he remained a
moment listening as the volley of knocking was repeated.
Then there was silence for a long time.

"Whoever the party is, looks as though he's given up for now," Ronald was just saying when there came another, sharper rap from below. The rap was twice repeated and was followed the third time by the unmistakable sound of breaking glass.

Ronald swore loudly. "Damn it," he said, "damn it!" He started for the door, trying to rebutton his clothes as he went and making a poor job of it in his haste. He seemed to have forgotten all about Emily. Emily drew in a deep breath, then screamed for all she was worth.

"Help!" she screamed. "Help! Help!"

Almost immediately footsteps came pounding up the stairs. Ronald, outside on the landing, swore again, then spoke in a louder tone. "Here, you fellow, what d'ye mean by breaking into my house? I'll have the law against you, I will!"

There was no verbal reply to this challenge. Emily could hear various confused noises, however, some of which sounded irresistibly like fists impacting on flesh. An instant later, Ronald reentered the room, back first and in an obvious state of retreat. Blood was streaming from his nose, and his shirt was now torn as well as unbuttoned. He was closely followed by Sir Terrence, who was obviously in a state of murderous rage.

There is something about murderous rage that is very difficult for the average human to resist. Ronald was certainly making no effort to resist it. He retreated to the far corner of the room and stood there cringing, dabbing now and then at the blood that was flowing from his nose. "I didn't hurt her," he gabbled. "I haven't laid a finger on her, I swear to God."

"That had better be true," said Sir Terrence, speaking with icy clarity. "Because if I find you have injured her in the slightest degree, I'm going to kill you. Emily!" He had just caught sight of Emily lying on the bed. He hurried to

her side and bent over her anxiously. "Emily," he said
again, and there was a vibrant note in his voice that sent
a thrill chasing down Emily's spine. "Emily, has he hurt
you?"

"No," said Emily. The sight of Sir Terrence's rage had
had an effect on her, too. Her voice was soft and diffident
as she added, "He has done me no harm as yet except for
tying me up."

"Did he, by God!" said Sir Terrence, turning a fiery
look upon Ronald. He then bent to loosen Emily's bonds.
Ronald took advantage of his temporary absorption to slip
quietly out of the room.

"Don't think I can't find you again when I want you,"
Sir Terrence said, raising his voice but not bothering to
look around. "The only reason I am letting you go now
is because I must tend first to Miss Pearce. I shall settle
with you later, once I know the full score of your villainy."

For answer, there was only a sound of rapidly retreating
footsteps. Sir Terrence cocked his head, listening, then
bent over Emily again. "Emily," he said. "You don't know
how relieved I am to have found you. Do you think you
can walk out to the carriage, or shall I carry you? I must
get you home as soon as possible. I wouldn't put it past
that fellow to try some other trick once he's had time to
regroup his forces."

"I can walk, I think," said Emily, gingerly testing her
ankles. "But I don't think you need to worry about Ronald
trying any more tricks, Terrence." She herself had been
powerfully impressed by Sir Terrence's sincerity when he
had threatened to kill Ronald. It seemed probable that
Ronald, against whom the threat had actually been
directed, would be equally impressed and very reluctant
to risk any possibility of Sir Terrence's fulfilling it.

During the drive home, Emily was very quiet. Once more
she found herself shy in Sir Terrence's company, but not

for the same reasons as before. Then she had been shy
because he was her lover and her social superior and she
felt uncomfortable trying to reconcile the two roles. Now
he appeared to her in the light of an avenging angel. She
was so overwhelmed with love and gratitude, coupled with a
sense of overpowering inferiority, that she felt like weeping
whenever she looked at him.

Finally, in a timid voice, she ventured to ask how he had
known where to find her. Sir Terrence looked at her in
amazement.

"I heard you calling for help, of course. I came as quickly
as I could, but when I arrived, Ronald had already got you
in the carriage and was just driving off. If you had looked
out the carriage window, you would have seen me back in
the roadway shouting and shaking my fist after him."

"I couldn't look out the window," said Emily with a
shiver. "I was lying on the floor of the carriage trussed
like a Christmas goose."

Sir Terrence's eyes darkened. "Damn him," he said in
a low voice. "I owe him something for that as well as for
the effrontery of having abducted you from my property.
And for general principles as well."

Emily shook her head. "No doubt he deserves punishment, Terrence," she said. "But unfortunately the situation is much as it was before. There's no good way to
punish Ronald without the punishment rebounding on
me."

Sir Terrence still looked very dark, and Emily hurried
on in an effort to change the subject. "So you saw him
drive off with me? I wish I had known it at the time. As it
was, I was afraid you wouldn't notice I was gone until
dinner was served and I came up missing at table."

"No, I knew where you had gone. At least I hoped I
knew. I was hoping Ronald would take you back to his
house, but I didn't know for certain. If he had taken you

somewhere else—'' Sir Terrence stopped, shaking his head as though trying to rid his brain of an unpleasant picture. "But I guessed right, thanks be to heaven. Emily, I would have died if he had harmed you in any way."

Emily found she could not speak, so she nodded instead. Sir Terrence gathered the reins into one hand and drew Emily closer to him with the other. "Emily," he whispered. "Emily."

Emily shut her eyes. To ride in an open carriage with a gentleman's arm around her was an improper proceeding, she knew. If any of the neighbors saw her, they would be scandalized, and justly so. But she felt so safe and comfortable that she could not bring herself to protest. She rode with Sir Terrence's arm around her all the way back to Honeywell House.

By great good fortune, the two of them encountered none of their neighbors during the drive, so there was no one to be scandalized by their behavior. Sir Terrence removed his arm just before they turned into the gates of Honeywell House. It was as well that he did, for when they reached the court before the house a strange carriage was standing there. A coachman in a splendid livery of scarlet and gold was seated on the box, while several gargantuan footmen, similarly attired, were standing beside the carriage. They stared incuriously at Sir Terrence and Emily as Sir Terrence maneuvered the curricle around the carriage.

"Now who can this be?" Sir Terrence wondered aloud. "It's a deuce of a time for visitors to be calling!"

Emily said nothing. But as she looked back at the carriage with its magnificent appointments, she felt a strange certainty that it portended nothing good.

Chapter 19

Wishing to avoid the unknown visitors until he and Emily had had a chance to make themselves more respectable, Sir Terrence did not stop the curricle in the court before the house but took it around to the side entrance. "I wonder who is calling on us," he said again as he helped Emily down from the curricle. "Whoever it is, he or she has a devilish poor sense of timing. I'm hardly in a fit state to receive social calls."

"Nor I," said Emily, looking down at herself. She had lost her hat during her initial struggle with Ronald, and her hair was falling over her shoulders. There were red marks on her wrists where the bonds had chafed them, and her dress was rumpled and soiled. "I don't think I'm in a state to receive visitors at all," she told Sir Terrence as they entered the house together. "If you would kindly make my excuses to—"

"Terrence!" came a rapturous voice.

Both Emily and Sir Terrence spun around. A lady was

standing there, regarding them from the doorway of the drawing room.

She was a very small lady, but nobody could have called her too small. From the top of her bonneted head to the soles of her dainty slippers, she was as perfectly proportioned and exquisitely turned out as a French doll. Curls as golden as new-minted guineas peeped beneath the lace flounce of her bonnet. Her eyes were as blue as a summer sky, her cheeks were flushed with hectic pink, and her cupid's bow mouth was as red as a cherry.

Looking at her made Emily feel more conscious than ever of her own bedraggled appearance. She put a hand to her hair, then dropped it again. The lady threw her a sharp look, but the chief of her attention was centered on Sir Terrence. She came toward him, holding out her small gloved hands with wistful appeal.

"Terrence!" she said again. "Terrence!"

Her voice was low and sweet and held the faintest traces of an Irish brogue. Emily was suddenly seized by a chill certainty. It did not need Sir Terrence's stupefied "Moira!" to complete the identification.

This, then, was Lady Moira. This was the lady who had won Sir Terrence's heart, only to break it when she had married another man. Looking at her, Emily realized she had done Sir Terrence an injustice. In reading his novel, she had supposed the fulsome descriptions of his heroine's beauty had been merely a lover's exaggerations. But now that she had seen Lady Moira in the flesh, she decided that Sir Terrence's praises had been inadequate rather than excessive. There was nothing shy or subtle about Lady Moira's beauty. It was a flaunting, flaring thing that forced itself on the eye like a lurid sunset or a bed of red poppies. Even the black crepe that draped her from head to foot did nothing to diminish it.

Black crepe? wondered Emily. *Why is she in mourning?* The answer came to her with the same chill certainty that had accompanied her previous deduction. Even before the words came spilling from Lady Moira's mouth, Emily knew what she was going to say.

"Terrence, you will think me very brazen, but indeed I had to come. Duncannon is—is *dead*, Terrence! Heart failure, they said it was—he died in his sleep just last Friday. And so I am free again, Terrence—free! You must forgive me for all that happened before. It was all a mistake—a dreadful mistake—I knew it as soon as I had done it. But now we have a second chance. We will start anew, and it will be as it was meant to be." Weeping tempestuously, she threw herself into Sir Terrence's arms.

Judging from the astounded look on Sir Terrence's face, he had not expected this turn of events. It would have been an understatement to say that Emily, too, had not expected it. Yet even in the midst of her shock and disgust, she felt sorry for Sir Terrence. She set about effacing herself as quickly and quietly as possible.

"Of course, I am very sorry to hear of your loss, Moira," Sir Terrence was saying as Emily drifted away. "But you shouldn't have come here. People will think it very odd—"

The rest of his words were lost as Emily turned a corner of the hallway. She wondered how Sir Terrence would have completed the sentence. "People will think it very odd that you came to me, your former fiancé, instead of seeking refuge with your family in your time of trouble" was the first and most obvious possibility. But it might equally well have been "People will think it very odd that you did not wait a decent interval before coming to me," or even, "People will think it very odd, but I am glad you came to me all the same."

Having thought these possibilities over, Emily decided she was glad that Lady Moira had arrived when she did. Her arrival had coincided with a crisis in Emily's relationship with Sir Terrence. Jealous and even angry as she might feel toward her, she was forced to admit that Lady Moira's appearance had simplified her decision. She had sliced through the tangled perplexities of Emily's affairs like a sword through a Gordian knot. One look at Lady Moira had assured Emily that she would get what she wanted despite her former atrocious conduct and her present astounding disregard of the conventions. She was so obviously the kind of woman who got everything she wanted.

There was nothing left for Emily to do now but pick up the pieces. She set herself to do just that. She blessed heaven that she still had her pride, no matter what else Lady Moira might have taken from her. Pride had been her mainstay for the past three years, and she trusted it might still serve her in this extremity.

So she went to her bedchamber, rang for bath and bathwater, and proceeded to scrub away as far as possible the evidences of her recent ordeal. Once bathed and her hair freshly arranged, she dressed herself in a long-sleeved blue muslin dress that hid the marks on her wrists and tapped on the door of Aunt Katie's sitting room.

Aunt Katie admitted her at once, a grim look on her cameo face. "I never thought I'd see the day," she said as she ushered Emily into the room. "You'll have heard who's visiting us, I doubt not?"

"Yes, I have heard," said Emily. She hesitated a moment, then went on resolutely. "In fact, I have seen her—seen Lady Moira, I mean. I was—I was out driving with Sir Terrence, and when we came in, she was there in the hall."

Aunt Katie shook her head. "Poor boy! It must have been the devil of a shock to come home and find her here. For sheer, unadulterated brass, I've yet to meet her match. Why, she didn't even wait for her husband to be cold in his grave before she comes here, flinging herself at Terry!

She thinks to force his hand, you see—and the devil of it is that she might well do it.''

Emily merely nodded. Aunt Katie went on fulminating against Lady Moira, describing what she herself would do if the situation were solely hers to handle. Emily gained some small satisfaction in hearing her rival denounced, but it was a hollow satisfaction. In her heart she felt she would rather Lady Moira was as good as she was beautiful if Sir Terrence were truly to marry her. It made her sick to think he could be taken in by a scheming adventuress. Not just any adventuress, either, but one who had already once betrayed him.

It did occur to Emily, as she reflected on these matters, that perhaps she was taking an unnecessarily dim view of the situation. In the time she had known him, Sir Terrence had seemed to throw off his infatuation and come to recognize Lady Moira's true character. He had revised his book to reflect this discovery and spoken of his former gullibility with self-deprecating humor. Most importantly, he had gone so far as to imply that the heart Lady Moira had rejected was now in Emily's keeping.

But much as Emily longed to believe this was true, there were several things that kept her from putting much faith in it. One was Lady Moira's staggering beauty. Emily had been thinking a little better of her own looks lately, but now all her old sense of inferiority came flooding back. Even if she were not quite the antidote Miss Morris had implied, she knew she was still not a beauty of the caliber of Lady Moira. The idea that Sir Terrence could really prefer her to such an Incomparable was laughable. Even if he were to maintain against all reason that he did prefer her, she must have always felt he was comparing her unfavorably with his former lover.

Nor were looks the only way in which Emily felt inferior. There was also the matter of social position. When Sir

Terrence had first become engaged to Lady Moira, everyone in his home county had thought it a suitable match.
What would they think if he were to marry Emily? Emily
smiled bitterly. They would think exactly what Isabel had
thought. They would think that she had set her cap at him
and been clever enough to win him.

Even if Sir Terrence was right in saying that her scruples
on this score were false pride, Emily did not feel inclined
to abandon them on that account. Indeed, after meeting
Lady Moira, she was more than ever resolved to be true
to her convictions. Whether her pride was false or not, it
had been her sole mainstay for many years. She made up
her mind now that she would cling to it until the bitter
end.

Such were Emily's conscious arguments. But the thing
that most convinced her that her love for Sir Terrence was
doomed—what made her relinquish him to Lady Moira
without even considering the choices—was not a reason
at all but her own sense of fatalism. Ever since her parents'
deaths, the trend of her existence had been steadily down-
ward. She had come to believe it was fated that she should
be unhappy all her life. In a strange way, the happiness
she had known since coming to Honeywell House had
only confirmed her in this belief. It had seemed a kind of
thwarting of fate, a temporary state that would have to be
paid for in time with something more than mere unhappi-
ness. It would, in fact, have to be paid for with misery on
a grand scale. And since Emily could imagine no greater
misery than losing Sir Terrence to Lady Moira, she
promptly assumed the worst would happen and gave up
her own cause as hopeless.

In her mood of hopelessness, she was oblivious to smaller
miseries. When the dinner bell rang, she never even
thought of excusing herself from the table, though her
experiences that afternoon would have certainly entitled

her to do so even leaving Lady Moira out of the equation. Emily never thought of this, however. She merely rose dully and accompanied Aunt Katie downstairs to the drawing room.

Lady Moira was there, changed from her traveling clothes into a splendid evening toilette that proclaimed its extreme fashionableness in spite of being black. She was seated on a loveseat, thumbing disdainfully through an old copy of *La Belle Assemblée*. When she saw the other ladies, however, she bounced up at once and came over to seize Aunt Katie by the hand, her cherry lips parted in a doll-like smile.

"My dear Miss O'Reilly!" she exclaimed. "Or may I call you Aunt Katie? You can't think how happy I am to see you again."

Aunt Katie, smiling frigidly, said, "You needn't bother with your Aunt Katies. Miss O'Reilly will do well enough between such as you and me." Nodding toward Emily, she asked, "Are you acquainted with Miss Pearce, Lady Moira?"

"No," said Lady Moira, looking also at Emily. "Is that her name? I saw her with Terrence earlier, but he didn't bother to introduce her to me."

She made the slight sound a deliberate one. Aunt Katie, however, merely gave a short laugh. "No," she said, "no, I'll wager Terry had other things on his mind when he saw you. Then, too, he's a regard for Miss Pearce, and that would make him careful about who he introduced her to."

This riposte made Lady Moira flush deeply. She gave Aunt Katie a furious look but apparently judged it better not to exchange any more words with her. Instead, she merely said, "Miss Pearce, is it? I am pleased to meet you, Miss Pearce."

"Lady Moira," said Emily in a colorless voice, and dropped

a slight curtsy. She then went over and sat in a corner until
Sir Terrence arrived in the drawing room.

It was with extreme reluctance that Sir Terrence came
down to the drawing room that evening. He had been
tempted not to come down to dinner at all, but the thought
of what Lady Moira might say to Emily in his absence had
driven him to do his duty. No end of misunderstandings
might result from such an interview, and on the whole he
thought it would be better to take part in the scene, however painful it might be, rather than avoid it. Still, he
shrank from seeing Lady Moira again, especially in Emily's
company. There was something about seeing her side by
side with Emily that had made Moira appear very crude
and obvious. So crude and obvious had she appeared, in
fact, that he wondered now how he had ever thought
himself in love with her.

It would have been bad enough merely to be reminded
of his past folly. But what Sir Terrence feared now was that
his folly, not being content to blight the past, would go
on to poison the present and future. Indeed, he had not
been in the drawing room two minutes before he began
to wonder whether the poison might not already be at
work. Emily had looked up as he came in but then had
looked away immediately and had refused to look up again,
though he made numerous attempts to catch her eye.
Moira, on the other hand, came fluttering over to him as
soon as he appeared and proceeded to make a truly revolt-
ing display of herself. She stroked his arm and said he
must take her in to dinner; cooed and coquetted; and
otherwise behaved in a manner totally at odds with her
widow's weeds.

Sir Terrence stood it because it was either that or tell
her to go to hell, and his conscience revolted against telling

any woman that, even one who deserved it as richly as Moira. At the same time, however, he resolved to tell her at the earliest opportunity that she was wasting her time. He had already tried to tell her so that afternoon; it had been almost the first words out of his mouth as soon as he had understood what she had come for. But she had brushed his words aside, saying they would have a nice long talk that evening and get everything settled between them.

Sir Terrence had been willing to wait until evening to make his point. He knew Moira well enough to know that it would take a lot of convincing to make her believe he no longer cared for her and that she would probably cause a scene once she *was* convinced. He preferred to have such a scene take place in private rather than a public location like the hall, with servants passing by and Emily and his aunt perhaps within earshot. But though he had been glad at the time to postpone his interview with Moira, now he began to wonder whether it would not have been better to get it over with and get her out of the house, even at the cost of a public scene. With every passing minute she seemed to reveal more and more of the ugliness of her character, showing herself to be at heart an ignorant, greedy, and unprincipled woman.

And Emily was witnessing the whole thing. She was seeing firsthand the woman to whom Sir Terrence had previously given his heart. It seemed to him a certainty that she must think less of him after such a spectacle. Quite possibly she would reconsider the value of a heart that could be so indiscriminately bestowed. And so, when Emily sat quietly in the corner and refused to meet his eye, he supposed her actions motivated by disgust and not by despair. He was furious at Moira for injuring him in Emily's eyes, but he trusted that once she was gone, he would be able to repair the damage. What would happen if the damage proved irreparable, he did not like to think.

Dinner was announced, and the party went into the dining room. They were a silent party apart from Lady Moira. She, however, made enough noise for all of them. She laughed and chattered during the meal, reminding Sir Terrence and Aunt Katie of other meals she had eaten in their company. To Emily she said nothing, and Emily said nothing to her. Emily did not even look at Moira, as far as Sir Terrence could tell. But the reverse was certainly not true. He several times caught Moira studying Emily with a spiteful expression. Inwardly, he trembled at the prospect of how her spite might express itself. As soon as the dessert had been served, he rose to his feet.

"I am going to the library," he said. "You had better come with me, Moira. As you pointed out earlier, we need to talk."

Lady Moira rose to her feet. "Certainly, Terrence," she said. "Do please excuse me, Miss O'Reilly, Miss Pearce. I doubt I shall be joining you in the drawing room this evening."

"Hussy," said Aunt Katie distinctly as Lady Moira swept out of the room on Sir Terrence's arm. "Did you ever see such a hussy, Miss Pearce? It's amazing to me that even Moira could behave so brazenly. Before she married Duncannon, she made at least a show of respecting the conventions. But now she acts as though she's above 'em all. Below them all would be more like it, I daresay. Shall we go to the drawing room?"

Emily shook her head. "No, I beg you will excuse me, Aunt Katie. I am not feeling well, and I believe I shall retire early tonight."

Aunt Katie did not express any surprise at this. She merely observed that anybody might feel unwell after such a brazen display as Lady Moira's. She also made Emily promise to let her know if she could do anything for her. Emily gave this promise willingly, for she was privately assured that she would never have any cause to fulfill it. She had been revolving a plan in her mind ever since she had sat down to dinner that evening, and as soon as she reached her bedchamber, she set about putting it into action.

She removed her muslin dinner dress and slippers, replacing them with the plum-colored poplin and half boots she had worn when she first arrived at Honeywell House. Having folded her dinner dress, she then took her other dresses one by one from her wardrobe, folded them, too, and packed them away in her trunk.

Next she set about gathering up her books, papers, and other personal possessions. Most of these went in her trunk, too. When everything was stowed in its proper place, she locked the trunk, corded it, and left it sitting prominently in the center of her room with a note on top saying, "To be left until called for." There was no way she could take her heavy baggage with her at present, but she trusted Sir Terrence would be generous enough to send it on once she had settled on a place to go. She then packed her toiletries and a change of linen in her dressing case, put on her pelisse, hat, and gloves, and stole noiselessly downstairs. As she passed the library door, she could hear Lady Moira saying something to Sir Terrence. There was an emotional throb in her voice that made Emily hasten her steps to avoid the temptation of listening in.

She went quickly down the stairs and out the side door of the house. The sun had set only a short time before, and twilight was falling as Emily made her way through the gardens surrounding the house. It was nearly dark when she reached the woods beyond, but she went on steadily until she reached the clearing where the well stood. It was her intention to continue into the village that night, where she hoped to arrive in time to catch the stagecoach that left each evening from the village inn. She had no time to spare if she wished to catch it, but she paused a moment at the entrance to the well pavilion and stood looking at the place where she had first encountered Sir Terrence.

"It would have been better if I had never met him," she said aloud.

Her words rang out loudly in the quiet evening air. In spite of her heavy heart, Emily could not help smiling at the sound of them.

I sound a melodramatic fool, she reflected. *Looking at the matter rationally, I am sure I am very much better off for having met him. If he hadn't helped me as he did, I would probably have starved to death, and at the very least I would have endured weeks of anxiety about having injured Ronald. And I would have lost all my money and clothes and other belongings because I would have been too frightened to inquire about them.*

By contrast, I am in a very good position right now. I have a fair bit of money saved, enough to take me someplace where I can make a new start in life. And I have all my clothes and other possessions, because I am sure Terrence will send my trunk on whenever I ask him to. I expect he would even give me a reference if I asked for one, but I would rather get by without if I can. There's only so much I am comfortable asking of him after leaving him like this.

The thought of her unceremonious leave-taking made Emily feel a little guilty. She had originally meant to go away without leaving any word at all, but then it had occurred to her that such an action might be subject to misunderstanding. Sir Terrence might think that Ronald had abducted her again, and the complications that might arise from such a mistake made Emily shudder to consider. It would be better by far simply to write him that she had gone without specifying any reason for her going. In addition, writing him a note would give her an opportunity to express her thanks for his kindness and hospitality and that of Aunt Katie.

So Emily had written her note, but the results had not satisfied her. She was forced to be vague when it came to describing her reasons for leaving Honeywell House. All the while she was writing, she had a strong feeling that Sir Terrence would not be taken in by her polite excuses. But she counted on his preoccupation with Lady Moira to keep him from objecting too violently to her actions. As it was, there was definitely one woman too many at Honeywell House, and if one of them had to go, she felt she was the natural choice.

She closed her note by wishing him and his aunt every happiness in the future. She had hesitated a long time over this closing, feeling that she ought to say something about Lady Moira, but in the end she let it stand as it was. She might be resolute enough to step aside and let Sir Terrence take up with Lady Moira again, but she simply could not put pen to paper in order to congratulate him about it. Besides, she reasoned, to do so might seem like a reproach of sorts. It might even seem like a sneer. There had been a time when he had spoken of his courtship of Lady Moira as an act of folly. If he chose to indulge in the same folly a second time, it was not for her to reproach him.

"And I don't reproach him," Emily whispered. "It's not as though there was ever any formal understanding between us. And yet—and yet, even if there had been and he had broken it, I would still want him. Fool that I am." For a long time she stood looking at the well until it blurred suddenly in a rush of tears. "Fool," she said again in a choked voice. Turning away, she picked up her dressing case and set off once more in the direction of the village.

Chapter 20

Emily had not gone halfway to the village before she realized she had tarried too long at the well. By the time she reached the village, she was certain of it. She half-walked, half-ran to the Blue Boar, the village's sole inn and coaching house, but when she breathlessly demanded of the landlord whether the London stagecoach had left yet, she was hardly surprised to be told, "Ah, you've come too late, miss. That coach left here a good ten minutes ago. There won't be another along until tomorrow night."

"I see," said Emily. "Is there another one leaving sooner? Not a London coach, that is, but one going somewhere else?" Although she had settled on London as a good place to begin her new life, she saw no reason why another city would not do as well. All places were much alike to her as long as they did not contain Sir Terrence—and Lady Moira.

The landlord rubbed his chin. "There's one leaving for

Plymouth that'll be along in a couple of hours," he said. "Were you wishful to take that, miss?"

Emily considered. Plymouth was rather a small town for her purposes and rather closer to Langton Abbots than she would have liked. "I don't know," she said uncertainly. The strain of that afternoon and evening was beginning to take its toll on her. Since her first plan had been thwarted, she found herself incapable of making another one. "Perhaps I should have a cup of tea and think about it. Is there a private parlor where I can sit?"

"Just down the hall, miss, first door on the left. I'll bring you your tea as soon as I'm done serving these gentlemen here."

Emily thanked him, picked up her bag once more, and walked slowly down the hall. Locating the first door on the left, she opened it confidently, supposing it to be the private parlor the landlord had spoken of. She was therefore much surprised to be greeted by a querulous feminine voice. "Is that my tea at last? Bring it in, girl, and close the door behind you. There's a dreadful draught coming in from the hall."

"I beg your pardon, ma'am," said Emily, hastily shutting the door. It swung open again an instant later, however, and a middle-aged lady thrust her head out, looking extremely vexed.

"I said to bring the tea in—oh!" She broke off when she saw Emily and looked as embarrassed as she had looked vexed before. "Why, you're not a maidservant, are you, my dear? I was thinking you were the girl with my tea."

"No, I'm afraid not, ma'am," said Emily, smiling. "I was merely trying to find a private parlor and opened the wrong door by mistake. Do forgive me for disturbing you."

"It's no matter," said the lady graciously. "But I wonder what can be keeping my tea? I am sure I have been waiting an hour for it, and the landlord said he would bring it to me directly."

"Do you wish me to inquire about it?" asked Emily. "I must go and speak to him, anyway, since I seem to have mistaken his directions."

"If you would be so kind, my dear. Tell him that Mrs. Engelbright is still waiting for her tea. And ask him also if there is any word whether my carriage will be ready soon. I declare, it's just been one thing after another this journey."

Mrs. Engelbright went back into her parlor, and Emily went down the hall to find the landlord. She found him trying to serve a party of young gentlemen who were noisily calling for beer.

"Mrs. Engelbright? Oh, yes, her tea's here, but the girls and I have been so busy we haven't had a chance to take it to her yet." He gestured toward a tray sitting on the counter. "As for her carriage, the wheelwright didn't think it would take much to set it to rights, but he hasn't sent word yet to say it's done, so more than likely it's not. And beg pardon, miss, it's the second door on the left I meant to direct you to, not the first. I've been so busy, I clean forgot I'd already put Mrs. Engelbright in the first parlor."

Emily thanked the landlord for this information and promised to pass the relevant facts on to Mrs. Engelbright. "And shall I take her her tea tray, too, as long as I am going by her room?" she suggested.

"That would be very Christian of you, miss. In the normal way I would have already done it myself, but we've had an unusual amount of traffic this evening."

As though to confirm the truth of these words, a gentleman on the other side of the room set up a cry for the porter. The landlord hurried away to serve him, and Emily picked up the tray and carried it down the hall to Mrs. Engelbright's room.

Mrs. Engelbright appeared to have been on the lookout

for her, for she opened the door before Emily could even knock. Her face, which wore a look of anxiety, brightened when she saw the tea.

"Why, if you haven't gone and brought me my tea yourself! I'm sure I'm much obliged to you, my dear."

"Not at all," Emily assured her. "I was coming to your room, anyway, and it was as easy to bring the tea with me as not." Setting the tray on the table, she added, "I'm afraid I wasn't able to obtain any definite word about your carriage, ma'am. However, the landlord seems to think the wheelwright will be done with it soon."

"Ah, that's good news! I only hope he is right. What with one thing and another, this has been the most awkward journey of my life. Everything has gone wrong from start to finish."

Emily said politely that she was sorry to hear it and began to move toward the door. "I had better be getting to my own room now," she said. "The landlord is supposed to be bringing me some tea, too. Though I suspect he won't be any quicker with mine than he was with yours!"

Mrs. Engelbright, who had already poured and drunk one cup of tea, now paused in the act of filling her cup a second time. "Oh! Oh, well then, you must stay and have some of mine," she told Emily. "Why don't you, my dear? I'd be glad of the company, I promise you. And I'm sure sharing my tea is the least I can do in return for the favor you've done me."

Emily said dubiously that she did not like to intrude. Mrs. Engelbright said firmly that she was not intruding, poured her a cup of tea, and insisted that she sit down to drink it. "It's as I said before, my dear—I'm glad of the company," she assured Emily as she settled herself into her own chair again and took a sip of tea. "I'm all alone on this journey, and not by choice. My maid was to have come with me, but she fell and broke her collarbone two days before I was to leave, so of course she couldn't come."

"What an unfortunate thing to happen," said Emily with sympathy.

"You may well say so, my dear. Of course, I know people do break bones; one hears of it happening quite often nowadays. But I still cannot conceive how Beatrice, of all people, came to break one. She is such a careful girl in the ordinary way. And to break her collarbone, too, of all things!" Mrs. Engelbright shook her head with an air of amazement. "It still seems most remarkable to me. When my own brother broke his collarbone years ago, I'm sure we all thought nothing of it, for he was hunting-mad, and broken collarbones are no more than what's to be expected when one is hunting-mad. But Beatrice! I am sure she has never hunted in her life."

Emily, greatly entertained by this speech, said there was no accounting for the vagaries of fate. Mrs. Engelbright agreed that there was not and spent several minutes describing the other accidents, major and minor, that had afflicted her in her life. "But I do believe this business of Beatrice is the unluckiest thing that ever happened to me. I didn't realize it at the outset, for I've never traveled alone before, so I never knew how much she did to make me comfortable."

"Traveling alone can certainly be uncomfortable," said Emily, repressing a sigh.

"That it can, my dear," said Mrs. Engelbright, patting her hand in a motherly way. "So you're traveling alone, too, are you? I wondered if you were but didn't like to ask. May I inquire where you are going?"

"Well, I meant to take the London coach," said Emily. "But since I seem to have missed it, I am thinking of going to Plymouth instead."

"Don't you know where you are going?" said Mrs. Engelbright, looking amazed.

Emily shook her head. "No, for it doesn't much matter where I go. Or rather, it does matter, but I'm not in a position to know where I would be best off."

"That sounds very mysterious," said Mrs. Engelbright, eyeing her with curiosity. Emily thought there was also a touch of suspicion in her glance. Thinking it best to allay her suspicions, Emily explained a little about who she was and why she was traveling alone with no special destination in mind. Mrs. Engelbright was sympathetic at once.

"So you are out of a position? I'm sure that must be very uncomfortable. But if you'll forgive me for asking, my dear, why did you not secure a new position before you left your old one? It seems to me *that* would have been the most sensible way to go about it."

She spoke with such an air of näiveté that Emily had to laugh in spite of herself. "No doubt that would have been the most sensible way, ma'am," she agreed. "But as it happened, my old position came to an end quite suddenly, and I did not like to linger in the household. They had company staying with them, for one thing, and—and it would have been very inconvenient."

"I see. I see." Mrs. Engelbright nodded her head, looking very worldly wise. "Well, it ought not to be difficult to find you a new place. You seem a clever sort of girl, and I don't doubt you perform your duties admirably. I wonder if I know anyone who is looking for a companion?" She frowned a moment, and it was apparent she was thinking deeply. Then suddenly her eyes opened wide. "Oh! Why, I do know someone. How foolish I am! It's me, of course— or do I mean it's I?"

"*You* are looking for a companion?" said Emily in amazement.

"Well, I wasn't, but now that I have met you, I see how

splendidly we would suit. Here I am all alone, as I said before, and gracious knows when Beatrice will be well enough to join me."

"You want me to take her place?" said Emily. Now that her first shock was past, her mind was beginning to work again. She was not a maidservant, of course, but she had frequently performed the tasks of one while working for Miss Morris. She had no doubt she could do so again if necessary. The question was whether it really was necessary.

"I would not expect you to take Beatrice's place, my dear," said Mrs. Engelbright, just as though she were reading Emily's thoughts. "I do realize you are a gentlewoman, and of course I would not expect you to fetch and carry like a servant. But you might keep me company and attend to all the little tasks, like changing my books and straightening my workbasket—all the things that I am too stupid to do myself. I'm not a clever woman at all, I'm afraid. Mr. Engelbright used to say I had more hair than wit, and I don't doubt he was right. Only look how badly I was managing today until you came to my rescue! Why, I couldn't even get myself a pot of tea."

"That wasn't because you were stupid, ma'am, but rather because the landlord was busy," said Emily. "But if you think I can be of service to you, I am willing to try."

It seemed to her that the position Mrs. Engelbright was offering her was too good to pass up. She could leave Langton Abbots in Mrs. Engelbright's carriage instead of paying for a stagecoach ticket; she would have meals and housing provided; and she could earn a little more money instead of spending what she already had. Probably Mrs. Engelbright would have no further use for her once Beatrice was well, but by that time she might have found another situation. Even if she had not, she would be in a better position than she was now, with a little more money in her purse and an ex-employer whom she did not mind asking for a reference.

Her only qualm was whether Mrs. Engelbright was as respectable as she seemed. Emily had heard of women who, representing themselves as ladies of fashion, would approach young women and offer them positions in their service—positions that later proved to be not respectable at all. But Emily was fairly certain Mrs. Engelbright was not a woman of this sort. Her dark blue dress and pelisse had probably cost her a fair sum, but the cost had been expended on material and fit rather than on showy trimmings. Her manners, too, were of this sort, devoid of vulgarity but likewise lacking any attempt at false refinement.

But the thing that most convinced Emily of Mrs. Engelbright's respectability was her helplessness. When the landlord arrived presently to inform her that her carriage was ready, Mrs. Engelbright jumped up in such haste that she knocked her teacup off the table. Uttering a stream of disjointed exclamations and apologies, she took out her purse to reimburse him for the damage and proceeded to spill the contents of her reticule on the parlor floor. By the time this had been remedied and the tea and teacup paid for, she was so much flustered that she would have gone out to the carriage leaving her hand valise behind her if Emily had not been there to remind her of it. Emily, following her out to the carriage with the valise in one hand and her own dressing case in the other, decided her new mistress was too scatterbrained to be a successful procuress or anything else.

Like its mistress, Mrs. Engelbright's carriage was large, solid, and respectable without any attempt at show or elegance. Emily tucked her own bag beside her on the forward seat, then settled herself for the journey. With a sense of melancholy amusement, she reflected that she did not even know where she was going. Mrs. Engelbright had said

nothing of her final destination, but it was enough for
Emily merely to be leaving Langton Abbots. Nevertheless,
she looked wistfully out the carriage window until the last
sight of the village was lost to view.

She had little time for wistful reflections once they were
on the road. Mrs. Engelbright proved to be an inveterate
talker and chattered away during the drive as though she
and Emily had known each other all their lives. By the
time they had been riding an hour, Emily was beginning
to feel that they had, or at any rate as though she knew
all there was worth knowing about her new mistress. She
knew, for instance, how Mrs. Engelbright had met the
late Mr. Engelbright and what had been that gentleman's
opinions on any number of subjects; she knew the exact
amount of the jointure he had left his widow and in what
funds it was invested. She also learned more about the
injured Beatrice and the circumstances of her accident.
Emily, not caring to dwell on her own thoughts, was glad
to listen to her mistress's artless chatter. It was not until
the carriage slowed to negotiate a turn that she noticed
where they were. "Why, this is Wybolt!" she exclaimed. "I
can see the church tower from here."

Mrs. Engelbright glanced out the window. "Yes, I see it,
too. We should reach Orchard House any minute now. I
hope Mrs. Hinchley remembered to air the linens in my
bedchamber."

Emily stared at her. "Orchard House!" she said. "You
don't mean to say you live at Orchard House, ma'am? That
big place just outside Wybolt?"

"To be sure I do, my dear, though only part of the year.
I usually pass winter and spring in London and summer
at a watering place. But I like to come back to Wybolt for
the autumn months. Why? Do you know Wybolt?"

"Yes, I know it," said Emily in a strangled voice. "I used
to live here."

"Did you indeed, my dear! And when was that?"

"Not so very long ago. Before I got the situation at Honeywell House, I worked as a companion to a Miss Morris."

Mrs. Engelbright said that she had been slightly acquainted with Miss Morris, though they had never moved in the same circles. She then remarked with pleasure that it was a very small world. Emily returned no answer to this remark. She sank back on the carriage seat and gave herself furiously to think.

Of all the places she would have chosen to live after leaving Langton Abbots, Wybolt would have been her very last choice. She had no knowledge of Ronald's recent activities, but even assuming that Sir Terrence's threats had frightened him away from Wybolt, there was nothing to keep him from coming back again. Indeed, the news that Emily was living in Wybolt once more might be of itself enough to bring him back. And Emily knew Wybolt and Wybolt society too well to doubt that Ronald would hear the news somehow no matter where he might be living at present. One of Miss Morris's friends would write it to him, or some servant would mention it as a piece of gossip, and then she would never be safe for a minute from the threat of Ronald's continuing persecution.

This idea so much dismayed Emily that she sat silent for the rest of the drive, not hearing a word of Mrs. Engelbright's chatter. She supposed she ought to say or do something to avert the approaching disaster, but it was as though this final blow had paralyzed her. She could think of nothing except that fate had once more played her for a fool. When at last the carriage came to a stop in front of Orchard House, she picked up her bag and followed Mrs. Engelbright down the carriage steps like someone in a dream.

Chapter 21

Orchard House was a square, solid house of red brick, with a neat garden plot in front and the orchard from which it had gotten its name sloping up toward the hills behind. It was not so grand an estate as Honeywell House or the Abbey, but it was an attractive and comfortable-looking property. Emily had admired it many times when out driving with Miss Morris, but she was impervious to its charm now as she followed Mrs. Engelbright into the house.

An elderly butler opened the door to them. He smiled all over his wrinkled face when he saw his mistress and bowed familiarly both to her and to Emily as he ushered them into the house's snug entrance hall. "Good evening, Walker," said Mrs. Engelbright. "This is Miss Pearce. She will be staying with us as my companion. Please tell Mrs. Hinchley to make up the blue bedroom for her and have one of the maids bring us both some tea in the parlor. I am sure we are both parched with thirst."

Emily wanted no tea, but she was too beaten down to protest. Silently, she accompanied Mrs. Engelbright to the parlor and sat stiffly in a straight chair while that lady drank tea and chatted with the maid who brought it about all the events that had passed at Orchard House since she had left it in January. They had only got as far as midsummer when the housekeeper appeared and announced that the blue bedroom was ready for Mrs. Engelbright's young lady guest.

Mrs. Engelbright insisted on taking Emily to the blue bedroom herself. She showed Emily all its amenities, begged her to ring if she wanted anything more, and then wished her a good night, saying that she herself was tired to death and was sure Emily must be also.

The blue bedroom was a comfortable chamber, low-ceilinged and cozy, with its chintz hangings and sturdy, old-fashioned oaken furniture. As soon as Mrs. Engelbright was gone, Emily took off her hat, gloves, and pelisse, sank down on a convenient chair, and tried to think what she had better do. It was a knotty problem. She had run away from one set of problems, only to encounter another and even more impossible set.

It's no use, Emily, in the grip of fatalism, told herself. *No matter what I do, things always go amiss. I might as well put an end to myself and be done with it.*

Fortunately, she felt so weary and dispirited that even the act of putting an end to herself seemed too much exertion. She decided she might as well go to bed as spend any more time pondering a problem that appeared insoluble. Weary as she was, she did not even bother to undress, but merely removed her dress and shoes and stockings and threw herself down on the bed.

In spite of her depression, or perhaps because of it, sleep came almost at once. And when Emily awoke to a glorious autumn morning with sunlight streaming through the windows, she was glad she had not put an end to herself the night before. Her problems still remained, but somehow, with the light of day, she no longer despaired of finding a solution to them.

After all, I was in a much worse predicament before, when I thought I had killed Ronald, she reminded herself. *It's worrisome to be back in Wybolt when he still has a house here, but it is not established that he still lives in it. And even if he does, it is not proven that he will try to molest me again. I may as well see what happens before I begin to fret about it.*

As for her other problem, the demise of her relationship with Sir Terrence, Emily told herself there was no use fretting about that at all. As a problem, it was already resolved, and though she might not like the way it had been resolved, she would have to accept it. She would have to acknowledge the fact that Sir Terrence still loved Lady Moira, and that whatever feelings he had sustained for her had not been able to stand up against the return of his former love. It was a heartbreaking realization, but women other than she had doubtless endured similar heartbreak and recovered to live productive lives. She would try to do the same. It was weak and contemptible to think of suicide because a man had proved faithless. She, Emily Pearce, was neither weak nor contemptible. She had been enduring the slings and arrows of outrageous fortune for many years now, and she trusted she would live to endure them for many more.

Strong in this spirit, Emily dressed and went downstairs to see what her new life would ask of her.

What she discovered, in a very short time, was that it was not likely to ask much at all. Mrs. Engelbright had even less need of a hired companion than Aunt Katie. What she really required was a sympathetic listener and someone to assist her in the small predicaments that continually befell her owing to her hen-wittedness. Almost the only real and regular tasks Emily had to perform for her were to fetch novels from the Wybolt Lending Library and read aloud to her of an evening. Mrs. Engelbright loved novels, the more sensational the better, and no plot was too improbable to tax her credulity. She hung on every word with breathless enthusiasm, exclaiming at the hero's bravery, shedding tears at the heroine's perils, and denouncing the villain's wickedness with passionate indignation.

Emily found all this very entertaining. Yet despite the entertainment provided by Mrs. Engelbright's literary tastes, there was a certain vapid sameness to her days at Orchard House. Often she found herself longing for the intellectual stimulation she had enjoyed living with Sir Terrence and Aunt Katie.

But she reminded herself that they were lost to her now. Doubtless Lady Moira was taking her place at the evening gatherings at Honeywell House. If Sir Terrence thought of her at all, it was probably only to wonder how he could ever have fancied her a replacement for Lady Moira. Altogether, she was fortunate to have fallen in with such a companion as Mrs. Engelbright and to be enjoying a life as comfortable, safe, and secure as the one she was now living.

For despite her early fears, life at Orchard House did seem to be safe and secure. She had not seen Ronald at all since her arrival. He did not even appear to be living in Wybolt at present, for when she and Mrs. Engelbright once happened to drive past Miss Morris's house, she had seen that the blinds were drawn and the knocker off the door, as though the house were untenanted.

Having a suspicious mind where Ronald was concerned, Emily was not convinced this meant she was safe. He might be conniving enough, desperate enough, or vengeful enough to try to lull her into thinking he posed no threat to her before pouncing on her again. Emily was therefore

resolved against being lulled, and she was careful never to
walk or ride out alone. Fortunately for her, Mrs. Engelbright had old-fashioned prejudices about young ladies
walking or riding out alone and felt no lady of any age
was safe outdoors without at least one stout footman in
attendance. So Emily was able to run errands or take exercise while feeling tolerably secure against any threat of
abduction.

It was therefore a great shock to her, upon returning to
Orchard House one afternoon, to find Ronald waiting for
her in the parlor.

She came in unsuspectingly, addressing Mrs. Engelbright, who was seated in her usual place beside her workbasket. "I spoke with the dressmaker about your new
pelisse, ma'am. She says if you wish to change from a cloth
to a kerseymere, you should have spoken to her sooner.
The pattern is already cut out."

"Dear, dear, to be sure that is very unfortunate. I can't
think how I came to say cloth when kerseymere was what
I wanted." Mrs. Engelbright shook her head, then stopped
short with an exclamation of vexation. "But never mind
that dull business right now, Miss Pearce. You have a visitor,
and he has been waiting so patiently to talk to you that
it would be cruel to keep him waiting any longer. Mr.
Bartholomew, I do apologize for forgetting you. If you
knew me better, you would realize I am the most scatterbrained creature alive and not hold it against me, I am
sure."

"No more do I now, ma'am," said Ronald, rising to his
feet.

Emily, upon hearing his voice, had stiffened. She continued to stand frozen, her eyes wide with shock, as he
advanced toward her. There was a smile on his lips, but
he looked nonetheless a little uncertain of the reception

he might meet. He stopped some six feet away from her without making any attempt to come closer.

"Miss Pearce," he said. "I am pleased to see you again. I was back in Wybolt to see about some business connected with my late aunt's estate and heard from her attorney that you were living at Orchard House."

He bowed as he spoke and smiled at Emily again. Emily did not return either smile or bow. She merely went on looking at him in frozen silence. Mrs. Engelbright looked from one to the other of them, cleared her throat, and rose to her feet. "Dear, dear, only see what time it is," she said. "I had better go talk to Cook about the dinner."

"No," said Emily. She spoke the single word loudly, and Mrs. Engelbright paused in mid-retreat to stare at her. "No, don't go, ma'am," said Emily, moderating her voice but still speaking with emphasis. "I would rather you stayed until Mr. Bartholomew has gone."

"Why, if you like, my dear," said Mrs. Engelbright dubiously. She returned to her seat once more, and Emily turned to Ronald.

"You had better not have come, Mr. Bartholomew," she said. "I have nothing to say to you."

Something like a flush stained Ronald's cheeks. "You are angry with me," he said. "I suppose you've a right to be. Indeed, I have regretted that I behaved the way I did last time I saw you." Flushing deeper, he went on in a halting voice. "But Emily—Miss Pearce—you must believe I meant no disrespect. I simply allowed my—my feelings to get the better of me."

Emily's only reply was to lift her eyebrows incredulously. Ronald went on, his voice sounding remarkably humble and apologetic for Ronald. "I wanted to apologize. I have been thinking a great deal about—about what happened and what you said. And I decided if I ever got the chance, I'd come and beg your pardon."

He paused, looking at Emily. She inclined her head very slightly but made no other reply.

In a slightly sharper voice, Ronald went on. "Look here, Emily—Miss Pearce," he said. "If I could speak to you alone—" He threw a frustrated look at Mrs. Engelbright.

"I see no point in that," said Emily. "You have made your apology, Mr. Bartholomew. As far as I am concerned, there is nothing else you can say that would be at all to the point."

"But damn it all—dash it all, Emily—Miss Pearce—" Ronald swallowed. "Very well, if you will have it so. The reason I came here today, besides to apologize, is to ask you to marry me."

He brought the words out defiantly. Surprised as Emily had been to see him in the first place, it was nothing compared to what she felt now. She took an involuntary step backward, regarding Ronald with incredulity.

Mrs. Engelbright, in her chair, drew in her breath and said, "Oh, my!" in a gratified voice.

Ronald looked pleased by this response. His manner relaxed slightly, and he went on, smiling at Emily as he spoke.

"Aye, I don't wonder you're surprised. I know I said before that I wasn't looking to be married, but you see I've changed my mind. I really am wild about you, Emily—Miss Pearce. I've done my best to put you out of my mind, but the fact is you've got under my skin somehow. If it takes marriage to get you, I—" He broke off with an embarrassed look at Mrs. Engelbright, but observing that she did not seem to have noticed his slip, he went on in a more confident voice. "Anyhow, I made up my mind I'd pop the question. So you see you've won, Emily—Miss Pearce. You've caught me fair and square, and now I'm here to make you an offer. I'll even go down on my knees for you if you wish. There, does that make you happy?"

Smiling, he knelt on the parlor floor. Mrs. Engelbright sighed with sentimental pleasure, and both of them looked expectantly at Emily. But all Emily said was, "No, I thank you, Mr. Bartholomew. Your apology is very welcome, but the rest of what you offer me is entirely superfluous."

Ronald did not quite cease to smile at these words, but his smile lost a good deal of its buoyancy. "Come, you don't mean it, Emily," he said. "You can't say I'm not doing the thing handsomely! I should think you wouldn't be so cruel as to throw my past mistakes in my face."

"You misunderstand me, Mr. Bartholomew. I have no intention of throwing your past mistakes in your face. Indeed, I would rather not allude to them at all. You have apologized for them, and I will accept your apology—with reservations. But there is nothing more I want from you, an offer of marriage least of all."

Ronald's smile had quite vanished now. He bounded to his feet, staring at Emily. "You don't mean it!" he said. "You are refusing me?"

"Yes," said Emily.

"But I tell you it's marriage I'm offering you!"

"I quite understand that, Mr. Bartholomew. The answer is still no."

Ronald stood still a moment staring at her. Then his face hardened. "Very well," he said. "But I tell you plainly that if I once accept your answer, Emily—Miss Pearce—I won't be coming back. Do you understand?"

"I understand," said Emily.

Ronald regarded her a moment longer, then shook his head in a baffled manner. He then turned and stalked from the room. Both ladies heard the front door slam and then the sound of rapid footsteps going down the walk.

"Well," said Mrs. Engelbright, letting out her breath in a sigh. "I don't see how you could be so cruel to him, my dear. When he came here and made you that lovely proposal—and even got on his knees to do it! I declare my heart quite melted.''

"It wouldn't have if you knew more about him," said Emily. "If you knew him as well as I do, your heart would have remained perfectly unmoved.''

"But I am sure it would not, my dear. Such a handsome young man, and with such an air about him. Is he well-off?''

"Yes, very well-off. But he is also very selfish and unprincipled. Of all the men in the world, he is the very last I would choose to marry.''

Mrs. Engelbright clucked her tongue at this and said she would never have suspected it of such a handsome young man. "But of course handsome is as handsome does, and there's many that don't do half so handsome as they look," she admitted. "Still and all, Mr. Bartholomew did seem sorry for what he'd done before (whatever that may have been, my dear). And he seems most sincerely attached to you. There's no saying but that if you married him, you might be able to reform him.''

"I don't think Mr. Bartholomew is attached to anything but getting his own way," said Emily. "As for reforming him, I wouldn't care to undertake such a labor even if I thought it likely to do any good. And let me say, I don't think it at all likely. I don't believe people can ever change their basic natures, and certainly not because of anything other people can say or do.''

Mrs. Engelbright shook her head firmly. "Ah, you're wrong there, my dear. Mr. Engelbright was sadly addicted to brandy and cigars before our marriage, but I soon saw to that. After we were married, he never smoked a cigar or took a glass of brandy again, except it might be of an evening in the bookroom—or in the stable when he was looking over the horses—or at his club, when he was staying in London.''

Emily smiled at Mrs. Engelbright's notions of reformation but said merely that she thought Ronald unlikely to respond so amiably to a wife's guidance. Mrs. Engelbright sighed at this but acknowledged that Mr. Engelbright had possessed a strong character and that Emily was right to refuse a young man whose character had been demonstrably less strong. "But it's a very romantic situation all the same," she added with a shake of her head. "It put me in mind of the duke's proposal in that last novel but one we were reading. It's cheering to know such things happen in real life as well as in books."

Emily, for her part, was merely relieved to have seen the last of Ronald. She hoped it was the last, though in her weaker moments she could not help fearing that this episode had been merely a prelude to another round of badgering. But on the whole, she felt Ronald had probably been speaking the truth when he said he would not be coming back. He had suffered a severe blow to his pride by having his proposal refused in front of a witness, and knowing him as she did, she was convinced that his pride was much the strongest and most cogent part of him.

As she pondered the depths of Ronald's pride, however, it occurred to her that she herself was not wholly guiltless in this respect. *It was at least partly pride that made me run away from Honeywell House as I did,* she acknowledged to herself. *I could perfectly well have stayed a day or two longer and taken my departure in a more seemly manner.* Instead, she had left in the night like a second-rate servant, without notice and without saying good-bye, merely because she could not stomach being second to Lady Moira.

That had been wrong, as Emily admitted now. Even if Sir Terrence did not love her, he might have maintained some shred of respect for her if she had behaved in a sensible manner. As it was, he could have no respect for her at all.

Then there was Aunt Katie. Emily was not conceited enough to suppose she had been indispensable to Aunt Katie, but she thought the elder woman had liked and esteemed her. It made her feel guilty to think she had left her with no more than a hastily written postscript to Sir Terrence's note. And when she thought about it, she realized that her departure had left Aunt Katie virtually friendless in the household. Aunt Katie did not like Lady Moira any more than Emily did, and at the time of Emily's departure it had looked strongly as though she would be forced to endure Lady Moira not only as a niece by marriage but as mistress of the house. In that case, her position would be much worse than Emily's own.

Moved by these reflections, Emily decided at last to write Aunt Katie a letter. She reasoned that there could be no objection to such a harmless action. She had a home and another position, so it would not look as though she were seeking her old ones back, and she could express in a letter all the sentiments of gratitude and regret that her hasty flight had forced her to leave unsaid. And if Aunt Katie was at all worried about where she was and what had become of her, she could set her fears at rest.

In the back of Emily's mind was a hope that Sir Terrence might have similar concerns. She and Sir Terrence had been not merely friends but lovers, and twice he had rescued her from situations of peril. Yet she could not in conscience give this hope any sort of encouragement. It seemed to her that if Sir Terrence had really cared about her, he would have made some effort before now to communicate with her. Her journey from Langton Abbots to Wybolt could easily have been traced if he had cared to go to the trouble to do it. That he had not cared to do so seemed to show he had no further interest in her. So she was careful to make no reference to Sir Terrence in her letter apart from a formal expression of thanks and compliments that included both him and Aunt Katie.

Having sent this epistle off, she waited impatiently for a reply to it. Sometimes, as she busied herself with her small duties for Mrs. Engelbright, it struck her that she was anticipating it with an eagerness that its response could hardly justify. When a response came, however, it came not in the form of a letter but as a neatly tied brown-paper parcel addressed to her in a very familiar masculine hand.

Upon receiving this parcel, Emily sat regarding it with almost superstitious fear. "What have you there, my dear?" said Mrs. Engelbright, who was as inquisitive as a child where parcels were concerned. "Aren't you going to open it?"

With fingers that trembled slightly, Emily untied the string and tore the wrapping paper aside. It disclosed a stack of neatly written manuscript and a note. Emily picked up the note and read it through with growing bemusement.

Honeywell House, Devon

Dear Emily,

   As ever, there are at least a thousand things I would like to say to you. For the purposes of this letter, however, I shall limit myself to only three of them, to wit:

   Item one: Both my aunt and I were glad to get your letter. It was a relief to hear your new situation is a good one and that you are well and happy. I have taken the liberty of passing the information on to Lady Meredith, who has besieged Honeywell House with frequent queries concerning you in the weeks since your departure. I believe both Lady Meredith and my aunt plan to write to you, but I have taken the liberty of writing first, for reasons which I shall subsequently attempt to make clear.

Item two: In your letter, you allude to your regret at having had to leave Honeywell House so suddenly. I do not question your reasons for leaving, Emily, because I think I know them. Likewise, I do not question whether such reasons were adequate. Clearly they were adequate for you or you would not have thought it necessary to go. I can only assure you that much as you may have regretted the necessity of your departure, I have regretted it even more.

Item three: You may be wondering at the enclosed manuscript. I trust you have not forgotten the literary work to which you devoted so many hours of labor? There have been countless times during the past few weeks when I have longed for your assistance once again. But remembering a certain conversation that passed between us weeks ago in which you forswore assisting me in any way save for the copying of the finished manuscript, I thought it better to wait until the manuscript was indeed finished before approaching you again.

Here, then, is the finished manuscript. It may be that you will decline to undertake the task of copying it now, feeling that your change of employment has rendered my request impertinent. Of course, you are entitled to decline it if you choose. But I humbly entreat you not to so choose, at least not until you have had a chance to read it through and weigh its merits.

Once you have done this, I hope we may meet to discuss your decision. You can either send me word and I will come to you, or you may meet me this coming Friday at three o'clock at the well pavilion at Honeywell House, where we first met.

If I do not see you this Friday, I will assume that some previous engagement has prevented you from keeping our appointment. I will therefore expect you at the pavilion the

*following Friday. If you do not come that Friday, I will
expect you the Friday after that, and so on ad infinitum,
so you see if you do not wish to keep me dangling forever
in a state of uncertainty, you must either come to the pavilion
or send for me. Hoping the manuscript meets with your
approval, I am*

> *Yours in expectation,*
>
> *Terrence O'Reilly*

Emily read this letter through, and did so a second time,
then laid it on the table and stared dumbfounded at the
pile of manuscript. "What have you there, my dear?"
repeated Mrs. Engelbright. "I can see it is papers—a great
many papers, upon my word. Who is sending you such a
lot of papers?"

"It's a manuscript," said Emily in a voice that was hardly
audible. "The manuscript of a book."

"Indeed?" said Mrs. Engelbright. She looked suspi-
ciously at the stack of papers. "It doesn't look much like
a book to *me*."

"That's because it is not published and bound yet,"
explained Emily. "After it is published and bound, it will
be just like the novels you get from the library."

"Indeed? Well, then, why don't you read me a little of
it? I am quite longing for something new. *The Rose in the
Storm* was very good, only a great deal like *Child of Destiny*
and *The Mistress of Morville Manor* and half a dozen others
I have forgotten the name of."

Emily hesitated. She wanted to read the manuscript in
the worst way but would have preferred to do so in private.
After a moment's reflection, however, she realized there
would be advantages to beginning it now. It might take
her several nights or even a week to read it under ordinary

conditions, and Mrs. Engelbright was so unsuspicious a person that she would not be likely to notice if Emily betrayed undue emotion during the reading. "Very well, ma'am," she said. Picking up the manuscript, she turned over to its first page and began to read.

Chapter 22

For the rest of that afternoon and into the evening, Emily read Sir Terrence's novel to Mrs. Engelbright. Even after three hours she desired only to go on reading, and it was obvious that Mrs. Engelbright shared her desire.

"Go on, my dear," she urged whenever Emily paused to clear her throat or turn over a page. "I cannot bear for you to stop now. I must know how it all comes out."

When dinnertime came, she made the servants bring food to the drawing room so that she and Emily need not interrupt their reading longer than was absolutely necessary. Her normal hour for retiring came and went, and still she pressed Emily to read on. "Bring wine for Miss Pearce—wine and water," she told the butler, who had come to see what was keeping his mistress up so late. "And bring enough for me, too. Then you may as well go to bed, Walker. I don't know how late we'll be, but Miss Pearce and I can put out the lights when we go upstairs."

It was past three o'clock in the morning when Emily

turned the final page of the manuscript over. Her throat was dry despite the wine and water, her voice was hoarse, and her eyes were wet with tears. Mrs. Engelbright was weeping, too, but laughing at the same time, dabbing at her eyes with her handkerchief and making little disjointed utterances.

"What a charming story—so affecting—yet so diverting, too. I never laughed so hard in my life—but it was very sad, too, in places. But then the ending was so droll and the whole of it utterly delightful. To think of the heroine never realizing that the hero was in love with her right along! She was a bit of a ninny, I think, though a delightful girl in most respects. I do like a heroine with spirit."

"I suppose she had spirit," agreed Emily, looking down at the manuscript. "But I agree with you that she behaved like a ninny."

"Ah, well, she was sensible enough to take the hero back once he had explained everything to her. And of course it *was* against him, having his former love visiting him like that and making those nasty, insinuating remarks. But the heroine should have waited to see what he did before she ran away. I am sure I would have if I were in her place."

"Probably," agreed Emily. "You are more intelligent than she was, ma'am."

"No, I am sure I am not, my dear. However, it's very good of you to say so. I declare, I think I shall have to have you read the whole book over to me again. Not tonight, to be sure, and not all in one sitting! My poor, dear Miss Pearce, I am sure you must be perfectly exhausted. It was so good of you to humor me as you did. Indeed, I never fancied a book so much in my life. You must be sure to ask at the lending library if the same author has written other books."

"He has," said Emily. "He has written a number of other books, all of them delightful."

"But none so good as this one, I am sure," said Mrs. Engelbright firmly. "I'll make a point of reading them all after this, but I am sure I shall always like this one best."

Emily felt the same way. She was careful to take the manuscript with her when she went upstairs to bed. Once she was in her room, she lit all the candles and sat down to look through it again.

Every paragraph that her eye fell upon seemed to be written directly to her. And some, if she mistook not, were even written about her, though the novel was not, strictly speaking, biographical. The setting was Ireland, many incidents and characters had been added, altered, or omitted, and the dialogue was much more witty and sparkling over-all. But the bare bones of the truth were clearly discernible beneath the veil of invention Sir Terrence had cast over them.

The novel began, as it had before, with the hero fancying himself in love with Lady Moira's character. But instead of being a heavy-handed tribute to Lady Moira's beauty and virtue, those early chapters had become satire, biting in places but showing mainly a humorous forbearance toward the hero and his mistaken passion.

Having reduced Lady Moira to a minor and comic character, Sir Terrence had left himself free to introduce another heroine in her place. And Emily could not doubt that she was that heroine in every respect that mattered. There were differences between her and the fictional girl in the novel, of course. But the heroine's feelings and motivations were her own, and to some extent her appearance, too.

"He cannot really see me like that!" said Emily softly, turning over the pages of the manuscript. But she felt in her heart that he did. The book was only a confirmation of the things Sir Terrence had said before. If she accepted the fact that his feelings were those of his fictional hero, then she must also acknowledge that he admired her wholeheartedly as well as being deeply and sincerely in love with her. The entire progress of his thoughts and feelings was there, from the moment he had first seen her through the moment when she had opened his eyes to Lady Moira's false conduct, to the moment when he had recognized her as the woman he wanted for his wife.

But it's still fiction, Emily argued to herself. *He has taken an author's liberties with the truth and skimmed right over such difficulties as the difference in our stations. And there are other objections to our marrying that he has not even mentioned. In real life the situation is not so simple as he has made it.* She had a strong urge to tell Sir Terrence so and not to wait until Friday to do it. *But perhaps it would be as well to wait until Friday, since he mentions it in his letter,* she conceded. *That will give me time to decide exactly what to say to him. I am tired and overexcited just now and in no condition to decide anything. It would be all too easy to let myself be carried away by a romance that is, when one considers it, as much fiction as fact.*

Friday was still several days away, leaving Emily plenty of time to decide exactly what to say to Sir Terrence when she saw him. Yet despite all that infinity of time, she had still not made up her mind what to say to him when Friday finally came around. She had arranged to borrow Mrs. Engelbright's carriage to take her to Langton Abbots, a measure Mrs. Engelbright gladly consented to when Emily explained she was taking the manuscript back to its owner. "Tell him how much I admired it. And tell him, too, that his publisher may put me down for three copies of it when it comes out. I should like always to have a copy of it about me so I can read it no matter where I am."

Emily agreed to do this and set off for Langton Abbots with the manuscript bound once more in its brown-paper wrapping. She thought it best for the coachman not to take her directly to Honeywell House but to set her down in the village. From there she could easily walk to the well pavilion, an approach she preferred, since her errand was such an unconventional one.

The way to Honeywell House had changed a great deal in the weeks since she had seen it. The grass of the common was sere and brown, while the trees were beginning to blaze in the glory of their autumn colors. Emily forced herself to walk slowly and observe all these changes despite her impatience to reach the well. In truth, there was something remarkably like dread mingled with her impatience. Within a few minutes she would be seeing Sir Terrence again after an absence of more than a month. It was entirely possible he might have changed in that time. Or it might be that *she* had changed. She might find her memories of him were idealized and that he was merely an ordinary man with whom she was no longer in love at all. In a way, such a discovery would be a relief, because she was not convinced that a happy ending was possible even if she and Sir Terrence did love each other. Sometimes she thought it was; at other times, she was certain it was not.

Of course, there was no longer any Lady Moira to complicate the situation. Emily took it for granted that this was so, though she had no grounds but Sir Terrence's novel to suppose it. Still, if the novel had been sent to her for the reason she imagined, then that was grounds enough. Lady Moira had been sent away—courteously but with finality—and it looked as though Ronald were finally out of the picture, too. Yet the departure of these two obtrusive characters had made curiously little difference in her and Sir Terrence's situation.

In the last few days, Emily had read his novel through twice more. Each time had left her so deeply affected that she was ready to throw herself into his arms and declare herself unequivocally his. But then the same doubts that had troubled her all along would resurface, and she would

become convinced she would be doing him a disservice if
she allowed him to sway her in her convictions.

Back and forth, back and forth Emily argued these issues
in her mind, all the way across the common and past the
spinney where she had once run in fear from a workman's
dog. She passed the quarry without even sparing a glance
at its dark menace and took the turning into the woods
of Honeywell House without conscious thought. When she
reached the clearing surrounding the well and well pavilion, however, she halted. There was someone already
inside the pavilion, and even before she drew close enough
to see, she knew it was Sir Terrence.

He was leaning on the well curb, looking down into the
water. He seemed to sense her presence in the same way
she had felt his, for he turned around quickly at her
approach, even though her feet had made no noise on
the earthen path. "Emily," he said.

"Terrence," said Emily, and felt a rush of relief. He had
not changed at all. He looked just as he had before, tall
and rangy with vivid blue eyes and a mouth that was made
for smiling. His voice sounded the same as before, too, a
musical baritone that made every word poetry. And the
net effect of his presence on Emily was likewise the same
as it had been before. Every fiber of her being was intensely
aware of him, not merely as a man but as the one man
who held the key to her heart and happiness.

Sir Terrence, intimately attuned to Emily's thoughts and
feelings, caught some of this in her voice. "Emily," he said
again, coming toward her with hope surging in his voice.
"Emily!" But he saw the negative in her face even before
she took a step backward, and he came to a stop a few
paces away. They stood studying each other.

"You received the manuscript?" said Sir Terrence,
breaking the silence at last. "You have had a chance to
read it?"

"Yes, several times. Terrence, I hardly know what to say. It is a wonderful book—a magical book."

Sir Terrence made a gesture of impatience. "It is well enough, I daresay. I am glad to hear you enjoyed it. But it happens at the moment that I am more concerned to know if you understood it. Did you? But of course you did," he said, answering his own question. "You understand me better than anyone ever has. Now if only you could bring yourself to trust me as well."

"I do trust you," said Emily.

Sir Terrence gave her a very direct look. "Do you? Then it must be yourself you don't trust, mustn't it?"

"I—I don't—" Emily choked on the denial, then went on with gathering wrath. "I don't know what you mean!"

"Perhaps not. But it's either one or the other, isn't it? Why else would you have run away after Moira came without even giving me a chance to explain?"

"Terrence, I am sorry about that." Emily hung her head. "It was all so clear to me after reading your book." She was silent a moment, looking down at her feet. "Perhaps I did fail to trust you. I assure you, I feel very badly now that I ran away as I did, without saying good-bye to you and Aunt Katie."

"You needn't worry about Aunt Katie. She doesn't hold it against you in the least. In fact, she said she was tempted to do the same thing as soon as Moira showed her face at Honeywell House."

Emily smiled a little. Sir Terrence went on, his voice low and earnest once more. "Indeed, I didn't wonder that you were disgusted with me, Emily. Listening to Moira go on and on at the table that night, I was disgusted with myself. I was a fool to have ever been taken in by her. And when you ran away, I was sure it was only because you didn't feel a man who could be so taken in was worth bothering about."

"It wasn't that," said Emily. "It wasn't that at all, Terrence."

"Then what was it? Was it simply that you didn't trust me? You thought I would allow myself to be deceived by Moira again?"

"No, I don't think it was that, either." Again Emily looked at her feet. "Perhaps you are right, Terrence. Yes, I think you are. It was myself I didn't trust all along. But not in the way you think!" She looked up at him quickly. "It was only that I knew what I ought to do and was afraid I couldn't make myself do it if I stayed with you any longer."

"Yes." Sir Terrence let out his breath in a long sigh. "Yes, I rather thought it was something like that. But Emily, don't you see it's the same thing? The same thing I meant by saying you don't trust yourself?"

"No," said Emily stubbornly. "I don't see that they're the same things at all."

"But they are. Emily, look at me! I love you, Emily. I love you and want you to be my wife. Why won't you agree to that? Is it that you don't love me?"

"No," said Emily in a low voice. "You know that I love you, Terrence."

"Then will you marry me?"

Emily twisted her hands. "I can't," she said. "Terrence, it would be taking advantage of you! And I am sure you would come to regret it."

"And I am equally sure I would not," said Sir Terrence. "Why would I? Don't you know how I feel about you? I have certainly tried to tell you enough times—and I tried to put a little of it in my book there, too. But it's so futile to attempt to put such things into words. I only know that if you refuse to marry me, it will be as though I must be forever incomplete—as though a part of myself had died."

Emily glanced up at him. It was clear he was perfectly serious. Again she twisted her hands. "You say you would not regret it. But you cannot know that, Terrence. What if you came to realize later you had made a mistake?"

"It seems to me that you are more concerned whether *you* might make a mistake," he replied calmly. "It's exactly what I said before, Emily. You simply don't trust yourself. Perhaps you feel you have already made a mistake by allowing matters to go so far between us. That night in the library, for instance—"

"I don't regret that!" said Emily hotly. "I don't regret it in the least, Terrence! Not in the least!"

She stood regarding him with her chin held high. Sir Terrence drew a deep breath. "Then prove it," he said. "You once asked me to prove my feelings for you. I ask you now to prove yours for me. Will you let me make love to you again?"

For answer, Emily dropped the manuscript onto the nearest wicker chair, threw off her hat and shawl, and came to him. His arms reached out to enfold her. With a shuddering sigh, he buried his face in her neck. "Emily," he whispered. Emily shuddered in her turn. For a moment they merely stood, locked in each other's arms as though reluctant to risk anything more.

At last, Emily raised her face. Sir Terrence immediately kissed her. It was a formal, almost ritualistic kiss, but the one that followed was considerably less formal. Before long, Emily found herself crushed against Sir Terrence's chest as his mouth ravished hers with persuasive force. All the while his hands were taking liberties with her back, her neck, her shoulders. Each touch seemed to heap more fuel on the fire his kiss had kindled within her. Emily drew a deep sigh. She had a sense of melting from the inside out. She burned for him, not merely for his touch and his kiss but for the pleasure he had given her before.

"Emily," he whispered again. His hands were fumbling with the fasteners on her dress. Emily shut her eyes. She felt the fabric slip from her shoulders and the brush of cool air on her breast and shoulders. Then Sir Terrence's mouth touched the newly bared skin, and the contrast between the cool air and the heat of his mouth made her gasp. All the stiffening seemed suddenly to go out of her legs. She swayed and would have sunk to the ground had not Sir Terrence caught her in his arms and carried her over to a wicker settee—the same settee on which she had slept that June night so many weeks before.

"Emily," he said again. He laid her on the settee, and Emily put out her arms to draw him to her. She shut her eyes as his lips touched her skin again, feeling their soft and insinuating caress as they slipped lower and lower. She drew a deep sigh, caught her breath, then sighed again. His hands were busy at the same time, working aside her skirts and petticoats, and she felt a trembling excitement as more and more of her body was laid bare. One hand brushed the bare skin of her leg above the stocking. It was all Emily could do to keep from crying out. When the hand moved deliberately to caress her between the legs, she could not repress a soft moan.

"Terrence," she said. "Oh, Terrence!" It was just as it had been before, a flood of sensation so strong that she was borne along on it like a spar on a wave. Then suddenly the sensation was suspended, and she heard as though from a distance Sir Terrence speaking in a calm, regretful tone.

"It's no good. I can't do it."

Emily's eyes flew open. Sir Terrence was kneeling atop the settee with his legs astride hers. His hands still rested on her thighs, and all the while he spoke, they continued to trace idle patterns on her bare skin. His expression, however, was regretful. "I can't do it," he said again.

"Why not?" demanded Emily in bewilderment. "What do you mean, Terrence?"

Sir Terrence looked solemn. "I mean I cannot make love to you. It seems I have developed conscientious objections to making love to women who are not my wife—or at least my fiancée."

Emily stared at him a moment, then began to laugh helplessly. "Terrence!" she said. "Terrence, you are a scoundrel! This is iniquitous!"

"I will allow it is a bit inconvenient. But if you were to agree to marry me—well, then, my objections would be removed, and I might proceed in good conscience."

"Terrence, this is iniquitous!" repeated Emily. One of Sir Terrence's hands chose that moment to stray close to its former seat of operations, and she had to swallow hard before she could speak again. "How can you take advantage of me this way?"

"I am only acting for your own good," said Sir Terrence. His voice had dropped to a low, persuasive murmur. His hands continued their own persuasion as he added, "Cannot you trust me, Emily?"

"Yes—oh, yes! It's not that. It's not even that I don't trust myself. It's *fate* I don't trust, Terrence. Being with you is like heaven. It's like a happy dream come true—and I don't think I was meant to be happy, Terrence. I feel that if I were to marry you, it would be defying fate."

Sir Terrence pondered these words, his hands still absently caressing her as he thought. "You have had misfortunes in your life, I know," he said. "You have told me enough to give me some idea how difficult these last few years have been for you. All the same, I have never heard you complain about it. And if I know you as I think I do, Emily, I would be willing to wager that even when things were at their worst, you did not rant and rave against heaven because you had been afflicted. Did you? Did you rant and rave, or did you simply set your teeth and endure?"

Joy Reed

Emily could see clearly where this was tending. "Of course I did not rant and rave," she said reluctantly. "There would have been no point in it. It was my fate, and I accepted it because I had to. But—"

"Then why cannot you accept happiness when it offers? I don't suppose there's anyone on earth who hasn't suffered at some time or other. I have suffered myself, but I've always observed that even the worst period of misery is eventually succeeded by a period of happiness. As Father O'Donnell used to say when the pigs got into the potatoes, ' 'tis all part of the fair and equitable workings of a just God, ye see, and naught to put a body in a temper.' "

Emily gave a shaky laugh. "So it would be flying in the face of providence not to let you make love to me?" she asked.

"Yes," said Sir Terrence firmly. "It would."

"And you will not make love to me unless I agree to marry you?"

"No," said Sir Terrence, shaking his head. "Much as I'd like to, it'd be going against my conscience. And you wouldn't want me to go against my conscience, I am sure."

"So if I say I will marry you, you will make love to me, and events will take their proper course?"

"I'm certain of it," said Sir Terrence.

Emily put her arms around him and drew him toward her once more. "Then let events take their proper course," she said. "I have not strength enough to oppose the will of heaven any longer, let alone you, Terrence. Let events take their proper course!"

Having been relieved of the burden on his conscience, Sir Terrence went on to acquit himself in a gracious and generous manner. Emily acknowledged as much as they lay together afterward on the settee. He turned his face to smile at her.

"Naturally, I am gracious and generous. You haven't married me yet, and I mustn't give you any excuse to renege on our agreement."

"Of course I shall not renege!" said Emily. "I said I will marry you, Terrence, and I meant what I said." She laughed. "Although I still think it was iniquitous of you to extort a consent from me that way!"

"Yes, I feel a little remorse, but not much." Sir Terrence joined in her laughter. "Indeed, I flatter myself that not many men can have proposed marriage to a woman and obtained her consent in such a novel manner. It would make a good story, but not, I fear, a suitable one for public circulation. You will not be able to tell it to our children, for instance, when they beg to know how Father proposed to you!"

Emily laughed. "No, it wouldn't be suitable for that," she said. "When they ask, I will merely have to assure them he was very eloquent, very persuasive, and perfectly unanswerable in his arguments."

Sir Terrence was so pleased by this praise that he kissed her again, though he warned her that she must not try to tempt him into doing anything more. "It's getting late. And though we seem to have got away with the indiscretion of making love in broad daylight in a marginally private place, to do so twice would be tempting fate." He smiled at Emily.

"Yes," agreed Emily, returning his smile. It was a pensive smile, however, and Sir Terrence observed that her face remained pensive even after they had both risen and made themselves respectable once more. He came over to her as she stood beside the well, which she had been using as a mirror to straighten her disheveled hair. For a moment they both stood there, side by side, looking at their reflections in the water.

"You look beautiful," he said softly. "I thought so the first moment I saw you here. But you also look very thoughtful, my love. No regrets, I hope?"

"No, no regrets," said Emily, smiling at him in the water. "Indeed, I am very happy, Terrence. Only—I am not used to thinking I deserve to be happy. And it may be that you shall have to reconvince me of it now and then."

"I shall tell you as often as I need to with the greatest pleasure," said Sir Terrence, kissing her. "But perhaps wearing this will help you to remember."

Emily looked down at the emerald flashing on her third finger. "Oh, Terrence," she whispered. "What a beautiful thing. It's like green fire."

Sir Terrence smiled. "Green as the hills of Ireland. You're to be Irish by proxy now, you know. Do you really like it?"

"I love it. Only you must have been very sure of me to come here with a betrothal ring in your pocket!" Emily looked at him, smiling but reproachful. "Do you always get what you want?"

"No, indeed. But I like to think I get what I deserve. And I hope I deserve you, Emily. If I don't now, I shall certainly try to deserve you in the years to come."

"In the years to come," repeated Emily, and smiled. "I shall try to deserve you, too, Terrence. It will be something to look forward to, I think. But for now, I am afraid I must be getting back to Mrs. Engelbright. How providential that Beatrice's collarbone is almost healed! In another week or two, I should be able to leave her with a clear conscience."

"A week or two!" said Sir Terrence. "I want you now, Emily—now, if not sooner. Cannot you—?"

Emily cut short this plea by putting her hand over his mouth. "No, no! You must not try to persuade me into anything else today, Terrence. I should think you would be satisfied with what you have got already!'' Smiling, she looked up at him. ''Indeed, you are dangerously persuasive when once you begin talking.''

''Talking,'' said Sir Terrence, removing her hand and kissing it, ''is what I do best. It's the Irish in me, I suppose.''

''Yes, perhaps. But though you do talk very well, I wouldn't say it's what you do best, Terrence.''

Emily paused, looking at him provocatively. ''Oh, no?'' said Sir Terrence, regarding her with a gleam in his eye. ''And what do I do best?''

''Why, writing, to be sure!'' said Emily, opening her eyes very wide.

Sir Terrence laughed and kissed her. ''There's a leveler for me! But thank you for the compliment, all the same.'' He leaned over to pick up the manuscript from the wicker chair. ''I must say, I am rather proud of this, though it doesn't become me to say so, perhaps.''

''You should be proud of it,'' said Emily. ''I believe it's the best thing you've done, Terrence. I read it to Mrs. Engelbright, too—without telling her it was a *roman à clef*, of course—and she thinks it the most wonderful book ever written. She wants to be put down for three copies whenever it is published.''

''Does she? That *is* a compliment. I wouldn't go so far myself as to say it's the most wonderful book ever written, but I am very pleased with it. I think my publisher will be pleased with it, too. And I owe it all to you, Emily.'' Coming over to Emily, he took her in his arms once more. ''You are my inspiration. My muse. My goddess.'' His eyes were sparkling as he leaned down to kiss her. ''And I ask nothing better than to spend my life worshiping you.''

Emily was a little embarrassed at this sort of extravagant talk. She opened her mouth to object. Then she shut it again. It had just occurred to her that after all those years of being called a stupid girl, she might have earned the right to be called a goddess once in a while. It was all part of the fair and equitable workings of a just God, and as such she had no right to complain. So she said merely, "I freely grant you that right, my love," and proceeded to kiss him right back.

ABOUT THE AUTHOR

Joy Reed lives with her family in Michigan. She is currently working on the third installment of her Wishing Well trilogy. Look for *Anne's Wish*, coming from Zebra Books in May 2001. Joy loves hearing from readers, and you may write to her c/o Zebra Books. Please include a self-addressed stamped envelope if you wish a reply.

COMING IN DECEMBER FROM
ZEBRA BALLAD ROMANCES

___A SISTER'S QUEST, Shadow of the Bastille #3
   by Jo Ann Ferguson   0-8217-6788-7 $5.50US/$7.50CAN
When Michelle D'Orage agreed to be Count Alexei Vatutin's translator at the
Congress of Vienna she was excited, but then she learned the handsome
Russian's true reason for hiring her. Shaken and confused, she has little choice
but to trust this mysterious stranger who holds the key to her past . . . and her
dreams for the future.

___REILLY'S GOLD, Irish Blessing #2
   by Elizabeth Keys   0-8217-6730-5 $5.50US/$7.50CAN
Young Irishman Devin Reilly had just arrived in America seeking riches to
bolster family business, but his fortune was about to change. After rescuing
fiery Maggie Brownley he sees in her eyes that "Reilly's Blessing" will bind
them together. Devin soon realizes that in Maggie's embrace he will find a
love more precious than gold.

___THE FIRST TIME, The Mounties
   by Kathryn Fox   0-8217-6731-3 $5.50US/$7.50CAN
Freshly graduated from medical school and eager to bury his sorrow over the
tragedy in his past, Colin Fraser impulsively joins the Northwest Mounted
Police. During a raid on a bootleg whiskey operation he finds Maggie, an ill
bootlegger. Colin finds, while nursing the patient, the way to heal his own
heart.

___HIS STOLEN BRIDE, Brothers In Arms #2
   by Shelley Bradley   0-8217-6732-1 $5.50US/$7.50CAN
Wrongly accused of murdering his father, Drake Thornton MacDougall wants
nothing more than to take revenge against his duplicitous half-brother. So he
strikes at the fiend the only way that he can . . . by abducting, Averyl, his
bride-to-be. In Averyl he finds the key to forgiving past wrongs and healing
his tormented soul through pure love.

Call toll free **1-888-345-BOOK** to order by phone or use this coupon to order
by mail. ALL BOOKS AVAILABLE DECEMBER 1, 2000.
Name _____
Address _____
City _____ State _____ Zip _____
Please send me the books I have checked above.
I am enclosing $ _____
Plus postage and handling* $ _____
Sales tax (in NY and TN) $ _____
Total amount enclosed $ _____
*Add $2.50 for the first book and $.50 for each additional book.
Send check or money order (no cash or CODS) to:
Kensington Publishing Corp., Dept. C.O., 850 Third Avenue, New York, NY 10022
Prices and numbers subject to change without notice. Valid only in the U.S.
All orders subject to availabilty. **NO ADVANCE ORDERS.**
Visit our website at **www.kensingtonbooks.com.**